Domingo Villar grew up in Vigo, Galicia, and now lives in Madrid. His two novels have been top-ten bestsellers and shortlisted for several awards. *Death on a Galician Shore* won Spain's Brigada 21 Prize for best crime novel in 2009, and Domingo Villar was named Galician author of the year. His first novel, *Water-blue Eyes*, also featuring Inspector Leo Caldas, was published by Arcadia Books. *Death on a Galician Shore* is his second novel, and was shortlisted for the UK's Crime Writers Association International Dagger award in 2011.

Praise for *Death on a Galician Shore*

'A Spanish writer who does not set his novels in Madrid or Barcelona is to be welcomed, and the rugged coastline of Galicia makes a suitably unsettling setting . . . Caldas is an engaging copper and his loud, unsophisticated sidekick, Estevez, an amusing one'
Marcel Berlins, *The Times*

'A satisfying read . . . laced with gothic menace, mouthwatering descriptions of Galician cuisine and some wonderfully tetchy sparring between Caldas and his undiplomatic deputy, Estevez'
John O'Connell's Choice, *Guardian*

Death
on a Galician
Shore

DOMINGO VILLAR

Translated from Spanish by
Sonia Soto

ABACUS

First published in Great Britain in 2011 by Abacus
This paperback edition published in 2012 by Abacus
First publishing in Spanish with the title *La Playa de los ahogados* in 2009 by
Ediciones Siruela S.A.

A CIP catalogue record for this book
is available from the British Library.

ISBN 978-0-349-12342-4

Typeset in Berkeley by M Rules
Printed and bound in Great Britain by
Clays Ltd, St Ives plc

Papers used by Abacus are from well-managed forests
and other responsible sources.

MIX
Paper from
responsible sources
FSC® C104740

Abacus
An imprint of
Little, Brown Book Group
100 Victoria Embankment
London EC4Y 0DY

An Hachette UK Company
www.hachette.co.uk

www.littlebrown.co.uk

To my father

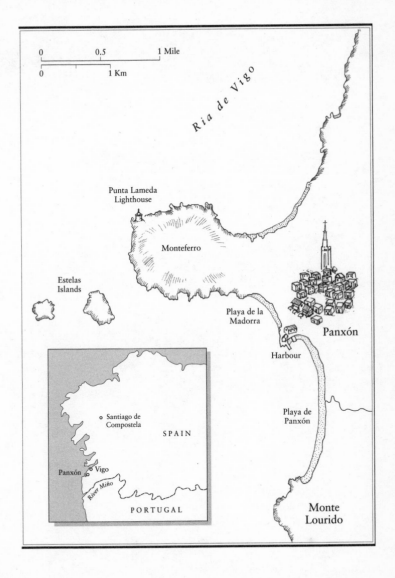

The Green Mask

Inspector Leo Caldas got out of a taxi and, stepping over the large puddles on the pavement, entered the hospital. He made his way through the crowd of people waiting by the lifts and headed for the stairs. He went up to the second floor and walked along a corridor lined with closed doors. Stopping at the one numbered 211, he opened it a crack and looked in. A man in a green respiratory mask was asleep in the bed nearest to the window. The television was on, with the sound turned down. The other bed was empty and sheets were folded on top of the bedcover.

Caldas glanced at his watch, closed the door and went to the waiting room at the end of the corridor. There he found only an elderly woman, her black clothes contrasting with the white of the walls. She looked up expectantly as Caldas put his head round the door. Their eyes met briefly before she looked down again, disappointed.

Caldas heard footsteps behind him and turned around. His father was hurrying towards him down the corridor. Caldas raised a hand in greeting.

'Have you seen him?' asked his father in a whisper once they were standing outside the room.

'Only from out here,' answered Caldas. 'I was late too. Have you spoken to the surgeon?'

His father nodded: 'He said it's not worth operating.'

Entering the room, the inspector's father went to sit on the empty bed, wrinkling his nose in distress as he looked at his brother. Caldas remained standing.

1

A drip was dispensing the contents of several vials into the emaciated arm of Uncle Alberto. Beneath the sheet, Alberto's chest rose slowly, and then fell abruptly, as if each exhalation were a deep sigh. The sound of oxygen bubbling through distilled water and air whistling as it escaped from the sides of the mask drowned out the murmur of the rain outside.

Caldas crossed to the window. He parted the net curtains and, through the double glazing, watched the lights of the cars stuck in traffic and the procession of umbrellas along the pavement.

He turned, alerted by the hissing of the mask, which his uncle had removed in order to speak.

'Is it still raining?' Alberto whispered before replacing the mask.

Caldas nodded, gave a small, close-lipped smile and jerked his head towards his father. His uncle was about to take off the mask again when his father stopped him.

'Come on, leave that alone. How are you feeling?'

The patient waved a hand and placed it over his chest to convey that it hurt.

'Well, you're bound to be uncomfortable,' said his brother.

After a moment's silence, Alberto gestured towards the radio on the bedside table and looked at the inspector.

'He says he listens to your programme,' his father explained.

'Right.'

Alberto nodded and gave a thumbs-up.

'He says he likes it,' his father translated once again.

'Right,' said Caldas, then he indicated the muted television, tuned to a news bulletin: 'I think TV's more entertaining.'

His uncle shook his head and gave another thumbs-up at the radio.

'He says your programme's better.'

'Do you really think I can't understand him?' Caldas asked his father. 'Anyway, it's not my programme. I'm only on occasionally.'

Caldas's father looked at his brother – whose eyes were smiling behind the mask – and the inspector watched, fascinated, as they began to converse without the need for words, using only glances and facial gestures, communicating in the private tongue of those who have shared a childhood.

*

A doctor entered, to the evident annoyance of the patient.

'How are things going, Alberto?' he asked. The only answer was a flutter of the hand.

The doctor lifted the sheet and felt several points on the patient's abdomen. Beneath his green plastic mask, the patient grimaced each time the doctor touched him.

'In a month you'll be as good as new,' the doctor said as he finished his examination and, after winking at Caldas's father, he left the room.

The three men remained in uncomfortable silence until Uncle Alberto gestured for his brother to approach. The inspector's father went over to the bed and Alberto removed his mask.

'Can you do me one last favour?' he said in a weary voice.

Father and son exchanged glances.

'Of course.'

'Have you still got your Book of Idiots?'

'What?'

'Have you still got it or not?' insisted the patient, straining to raise his murmur of a voice above the hissing of the oxygen.

'Yes, I think so.'

'Well, add that doctor to it,' he said, pointing feebly at the door through which the doctor had departed.

He breathed through the mask for a few moments before removing it again and whispering: 'His name's Doctor Apraces. Will you remember that?'

Caldas's father nodded and gently squeezed Alberto's arm. His brother's face wrinkled around the mask as he smiled. His breathing resumed its jerky rhythm when he fell asleep and the gurgle of distilled water continued.

Outside the hospital, the inspector lit a cigarette and his father opened his umbrella.

'There's room for both of us under here,' he said.

Caldas moved closer to him and they set off towards the car park, to the accompaniment of a chorus of honking horns from drivers exasperated by the traffic jam.

'You've got a Book of Idiots?'

'Didn't you know?' his father replied, not looking at him, and Caldas noticed that his eyes were moist.

3

He was surprised because, though he had spent many nights after his mother's death listening to the sound of his father weeping, he had never actually seen him shed a single tear. He decided to hang back a few steps despite the rain, and let his father give vent to his grief.

In the car park, before getting into the car, his father asked: 'Can I drop you anywhere, Leo?'

'Where are you going?'

'Home. It's quiet there.'

'Will you be visiting him tomorrow?'

'In the afternoon,' said his father. 'After lunch.'

Caldas reflected that he could phone the superintendent first thing and take the morning off. And, with any luck, he'd get to the radio station late and that fool Losada would have to manage without him.

'Well, I'll come with you, and you can give me a lift back.'

His father stared at him. 'Are you going to stay at my house tonight?'

'If you ask me . . .' said Caldas.

'Don't you have work tomorrow?'

Caldas shrugged, took a quick drag on his cigarette, threw it on the ground and climbed into the car.

Embers

In the months of anguish following the death of his wife, Leo Caldas's father had sometimes visited the manor house where she had lived as a child, an old ruin consisting of little more than stone walls. Only the winery had withstood the years of neglect, half sunk into the ground so as to avoid sudden changes in temperature. Inside there remained some barrels, an ancient wooden press, a hand-operated bottle filler and a few other old implements. Walking around the estate, its terraced vineyard descending like an amphitheatre to the River Miño, the inspector's father had found balm for his sorrow, a solace that the city denied him.

One October, seeing the grapes ripen and rot on the vines, and cheered by the thought of spending more time there, he decided to start making wine again in the old winery. After several months of reading and seeking advice, he starting working a small plot of land close to the house.

Every Saturday and Sunday, on the pretext of tending the vines, father and son rose early and drove out to the estate, a journey of almost fifty kilometres on winding roads that had to be made in stages, with the windows open, due to the young Leo's carsickness.

That March at weekends they cleared the land and, in April and May, they tore out the old barren vines. In the summer, making the most of the holidays and longer hours of daylight, they put up posts and wires to support the remaining healthy vines and the new ones to be planted that winter, after the harvest.

For the first few years, as he extended the land under cultivation,

Caldas's father sold wine from the barrel or gave it to friends. Later, as the new vines began producing, he put his savings into modernising the winery so that he could bottle and sell the wine under label. He soon recouped his money, as the wine was acquiring a good reputation and, though the quantity increased with every harvest, he had no trouble selling it all.

As soon as he was old enough to stay at home on his own, Leo gave up the torture of the winding roads and stopped accompanying his father to the estate. When he went to university, his father left his job in Vigo and moved permanently to his wife's old family home, which he had gradually restored.

The land, initially providing comfort in his time of affliction, was now a profitable business, and the nights of weeping were no more than a shadow in the memory.

Wine, the downfall of so many men, had been his salvation.

They hardly spoke during the drive. The modern roads were less tortuous, but Caldas still opened the window a crack and closed his eyes for the journey. He sank back in the seat and didn't move, even when raindrops got in and spattered his face.

Beside him, his father drove one-handed, gripping the nails of the other between his teeth without breaking them, while in his mind he travelled from his childhood to the hospital room.

When they reached the estate, Caldas got out to open the gate and waited in the rain while his father drove through. Back in the car, on the way up to the house, he thought he saw a dark shape moving behind them. Through the rain-streaked rear window he made out an animal running after them.

'Have you got a dog?' he asked, surprised.

'No.'

'Isn't it yours?' he insisted, motioning behind them.

Caldas's father looked in the rear-view mirror for a moment and then said firmly, 'No, it's not.'

All the way from the car to the front door, the dog bounded around Caldas's father, barking. It leaped and shot off in all directions in the rain, spinning around within a few metres and galloping back, howling with delight, thrashing its tail and trying to lick the inspector's father's hands, face or whatever else he saw fit to proffer.

6

'Look at the mess he's made of my clothes,' he complained as they entered the house. He shook his trousers and shirt, which the dog had smeared with dark mud, and went up to his bedroom. Caldas stayed downstairs.

'Lucky the dog isn't yours, then,' he muttered.

Circling the large dining-room table he made his way to the sitting room. He sat down on the sofa, facing the fireplace, which still contained the ashes and dead embers of a recent fire. Next to the coffee table, beside a pile of old newspapers, stood a basket of logs.

His father returned, wearing a fresh change of clothes.

'Shall I put some dry things out for you?'

'Maybe tomorrow. I'd rather dry off in front of the fire. Can I light it?' Caldas asked, pointing to the firewood.

'If you think you know how . . .' said his father disdainfully before slipping off to the kitchen.

Caldas sighed and knelt down by the fireplace. He took two large pine logs from the basket and placed them in the hearth. Crumpling up a few sheets of newspaper, he pushed them between the logs and laid pine cones and vine prunings on top. He rummaged in his pocket for his cigarettes and lighter, and lit up with the same flame he held to the newspaper. Once it was alight, he sat on the sofa, smoking in front of the fire.

His father returned with an unlabelled bottle of white wine. After opening it with the bottle opener on the wall, he left it on the coffee table and went to get two glasses from the cupboard.

'This is the latest vintage,' he said, filling the glasses with wine that was still cloudy. 'See what you think.'

Caldas laid his cigarette on the ashtray and thrust his nose into his glass. His father did the same.

'It stills need to clarify, but as far as the nose goes, it's ready,' he said.

'Right.'

'How do you like it, Leo?'

The inspector raised the glass to his lips and swilled the wine around in his mouth for a few seconds before swallowing.

'What do you think?' asked his father, standing waiting for his son's verdict.

Caldas nodded several times then emptied his glass in one gulp.

*

They opened another bottle, from the previous year this time, and heated some of the soup from the fridge, made with slab bacon, beef broth, turnip tops, broad beans and potatoes. Afterwards they ate a local cheese with some of Maria's home-made quince jelly.

When they'd finished eating and had cleared the dishes, Caldas carried the wine to the coffee table and refilled the glasses. He sat on the sofa, facing the fire; he could have stared at it for hours. His father went to the bookshelves and stood searching for a couple of minutes, cursing under his breath until he found a small notebook behind the books. Its cardboard cover was so worn it was difficult to tell its original colour. Taking his glass, he went to sit at the dining table and leafed through the notebook for a while.

When Caldas got up for more wine, he asked: 'Is that the Book of Idiots?'

His father nodded. 'I wonder how Alberto remembered it. I haven't looked at it for years,' he said, turning pages full of names, of the fragments of life associated with each one. Then he took a pen and turned to the last entry in the notebook.

'It was Dr Apraces, wasn't it?'

'Yes,' said the inspector and, glancing at his father, once again saw eyes glistening with unfamiliar tears.

Caldas stretched out on the sofa and remained there for the rest of the evening, staring at the fire so that his father could weep with each glass of wine he drank.

A Call from Estevez

The next morning, Caldas took a change of clothes from his father's wardrobe, had a long shower and went out into the courtyard between the house and the winery. After weeks of rain, autumn had called a truce and, though the sun was hidden by clouds, the new day was bright and still.

Approaching a flowerbed, he pinched a sprig of lemon verbena in his fingers and inhaled the fragrance.

'I hear you enjoyed the soup,' said a voice behind him.

Maria, who came every morning to clean the house and prepare his father's meals, was sweeping up the russet leaves shed overnight by the sweetgum tree.

'Very much, Maria,' said Caldas.

'The trick is to skim it well,' she said, still sweeping. Then, wanting to return the compliment, she added: 'I really enjoy *Patrolling the Waves*. We never miss it.'

The inspector wondered how on earth they received the show out there. Surely Radio Vigo only covered the city itself?

He thanked her and changed the subject: 'Have you seen my father?'

'He was heading that way, with the dog,' she said, pointing beyond the winery to the river. 'Don't you want breakfast? There's hot coffee in the thermos.'

'Maybe later,' said Caldas, slipping out of the courtyard.

He made his way around the house. Leaning with his elbows on the stone parapet, he looked out over the seven hectares of terraced vine-yards sloping down to the river.

A few hundred metres below, a tractor was parked on the path beside one of the plots to the right. Caldas could make out a few people among the vines and remembered his father saying over supper that they had begun pruning.

He lit a cigarette and remained leaning on the parapet, savouring the peace and quiet. He was about to call the station, to tell them not to expect him until the afternoon, when his mobile rang shrilly in his pocket. He answered, seeing his assistant's name on the display.

'Are you on your way here, boss?' asked Rafael Estevez by way of greeting, before Caldas could speak.

'Is something up?'

'We got a call about half an hour ago from Panxón. A man's body's been found in the water.'

'A fisherman?'

'How should I know, Inspector?'

Caldas's assistant, who came from the province of Aragon, was obviously in fine form from first thing in the morning.

'Had we had a report of anyone missing?' asked the inspector, aware that sometimes it took days for bodies to be washed ashore.

'Not as far as I know.'

'Right.'

'D'you mind telling me how long you'll be?' asked Estevez with customary impatience. 'The coroner set off for Panxón ten minutes ago, and the pathologist called to ask if we could pick him up en route.'

Caldas glanced at his watch and reflected that all the hassle was starting much too early this Monday. He was glad to be well away from the city.

'Well, you pick him up en route.'

'What about you?'

'I don't think I'll be able to get there till this afternoon, Rafa.'

'You don't think so, or you know so for a fact?'

'Don't start, Rafa. I was just about to call to let you know.'

Estevez hung up with a grunt. Caldas thought of phoning the superintendent to let him know he wouldn't be in that morning and

10

have him assign someone to go with Estevez, but changed his mind. It was only a drowned man after all.

He headed along the path between the vines that cut through the estate to the river like a sinewy scar. The vines in the upper part had yet to be pruned, though autumn had already divested them of their foliage, with only a few branches retaining a languid leaf or two.

He stopped when he was level with the tractor and stood watching in silence as the workers took five or six stems on each vine and tied them to the wires. They chose stems that already had several buds, from which shoots would sprout in the spring, and cut off the others. Later, before moving to the next section of vineyard, they would collect in the tractor any pruned branches that might serve as kindling and leave the rest to rot on the ground.

The osier bindings with which he'd helped his father tie in the first stems were now made of plastic, but nothing else seemed to have changed.

Ten metres or so further down, the brown dog that had greeted them the day before appeared on the path. A moment later, Caldas's father emerged from the same row of vines holding a pair of pruning shears, his rubber boots glistening with dew.

Caldas went to meet him.

'There are spare boots in the storeroom,' said his father, looking at his son's shoes.

Caldas shrugged. 'I'll stay on the path.'

'It's up to you. Have you seen the new planting?' asked his father, motioning towards the river.

Caldas had seen it but said he hadn't. They set off that way, with the dog ahead of them, nose to the ground, scurrying among the vines. Now and then the brown shape reappeared on the path, its head erect, making sure they were still following, before resuming its distracted scampering.

'What's its name?' asked the inspector, pointing at the dog during one of its appearances.

'I don't know. It's not mine,' said his father without stopping.

They continued down the path, which turned right at an angle, parallel to the river, as it reached the lower part of the estate. On either side there were several rows of white posts with wires stretched between. At the foot of each post, a new vine was just visible.

11

Caldas's father explained that they'd had to use a digger to level the ground and that they'd left a larger than usual gap between vines so that the tractor could manoeuvre more easily. The inspector listened in silence, nodding as if he were hearing it all for the first time.

While his father stopped to tie a loose stem to a post, Caldas headed through the rows of vines to look out at the river that flowed several metres below.

The stretch of river that ran past the estate had many whirlpools. If they wanted to swim they had to walk upriver for half an hour, to a bend with a beach where the water slowed. They'd set out after lunch and return along the bank, as it was growing dark. In childhood the days had seemed longer.

Seeing the water and hearing the murmur of the current, he remembered Estevez's call about the man swept away by the sea. He thought of the night the pharmacist had drowned in the rapids. He had waited in the car while his father had helped the police as they scoured the riverbank, probing beneath the water with wooden poles. Later they'd driven back to Vigo for the night while the police continued their search downriver.

The pharmacist's body hadn't turned up for another three days. She was found by men fishing for lampreys eight kilometres from the spot where she'd fallen in.

Years later, the inspector learned that the pharmacist had jumped into the river and that she couldn't swim. But for months, she had swum beside him in his childhood nightmares, begging him to save her from the swirling current that always swallowed her in the end. The young Leo would wake, terrified and drenched with sweat, as wet as if he really had been swimming.

Caldas looked at his watch: Estevez would have got to Panxón by now and he was sure he wouldn't hear any more about the case until the afternoon, when he was back at the station.

His father joined him and they stood watching the river, the leaves and branches swept along by the current.

'You should have put on boots.'

'Right,' said Caldas, staring at the water.

'Have you had breakfast?' asked his father after a pause.

12

Caldas shook his head.

'Shall we go back for coffee?' said his father.

As they made their way up to the house, he lamented: 'I don't know why I didn't think of planting in this area before.'

'I thought you didn't think sandy soil was good for vines.'

'Well, you'll see, it'll make wonderful wine. Not this year, obviously, or next, but in five years time I think the best wine on the estate will come from these vines. And if I'm right, I'll plant over there too,' he said, pointing to the other side of the path.

'Five years?'

'Five or six. Once the vines have grown.'

'Isn't that too long?'

'I don't set the schedule. That's how long they take to mature.'

'I know,' said the inspector. 'I meant, aren't you planning to retire before then?'

'Retire? And do what?'

Caldas shrugged. 'Anything . . .'

'Isn't all this anything?' said his father, spreading his arms to encompass the vine-clad slopes on either side of the path. 'At my age, the only way to have peace of mind and not dwell on things is to keep busy. The alternative is to resign yourself to living through other people and sit waiting for time to pass and do its work.'

Caldas felt he'd ruined his father's morning. He was sorry he'd spoken. His father, however, added with a smile: 'Besides, when you're retired, you don't get holidays.'

In the kitchen Caldas's father poured two cups of coffee from the thermos. He added a little milk and sugar to one, and handed the other to his son.

'Shall we go outside?' he asked, indicating the door as he rummaged around on the countertop.

In the courtyard they met Maria, returning to the house, broom in hand.

'Maria never misses *Patrolling the Waves*,' said his father.

'Yeah, she told me,' replied Caldas, grimacing in an attempt at a smile.

They walked around the house and went to lean on the stone parapet overlooking the estate. His father was about to say something

13

when the inspector's mobile rang. Caldas gave a deep sigh on seeing Estevez's name on the display.

'Work?' whispered his father.

'My assistant,' said Caldas, moving a little distance away and taking his cigarettes from his trouser pocket before answering the call.

'How did it go?' he asked, holding a cigarette between his lips and lighting it.

'I'm still here at the harbour.'

'With the dead man?'

'Looks like he had help.'

'How d'you mean?'

'His hands were tied.'

People throwing themselves into the sea to commit suicide often tied their hands or feet to make sure they succeeded.

'He could have done it himself,' the inspector pointed out.

'No, boss. For some reason the pathologist doesn't think he killed himself or drowned fishing for trout.'

'Not many trout in the sea,' said Caldas drily.

'You know what I mean.'

'Yeah.'

Caldas took a drag on his cigarette. He had a feeling he was going to regret letting his assistant go to Panxón alone.

'Do you know who he was?'

'He was from the village. A fisherman. They're going to transfer the body to Vigo for identification and autopsy. And someone from Forensics is going to come by, to look for clues.'

'Nobody recognises him?'

'Not with any certainty, no. You know what these people are like,' said Estevez. He'd lived in Galicia for several months but he still wasn't used to the locals' ambiguous way of expressing themselves.

'See if you can get them to give you something more definite,' said the inspector, then regretted it instantly, knowing how forcefully his assistant could go about things. 'But be gentle, Rafa,' he added. 'I don't want any trouble.'

'Don't you worry, boss. Leave it to me,' said his assistant, in a tone that Caldas found far from reassuring.

*

14

The inspector rejoined his father and picked up the cup he'd left on the parapet.

'Is your assistant getting used to things here?'

Caldas sipped his coffee. 'No, I don't think he ever will.'

His father traced letters in the air with his pen.

'Shall I enter him in my book?' he asked, as if there could be no more cruel punishment.

When Caldas didn't reply, he added: 'I can always erase his name later. He wouldn't be the first I've removed.'

'It's up to you,' the inspector said, and his father noticed his pre-occupied air.

'Something up, Leo?'

'A client,' Caldas said, clicking his tongue.

'Murdered?'

'Could be,' said Caldas.

'Would you like us to drive back to Vigo now?' asked his father.

'No, don't worry,' replied Caldas, well aware that his father didn't like spending any more time than he had to in the city.

'I could try to get in to see your uncle this morning.'

'There's no need. Really.'

'It would almost suit me better, Leo,' insisted his father. 'I've got things to do here this afternoon.'

'All right then,' said Caldas gratefully, knowing his father was lying.

They contemplated the rows of white posts supporting the vines, while the inspector finished his cigarette.

'It's looking pretty, isn't it?' said his father proudly.

'Yes, it is,' whispered Caldas. 'Even though autumn doesn't suit vines.'

His father gathered up the cups and headed back to the house. Caldas heard him muse: 'Does autumn suit anyone?'

Excuses

Just before they reached the police station, and as the traffic lights turned red, Caldas suddenly made a vague excuse and got out of the car. He watched it disappear into the Vigo traffic, feeling guilty. This was a difficult time for his father.

As they left the estate they had exchanged a few words about his uncle, lamenting the illness that was consuming him from within, forcing him to breathe through a machine. They had spent the rest of the journey in silence, Caldas with eyes closed, his father with his eyes on the road and mind on the hospital.

Only once they were in the city, driving down the sloping streets to the police station, did the inspector's father ask about Alba. To cut the conversation short, Caldas had said he had no news, that he hadn't heard from her for several months. But his father persisted with his questions despite these evasive answers. Why did he always insist on raising the most awkward subjects at the last minute? If the aim was to prolong their time together, he should have learned his lesson by now. The unwelcome questions only precipitated Caldas's departure, leaving them both with a bitter aftertaste.

In the police station Caldas made his way down the aisle between the two rows of desks to the far end of the room. He opened the frosted glass door to his office, hung his raincoat on the coat rack and sank into his black desk chair.

Gazing at the piles of papers on his desk, he continued thinking about his father until Superintendent Soto came in and brought him back to reality.

16

'How did you get on in Panxón?'

'I didn't have time to go, Superintendent. Estevez is dealing with it.'

'You sent Estevez on his own for the removal of a body?' asked Superintendent Soto.

When Caldas's silence confirmed this, the superintendent shook his head disgustedly and left the room, muttering.

Caldas picked up the phone. He dialled Olga's extension and told her to send Estevez straight into his office as soon as he got back to the station.

He remained at his desk, ignoring his stomach, which was informing him noisily that it was well past lunchtime. He took the opportunity to go through some of the papers that had accumulated on his desk, pencilling notes in the margins before placing them on a different pile. Every time he put down a document, he checked his watch and glanced at the door. He wondered how his assistant was getting on with the recovery of the drowned man's corpse. He also thought about his father and his own abrupt exit.

At a quarter to three, as he was leafing through the statements of witnesses to the hold-up of a jeweller's in the Calle del Principe, the city's main shopping street, Rafael Estevez's bulky form appeared at the glass door.

'That was some morning I've had, boss,' he snorted as he came in.

Caldas was starving. And he thought he'd rather hear what Estevez had to say somewhere else, safe from interruptions. He put the robbery statements down on top of a heap of papers and stood up.

'Have you had lunch yet?' he asked. 'My treat.'

'Thanks, but I couldn't eat a thing,' replied Estevez. 'You can't imagine the state that guy's body was in.'

Before his assistant had a chance to go into detail, Caldas took his raincoat, folded it over his arm and went to the door.

'Do you mind filling me in on it while I have something to eat?' he said. 'All I've had this morning is coffee and if I leave it any later I won't get served.'

'It's not raining today,' said Estevez, pointing at the raincoat.

17

'I know,' said the inspector, hurrying out.

Estevez followed him out into the street, where the sun was just peeking between clouds.

They crossed the Alameda, stepping through fallen leaves, and headed along the Calle del Arenal with its elegant stone buildings. The façades with their ironwork balconies had overlooked the container port for several decades now, but still seemed to be wondering where the beach and sea had disappeared to.

The Bar Puerto was still packed. As usual at lunchtime, the customers wore a mixture of suits, blue overalls and thick fishermen's clothing. Caldas glanced at the plates being emptied at the nearest tables.

'Pity you're not hungry,' he said.

'There was foam coming out of his nose,' Estevez recalled, wrinkling his nose in disgust.

'Later, Rafa,' said the inspector. There would be plenty of time to hear the more macabre details once he'd eaten.

Cristina came to fetch a bottle of brandy from the bar near the door.

'Can we still get something to eat?' asked the inspector, raising his voice above the din of overlapping conversations.

'We've always got something for a radio star,' teased the waitress. Then she took the bottle to the back of the dining room so that two dockworkers, lunchtime regulars like Caldas, could add brandy to the coffee with which they were rounding off their meal.

When she returned, she indicated a couple of tables with empty places.

'Would you rather sit here or over there?'

At the table nearest to them, three veteran seafarers were sitting with a young man in a dark suit who was avidly devouring a bowl of soup and a sports paper. At the other sat the dockworkers to whom Cristina had taken the brandy.

'The one at the back,' said Caldas. 'And would you mind not seating anyone else with us once those two have left?'

'Don't worry, Leo. At this time of day we only get the odd straggler.'

As they headed to their table they passed the kitchen. The white-tiled walls were hung with cooking pots, awaiting their turn on the stove. The dented metal revealed many years of use, but they gleamed as if they had been polished.

Caldas and Estevez stopped before the low counter separating dining room and kitchen. The inspector leaned over to examine the chiller cabinet where the shellfish was usually displayed. It was empty.

'No point in looking. There's no shellfish on a Monday,' said one of the cooks behind the counter. She was washing a pan before returning it to its place on the wall.

'What do you use to make them shine like that?' asked Estevez, pointing at the pan.

'Plenty of elbow grease, son,' said the cook. 'Like to have a go?' she added, holding out the soapy pan.

Estevez declined the offer with a smile and followed Caldas to the back of the restaurant. He exchanged a glance with the dockers sharing their table and settled back in the chair facing the inspector.

Cristina brought a tureen and placed it between them. When she removed the lid, fragrant steam spread across the table making Estevez sit up, nostrils flaring.

The waitress returned with a carafe of chilled white wine in one hand, and plates, glasses and cutlery in the other.

'Rafael doesn't need a plate,' Caldas said. 'He won't be eating.'

Estevez looked at the tureen like a little boy peering up into the sky for the balloon that's just got away.

'Why don't I leave one just in case?' asked Cristina.

'OK. Just in case,' agreed Estevez.

Caldas filled his bowl with soup and returned the ladle to the tureen. Estevez helped himself immediately.

'I thought you couldn't eat a thing,' the inspector remarked.

'A little soup can't hurt,' replied his assistant, filling his bowl to the brim.

Caldas blew on his first spoonful to cool it before lifting it to his lips: 'You're right about that.'

Estevez had had a second helping and was refraining from a third by the time Cristina came to take their order for the main course. She offered them *bacalao a la gallega*, cod with potatoes, or squid in its ink with rice. Caldas chose the squid.

'Would you like something else?' Cristina asked Estevez.

The soup had blotted out all thoughts of the drowned man's foaming nose and restored the policeman's habitual voracious appetite.

'What do you recommend?' he asked.

'The squid's turned out really well,' said Cristina, adding almost immediately: 'But the cod's been popular, too ...'

She left her words hanging and Estevez stared, awaiting her verdict. After a few seconds, as none came, he asked:

'Well?'

'They're different,' the waitress said simply.

'I know that. But one of them must be better,' insisted Estevez.

'They're both really good,' said Cristina with an open smile. 'Which do you like best?'

'Forget it,' muttered Estevez, realising he wasn't going to get a definite answer. 'I'll have the same as him – the squid. And a salad.'

As soon as Cristina was out of earshot, Estevez complained: 'I don't know why the hell I bother asking these people anything.'

He realised that Caldas was staring at him in silence across the table.

'Sorry, boss,' he said. 'Sometimes I forget you're one of them.'

The Drowned Man

At four in the afternoon, when all that remained of the policemen's squid in ink were dark stains on their paper napkins, the last few customers of the Bar Puerto stood up. Caldas watched them as they left.

'Tell me about the drowned man,' he said to his assistant, picking up a teaspoon to stir his coffee.

'He was found floating at the water's edge, but by the time I got there he'd been laid out on the sand. There was foam coming out of his nose and mouth.'

'You've already told me.'

'I just can't get it out of my head. And he was icy,' Estevez explained, clenching his teeth as if a shiver had just run through him.

'Haven't you ever seen a drowned man before?' asked Caldas, surprised.

'Back in Zaragoza, occasionally we had to fish someone who'd committed suicide out of the river, but I never got too close. You know I'm not keen on dead people, Inspector,' said Estevez a little sheepishly.

'And the living aren't too keen on you,' murmured Caldas, picturing, for the second time that day, the drowned pharmacist about whom he'd dreamed so often as a child. 'Come on, get on with it. Did you find out who he was?'

'His name was Justo Castelo. He was a fisherman from the village.

He went out in his boat yesterday morning and wasn't seen again. The boat hasn't turned up yet.'

'What kind of boat is it?'

'I don't know – one of those small ones. He worked on his own. He fished for shrimps and crabs using those mesh crates they drop on the seabed. You know the kind of thing.'

'Traps,' said Caldas.

'That's right – traps. He sold his catch at the market in Panxón.'

'Age?'

Estevez shrugged: 'Early forties. I've got his details back at the station. Single, no partner or children. Mother lives in the village, with the sister and her husband.'

'Did you speak to them?'

'I saw the sister, but I didn't interview her, if that's what you mean. Bad enough for the poor woman to get that news. I said we'd transferred her brother's body to Vigo for an autopsy. She was anxious to know when they'd be able to have the funeral and I told her we'd release the body as soon as possible. She's agreed to come by this afternoon to identify him.'

Caldas was reassured to hear that his assistant could behave with tact when required.

'You didn't see the husband or the mother?'

'No. The husband's away on a fishing boat somewhere off the coast of Africa. The mother's a semi-invalid. Not the day to go and pay a social call.'

'No, of course not. On the phone you said the man's hands were tied, didn't you?'

'That's right, boss. Wrists bound with a plastic tie, like the kind used for fastening cables and pipes. It's a flexible strip with a hole at one end. You insert the tip and pull to adjust it,' he explained, miming the gesture. 'You know the sort of thing I mean. Once you pull it tight you can't loosen it without breaking it,' he said, repeating the motion.

Caldas nodded, still stirring his coffee. He'd rather have lit a cigarette, but in the Bar Puerto they were as strict about not smoking as they were with the cooking times of their shellfish, so he had to make do with stirring coffee.

'What about the legs?'

22

'They were bent back. And stiff as a statue's.'

'Were they tied as well?' the inspector asked.

'No, only the hands.'

'What about the face?'

'A complete mess – bloated, with eyes wide open as if he'd seen a ghost,' said Estevez, opening his own eyes wide. 'It was all bashed up. And I've already mentioned the foam ...' He now shut his eyes tight as if trying to erase the memory.

Caldas knew exactly what his assistant was talking about. On one occasion, weeks after a freighter had sunk, some fishermen had found the body of one of the crew. It had been pounded against the rocks for days and served as fish food, so the Forensics people had had to identify it from dental records.

'He was clothed, wasn't he?'

'Of course, boss. He'd gone fishing.'

Beyond the counter, the cook had finished washing up the last pan from lunch. After drying it carefully with a cloth she returned it to its hook on the wall.

'I don't think so,' said Caldas, watching the woman.

'What d'you mean, you don't think so?' said Estevez, turning around. 'You don't think I can tell the difference between a guy who's clothed and one who isn't?'

'Don't be silly, Rafa. I don't think he'd gone fishing,' said Caldas, indicating the empty display cabinet between kitchen and dining room. 'There's no seafood on a Monday because fishermen don't fish on Sundays.'

'Well, this one was spotted in his boat early in the morning. You tell me where he was off to otherwise.'

'I don't know. Who did you say saw him?'

'I didn't say,' replied Estevez. 'Someone mentioned it this morning.'

'And did you confirm it?'

'No.'

Caldas reflected that maybe it was a good thing that he hadn't. Estevez didn't exactly resemble a tame bloodhound when he was following a trail. They'd have time to check all the details in due course.

'D'you know if there were any marks on the body?'

'Any marks? I told you, the face was all beaten up.'

'Apart from that, Rafa. Did anything else show up when he was examined?'

Estevez hesitated: 'The body was covered in green seaweed so you couldn't really see, but, no, I don't think there was anything else. Anyway, it was the pathologist who looked at him.'

'Dr Barrio?' asked Caldas, and his assistant nodded.

'And the Forensics people filmed it all,' added Estevez. 'You know they never go anywhere these days without that camera of theirs.'

'Did they find anything?'

Estevez shrugged. 'They looked around, but the guy was washed up by the sea so I doubt they'll find any clues.'

'Right,' said Caldas, reassured by the flashes of common sense in his assistant's account.

'And you say he was found on the beach at Panxón?'

'Yes, but not the bigger one. Another one beyond it, between the harbour and the mountain with the monument at the top.'

'Monteferro,' said Caldas.

Estevez nodded.

'It's a smaller beach, with loads of seaweed on the shoreline. Apparently it's not the first time a corpse has washed up there.'

'Do you know who found him?'

'A pensioner from the village. He goes out for a walk every morning and saw the body in the seaweed, from the road, and called the local police. It was them who called us. I've got the old boy's name back at the station.'

'Did you speak to him?'

'Yes, of course. To him and others. But they didn't tell me much. You know people here . . .'

'I know, I know,' interrupted Caldas.

'Would you do me a favour, boss?' asked Estevez suddenly.

'Of course.'

'Could you stop doing that with your spoon? You're making me nervous.'

The sound of the spoon scraping the sides of the cup stopped instantly and Caldas reddened slightly.

'Of course,' he said again, downing the rest of his now almost cold coffee.

Then he left enough money on the table to pay for both him and Estevez, and stood up. He was keen to see Guzman Barrio and hear the pathologist's findings first hand. He'd go there after the radio station.

The Jingle

By the time they left the Bar Puerto, autumn had resumed its hostilities. After a few hours without rain, a vault of clouds had settled overhead and now emptied itself upon the city.

Estevez walked close to the buildings, trying to shelter from the rain. His raincoat was hanging on a hook back at the station. He wondered aloud how Galicians could make sense of weather that went from springlike to wintry in a few hours, and cursed whenever a large drop landed on his head.

The inspector walked beside him in silence, not admitting that they didn't try to make sense of the climate, they simply lived with it.

At the entrance to the building on the Alameda, Caldas checked the time and lit a cigarette. He watched his assistant run through the park back to the police station, dodging puddles and cursing, and then just stood staring at the rain lashing down. When he'd finished his cigarette, he greeted the doorman and ascended the stairs to the first floor. He pushed open the door to the radio station, took his notebook from the pocket of his raincoat, hung the coat on the rack at the entrance and made his way down the long corridor to the control room where a technician was going over the order of calls with Rebeca, the producer.

'Come in, come in,' she said when she saw the inspector. 'Santiago's already asked for you twice.'

Through the glass Caldas could see that fool Santiago Losada

26

already at the microphone. With a sigh of resignation, he slipped inside the studio. The host welcomed him with his customary friendliness:

'Late as usual,' he said, signalling to the technician to start the programme.

'As usual,' replied Caldas, choosing the seat closest to the window.

He took out his mobile phone and, switching it off, placed it beside his notebook on the desk. Then he turned to look out at the Alameda where a small group of foreign cruise passengers were braving the bad weather. They walked with heads down, the hoods of their yellow raincoats up, determined to see the sights featured in their guidebooks before returning to the liner and sailing on to the next port.

That morning, when he'd mentioned retirement and his father had turned around and asked what he would do if he gave up the vineyard, Caldas had been about to suggest that he travel, see the world. Now, watching the tourists wandering in the rain in a foreign city, he was glad he'd kept quiet.

'Off we go,' announced Losada drily. The inspector opened his notebook and put on his headphones, wondering if the host's set was as uncomfortable as his. He'd have to swap them one day to check.

As in every other edition of the show, call after call related to matters that fell within the remit of the City Police: potholes, zebra crossings that were slippery in the rain, drivers crashing into parked cars and speeding off . . . Caldas simply listened and took down the details in his notebook, wondering how a radio phone-in show could be so popular when the callers' problems were so rarely solved.

After the seventh call, he tallied the score: City Police seven, Leo nil.

The *Patrolling the Waves* theme tune played until Rebeca, on the other side of the glass, held up a slip of paper with the name of the eighth caller of the day.

'Good afternoon, José,' said Losada.

'Good afternoon. I've called in before,' declared the man.

'Could you refresh our memory?' the presenter urged. 'The show does get hundreds of calls.'

'Your head's bigger than your audience,' thought Caldas, feeling the urge to insult the host on air. He wished the caller would put Losada in his place, but the man on the line sounded like a wimp:

'It's about police vehicle stops,' he said. 'They keep picking me. I don't even use the car much – only at weekends.'

Caldas remembered the man. He'd called the show recently, accusing his local police of ordering him out of the car and breathalysing him at every turn.

'I remember you, José,' said Caldas, to move things along. 'Have you been breathalysed again?'

'This Saturday. Three times.'

'Three?'

'Yes, Inspector, three. Once in the morning and twice in the afternoon.'

'Good heavens.'

'On Sunday I saw the officer out of the window so I left the car at home. Just in case. And would you believe it, when I walked past him in the street, he was watching me the whole time. I thought he was going to breathalyse me again.'

'Tell me something, is it always the same officer?'

'This Saturday, yes. But last week it was a different one.'

'And what were the results?'

'The results?'

'Of the tests,' said Caldas. 'Were any positive?'

'No, Inspector.'

'None of them?'

'None, Inspector. I hardly drink.'

Caldas thought the caller sounded puzzled rather than angry with the police. Caldas shared his bewilderment.

'What can I do, Inspector?'

While he was trying to come up with an answer for the caller, Caldas saw Losada signal to the sound technician. A tune, more suited to a cartoon than a police phone-in, began to play in his headphones. It was highly distracting, and he had to glance at the caller's name on the sign again before he could answer him.

'Here's what we're going to do, José,' he said. 'Why don't you come down to the radio station the day of our next show and afterwards we can go and have a word with the chief of the City Police. Let's see if he can persuade his officers not to stop you all the time. How's that?'

The caller hung up and Caldas wrote in his notebook: *City Police eight, Leo nil.*

After another two calls, *Patrolling the Waves* came to an end. Caldas freed himself from the oppressive headphones while Losada sonorously exhorted his audience to tune in for the next show.

When the red light indicated that they were off air, Caldas asked Losada: 'What was that music?'

'What music?'

'The jingle you had playing when I was about to answer the breathalyser man, and all the callers after that.'

'Ah!' smiled the presenter. 'I thought it would be a great idea to play a tune while you're thinking.'

'What?'

'To make it more fun for the audience. Just while you're thinking,' he said, smugly sure of himself.

Caldas was horrified. If he didn't stop this arrogant fool right now, pretty soon there'd be a trumpet fanfare after each answer.

'Didn't it occur to you that it might do the exact opposite – that a silly little jingle like that might actually distract me?' said Caldas. 'Anyway, what do you mean "while I'm thinking"? What the hell do you suppose I'm doing the rest of the time?'

'Look, Leo, if that's how you're going to be about it, no more music for you.'

Caldas left the studio and, as he looked in on the control room to say goodbye to Rebeca and the technician, he switched his phone back on. He'd missed two calls. The first was from Guzman Barrio. The pathologist had agreed to phone as soon as he finished the autopsy on the drowned man. The second call was from his father.

'See you Thursday,' said Rebeca with a wave.

Justo Castelo

The rain was still pouring down when Caldas got back to the police station so he asked his assistant for a lift to the Town Hall. Estevez waited with the engine running while the inspector delivered the string of complaints gathered during the radio show to the City Police. Then they went to see the forensic pathologist.

'Go and see if he's in his office,' said Caldas, checking his mobile again.

Estevez peered round a door abruptly, then looked back to Caldas and shouted: 'Yes, boss, he's here!'

'Bloody hell, Estevez,' said a startled Guzman Barrio. He'd been slouching in an armchair, trying to catch up on his sleep. 'Do you always burst in like that?'

'No, he usually kicks the door down,' said Caldas from behind his assistant. 'You left me a message on my mobile.'

'It's about the man who was washed up this morning in Panxón,' said the pathologist. 'You know about it?'

Caldas answered with a question: 'Have you finished the examination?'

The pathologist rose, stretching discreetly, and made his way towards the door past the two policemen.

'If you'd like to see the body . . .' he said, heading out into the corridor. 'It's just been stitched up, so it can be handed over to the family.'

'Nice work,' muttered Estevez.

'Well, our customers don't complain,' said the pathologist.

As always on these occasions, Estevez grumbled all the way to the swing doors of the autopsy room. He really didn't want to see the drowned man again, especially now that he'd been cut open. Taking a deep breath, he followed the inspector and the pathologist inside.

'Where's the drowned man?' Barrio asked two auxiliaries who were washing a female cadaver in preparation for an autopsy.

'In the freezer, Doctor. Shall I bring it out?' asked one of the auxiliaries.

'No, that's OK. You carry on with what you're doing.'

Barrio headed towards a large metal door and, pulling the handle firmly, entered the cold room. He came out a few seconds later pushing a trolley. On it lay a body in a grey plastic cover. Barrio took a pair of latex gloves from a box on a shelf, and also found some disposable masks, which he handed to the policemen.

Having donned the gloves, the pathologist unzipped the body bag in a single motion and let it fall open, revealing the naked body of the fisherman.

'Meet Justo Castelo,' he said.

'We've already met,' said Estevez, hanging back. He had no intention of coming any closer.

The stitched-up autopsy incision stood out like a zip against the corpse's chalk-white skin. The Y-shaped wound started on either side of the neck, merged below the sternum and descended in a single line, circling the navel and ending just above the pubic bone.

Though wearing a mask, Caldas recoiled at first from the smell. Then he looked at the corpse's wrists. Only after examining the deep grooves left there by the plastic cable tie did he look at the head. A row of stitches circled the scalp like a crown.

Justo Castelo's forehead, cheeks and chin had suffered multiple blows. His eyelids were taped shut. The pressure of the water had burst the blood vessels of his nose and eyes. His lips were swollen and turned outwards, as if he'd greeted death with a kiss, lending the face a grotesque aspect.

'He drowned,' said Barrio solemnly.

'Some sleuth,' muttered Estevez from behind.

Inspector Caldas turned to his assistant with a furious glance.

31

'What?' said Estevez defensively. 'You don't need a bloody autopsy to tell you that.'

'I meant he was still alive when he entered the water,' said Barrio. 'That's not always the case. The sea is a good place to dispose of a corpse.'

'Right, right,' Caldas interrupted and then, turning to his assistant, he said: 'Why don't you wait outside?'

Estevez's face lit up: 'Sure,' he said, tugging off the mask with a sigh of relief. 'What with the young lady those two are cleaning up and our fair-haired friend here, I was starting to feel sick.'

Dr Barrio waited for Estevez to leave the room before continuing:

'As I was saying, there's evidence of vital reactions. See the ecchymoses here?' he said, indicating small red marks on the eyelids. 'And when we got there, there was still foam exuding from his mouth and nose. So there's no doubt he was still alive when he entered the water.'

Caldas grimaced, imagining the dead man's face with eyes wide open and foaming at the nose and mouth. Familiar with his assistant's reaction to dead bodies, he wasn't surprised at the effect this one had had on him.

He examined the grooves on the dead man's wrists. The pathologist told him what he already knew:

'They were bound with a plastic tie.'

'Estevez said you don't think he tied his hands himself.'

'No, I don't,' confirmed the pathologist. 'It was a cable tie – you fasten it by inserting one end into an eyelet in the other.'

Apparently the only way to explain how these ties worked was by miming the action. Like Estevez at the Bar Puerto, Barrio put both hands together in the air and then tried to jerk them apart.

'You know the kind I mean?'

Caldas nodded.

'And he couldn't have fastened it himself?'

'His palms were pressed together. How would he have fastened the tie?' asked Barrio, indicating the indentations on the dead man's wrists.

Caldas brought his own hands together. 'I suppose first I'd try to insert the end into the hole.'

'How?'

'With my fingers,' Caldas said doubtfully. 'No?'

'Maybe,' conceded Barrio. 'And how would you tighten it?'

'With my teeth?'

'Exactly – with your teeth.'

'So what's the problem?' asked the inspector.

'Would you mind putting your hands together again?' the doctor asked.

Caldas once again pressed his palms together.

'How would you go about fastening a tie around your wrists using your teeth?'

'Like this,' said the inspector, raising his hands to his mouth.

'But to do that the eyelet would have to be there, by your thumbs,' said Barrio, indicating the part of the inspector's wrists closest to his mouth. 'Yet the tie binding this man's hands was fastened around the other side, by his little fingers.'

Caldas rotated his hands and held them up to his mouth as the pathologist had described.

'You could do it like this, too,' he said.

Barrio disagreed: 'You could tighten it like that, Leo, but it would be unnatural.'

'But you could do it,' insisted Caldas.

'Maybe,' said the doctor. 'But it would be more or less impossible to insert the end of the tie into the eyelet using your little fingers. Almost as hard as threading a needle with them.'

Caldas stared at his hands and nodded, separating them.

'Couldn't he have moved the fastener round after tightening the tie?'

Barrio shook his head. 'It was too tight, Leo. See the marks it's left on the wrists? I'm sure it didn't move at all. I had to cut it to release his hands,' the doctor went on. 'Clara Barcia has taken it away to examine it, but I doubt she'll find anything useful after so many hours in the sea.'

'Couldn't he have got someone else to tighten it and then jumped into the water?' asked Caldas.

'He could have . . .' said Dr Barrio, but his expression showed doubt. In his experience, people who decided to end their lives by throwing themselves into the sea had access to too many ways of tying themselves up to choose one that required another's help.

'Right,' said Caldas, then pointed to the dead man's face: 'What about these injuries?'

'Most of them are post mortem. But there are two contusions that were inflicted while he was still alive. This is one of them,' said the pathologist, showing Caldas a wound surrounded by a large bruise on the dead man's right temple.

'And the other one?'

'Behind, on the occipital bone,' said Barrio, lifting the corpse's head to show Caldas the back.

The inspector walked around the trolley to look more closely at the area.

'The blow on the back of the head was severe enough to make him lose consciousness. It was caused by a long object, probably metal,' explained the pathologist. 'See?'

Caldas was having trouble distinguishing this particular injury from all the others. 'Sort of,' he said.

Barrio took a pen from the pocket of his white coat and went over to fetch a notebook from a shelf.

'The contusion's narrow at first, then thicker and rounder at the end,' he explained, resting the notebook on the trolley and drawing the outline of the injury on a blank page. 'It could have been made by the kind of spanner used for tightening wheel nuts, or any other object with a rounded end.'

Barrio tore out the page and handed it to the inspector.

'And the wound on the forehead?' asked Caldas, folding the paper and tucking it in his back pocket.

'That one has a very uneven shape. It could have been caused by a rock,' said the pathologist. 'I'd say he was struck with the bar from behind and the injury on the forehead happened when he fell forwards on to a rock. Then he was tied up and thrown into the sea. Though the blow on the temple could have been caused by the waves dashing him against rocks while he was still alive.'

Caldas continued to stare at the wound, partly hidden by his fair hair, on Justo Castelo's forehead.

'That seems more likely than him falling on to a rock while he was on a boat,' he pointed out.

'Yes, it makes more sense.'

'But there's something I don't quite understand,' said the inspector.

34

'If he was unconscious, there was no need to tie him up. Simply throwing him overboard would have been enough for him to drown.'

'They wanted to make sure. Contact with the cold water might have brought him round, but no one can swim in the sea with their hands tied. In fact, there was foam in his bronchi, so he drowned trying to breathe in the water. Have you ever watched a fish die out of water, Leo?'

'Once or twice,' said Caldas. 'So you think he was murdered?'

'Don't rule out other possibilities yet,' said the doctor hastily. 'If for some reason this man was on a boat with his hands tied, he could have lost his balance and hit his head on some part of the hull before falling into the sea. Maybe he was trying to escape. There's no sign of the boat yet, is there?'

There wasn't.

'Do you really think it could have been an accident?'

'No,' said Barrio, before adding: 'But I can't rule it out.'

Caldas moved closer to take another look at the fisherman's hands, the wounds on his wrists and the skin of his palms corrugated by sea water. Barrio might not rule it out, but the possibility of Justo Castelo's death being an accident was too remote. Caldas didn't need to wait for the boat to turn up to know that he was dealing with murder. He noticed the man's elbows. They were marked in a way he couldn't identify so he asked the pathologist about them.

'The elbows, shoulders and knees are our fault,' admitted Dr Barrio with a rueful smile. 'He was so stiff we had to coax him on to the stretcher with a hammer.'

'I'm not surprised he's got gooseflesh,' said Caldas, remembering that his assistant had been struck by how cold the body was. 'He was icy', Estevez had said.

'Do you know the exact time of death?'

'For a drowned man, Leo?' said Barrio, spreading his arms. 'He'd been in the water over eighteen hours, I can state that definitely. A day, maybe two . . .'

'Estevez remarked that the body was very cold.'

'It wasn't particularly,' said Barrio, shaking his head. 'It was soaked with sea water, of course, so perhaps that's why the skin felt so cold to him.'

'Right.'

35

Superintendent Soto always said that the bodies of the drowned were the only ones that could bamboozle pathologists. Caldas was learning the truth of this.

'When was he last seen alive?' Barrio asked.

'Seems like it was Sunday morning, in his boat in the harbour.'

'Well, there you have it: a day,' concluded the doctor. 'Can I cover him up now?'

'If there's nothing else.'

'Nothing you can see with the naked eye,' said the pathologist, starting to zip up the grey plastic body bag.

'And the stuff you can't see?'

'When he was searched, a sachet of white powder was found in one of his pockets.'

'Cocaine?'

'That's what I thought but it just tasted like salt. Maybe the sea water had tainted it,' he said. 'We've sent it off to the lab, together with a blood sample. I'll let you know as soon as I get the results back.'

'Anything else?'

The pathologist shook his head.

'Clara Barcia has got the full list of his clothes and personal effects, but there was nothing noteworthy. Apart from the sachet, I think all he had on him was a bit of money, keys and a *figa*.'

'A what?'

'A *figa*,' repeated Barrio. He clenched his fist with his thumb protruding between his index and middle fingers, and held it up. 'Haven't you ever seen one?' he asked. 'It's a kind of amulet.'

'Of course I have,' said Caldas, clenching his own fist in the same way. 'I just didn't know that's what they were called.'

Shadows

The shirt, sweater and corduroy trousers that Justo Castelo had been wearing when he was pulled out of the water sat carefully folded on a metal table at the Visual Inspection Unit. Beside them lay a navy-blue waterproof jacket, together with his socks and underpants.

On the floor, Caldas saw a pair of rubber boots, similar to those his father had been wearing when he had emerged from the rows of vines preceded by the brown dog that accompanied him everywhere. The inspector looked down at his shoes. He'd wiped them with a paper towel when he got to the office, but they retained traces of the sandy soil from the riverbank where they'd walked that morning.

The inspector was still thinking about his father as Clara Barcia showed them each item of clothing and confirmed that nothing relevant had been found on the beach. He was still sorry he'd got out of the car so abruptly, and suddenly remembered that his father had called during the radio show. He looked at his watch. By now his father would have visited Uncle Alberto in hospital and left the city, returning to the sanctuary of his vines. Caldas pictured him sitting at the table, as he had been the night before, looking through his notebook, warmed by the fire and Maria's soup. He promised himself he'd call as soon as he had a moment.

Barcia brought over a tray. On it lay several transparent bags containing the items found in the drowned man's clothing. One contained some banknotes that had almost disintegrated in the water, another two keys on a simple metal ring, and a gold chain and medallion. In the third was the little fist with the thumb protruding between the fingers. It was made of a dark metal, and about the size of a grape.

'What's that?' asked Estevez.

'A *figa*,' said Barcia. 'They were supposed to ward off the evil eye and spells. They protected you against bad luck.'

'Well, a lot of good it did him,' muttered Estevez.

'No, it didn't protect him. But nowadays they're not worn for that, they're just jewellery,' said Barcia. She then repeated what the pathologist had already told the inspector: 'There was also a little plastic sachet containing a white substance. We've sent it off for tests. I expect Dr Barrio mentioned it.'

Caldas confirmed that he had.

'What about the cable tie?' he asked.

Barcia went to a shelf and returned with another transparent bag.

'It had to be cut off, to free the wrists,' she said, placing the sachet containing the tie, which had been cut in half, on the table.

The policemen leaned over to look at it more closely.

'It's green,' said Estevez.

Caldas saw he was right: the smooth side of the tie was green plastic. He didn't need to ask what the dark stains on the other, toothed side – the side that had been in contact with the skin – were.

'Is that unusual?' he asked.

'They're usually white or black, aren't they?' said Estevez.

'Yes, that's right,' said Barcia. 'The problem is I can't see any marks from which to identify the manufacturer.'

'I bet it was made in China,' said Estevez. 'Everything's made in China these days.'

'Quite possibly,' said Barcia. She indicated one of the dark stains like shadows in the indentations of the toothed side of the cable tie. 'We're going to get this tested as well, just in case. Though I'm sure all we'll find is blood and skin remains.'

Caldas was glad Barcia was working on the case. She had initiative and was extremely meticulous. She noticed things other people missed.

She indicated the bag containing the keys and medallion. 'He was wearing the chain around his neck. The medallion is of the Virgin of El Carmen, the patron saint of fishermen.'

Caldas nodded.

'The larger key looks like a front-door key,' Barcia continued, handing the bag to the inspector. 'The smaller one could be for a cupboard, a garage, a junk room ...'

'What about the keys for the boat?'

'Still on the boat, I suppose.'

'Of course.'

Caldas replaced the bag on the tray. He was about to pick up the one containing money when someone came in with a message for Barcia: Alicia Castelo had just arrived and the pathologist wanted Clara to be with her when she identified her brother's body.

Alicia

Justo Castelo's sister had identified the body. She'd been asked to wait for a moment before leaving, and she was sitting on one of the benches in the corridor. She was alone, leaning forward, resting her elbows on her knees, chin cupped in her hands and her gaze fixed on a point on the floor, between her feet. She was wearing dark clothes and her hair was as fair as her brother's.

As Estevez approached, she looked up, her blue eyes red from crying. On seeing the policeman who had spoken to her that morning she smiled faintly. Caldas was pleased to see that his assistant's visit to Panxón had not made a bad impression. At least not on her.

After exchanging a few words with her, Estevez beckoned to the inspector.

'Inspector, this is Alicia Castelo, the sister, you know ... I've told her you've only got a few questions.'

Caldas held out his hand. 'Please, don't get up.'

'Inspector,' she said, taking his hand.

'I'm sorry to trouble you at such a difficult time, but we need to speak to you,' began Caldas gently. 'If you don't feel strong enough we can leave it till tomorrow.'

Alicia Castelo looked at him and Caldas liked her face. Even though it was dulled by grief, the blue eyes ringed with shadows, he found it attractive. He thought she must be about ten or twelve years younger than her brother.

'Do you think he committed suicide, too?' she asked.

'What reason would we have for thinking that?'

'He went to sea and his body turned up on the beach with his hands tied,' she whispered. 'What else could you think?'

Caldas exchanged a look with Estevez.

'You don't believe it?' he asked.

'I know that my brother would never do such a thing,' she said. 'Not while our mother is still alive.'

'We're not convinced that it was suicide either,' Caldas assured her. 'It may be that someone tied your brother's hands and threw him ... Well ...'

The drowned fisherman's sister ran her hand through her hair and lowered her head, looking down at the floor again. After a few seconds, she looked up and asked: 'Do you have any idea who might have done it?'

'That's exactly what we wanted to ask you,' replied Caldas.

She thought for a moment, and then shook her head.

'You didn't live with him, did you?' asked Caldas.

The woman swallowed. Caldas realised that she had shuddered inwardly on hearing her brother referred to in the past tense.

'No. I live with my husband and my mother. She has trouble getting around so she lives with me. Anyway, my husband spends months at a time away at sea. She and I keep each other company.'

'Your brother lived alone?' asked Caldas.

She swallowed again. 'Yes, alone. In the house that used to belong to our grandparents.'

'Do you remember the last time you saw him?' asked Caldas.

Without needing to reflect, Alicia Castelo replied, 'He came to the house on Friday afternoon. He dropped in to see our mother almost every afternoon, before baiting the traps and setting them out at sea. She hardly ever goes out.'

'Did you notice anything unusual about your brother?'

She thought in silence. 'No.'

'Do you know if he'd had an argument with anyone or if anything was worrying him?' the inspector pressed.

'If it was, he didn't mention it.'

'Was he in a relationship with a woman?'

'I don't know. I don't think so. Justo was very reserved.'

'Any new or strange friends?'

Again, she thought not. Remembering the little plastic sachet in the dead man's pocket, Caldas tried another tack: 'What about drugs?'

Alicia looked down once more. 'I don't know what you've been told, Inspector, but Justo gave them up a long time ago.'

'How long is a long time?'

'Years,' she said. 'He did it for our mother. He came off all that junk because he wanted to stop hurting her. That's why I know he'd never have committed suicide while she was still alive. Never.'

'Can you think of anything that might have made him …?'

Caldas didn't finish his sentence. He saw the grief in the woman's eyes and decided not to push her further. He knew there was no point in continuing to question her when she was like this. Alicia Castelo needed time to rest if she was to think clearly and provide answers. Caldas granted it to her.

'Don't worry. I'll give you my number in case you think of anything,' he said, handing her his card. 'I'm afraid we'll have to trouble you again. I hope you understand.'

Alicia Castelo put the card away without looking at it. 'Do you know when we'll be able to bury him?'

'Soon,' the inspector assured her. 'Though it's up to the pathologist and the coroner.'

While they were seeing her out, Estevez placed one of his great big hands on her shoulder as she wiped her eyes on her sleeve. 'Try to get some rest, Alicia,' he said. 'You've got a difficult day ahead of you tomorrow.'

El Eligio

'At least someone doesn't mind all this rain,' said Estevez, indicating the statue as he stopped the car.

The inspector looked up. Through the rivulets coursing down the glass, he saw the merman on his pedestal, illuminated by streetlights. Estevez was right. With the scales of his tail glistening in the rain, the half-man, half-fish seemed to be smiling down on the city.

Caldas got out of the car. He made his way briskly down the Calle del Principe, turned right into the first side street and pushed open the wooden door of El Eligio.

'Good evening, Leo,' chorused the group of academics sitting at the table nearest to the bar.

'Good evening,' he called back, struggling to remove his wet raincoat. When he'd succeeded at last he hung it on the coat rack beside the iron stove and approached the bar.

Carlos was totting up a customer's bill. He always jotted down orders in pencil directly on to the marble counter. Once he'd finished he brought out a bottle of white wine and poured the inspector a glass.

'Everything OK?' he asked. Caldas responded with an ambiguous gesture.

Oroza, the poet, was standing at the bar beside him. He'd enjoyed the radio show that afternoon.

'That story about the man who was breathalysed every time he took out the car was very clever,' he remarked.

Caldas no longer bothered explaining that it wasn't his show and that the calls to *Patrolling the Waves* were unplanned and unscripted.

There had been a time when he'd tried to convince people of this, but he'd given up, realising it was futile.

'Thanks,' he said simply, and saw Carlos smile behind his moustache.

He was planning to have something quick to eat and then go home to bed. Estevez would be picking him up at seven the next morning for the drive to Panxón. The fish market opened at eight, and Caldas intended to get there in time to speak to the dead fisherman's colleagues. He also wanted to see the beach where the body had washed up and go to Castelo's house. He'd had it cordoned off until he could get to inspect it.

Dr Barrio would be releasing the body to the undertakers specified by the family in the morning. Unless absolutely necessary, Caldas preferred not to question the sister again until she'd had a little time to recover from the funeral.

'Have you got anything to eat?' he asked.

'How about some of the veal with chickpeas left over from lunchtime?'

Eating pulses late at night didn't agree with him, but the Eligio's veal with chickpeas was hard to resist. He'd been there a few times when they were preparing it and his mouth watered at the thought of it. Leg of veal, boned and chopped small, was simmered over a low heat all morning together with onions, leeks, carrots and seasoning. After about three hours on the hob, the chickpeas were added and, at the very end, a *sofrito* of onions, garlic and paprika.

'Is it very spicy?' he asked to salve his conscience.

Carlos gave him the answer he wanted. 'No,' he replied, 'it's the same as always.'

Caldas ordered a small portion and carried his glass of wine to his usual table in the corner. He leaned back against the stone wall which so many famous artists, habitués of the *tertulias*, the gatherings convening around the stove and wine barrels, had covered with paintings over the decades.

He stared at the floor between his feet while he waited for his meal, in the same position as Alicia Castelo had sat in earlier. He recalled her relief when she had found out that they too believed her brother had not committed suicide.

The inspector took his mobile phone from his trouser pocket and placed it on the table. Carlos arrived with a steaming earthenware dish of chickpeas.

'How's your uncle?' he asked.

'Not too good.'

'Careful – it's hot,' Carlos warned, putting the dish down. 'And your father?'

'I was just about to call him,' said Caldas, glancing at his watch and seeing that it was almost nine thirty.

'Give him my regards,' said Carlos before heading back behind the bar.

Caldas hadn't had time to get to the hospital that afternoon, so he did want to ask how Uncle Alberto had been that day, but mainly to know how his father was. He'd thanked his father for the lift back to Vigo with that rude departure, and hadn't even suggested they meet for lunch. He owed him an apology, so, lighting a cigarette, he pressed the call button on his phone.

'How are you?' he asked.

'Fine,' replied his father. 'Back home, getting all that traffic and noise out of my system. I don't know how you can all live there.'

'I didn't get a chance to drop in on Alberto after all,' Caldas apologised. 'How was he?'

'We had quite an enjoyable afternoon,' answered his father. 'Partly thanks to you: we listened to your show.'

'Glad to be of use,' said Caldas, not bothering to point out that he was simply a contributor to the programme.

'By the way, we like the new tune they play while you're thinking.'

Caldas felt like hanging up.

'Oh yes?'

'Yes, it's great,' his father assured him. 'I think it works really well. So does your uncle. Was it your idea?'

Caldas avoided answering by raising his cigarette to his lips. 'You called me, didn't you?' he said after a moment.

'Yes, from the hospital. When you didn't answer we realised you must be on air so we switched on the radio.'

'Right.'

'I just wanted to find out the name of that boy you were at school with who's now a town councillor.'

45

What did his father want with that bore?

'Pedro,' he replied. 'Pedro Moure.'

'That's right – Moure. I remembered it later.'

The last time Caldas had bumped into him, after years in which he'd done little more than raise his eyebrows in greeting, Pedro Moure had crossed the road and given him a big hug. That day Caldas had begun to worry about the growing influence of *Patrolling the Waves*.

'If you need something from the City Council, I know other people there. Pedro Moure's a moron.'

'That's exactly why I wanted his name, Leo. Remember that I'm updating my Book of Idiots.'

Was this all his father had called for?

'You had mentioned it, yes,' mumbled Caldas, concealing his bemusement. 'Will you be coming into town tomorrow?'

'Yes, of course. I'll be spending the afternoon at the hospital.'

'I've got to go to Panxón first thing and I'll call you when I get back. Let's have lunch together.'

Before he'd had time to put the phone down on the table it rang again. Dr Barrio's number flashed up on screen.

'Still there?'

'Yes, I've been on duty for the past two nights,' complained the pathologist. 'Have you got a moment?'

'Is something up?'

'Nothing serious,' said Barrio, 'just odd. Do you remember the substance we found in the drowned man's pocket that tasted like salt?'

Caldas didn't reply, waiting for the pathologist to answer his own question.

'Well, I've just got the test results: it is salt,' said Barrio.

'Salt?'

'That's right. Don't ask me why but the man was carrying around a little sachet of salt.'

'What about the blood test?'

'Clean,' said the doctor succinctly, confirming what Alicia Castelo had said.

Once he'd rung off, Caldas ate the veal with chickpeas, which had stayed warm in the earthenware dish. Carlos came over with a bottle

46

of white wine and an empty glass. He sat down, poured himself a glass and refilled the inspector's.

'Pretty good, wasn't it?' he said, lighting a cigarette and indicating the dish, which the inspector had scraped clean.

'Delicious,' replied Caldas. Turning towards the table where the academics were deep in conversation, he asked: 'Are they still on about the breathalyser man?'

'No, they've moved on to something else,' said Carlos with a smile.

Caldas reflected aloud: 'Why would someone carry a sachet of salt around in their pocket?'

Carlos thought for a moment, resting his chin on his fist. Caldas was tempted to start humming the jingle Losada had started playing on the show while he was thinking.

'I don't know,' said Carlos at last, pouring more wine. 'Why would they?'

'I don't know either, Carlos. It wasn't a riddle.'

'So why do you ask?'

'A client,' said the inspector laconically. 'He had a little bag of salt in his pocket.'

'Well, I haven't got a clue.'

They sat on for a few minutes at the back table of the Eligio, smoking and sipping their wine in companionable silence.

When he'd finished his cigarette, Caldas paid for the meal and went home.

Insomnia

By the time the alarm rang at six thirty on Tuesday morning, Caldas had been awake for a long while, lying in bed in the dark, listening to the rain dripping from the eaves and splashing on to the courtyard below. The Eligio's food was really good, but he'd spent all night tossing and turning, having bad dreams and getting up for water from the kitchen. As he headed for the shower, he swore he'd never order chickpeas again after midday.

Uncle Alberto's green face mask, his father and the Book of Idiots had filled his mind during his many wakeful moments. And, throughout, Alba's pendant had been in his thoughts, two metal balls that produced a jingling he now missed terribly. One night she'd told him that the sound was calming to babies in the womb, and Caldas had simply turned over. Only after it was gone did he realise it had soothed him, too.

His thoughts also gravitated to the drowned fisherman, the blows to his blond head and the green plastic cable tie scoring the flesh of his wrists.

The pathologist supposed that the fisherman had, first, received a blow to the back of the head. He'd been struck with a metal object with a rounded end so violently that it had knocked him out. Then, once he was unconscious, his hands had been tied and he'd been thrown overboard.

But there was something in this reconstruction that didn't quite fit: Justo Castelo had apparently set out in his boat alone. No matter how much he tried, Caldas couldn't see how Castelo could have been taken by surprise by someone approaching in another boat. Perhaps an attacker had lain hidden on deck, among the traps, waiting for a chance to jump the fisherman. But Castelo had sailed on a wet Sunday morning when he should have been having a day off. How could the murderer have known that he would be going out?

It was still dark when the lights of Estevez's car appeared outside Caldas's apartment block.

'Morning,' said the inspector as he opened the car door.

'Yeah, great,' grumbled Estevez, staring at the rain, soon to turn into a downpour, spattering the windscreen.

'Do you know how to get to Panxón?' Caldas asked, leaning back in the passenger seat and opening the window a crack.

Estevez shot him a look of contempt, before pulling out and setting off down the hill. They reached the fishing port as the working day was coming to an end and the rest of the city was only just waking up. The last few lorries were lined up on the docks, impatient to receive their cargoes of fish and depart. Across the road, at the counter of the Kiosko de las Almas Perdidas, fishermen and dockers were warming their bellies and trading gossip before going home to bed. Meanwhile, flocks of gulls hovered overhead, noisily demanding food.

They drove on, leaving the fishing port behind and passing the shipyards, where the glow of welding illuminated the bowels of ships under construction.

The inspector closed his eyes and Estevez switched on the radio, which was broadcasting a local news bulletin. There was no mention of the drowned fisherman, only a weather forecast and a report on the increasing number of pedestrians run over in the streets of the city.

'Well, I haven't run anyone over for ages,' said Estevez. 'The last time was in Zaragoza, but that was over three years ago.'

Caldas's eyes sprang open.

'Hope you don't miss it,' he said.

'Of course not.'

'Well, good. While you're working for me I forbid you to run anyone over.'

*

49

They followed the coast until they turned on to the ring road, which was almost empty that early in the morning, and then took the coast road out of Vigo.

The road kept the *ria* – the estuary – to the right and ran past all the small ports along the coast. The tarmac had been laid over the rails of a tram, which an enlightened mayor had decided to pension off decades earlier, replacing electric trams with modern diesel-powered buses.

They passed the island of Toralla, with its skyscraper guiding ships in the darkness like a lighthouse, and drove on until a black shape loomed up over the sea. Beyond the mountain of Monteferro lay Panxón, the end of the journey.

Low Tide

When they reached Panxón, just before seven fifteen by the inspector's watch, they found the fish market closed with no signs of activity.

'Are you sure we needed to arrive this early?' muttered Estevez, looking around. 'The place is deserted.'

Caldas didn't reply. It was the third time his assistant had complained about the same thing and, if Estevez had got it into his head that they'd arrived too early, nothing would make him change his mind. He seemed to be right, though: there wasn't a soul about.

The market stood in a dead-end street which led to a small yacht club; houses ran down to the right and the sea was on the left. Beyond, stretched the stone jetty that protected the harbour.

'Someone'll turn up soon,' said the inspector. 'Pull up over there.'

Estevez drove forward and parked facing the sea. It was still raining so they stayed in the car, with the wipers on and headlights off, staring out at the few boats slumbering in the harbour.

There were no floating docks in Panxón and vessels were moored to buoys fastened by chains to concrete blocks sunk on the sea floor. They were mostly *gamelas*, the shallow wooden boats used in and around the estuaries of that part of the Galician coast, and other small fishing boats, though the occasional mast was just visible in the darkness.

Caldas recalled that, in summer, when the water was crowded with motor boats and yachts, a boy in a dinghy shuttled people out to their boats and back to dry land. But now, in the rain, many buoys swayed empty, bereft until summer, when holidaymakers would once again moor their leisure craft to them.

Opposite the market building, a stone slipway ran down from the street to the water's edge. Near the top, by the parked cars, a few wooden boats lay beyond the reach of high tide.

Past the slipway, the beach stretched away to the lower slopes of Monte Lourido, forming an immense arc broken only by a creek that flowed into the sea, dividing the beach in two.

Monteferro and the Estelas Islands provided the harbour in Panxón with natural shelter. The beach there was protected and calm, but as it left the village it became exposed, so open to the Atlantic that old seafarers claimed that, sailing west in a straight line, America was the first obstacle one reached. For this reason, the stretch of sand beyond the creek was no longer called the Playa de Panxón but the Playa America.

There, away from the lights of the village and the street lamps of the promenade, the outline of the coast was only distinguishable by the white trail of foam from waves breaking on the shore.

Caldas remembered one August when they'd come here often. If the tide was out, Alba would walk the entire length of the beach, at the water's edge, insisting on placing a hand on the wall at either end, as if the walk were not complete unless she did so. He went with her, but stopped before reaching either end, defeated by the seaweed that covered the damp sand near the wall of the Playa America, and the seashells that scraped the soles of his bare feet by the slipway in Panxón.

Caldas was surprised to see how many other visitors shared Alba's quaint insistence on touching both walls, as if they thought their prints would remain on the stone for ever.

'Are you sure it's a market day, boss?' grumbled Estevez after a few minutes, bringing the inspector back from summer walks to a wet autumn morning.

Looking around the empty harbour, Caldas suddenly had his own doubts. What if the market was closed for the day out of respect for the drowned man? It had only just occurred to him, but now it seemed obvious that a small place like Panxón would cease trading when one of its fishermen died.

'Of course I am,' he replied, sinking into his seat. He tried to find a convincing excuse to give his assistant but ruled each one out as it came to him. He had just resigned himself to enduring Estevez's complaints all the way back to Vigo when, almost simultaneously, two lights doubled the jetty and entered the harbour.

The first boat switched off its engine as it approached a buoy where a small wooden rowing boat was moored. The fisherman on board leaned over the gunwale and plunged a boat hook into the water to retrieve a rope.

A lightbulb hanging like an oil lamp over the deck illuminated the man's wizened features. A few wisps of white hair protruded from the dark cap he wore to ward off the cold and rain.

Caldas remembered a crime novel by a French writer that Alba had given him a couple of years before. He'd forgotten the plot but remembered one of the characters, Joss, a former sailor who earned his living as a town crier in a Paris square. He read out the messages given him by local residents and, after each one, recounted the tale of a shipwreck. He'd describe the boat and the conditions at sea, and people held their breath as they waited to hear the number of victims. Caldas liked to imagine the sigh of relief from Joss's audience when he concluded: 'No dead or missing.'

After mooring the boat to the buoy, the fisherman began emptying the contents of his traps into a basket to transfer his overnight catch to dry land. The same operation was taking place in the other returning boat.

Seagulls wheeled above them and, through the open car window, the inspector could hear their cries as they clamoured for fish, and smell the pungent odour of low tide.

'His name's Ernesto Hermida,' said Estevez.

'The old man?' asked Caldas.

'No, the seagull,' muttered Estevez. 'What a question.'

Caldas smiled and watched the fisherman work. As he cleared out the traps, he placed them in order so as to make it easier to set them the following day. When he'd emptied the last one, he turned off the light and the boat was shrouded in darkness.

'Well?' asked Estevez.

'Well what?' said Caldas, wondering what his assistant meant.

Estevez indicated the old man's boat with a flourish.

'What now?' he asked.

Caldas looked at him out of the corner of his eye.

53

'Did you think he was going to let off fireworks at the end?'

'Bloody hell, of course not,' Estevez replied. 'But if he leaves the boat tied to the buoy, how is this Hermida going to get here? Swim?'

'Ah,' shrugged the inspector. There was no sign of the boy who ferried holidaymakers to and from their boats, or of his dinghy. 'I shouldn't think so.'

They next saw Ernesto Hermida rowing towards the slipway in the little wooden boat that had been moored to the buoy. A woman who looked as old as him was waiting by the water's edge, standing on the dark stone exposed by the tide. She wore a white apron over her clothes and held up a black umbrella against the rain. Some of the seagulls had settled on the slipway and stood around her.

As he drew level with her, the fisherman handed her the basket containing his catch. The woman took it from him with difficulty and dropped it to the ground, beside the open umbrella. The old man then jumped ashore and they carried the basket up the slipway, each holding a handle.

'Are we going in then?' asked Estevez, indicating the market, which was now lit up.

Out on the water, the other boat had also switched off its light. Caldas looked at his watch. There were still twenty minutes to go before the start of the auction and he thought he'd rather wait in the car.

The second fisherman's rowing boat appeared among the other craft soon after. It looked smaller than the old man's, like a toy.

'That one's called Arias,' said Estevez, and added: 'He's taller than me.'

Arias needed no help transferring his catch. Seemingly without effort, he started up the slipway with a basket in each hand.

The policemen watched him cross the road and enter the market, then got out of the car.

The Fish Market

The sign above the entrance to the market read in letters set in relief: MUNICIPAL MARKET, 1942. Inside, the single-storey stone building consisted of a light and airy hall with a green-painted cement floor. A long metal table ran down the middle of the hall, beneath a notice that cautioned: *No eating, drinking, smoking or spitting.*

Beside the scales, José Arias was kneeling next to one of his baskets. As the policemen approached, they saw that it contained dozens of crabs. The huge fisherman was taking them out, one by one, grasping them firmly by the back legs to avoid being nipped by the claws. He laid them out on various plastic trays according to size and condition – larger ones on one tray, smaller ones on two other trays and the less valuable crabs (skinnier ones or those that had lost a leg) on yet another. He set a few aside in a plastic bag which he knotted and placed on the floor, resting against the wall. Caldas assumed these were the ones he'd be taking home.

After sorting the crabs, Arias went to the other basket, which was full of hundreds of squirming shrimp. He tipped them out on to three trays and went through them carefully, discarding the dead ones and removing seaweed, small crabs and starfish. As he finished, he placed each tray on the scales for the auctioneer to mark them with their weight. Finally, he set them out on the metal table.

A few feet away, Ernesto Hermida and the woman in the apron were also sorting through the catch, but his traps contained only crabs. They graded and weighed them and then placed them on the table alongside Arias's. Hermida had also caught some fish – six pollock and a couple of mackerel – which he laid on another tray, before standing aside with the woman to wait for the auction to begin.

A man with long grey sideburns and two women were leaning over the table, carefully inspecting the catch. Caldas assumed they were choosing which trays they would bid on.

Another two men, about the same age as Hermida, stood at the entrance, looking out at the rain and the sea, with little apparent interest in the auction.

In the course of his work Caldas had been to the fish market in Vigo a few times. He'd always been struck by the noise of the auctions, the hustle and bustle of boats, lorries, people and crates. He'd enjoyed listening to the shouts and laughter of these men of the sea, aware that the city slept beyond, indifferent to the wakefulness of these nocturnal beings. That morning, however, at the market in Panxón, the only sound disturbing the silence was the rumble of waves breaking on the shore, and Caldas assumed that it must be Justo Castelo's very recent death that was silencing the place.

The auctioneer approached the table, ran a hand over his black goatee, and indicated the trays on which the shrimp from Arias's traps wriggled.

'Excellent shrimp,' he announced. 'I'll start at forty-five euros. Forty-five, forty-four and a half, forty-four, forty-three and a half, forty-three . . .'

Panxón was a small port, with few fishermen or buyers. No one had deemed it necessary to modernise the auctions with electronics, as they had done in most ports in Galicia. Here, the auctioneer still called out the prices.

'It's going down,' whispered Estevez.

'Of course,' replied Caldas.

'Some system. You just have to wait . . .'

The two women and the man with the sideburns seemed to confirm Estevez's theory, remaining silent as the auctioneer called out ever-lower prices.

'Thirty-two and a half, thirty-two . . .'

One of the women raised a hand. 'Yes,' she said.

The auction stopped and the woman inspected the trays of shrimp again, choosing which to buy at the price.

'I'll take them all,' she said. Beside her, the man with the side-burns flashed her an annoyed look.

'See?' whispered the inspector. 'If you wait too long, you can end up with nothing.'

The auctioneer pointed towards the crabs and began his chant again. Then he auctioned the fish. When it was over, the man with the grey sideburns and the women went to a small office at the side of the hall, where the auctioneer took payment and issued receipts.

At the door to the office, Caldas heard them exchange brief words of regret over Castelo's death. He wanted to speak to the auctioneer before he closed the market until the following day, and ask if he'd noticed anything odd about Castelo's behaviour. He'd have time to question the two fishermen later.

He looked round to check that they hadn't left. Hermida was over in the corner, removing his waterproofs, but there was no sign of Arias.

'Where's the tall one?' he asked Estevez.

'He was here a moment ago, carrying his plastic bag. He must have gone outside.'

Caldas was afraid he'd gone home to bed after the night's fishing.

'Make sure the other fisherman and the auctioneer don't leave until I get back,' he said to his assistant. 'I want to speak to them.'

He walked quickly towards the entrance, where the two old boys were still silently staring out to sea.

Emerging from the market building, Caldas looked around for Arias. Dawn was breaking and, with the tower of the Templo Votivo del Mar looming above it, the village was waking up. He saw a couple of people in the distance, walking along the promenade, but the fisherman hadn't had time to get that far.

He turned back towards the old men. Before he'd even asked, one of them jerked his head towards the slipway, and Caldas saw Arias crouching at the water's edge.

A Tall Man

Caldas hunched deeper into his cagoule as a fine rain fell on his head. A few paces away, the fisherman, in a waterproof hat, turned the plastic bag inside out to release the crabs. They dropped on to the stone slipway and, now free, scuttled down to the water and disappeared.

One of the crabs fell upside-down and Caldas saw that it was a female, its abdomen covered with roe. He noticed the same coral patch on all the crabs the fisherman was returning to the sea. They were females about to spawn, loaded with hundreds of tiny eggs the same colour as the fishermen's waterproofs.

'Not everyone does that,' said Caldas. He'd found crabs on his plate just as full of roe on too many occasions.

The man shrugged and shook the bag gently with his great big hands, emptying the last few stragglers. 'It's none of my business what others do,' he said in a voice that sounded as if it came from the bottom of a cave.

The last crab fell out of the bag and disappeared into the sea. It was dark, but Arias remained crouching for a moment, staring at the water as if he could see them crawling away on the sea floor.

When Arias stood up, Caldas realised that Estevez had been right: the fisherman was even taller than his assistant and, though he didn't have Estevez's bulk, he too was solidly built. He had dark skin and eyes, and the stubble on his chin was flecked with grey.

'José Arias?'

The man nodded.

'Do you have a moment?'

'I was about to bring the boat up on to the slipway,' he said, gesturing towards the small wooden craft in which he'd rowed back to land. It sat in the water beside Hermida's, a few metres from the slipway. Both vessels were moored to the same metal ring embedded in the stone.

'Is it OK if I hang around while you do that so we can talk? I'm Inspector Caldas, with the police. I'd like to ask you a few questions.'

The fisherman shrugged. 'Fine. If you don't mind the rain,' he said, and pointed to a platform on the slipway where other small boats like his lay. 'I'll go and get the trailer.'

It was too late to back out so the inspector unzipped the neck of his cagoule, and drew out the hood.

Arias returned, pulling a small, two-wheeled metal trailer. He left it by the water's edge.

'It's about your colleague Castelo, as you can guess,' said Caldas, and he saw Arias wrinkle his nose.

'Of course,' he said, untying the end of the rope. 'What do you want to know?'

'Did you know each other well?'

'As you can see, there aren't many of us fishing here. But we weren't friends, if that's what you're asking.'

Caldas wasn't particularly close to any of his colleagues at the station either.

'I still can't believe he's dead,' added Arias. 'Is it true that his hands were bound?'

'That's right.'

The fisherman pulled on the rope, hauling in the boat until it was lined up with the trailer.

'When did you last see Castelo?'

'Saturday. In there.'

'At the auction?'

'That was in the morning,' said Arias. 'I saw him later on at the Refugio.'

'Where?' asked the inspector.

The fisherman pointed a huge finger at the promenade. Next to the fish market, outside the last building before the yacht club, hung a sign: 'El Refugio del Pescador'.

'When was that?'

'In the evening.'

'What time?'

'It must have been seven or eight. I can't give you a precise time.'

'Was he alone?'

Arias nodded. 'He was at the bar, talking to the waiter. Then he left.'

'And you didn't see him again?'

'No, I didn't.'

'Did you speak to him?'

Arias shook his head and crouched down by the boat, holding it by the bow. He removed the oars and dropped them on to the seaweed-covered stone.

'How about at the auction, in the morning?'

'No, not then either.'

'Did he seem worried?'

Arias looked up. 'I didn't speak to him,' he insisted in his deep voice.

'Even so, did he appear anxious?'

'You didn't know him, did you?'

Caldas shook his head.

'El Rubio never seemed anxious,' said the fisherman, and in less time than it took him to say this, he lifted the boat out of the water, turned it over in the air and dropped it on to the trailer, upside-down. Water poured out of the boat and Caldas jumped aside so as not to get splashed.

'Can I help?'

Arias lifted the boat by its side and centred it on the trailer.

'No, thanks.'

Caldas recalled Justo Castelo's skull on the autopsy trolley. The pathologist believed he'd been struck with a metal bar before being thrown into the water. Caldas pictured the man before him brandishing just such a bar. He wouldn't have needed to exert his full strength to cause a wound like the one on the dead man's head.

'You say he never seemed anxious?'

'He never got agitated, no.'

'About anything?'

60

'That's how he was,' replied Arias, and began pulling the trailer up the slipway.

Caldas followed. 'Are you sure I can't help?'

The fisherman glanced over his shoulder. 'If you wouldn't mind grabbing the oars ...'

Caldas walked back to where the fisherman had left them and, as he bent down, he slipped on the seaweed that covered the lower section of the slipway.

'Watch it,' said the fisherman, scraping the sole of one of his rubber boots on the stone. 'Those shoes are no good here.'

They weren't much good for walking around a vineyard either, the inspector reflected, remembering the previous morning when he'd got them covered in mud by the river.

Stepping carefully, he followed Arias up to the platform where the fishermen kept their boats out of reach of high tide. Caldas counted six rowing boats. He noticed they all had the word *auxiliary* beside the name of the boat they served. On José Arias's boat it read: *Auxiliary Aileen*.

'What does that mean?' asked Caldas, pointing at the dark letters hand-painted on the stern.

'Aileen? It's a name.'

'I've never heard of it.'

'It's Scottish,' said the fisherman, dropping the trailer on the slipway. He took the oars from the inspector and rested them on the upturned boat.

Caldas enquired about the dead man again: 'Do you know if Castelo had had an argument with anyone recently?'

'No, I don't. As I said, El Rubio and I didn't talk much,' replied Arias in his deep voice.

This was the second time he'd mentioned that, though they were colleagues, they weren't friends.

'You didn't get on?'

The fisherman said no, it wasn't that, as he put a chain around the trailer, boat and oars.

'Well, what, then?'

Arias shrugged. 'Life,' he said, tightening the chain and securing it with a small padlock.

Caldas looked around. All the other rowing boats were chained up, too. He wondered who would want to steal these little old wooden boats.

'You're afraid they'll get stolen?'

'No, of course not, but sometimes the oars float off or get washed up on the beach.' Arias indicated the padlock. 'This thing can be kicked open, but at least the oars stay put.'

'Which one is Castelo's?'

'That's his trailer,' he said, glancing over at one that lay empty. Then he indicated one of the rowing boats bobbing on the water tied to a buoy. 'His rowing boat is moored there.'

The inspector went over to the empty trailer. It was chained up and the tiny padlock was locked. He recalled the two keys found on Justo Castelo's body when he was pulled from the water. Neither was small enough to fit the padlock.

He thought he'd call Forensics to request a thorough examination of the trailer and the rowing boat out on the water, but he looked at his watch and decided to call later. Not even the conscientious Clara Barcia would be at work this early.

'Whose is the other one?' he asked, pointing to another empty trailer beside Castelo's.

'It's the old man's. Hermida's his name. His rowing boat's tied up down there.'

Caldas turned to look at the boat moored to a rusty ring.

'Did you know that Castelo put out to sea on Sunday morning?'

'So I heard.'

'But there's no fish market on a Sunday, is there?'

'No.'

'Do you and your colleagues go out fishing on Sundays?'

'No,' replied Arias without hesitation. 'We rest.'

'But someone saw Castelo in his boat before dawn.'

Arias shrugged. 'If they saw him, then it must be true.'

'Don't you find it odd?'

'It's unusual,' Arias admitted.

'Why do you think he went out this particular Sunday?'

'You'd have to ask him.'

Unfortunately that was no longer possible.

'Do you know who saw him go out in his boat?'

'No,' replied the fisherman in his cavernous voice.

62

'Not you, of course.'

'No.'

Caldas felt for the packet of cigarettes in the pocket of his cagoule and held it for a moment.

'What were you doing on Sunday morning?'

'Sleeping,' Arias muttered, and Caldas realised he wasn't going to get any more out of him.

'Thank you for your time,' he said, holding out his hand. It disappeared in the fisherman's, huge and rough. 'I haven't got any more questions for now, but I may need to speak to you again.'

'I'll be here.'

'If you remember anything else, you can contact me on this number.'

Arias took the card Caldas handed him.

'El Rubio didn't commit suicide, did he, Inspector?'

Caldas replied with a question: 'Would that surprise you?'

The fisherman made a face, which Caldas was at a loss to interpret.

'Nothing surprises me.'

'Do you have any idea who—'

The fisherman answered before Caldas could finish the question: 'I don't know, Inspector. I don't know.'

The two old fishermen were still standing at the entrance to the market. Before he went inside, the inspector took one last look at the tall man in orange walking away, head bowed, down the empty street.

Caldas pushed back his dripping hood. It had stopped raining.

The Auctioneer

Caldas went back inside, shaking the rain from his cagoule. The auctioneer was hosing down the floor, directing the jet at seaweed stuck to the cement surface. Estevez was keeping his distance, making sure his gleaming shoes didn't get splashed.

'Where's Hermida?' Caldas asked his assistant.

'He's gone home for a bit,' Estevez replied. 'He said he'd be back in ten minutes.'

'He lives just round the corner,' said the auctioneer, turning off the hose.

'Hello. I'm Inspector Caldas.'

'From the radio?' asked the auctioneer, smiling through his black goatee.

Did *Patrolling the Waves* reach Panxón, or had his assistant blabbed?

Estevez raised his hands, palms upward, mutely declaring his innocence.

'Lots of people here tune in,' said the auctioneer.

Caldas forced a smile, trying to appear pleased.

'Did you speak to Arias?' asked Estevez.

Caldas nodded.

The auctioneer coiled up the hose and dropped it on the floor beside the tap.

'Are there always so few people here on market days?' enquired the inspector.

'In winter, generally, yes. Not many fishermen or buyers. Only

64

three men work from here on a daily basis. Well, two now.' He fell silent for a moment. 'It's some time since we lost a man at sea.'

'Did you know Castelo well?' asked Caldas.

'I saw him here almost every day,' said the auctioneer. 'El Rubio was a good man. '

'When was the last time you saw him?'

'At the auction on Saturday.'

'Did you notice anything odd about him that day?'

'No. He was the same as usual, going about his business. He had a good day on Saturday – he caught a lot of shrimp and they fetched a good price. He certainly didn't seem down enough to do something like that. I'm from Baiona, you know,' he gestured in the direction of the town across the bay. 'A few years ago, a fisherman there threw himself into the sea. The same as El Rubio, with his hands tied so that he wouldn't be able to swim.'

'It's possible Castelo didn't commit suicide,' said Caldas.

The auctioneer looked first at the inspector, then at Estevez, as if questioning what he'd just heard. 'Isn't it true that his hands were tied?' he asked when Estevez nodded to confirm his boss's words.

'It's true,' said Caldas.

'What then?'

'We're looking into it.'

'You think someone tied him up and threw him in the sea?' asked the auctioneer, increasingly curious and plainly dissatisfied with the inspector's answers. 'Why would they do that?'

'We don't know. It's just a possibility,' said Caldas, noncommittally. 'The market's closed on Sundays, isn't it?'

The auctioneer puffed out his upper lip, before expelling the air with a high-pitched sound.

'Sundays and Mondays, because there's no fishing on Saturday or Sunday nights.'

'But Castelo went out in his boat this Sunday. I understand someone saw him before dawn.'

'In theory a fishing boat can't put out to sea on a rest day,' the auctioneer explained. 'It's prohibited.'

'Even if it's not to go out fishing?'

'A fishing boat is a fishing boat, Inspector. It's illegal, but . . .' he left the words hanging.

'But ...' Caldas encouraged him to go on.

'There are things that are forbidden but people still go ahead and do them. You know more about that than me.'

'Right. Do you know of Castelo going out on other occasions? Fishing on a Sunday, I mean.'

'On a rest day? Not as far as I'm aware. Neither El Rubio nor the others. But I don't live here, Inspector.'

'But you are here every day.'

'On market days, yes. I arrive, like today, at five to eight, I auction whatever they've caught and I go straight back to Baiona. I have another auction there at ten,' he said, glancing at his watch. 'And that market's not like this one. They have a lot more boats, and a big fishermen's association, so I need to prepare thoroughly. I don't come to Panxón when there's no market, so I don't know what goes on then.'

'And nobody's ever told you about anyone fishing on a Saturday or Sunday night?'

The auctioneer again blew air into his upper lip, shaking his head, before expelling it and replying, 'This is a small port, Inspector. Only three men work from here. Anyone could see them in their boats and report them. They risk being fined, and losing their licence. It's too high a price for someone who earns a living from fishing. And, believe me, they need their rest days. The work's too hard to be doing overtime,' he smiled.

'I can imagine,' said Caldas. Then he asked: 'Do they always row out to their boats?'

'In winter, yes, they take the rowing boats,' the auctioneer explained. 'In summer there's a boatman on duty ferrying people to and from their yachts and he drops the fishermen off en route.'

'But there are more than three rowing boats on the slipway.'

'Because some belong to the people on List Seven.'

'The people on what?'

'The men who don't fish for a living. Most of them are retired, like those two,' he said, pointing at the two fishermen at the entrance. 'They can only go out from sunrise to sunset, without traps or gear. They use lines, you know, legering or lure fishing.' He closed his hand as if holding a fishing line. 'They're not allowed to catch more than five kilos in total per day. Unless it's a single fish, of course.

You can catch one fish of any weight. It doesn't matter if it's a conger eel that weighs fifteen kilos or twenty-five or whatever. Though there aren't too many of those left.'

'Do you know if any of them put out to sea on Sunday?'

'I don't know for sure, but I assume none of them did,' said the auctioneer, adding after a pause: 'The weather was bad. Like today.'

Caldas nodded and returned to the drowned man's last hours: 'You say that at the Saturday auction nothing unusual happened?'

The auctioneer replied without hesitation: 'Nothing.'

'What about the previous days? Anything that caught your attention?'

'No, nothing. It was a quiet week.'

'I see,' said Caldas. 'How did Castelo get on with the other fishermen?'

'I don't really know.'

'Any conflicts over fishing zones?'

'The sea is open to everyone, Inspector.'

'Never any problems between them? Friction within professions is not unheard-of.'

'Hermida can be a bit grumpy sometimes, but that's because his joints ache,' said the auctioneer. 'He should have retired by now, you know. But he won't hear of it.'

Caldas couldn't help thinking of his father, of his hopes for the newly planted vines even though there'd be no harvest from them for at least six years.

'What about Arias?'

'He and El Rubio didn't have much to do with each other.'

'They got on badly?' asked Estevez.

'I wouldn't say that exactly,' said the auctioneer. 'It's just that they each went their separate ways.'

This echoed what Arias himself had told Caldas on the slipway.

'They're both good guys. And good fishermen,' added the auctioneer. 'I think they used to be quite close. For a time, they even crewed on the same fishing boat. A bigger one, like the ones that go out for octopus.'

'Why did they give that up?' asked the inspector.

The auctioneer again puffed out his top lip and whistled. 'The boat sank. It was about ten or twelve years ago. Before my time.'

67

Again he gestured towards the two men at the door. 'Any of them can tell you the story.'

'Any dead?' asked Caldas, thinking of Joss, the sailor-turned-town crier in the French novel.

The auctioneer rapped his knuckles on the metal table and spat on the floor. Both policemen glanced at the sign cautioning against this.

'One man,' said the auctioneer, spreading the spittle with the sole of his shoe.

Arias had not mentioned this.

'What can you tell me about the buyers?'

'What do you want to know?' replied the auctioneer.

'Were they on friendly terms with Castelo?'

'Yes, on the whole. Everyone got on with El Rubio.'

'They never had any disagreements over price?'

'Not exactly disagreements,' said the auctioneer. 'Sometimes the fishermen complain if they don't get a good price for their catch. It's hard to spend all night fishing and be paid peanuts.'

'But the auction goes downwards,' said Estevez. 'What happens if no one stops it?'

'If the price goes down too far I halt the auction myself, or the fishermen signal for me to stop. The catch is kept for the following day, or else I take it to be auctioned in Baiona.'

'Has that happened recently?'

'No, the catches have been small this year. We haven't had that problem.'

'Have you got a list of regular buyers?' asked Caldas.

'Of course,' the auctioneer replied.

He went to the office and returned a moment later with a sheet of paper, which he handed to Caldas.

'It's always the same people who buy, is that right?' said the policeman, seeing that the list contained barely a dozen names.

'In winter, yes. Almost always. The people you saw here today plus a few others. When the holidaymakers are here it's another story, because lots of private individuals attend. The auction is a tourist attraction.'

Estevez made a sign to the inspector. Hermida was chatting to the other two fishermen at the entrance.

Caldas stood up. 'I thought only people in the trade could bid,' he remarked, recalling the rules at the Vigo fish market.

'Here private individuals are allowed to buy up to four kilos,' said the auctioneer. 'This is a small market and we're not as strict as Vigo or Baiona. Now you know, for next time.'

'One last thing,' said Caldas. 'Do you know who saw Castelo in his boat on Sunday morning?'

'I'm not sure, Inspector Caldas,' the auctioneer replied. 'But someone saw him – that's for sure.'

Captain Sousa

Ernesto Hermida was a slight man. Time, sun and sea had worn his skin, and his face was crazed with cracks like parched earth. He wore a white shirt buttoned to the neck and a woollen sweater that was too big for him. He was still in the boots he'd worn to go fishing, the grimy rubber a contrast with Estevez's shiny shoes.

'So you're the policeman off the radio,' said Hermida when Caldas had introduced himself.

'Yes,' replied Caldas resignedly.

'Another fan, boss,' laughed Estevez. Caldas didn't bother to respond.

'Mr Hermida, we'd like to speak to you about Justo Castelo.'

'You want to talk about El Rubio on the programme?' asked Hermida.

'No, no. This has nothing to do with the show. I'm here in my capacity as a police officer,' Caldas explained, feeling ridiculous at having to clarify this. 'We're investigating Mr Castelo's death and we need to ask you some questions.'

They were sitting at a table in the Refugio del Pescador, the last in a row of restaurants along Panxón harbour, and the place where Arias had claimed to have seen Castelo alive last. There were eight square tables, the three by the window marble-topped, the others wooden like the chairs. A television, switched off, was fixed to the wall beside a poster illustrating different sailing knots. Another similar one, a little distance away, showed all the species of fish in the *rias*, the estuaries of the Galician coast.

'Go ahead,' said Hermida, placing a float attached to two keys on the table. One was large with a black plastic grip, the other was small and smooth.

'Is that the key to your boat?' asked the inspector, reaching out a hand. 'May I?'

The old fisherman nodded and Caldas picked up the key ring.

'The black one is the ignition key,' said Hermida.

Caldas held up the smaller one.

'And this one's for the padlock for your rowing boat, isn't it?'

Hermida confirmed it with a nod.

'Do all the fishermen keep them together?'

'I suppose so,' replied the old man, looking at the float and keys. 'It's handy.'

The waiter arrived with their order: water for Estevez, coffee for the inspector and Hermida, and an ashtray. Caldas took out his first cigarette of the day. He lit it, took a couple of drags, and gestured towards the packet on the table.

'Help yourself . . .'

Hermida declined, tapping his chest. He sipped his coffee and, almost as soon as it touched his lips, grimaced, adding yet more lines to his face. 'The waiter must be asleep,' he complained and, holding his cup out, he said loudly: 'What the hell is this?'

'Black coffee,' replied the waiter from the bar.

'Forget that. Put a few drops in it,' grumbled the old man.

The waiter brought a bottle of brandy and poured a good splash into the fisherman's coffee.

'Would you like some?' he asked the inspector, who shook his head.

When the waiter had left, Caldas pointed at the brandy-laced coffee.

'Will you get to sleep after drinking that?'

'After a night at sea I can drink a cauldron of anything and still drop off as soon as my head hits the pillow,' the old man assured him.

'How did the fishing go last night?' enquired Caldas.

'It went,' replied the old man, causing Estevez to clear his throat.

Caldas smiled. 'I've heard there's not much of a catch these days.'

'Not much,' acknowledged Hermida. 'But there aren't too many of us fishing from here. Fewer every day.'

'That's true,' said Caldas. 'I'm sorry about your mate.'

'It's a shame. El Rubio was a good lad,' said the fisherman.

'What was your relationship with him?'

'We worked together,' said the fisherman.

'I know. But how did you get on?' pressed Caldas.

'Well, like everyone.'

Caldas had a feeling that if he wanted to get definite answers out of the wrinkled old man now draining his cup of coffee he'd have to drag them out of him.

'When did you last see Castelo?'

'El Rubio?' Hermida raised his eyebrows as he thought back. 'I think it was Saturday, at the auction.'

'You didn't see him after that?'

'No,' he said. 'But my wife saw him on Sunday morning, in his boat.'

'So it was your wife who saw Castelo go out fishing on Sunday morning?'

'Who said anything about fishing?'

'Didn't you just say your wife saw him in his boat?' asked Caldas.

'What's that got to do with it?' retorted Hermida and, with a liver-spotted hand, gestured towards the jetty that protected the harbour. 'See those traps?'

Caldas and Estevez looked where the fisherman was pointing. Through the window they saw several dozen traps piled up against the jetty wall.

'They belong to El Rubio,' said Hermida.

'So Castelo wasn't fishing?' asked the inspector, surprised.

'Would you go fishing and leave all your gear behind?'

Caldas drew on his cigarette and looked again at the stacked traps, forming a dark shape against the white wall.

'So what was he doing?'

The old man said nothing, simply spreading his arms in a shrug.

Until then, Caldas had assumed that someone had spotted Castelo setting out fishing, but seeing the traps had dispelled that possibility. So why, Caldas wondered, had Justo Castelo, the man everyone called El Rubio, put out to sea that morning?

'Had you noticed anything odd about Castelo lately?' he asked, expecting another of the vague answers that so annoyed his assistant.

Hermida, however, decided to stick his head above the parapet.

'Personally, I think he was scared.'

'Scared?'

'Yes, scared,' he said.

'Did he say so?'

'El Rubio didn't talk much.'

'So why do you think he was scared?'

'Strange things happened.'

'What do you mean?'

'Things,' replied the old man, retreating. He turned round and asked the waiter for another coffee.

Caldas waited for the coffee to arrive before asking: 'What kind of things?'

'Didn't you just speak to the auctioneer?'

'Yes, but he didn't mention anything strange going on.'

'Didn't he tell you about the shipwreck?'

'You mean the boat Arias and Castelo worked on?'

The fisherman nodded slowly.

'He said it foundered, that one man died, and that Arias and Castelo became estranged because of it. But that happened a long time ago, didn't it?'

'Over ten years ago,' confirmed Hermida.

'So what has it got to do with Castelo being scared?' asked Caldas.

'As I said, strange things had been happening for some time.'

'What kind of things? Caldas asked again.

'Things.'

'Could you be more specific?' the inspector pressed.

Hermida looked around. The Refugio del Pescador was empty. He leaned forward and said quietly: 'He's been seen again a few times.'

Estevez, who'd been quiet until this moment, interrupted: 'You call that being more specific?'

'Please ignore him, Ernesto,' said Caldas quickly. 'Who's been seen?'

'Who else?' said the fisherman, glancing around again. 'Captain Sousa.'

The name was new to the policemen.

'Who's Captain Sousa?' asked Caldas.

'Keep your voice down,' said Hermida. Then he whispered: 'He was the skipper of the boat that went down.'

73

'And you say he's been seen again?' asked Caldas.

Hermida nodded gravely.

'Where?'

'Several places.'

Mystified as to why it was strange that Captain Sousa had been seen again, Caldas asked: 'Had he left the village?'

'You don't understand, Inspector,' muttered the fisherman. 'Captain Sousa drowned when the boat went down.'

'Drowned?' repeated Caldas, puzzled.

'Yes. But he must have had old scores to settle so that's why he came back,' said the old man. 'And that's why El Rubio was scared. So scared he decided to kill himself.'

The policemen stared in silence at the fisherman's deeply lined face as he nodded slowly to add gravitas to his words.

'So you mean a ghost, an apparition?' asked the inspector.

Hermida knocked on one of the metal table legs and spat on the floor.

'Touch metal,' he muttered.

'What the hell d'you think you're doing?' yelled Estevez, springing out of his chair.

'Calm down, Rafa,' said the inspector. 'He wasn't giving you the evil eye.'

'I couldn't give a fuck about the evil eye!' said Estevez angrily, reaching for a napkin from the next table. 'He just spat on my shoe.'

Cold Sea Wind

With the first light of day the boats, no longer vague shapes in the darkness, could be seen, lined up, almost motionless, bows pointing towards the Playa de Panxón.

There were no more than twenty of them, mostly small *gamelas* with oars or small outboard motors. The policemen could make out Arias's and Hermida's vessels, which were a little bigger than the rest and had traps piled on deck. A dark-blue yacht, its mast pointing up at the sky and swaying slowly, stood out among the fishing boats like a glass of champagne on the counter of a roadside bar.

The dead man's rowing boat was still moored to its buoy. Caldas had called Forensics and officers would soon be arriving to remove the boat from the water and examine it, and the trailer.

Following old Hermida's claim that the fisherman's death was linked to the apparition of a skipper drowned years earlier, the policemen had spoken to the waiter at the Refugio del Pescador. His colleague who worked the afternoon shift (the waiter who, according to Arias, Castelo had been talking to the day before his death) wouldn't be coming in until four.

Two men sat at the end of the jetty, their fishing rods out over the water. The policemen headed towards them. Caldas looked at the village, where almost nothing stirred. It looked like a stage set someone had placed between the sky and the beach.

The gate of the yacht club was open and, opposite, so was the sliding door to the boathouse in which sat several small sailing boats under canvas covers. It would be a few months yet before anyone put to sea in them. From somewhere inside the boathouse came the sound of sawing.

They walked on. A cold sea wind, salt-laden, lashed their faces. For a moment, Caldas forgot why they were there. Justo Castelo's traps brought him back to reality, reminding him that someone had cruelly murdered the fisherman they called El Rubio, knocking him unconscious and then throwing him into the sea with his hands tied. Caldas was sure the intention had not been simply to prevent him swimming but to make the murder look like suicide, to convince the inhabitants of the village that the fisherman had decided to bring his own life to a premature end.

Estevez stopped in front of the traps. They were neatly stacked one on top of the other, leaning in two piles against the whitewashed wall.

'How do these work?' he asked.

'They're like cages with sides made of netting,' replied the inspector, pointing at one of the top ones.

'I can see that, Inspector.'

'Well, there you go. The bait goes inside and they're dropped to the sea bottom. When crabs go after the bait, they get trapped.'

Estevez pointed to a short, wide funnel in the top of the trap. 'Is that where they get in?'

'That's right. They're attracted by the bait and they climb up the sides until they find the opening.'

'Why don't they get out the same way they got in?' asked Estevez.

'Because crabs can't swim,' explained the inspector. 'They'd have to crawl upside-down to find the way out.'

'What about shrimp? They can swim.'

Caldas showed him the traps in the other pile. The netting had a finer mesh.

'They're pretty much the same, but the mesh's finer so they can't escape, and the funnel is smaller and conical, much wider on the outside than the inside.'

'To entice them in.'

'And make sure they stay in,' added Caldas. 'Because they can't get out.'

They made their way to the end of the jetty, where the two anglers sat humming to themselves, staring at their lines cast into the water.

Looking down, they could see fish swimming near the surface, circling the hooks, oblivious to the imminent danger. One of the rods suddenly bent violently and the man holding it stopped humming.

'First one,' he smiled, and winked at the policemen.

He started reeling in, carefully at first, then faster, until he pulled out a struggling fish. He unhooked it and dropped it into a metal crate. After baiting the hook again, he flicked the line back out to sea. Caldas approached the crate and saw a gleaming mackerel, writhing frantically.

After a couple of minutes, the thrashing subsided into intermittent spasms. The mackerel, mouth open and gills palpitating in a desperate effort to breathe, would remain motionless for a moment, then summon the energy for another convulsion, its death throes seeming interminable.

Caldas recalled Guzman Barrio's words in the autopsy room. 'Have you ever seen a fish die out of water?' he'd asked.

The mackerel shuddered once more, and Caldas imagined Justo Castelo struggling to breathe beneath the waves, water flooding his lungs. He wondered whether the murderer had struck him on the head out of mercy.

There were three more mackerel in the crate by the time Caldas spotted Hermida and his wife at the foot of the slipway, placing their rowing boat face down on its trailer. Arias had pulled his trailer up to the platform himself, but the elderly couple needed their car to tow the trailer up the small stone slipway and park it alongside the others.

'I'm going to have a word with the old boy's wife,' said Caldas quietly. 'Let's find out what she saw the other day.'

'If she hits the brandy at eight in the morning like her husband, she probably sees ghosts, too,' said Estevez. 'Shall I come with you?'

'No,' said Caldas, turning his head towards the two anglers. 'See if those two can tell you anything.'

A Solitary Boat

'It was half past six in the morning,' said Ernesto Hermida's wife, standing on the flat part of the slipway, next to her husband's trailer and boat.

'Did you check your watch?' asked Caldas.

'I didn't need to check anything,' said the woman. 'I look out every morning at half past six to see what the sea's like. I find it comforting. I've been doing it for years.'

'Do you still look out even when your husband's not going fishing?'

'It's all the same whether he's going out or not. It's a habit. I wake up and I have to go to the living room and see what the sea's doing.'

'I understand,' said Caldas, turning towards the buildings across the road. 'Which is your window?'

The woman pointed to a balcony on the second floor of a building near the fish market, the ground floor occupied by a small chandlery shop.

'So you got up at six thirty and looked out of the window.'

'That's right.'

'What did you see exactly?'

'I saw El Rubio.'

'Where did you see him? Here, in the harbour?'

'No, he was in his rowing boat, heading out between those first few boats.'

Caldas recalled that, first thing that morning, even though he and Estevez had been right by the water's edge, they could hardly make out the boats in the darkness.

'How did you know it was Castelo?'

'By the boat, son. Over time you learn to recognise boats better than people.'

'Did you definitely see it was him rowing?'

'He was well covered up in his waterproofs, like they all are when it's raining. And it's pretty dark at that time of day. But I was sure it was El Rubio,' she said sadly. 'Turns out I was right.'

'That's true.'

'Poor lad,' she added, as if talking about a boy rather than the adult whose stiff corpse Caldas had seen lying on the trolley.

'Was he alone?'

'Of course, Inspector.'

'You're sure?'

'Absolutely,' she said without hesitation, and pointed to the dead fisherman's rowing boat, swaying on the water by the buoy. 'El Rubio's boat is that tiny one over there. If there'd been anyone in it with him I'd have seen.'

Caldas looked at the dead man's rowing boat. Hermida's wife was right: there was no way anyone could have hidden in such a small craft.

'Weren't you surprised to see him rowing out to his fishing boat?'

'Why would I be surprised?'

'It was a Sunday morning and it was raining,' said Caldas. 'It wasn't a day for putting out to sea, was it?'

'If they stayed at home whenever it rained I don't know what we'd eat, son.'

'But fishing is banned on Sundays.'

'I thought he was going to fetch something from his boat. Ernesto often forgets his keys and has to go back to the boat to get them. He grumbles about his joints, but I think it's his brain that's bad. Even though he doesn't drink any more.'

Caldas smiled to himself and continued questioning the woman.

'Did you see him again after that?'

'Yes, a few minutes later. When he switched on the boat headlight.'

'Was there anyone else on board?'

'I already told you there wasn't,' she said unhesitatingly. 'I may be old but I can still see fine. I don't even need glasses for sewing.'

'Did you see anything else?' asked Caldas.

'No. I went to the kitchen to make coffee,' replied Hermida's wife, before lamenting: 'Poor lad! If I'd known the foolishness he was planning I'd have woken Ernesto.'

'There was no way you could have known ...'

A teenage boy came up the street and attached a flyer to the door of the fish market with four strips of adhesive tape.

'There's the death notice,' said Hermida's wife.

They crossed the road together. The name of Justo Castelo, aged forty-two, was printed in large letters, beneath a cross, followed by the announcement that the funeral would be held that afternoon. Caldas thought of the sadness in Alicia Castelo's eyes as she had asked when the body would be released, and he was pleased that the coroner hadn't delayed things longer than necessary.

'I feel sorry for the mother, you know. She lost her husband when she was young and brought up those two children on her own,' said Hermida's wife, after crossing herself. 'El Rubio was always a good boy – quiet, kept himself to himself. But he went through a bad patch. His mother neglected her own health to take care of him, but getting your son well again is more important than being able to walk, don't you think? She's been disabled for years now and lives with her daughter. The son-in-law is at sea so they keep each other company. I don't understand how El Rubio could have done this to them now.'

Caldas did not reply. He turned towards the end of the jetty. Estevez was talking to the fishermen.

'Can you tell me which is Castelo's house?' Caldas asked the woman.

'El Rubio's?'

Caldas nodded, and the woman pointed towards the street leading up to the Templo Votivo del Mar.

'Just before you reach the church, turn left. El Rubio's is a one-storey house painted green,' she said. 'You can't miss it. It's the only green house in the village.'

The Green House

Castelo's house was easy to find. Set into its green façade were a white wooden door and a window with a black wrought-iron grille. A local policeman was standing at the door, smoking a cigarette.

'Inspector Caldas,' said Caldas.

'Like the one on the radio?' asked the policeman.

'That's right,' Caldas replied, entering the house.

He found himself in a simply furnished room. A picture of the Virgin of El Carmen hung on the wall, her dark eyes fixing whoever came through the door. To the right there was a beige sofa and a coffee table. A glass-fronted shelf unit contained a television, stereo and stacks of papers. On the other side of the room were a dining table and four modest chairs and, against the far wall, a sideboard on which stood a line of glass figurines and a couple of photographs.

Caldas crossed to look at the photos. The first showed a football team posing for the camera before a match. Five of the players were crouching and the other six were standing behind them. It was an old photo and Caldas thought he recognised a teenage Justo Castelo in the long-haired goalkeeper. The other, more recent picture showed the dead man with his sister and his mother. White-haired and dressed in black, the mother sat beside her son and daughter, smiling timidly at the camera.

As he held the framed photograph, the inspector felt a familiar shiver. Dead bodies did not affect him, whether fresh corpses or decomposed remains. Unlike Estevez, whose gruff exterior crumbled before a cadaver, when Caldas encountered a murder victim he had no trouble focusing on the clues that could shed light on the case. To him, a corpse was simply the means of solving a crime, like a picture in black and white. But every personal detail about a victim was a brushstroke of colour that, gradually, revealed the human being hidden in the murder investigation.

He hadn't been troubled in the autopsy room the previous afternoon, when Dr Barrio had uncovered the body. But the smile on Castelo's mother's tired face made him swallow hard. Caldas felt sorry for the living, not the dead.

In addition to the front door, two other doors opened off the room. One led to a small kitchen, which was as clean and tidy as the rest of the house, the second to a tiny lobby.

In the bedroom, a crucifix hung above the headboard of a wide, neatly made bed. A wicker chair stood on one side while, on the other, by the window, was a bedside table with a lamp and radio. Caldas pulled open a drawer and found a veritable medicine chest inside. There was a pot of bicarbonate of soda, several packets of antacid tablets, sleeping pills, nasal inhalers, a thermometer and a number of other medicines he didn't recognise.

The window looked on to a small tiled patio with a shed painted the same green as the front of the house.

There was a glass door in the lobby and he went out through it on to the patio. A pergola covered the area closest to the house, sheltering it from the rain. A couple of boat hooks and other implements were leaning against one of the walls, which was also painted green. On the ground lay a few damaged traps and some large black baskets of the kind fishermen used to land their catch in the harbour, stacked one inside the other. In the top basket El Rubio kept fishing lines and a couple of floats like the one old Hermida used as a key fob.

Beside the baskets were coiled ropes and a transparent plastic toolbox. Caldas opened it. In its compartments, hooks and sinkers were arranged by size. There were also a number of reels and lures. Some hooks were threaded with plastic worms or other artificial bait. It seemed ridiculous to imagine that any fish with normal sight would be fooled by such crude imitations.

Caldas crossed the patio to the shed and looked up. The fisherman's house had been boxed in by blocks of apartments and was overlooked by windows whose blinds would remain drawn until the following summer.

The little wooden door to the shed had no handle and was locked. He looked through the window, shielding his eyes from the light so as to be able to see in.

'Inspector,' said a voice behind him, making him jump.

Caldas turned to find the policeman who had been standing guard outside.

'The sister of the deceased is at the door. She says she's come to get some of his clothes. Shall I let her in?'

The inspector went outside with the policeman. Alicia Castelo was waiting, her blue eyes swollen by crying and her hair gathered in a ponytail.

'Inspector Caldas,' she recognised him immediately. 'I didn't realise you were here. I need some of my brother's clothes. The body's with the undertakers . . .'

'Of course, come in,' said Caldas, so that she wouldn't have to say anything more. He stood aside to let her in. 'I've just got here. I was looking around.'

Alicia Castelo went to the bedroom. She opened the wardrobe, took a pair of dark-blue trousers from a hanger and laid them on the bed. She was weeping bitterly as she took a white shirt from a drawer, and Caldas returned to the living room.

On the shelf unit he found a framed newspaper cutting, dating from the previous November. It recounted how a fisherman had caught a species of tropical fish near Panxón that had never before been found off the coast of Galicia. The newspaper attributed the unusual find to the water temperature, which had been several degrees higher than usual for the time of year. In the accompanying photograph, Justo Castelo was smiling broadly, holding up an almost spherical fish dangling from a hook.

'It was his moment of fame.'

'I'm sorry?' Caldas turned to see Alicia Castelo carrying her brother's clothes draped over one arm. In her other hand she held a pair of shoes almost as shiny as Estevez's.

'Everyone saw that photo. They even came to interview him for

83

the TV. Justo was so nervous he could hardly speak,' she said, smiling and sniffing.

Caldas swallowed.

'Have you and your mother managed to get any sleep?'

'Not really,' said El Rubio's sister. 'The funeral's this afternoon.'

'I know. I saw the death notice on the door to the fish market just now.'

Alicia Castelo closed her blue eyes for a few seconds.

'Have you been able to find out anything, Inspector?'

'It's still too soon to say,' replied Caldas, replacing the framed cutting about the sunfish on the shelf. 'Did he own this house?'

'Why do you ask?' replied the woman.

'They could build an apartment block here.'

'Justo didn't want to sell.'

'Did anyone ever make him an offer?'

Alicia Castelo looked up at the ceiling.

'Plenty of people, Inspector. But my brother couldn't be bought. He just wanted a quiet life. Fishing is hard work but he enjoyed it. And he had very modest needs. When he wasn't at sea he could spend hours in his shed,' she said, gesturing towards the patio with the hand holding the shoes, 'just pottering.'

'I wanted to have a look around in there but it's locked. I don't suppose you've got a spare key?'

'No, I've only got one for the front door. But there's just a load of junk in there, Inspector. Old boat engines and bits and pieces like that. My mother says Justo only fixes useless stuff.'

Caldas smiled thinly. 'How is she?'

'Not too good,' she sighed. 'She can't stop crying and she hasn't eaten a thing since she got the news. I don't know how she's going to react when she finds out his hands were tied.'

'Don't tell her.'

Alicia Castelo looked at him just like his father did when he couldn't tell *albariño* from *treixadura* grapes.

'It's hard to keep anything secret in a small village, Inspector.'

'Right,' said Caldas laconically, and returned to the subject of people keen to purchase the house. 'Do you know if he'd received an offer for the house recently?'

She shook her head, swinging her blonde ponytail.

'He may have done, Inspector. I don't really know. Justo didn't talk much.'

'Maybe he mentioned it to your mother, or to a friend.'

Again Alicia shook her head. 'Justo didn't have friends.'

'Never?'

'Years ago,' she began, and went on to tell him what he already knew: 'When he got clean, he had several stints working on a fishing boat, the *Xurelo*. They would spend two or three days at a time out at sea. His crewmates were the only friends I ever remember him having. Justo was happy, but . . .'

'But?' Caldas prompted, keen to hear her version of events.

'Haven't you been told anything about it, Inspector?'

'No,' he lied. Castelo's sister sighed.

'The *Xurelo* went down one night in bad weather. The twentieth of December 1996. I'll never forget the date, or that Christmas. There were four men on board. My brother and his crewmates were young and managed to swim ashore, but the skipper didn't. My brother's a good swimmer but he couldn't help Captain Sousa. That's what everyone called him,' she explained. 'He never spoke of it, but from then on, my brother was a changed man.'

'Changed?' asked Caldas, inviting her to go on.

'Captain Sousa believed in him when everyone else treated him like a lost cause. He helped him, gave him an opportunity to feel useful. After his death, my brother became even quieter and, in a way, he became afraid of the sea.'

Caldas looked at her in surprise. 'Really?' he asked, and she nodded.

'He enjoyed fishing, but after that he never sailed out of sight of the coast, or even went out further than he could swim.'

'What happened to the others?'

'The others?'

'The other crewmembers of the *Xurelo*. What became of them?'

'One spent quite a long time abroad, on an oil rig. He came back to Panxón two or three years ago and now he's an inshore fisherman, like my brother. His name's José Arias. He's very tall. Almost as tall as your colleague.'

Caldas nodded. 'How did your brother and Arias get on?'

'When they were on the *Xurelo* they were close, but that ended.

When Arias came back, there was nothing left of their friendship. They hardly said a word to each other.'

'And the third?'

'The other one was called Marcos Valverde. He got out of fishing, but still lives in the village. Things have gone well for him. He's made a lot of money from tourism and construction. I don't think my brother ever had anything more to do with him either. After the *Xurelo* sank they each went their separate ways.'

Alicia fell silent but Caldas could see in her eyes that there was something else she wanted to tell him. She glanced at the photograph in which she was posing with her brother and mother, searching for the right words. When she found them, she said, 'Yesterday you asked if I'd noticed anything unusual about my brother's behaviour recently.' She paused and Caldas nodded. 'Well, there is something . . . though it might be trivial.'

'I'm sure it isn't,' the inspector said encouragingly.

'My brother had stopped whistling.'

'I'm sorry?'

'Do you know "Solveig's Song"?' she asked.

Caldas had never heard of it and raised his eyebrows enquiringly.

'It's Norwegian, but it sounds like a Galician song,' the woman explained. 'A man from Madrid taught it to us when we were children. My mother used to rent our house to him in the summer. We'd move here, to this house, which belonged to my grandmother at the time, and he and his family would spend the summer at ours. It was terribly inconvenient. My mother and I had to share a bed with my grandmother and Justo slept on the sofa, but with what they paid us we got by for the rest of the year.'

The inspector nodded, wondering where these childhood reminiscences were leading.

'The thing is, for years, my brother would drop by at the same time every day, give my mother a kiss, pick up the paper and sit down beside her to read.'

Caldas swallowed again and Alicia went on.

'Every afternoon was the same,' she said. 'He would pick up the paper from the table and sit down to read beside her. It was like a ritual. Then, not long after he sat down, he would start whistling "Solveig's Song". He did it without realising, as he read. It's a lovely tune, and Justo whistled like a bird. The same song every day. My mother and I would look at each other and smile when we heard it.'

Caldas listened in silence.

'But a couple of months ago he stopped, suddenly, from one day to the next. One afternoon, he arrived, kissed my mother and sat down with the paper as usual. But that day there was no "Solveig's Song". And he never whistled it again. Do you think it could be significant?' she asked, her eyes full of tears.

'I'm not sure,' replied Caldas, resisting the urge to put his arms around her.

'I'm sorry,' she said, wiping away the tears with the back of her hand, the clothes in which Justo Castelo would be buried still hanging over her arm. 'I'm just being silly. I don't know why I'm telling you all this,' she wept, and left hurriedly.

Caldas went back out to the patio and examined the lock on the shed. It was smaller than a normal lock. He thought of the two keys found in the dead man's pocket and was sorry he hadn't brought them. He was sure that the smaller one belonged to that door.

'I'm back,' said Estevez behind him.

'How did you get on with the fishermen on the jetty?' Caldas asked, without turning round.

'OK.'

'Did you get anything out of them?'

Caldas took his own keys from his pocket and selected one of the smaller ones.

'You're not going to believe this, Inspector. Those two think the same as the old boy: Castelo committed suicide because that captain drove him to it.'

'Captain Sousa?' asked Caldas, trying the key in the lock.

'Exactly. What do you think?'

Caldas didn't reply. He chose another key.

'They claimed Castelo had received messages from the captain,' added Estevez.

'Shit,' muttered the inspector. The key had slid easily into the lock but he couldn't turn it. 'Did they say what kind of message?'

'They said Castelo had found graffiti on his rowing boat one morning, and that he'd gone nuts when he saw it.'

'What did it say?' asked Caldas.

'They claim they didn't read it.'

Caldas turned towards his assistant. 'You expect me to believe that those fishermen saw something on a rowing boat on the slipway and didn't go and take a look ...'

'I don't expect anything, Inspector. It's what they said. Apparently El Rubio took the boat straight off to a ship's carpenter to have the graffiti removed.'

Gripping the key with white knuckles, the veins in his neck bulging from the effort, Caldas turned.

'So how do they know it was a message from Captain Sousa?'

Estevez shrugged. 'That's what I asked, but I didn't really get what they answered.'

'Right,' said Caldas, giving up on the key. 'Let's see if you can open this damn door.'

Estevez stepped back, swung his weight for momentum and kicked the door.

'Bloody hell, Rafa!' the inspector exclaimed, only just able to get out of the way.

'I thought you wanted it opened?'

Not only had Estevez opened it, he'd kicked it off one of its hinges. The inspector looked at the broken door, sighed and moved it aside as if it were a curtain.

He went inside the shed and, as Alicia Castelo had warned, found it full of junk. A dusty motorbike chassis was propped against one wall beside the shell of an old lawnmower. On a table, in a jumble of parts and tools, lay several dismantled boat engines.

'Do you know where that ship's carpenter is?' he asked, re-emerging on to the patio.

'There,' replied Estevez, pointing towards one side of the patio. 'He works at the yacht club.'

Caldas looked at Estevez's extended finger, then at the place he was indicating. Beyond the wall, between two houses, he saw a tiny patch of sea. How the hell did Estevez find his bearings like that?

'Did you speak to him?'

'I didn't speak to anyone else, boss. Getting spat at twice in under an hour is quite enough.'

'Twice?'

Estevez nodded. 'I only had to mention that dead captain and bam!' he said. 'I came this close to chucking the fisherman into the water with a hook through his lip.'

The Carpenter

The fish market was closed and only the pungent smell of the dust-bins at the entrance betrayed the morning's business. Up ahead, an old man stopped to read Justo Castelo's death notice. He perched a pair of glasses on his nose and tilted his head back to see through the lenses. Caldas smiled. For years his father had peered at him over his glasses. They had been thick and metal-rimmed, quite unlike the light pair hanging on a cord around the neck of the man reading the death notice. He had removed them only at night or when cleaning them, first misting them with his warm breath and then wiping them with a white handkerchief which he kept in his right-hand trouser pocket. He had long ago replaced them with a pair of bifocals, but Caldas could still clearly remember the way he squinted as he cleaned the old ones, and the red mark left by the frames, a dent that turned the end of his nose into a white blob.

The policemen walked past the old man and went through the gate to the yacht club. On the left, steps led up to the clubhouse. Like many other yacht clubs it had been built to resemble a ship, with a curved outline and round windows like portholes on the first floor. Across the courtyard stood the large shed that served as a boat-house. Through the open door, which was painted white and blue like the rest of the place, they could see the shapes of sailing boats beneath canvas covers.

'Are you sure there's a carpenter here?' Caldas asked Estevez, looking around as they mounted the steps to the building resembling a ship.

'So I was led to believe.'

A few seconds later they returned to the courtyard accompanied by a man who pointed to a sliding door at one end of the boathouse.

They slid it open and found a smallish workshop, lit by fluorescent tubes hanging from the ceiling and separated by a partition from the rest of the building. A carpenter's bench with two lathes fixed to it ran down the whole of one wall. Beside small boards all cut to the same size, the toothed blade of a circular saw protruded from a slot.

By the door, beside the ribs of a boat in the making, a grey cat lay dozing. It opened its eyes for a moment, looked at them with indifference and then curled itself tighter.

Estevez nodded towards the back of the workshop and, by the only window, Caldas made out the figure of the carpenter. He was sitting on a stool with his back to them, leaning over a small boat.

As they advanced through the workshop, avoiding a boat with a hole in its hull, the smell of the sea gave way to the odours of wood, glue and paint.

Caldas and Estevez stood behind the man leaning over the little boat, an old *gamela* that, despite having been thoroughly rubbed down, still retained a hint of blue from an original coat of paint. The carpenter reached into a bag and extracted a handful of fibres, remnants of old rope, which he inserted into the seam between two planks. He pressed the frayed bundle first with his fingers, then with a kind of chisel, which he tapped with a wooden mallet – one light tap followed by two or three harder taps, like drum rolls.

'What's he doing?' whispered Estevez.

'Caulking the boat,' replied the inspector quietly.

This explanation did not satisfy Estevez, who raised his eyebrows theatrically.

'Oakum is pushed between the planks and tamped down so there are no gaps for water to leak in through,' said the inspector. 'Then it needs a coat of pitch to protect the wood.'

The carpenter stopped hammering and turned slightly towards them.

'That's more or less it, isn't it?' Caldas asked him.

The carpenter bent over the boat again.

'More or less, though we don't treat the wood with pitch any more,' he said, pressing more oakum into a seam before striking it with the

91

mallet from different angles. 'You needed to know what you were doing when applying it, because if it was too soft it melted and if it was too hard it ended up cracking off. So now we use a vegetable tar.'

'Right.'

Caldas noticed that several fingers were missing on his right hand, the one he was holding the mallet with, and instinctively his eyes sought the circular saw on the bench. He wondered if it had been responsible for the injury. Then he turned back towards the carpenter, who continued pressing oakum into the seam until it was sealed. When he'd finished, he put his tools down on the floor and got to his feet.

'Did you want something?'

'I'm Inspector Caldas,' he said, resisting the urge to hold out his hand. 'And this is Officer Estevez. We're from Police Headquarters in Vigo. Do you have a moment?'

The carpenter nodded. His work clothes were as paint-spattered as the stool on which he'd sat. Medium height and thin, he had dark hair and a thick, untidy reddish beard, which made it hard to judge his age. Too young at any rate, thought Caldas, to have lost three fingers.

'How can I help you?'

The cat that had been dozing at the door suddenly appeared around the carpenter's legs and started rubbing against them.

Caldas thought of the brown dog greeting his father the previous evening. Though his father had claimed it wasn't his, the dog had howled and leaped with such joy on seeing him that Caldas had feared it would pee from excitement.

'Is it yours?' he asked, gesturing towards the cat.

'Of course,' replied the carpenter.

'Right,' said Caldas, staring at the creature, which was still rubbing against its owner's trousers.

'Have you come about the cat?' asked the carpenter, as puzzled as Estevez by the inspector's interest.

'No, no, we want to speak to you,' said Caldas, feeling foolish.

'It's about Justo Castelo. El Rubio,' added Estevez, getting to the point.

'You knew him, didn't you?' asked the inspector.

The carpenter nodded and with his maimed hand indicated the half-built boat by the entrance.

92

'That boat was for El Rubio,' he said.

The inspector looked at the boat, his assistant looked at the hand.

'When did he order it?' asked Caldas.

'It must have been a couple of months ago. He wasn't in a hurry because he was collecting the parts to build the engine himself. I had other more urgent jobs but at odd times, well ... If I'd known, I wouldn't have started on it.'

'Of course not,' said Caldas. 'I expect you spoke to him quite a bit during that time?'

'Not really, Inspector. We spoke when he placed the order and a few times after that. He was a quiet guy.'

Caldas thought the carpenter didn't seem too chatty himself.

'When was the last time you saw him?'

'El Rubio? He dropped in on Saturday at midday. But we didn't say a word to each other. He arrived, had a quick look at the boat, waved at me from the door and left. As I said, he wasn't the kind to stop and chat.'

Caldas decided to stop beating about the bush.

'We've been told that recently Castelo got you to remove some graffiti from his boat,' he said, and noticed the carpenter's expression change.

The carpenter ran his mutilated hand through his hair and Estevez's eyes followed it as if magnetised.

'Is that right?' Caldas pressed him.

'Not quite. El Rubio wheeled the rowing boat here on his trailer and asked for sandpaper to rub down the wood and then give it a coat of paint. He removed the graffiti himself.'

'Did you see what it said?'

'On the boat?'

Estevez cleared his throat and Caldas gave him a warning look.

'Yes,' said the inspector. 'Did you read it?'

'More or less.'

'More or less?'

'It was a few weeks ago,' said the carpenter apologetically.

'Try to remember,' urged the inspector.

The carpenter looked down at the cat, which was still twining itself around his legs.

'It was a date.'

'Can you remember it?' Caldas asked.

The man again passed his maimed hand over his hair.

'The twentieth of December 1996,' he said. 'In figures: 20/12/96.'

It couldn't be a coincidence. The twentieth of December was the day the *Xurelo* had foundered. El Rubio and the other crewmembers had survived, but it was the date of Captain Sousa's death.

'Are you sure?' he asked, and the carpenter replied with a small nod.

Caldas recalled that the fishermen Estevez had spoken to had mentioned a threatening message supposedly written by Captain Sousa on the rowing boat. Could a date alone constitute a warning? Numbers daubed on a boat would mean something to someone like Castelo, who had that tragic winter's night branded on his memory, but after all this time Caldas wasn't sure the other villagers would see them as a threat.

There had to be something else, so he decided to nudge the carpenter towards the right path.

'That date wasn't the only thing painted on the boat, was it?'

The carpenter looked straight into the inspector's eyes, but his beard prevented Caldas from fully reading his expression.

'What else was there?' he pressed. 'A sentence?'

'I only saw it for a split second,' replied the carpenter, glancing towards the closed door of the workshop.

'No one will know we've spoken to you about this,' Caldas assured him. 'Anyway, I get the feeling you weren't the only person who saw what was painted on the boat that morning.'

The man thought for a moment longer before finally muttering: 'It was one word.'

'Just one?'

The carpenter nodded, again looking down.

'Do you remember what it was?' asked Caldas, already knowing the answer. If he remembered the date painted on the boat so clearly, he couldn't have forgotten the word that went with it.

'"Murderers",' said the carpenter, sighing as if a weight were being lifted from him.

'"Murderers"?' asked Caldas.

The carpenter nodded slightly.

'"Murderers" in the plural?' pressed the inspector.

The man nodded again.

'I didn't tell you anything,' he said.

As they left the carpenter's workshop they were once again over-whelmed by the smell of the tide, which was now rising.

'Who the hell did you think it belonged to?' asked Estevez.

'What?'

'The cat, of course. Who did you imagine its owner was?'

'I don't know,' mumbled Caldas, walking on. 'It could have belonged to anyone.'

He stopped at the door to the Refugio del Pescador and glanced inside. There were a few customers leaning on the bar, while another was at a table reading a newspaper. Caldas looked at his watch and clicked his tongue. José Arias would be sleeping by now. The inspector needed to speak to him, but he'd have to wait a few hours. He crossed the street to the car and looked out at the boats moored in the harbour. The boys from Forensics hadn't yet come to collect Justo Castelo's rowing boat to examine it.

'Incredible how someone can work like that, isn't it?' remarked Estevez, joining him.

'Like what?'

Estevez pressed three fingers of his right hand against his palm.

'He had almost three whole fingers missing. Didn't you notice?'

'Oh, yes, right,' replied Caldas absently.

His gaze was fixed on the boats and his thoughts were very far from the carpenter's hand.

Horizon

Caldas took out his pack of cigarettes and lit one. They were leaning on the handrail at the Playa de la Madorra, watching the waves break on the dark strip of seaweed along the shoreline.

'Where did you say they found him?'

'Over there, in the seaweed,' replied Estevez, pointing.

Caldas looked at the spot his assistant had indicated and then to either side of it. To the left, a small spit of land sheltered the bay. On this, beyond the reed bed that they could see from where they were standing, were the fish market, the yacht club and a few houses. Panxón's huge expanse of sand extended beyond but was hidden from sight. To the right, at the end of the beach, rose Monteferro. That morning, the silhouette of the mountain was as grey as the sky and sea, and the monument at its summit was almost obscured by mist. Off the tip of the promontory, the two dark humps of the Estelas Islands emerged from the sea.

'There was foam coming out of his mouth,' added Estevez.

'Yes, you said,' replied Caldas, reflecting that Castelo's body could have been dragged there from anywhere, like the seaweed whose smell was almost stopping him enjoying his cigarette.

He descended the steps to the beach and headed towards the water. The rain had formed a dark layer on the sand, a crust that cracked with every step. Caldas stopped a few metres from the water's edge and stood contemplating the waves, with the cold sea wind making the tip of his cigarette glow more brightly. He pictured the fisherman's dead body caught in the tangle of seaweed, buffeted by the same waves now breaking before him.

They'd spoken to several locals after their conversation with the carpenter, all of whom described Castelo as a calm, quiet man, too reserved to have enemies among the people of the village. No one had ever seen him with any women other than his sister and mother, or knew of any friends apart from Arias and Valverde, the fishermen he'd broken off contact with after the shipwreck of the *Xurelo*. Although he sometimes spent evenings at the Refugio del Pescador like the other fishermen, El Rubio neither played cards nor drank too much. There seemed to be nothing in his life apart from fishing, the contraptions in his shed and his visits to his mother.

Caldas had been surprised not to hear the kind of excessive praise usually heaped upon the recently deceased, but there hadn't been any criticism either. He got the impression that they were neither sorry nor glad that Castelo was dead. The inhabitants of Panxón maintained the same cautious distance from the dead fisherman that he had kept from them in life.

However, like the damp crust cracking beneath his feet to reveal the white sand beneath, the civility that had surrounded Justo Castelo's life had been fractured by superstition upon his death.

No one in Panxón doubted that El Rubio had taken his own life and, though they didn't say so openly, they all sought culprits in the past, in the fear of the ghost of a skipper drowned years before, whose mere mention made seafarers touch metal and spit on the ground.

The word and date painted on the dead man's rowing boat also pointed to the sinking of the *Xurelo*. The carpenter had remembered the word and date daubed on the wood even though he'd only glimpsed them fleetingly. Caldas was waiting for confirmation from Forensics, hoping that some trace on the paintwork, the shape of the letters and figures, or some other clue might lead to the culprit.

He drew on his cigarette one last time before bending down to bury it in the sand. He remained crouching, admiring the waves. He could watch the sea, hypnotised, for hours, just like a fire. He loved watching the waves rise as they approached the shore and then collapse violently and continue towards the beach as a line of foam. He found it unspeakably cruel that someone had thrown the fair-haired fisherman into that same relentless sea, after striking him on the head and tying his hands.

Apart from Hermida's wife, no one had seen Castelo set out on Sunday morning. Most people were sleeping late on their day off, and the few awake at that early hour had been deterred by the wind and rain from leaving their houses before mid-morning. Hermida's wife had watched the fisherman from her window, as he rowed out to his boat. Then she'd seen him put out to sea, alone and with the boat's light on, at around six thirty.

The yacht club caretaker hadn't seen Castelo depart as he was only on night duty during the tourist season. His shift hadn't started till seven in the morning and no boat had left the port on that sad, grey October morning after that hour.

Estevez had telephoned the port of Baiona, across the bay, and there had been no activity there either. The weather had been too bad for leisure craft to set sail, and fishing boats were banned not only from catching fish but even from putting out to sea on a Sunday.

Caldas looked up from the crest of a wave to the horizon. It was just a blur between sea and sky. He couldn't believe that, on the morning of the murder, Castelo's boat – with no one but himself on board – had been the only vessel out in that area of ocean. The fisherman's body had been dragged by the tide on to that beach, but where was the boat? Forensics officers were searching every inch of the coast. It had to turn up sooner or later.

Caldas made his way back to the road across the crusted sand. His assistant was still leaning on the metal handrail.

'Find something, Inspector?'

Caldas looked at him grumpily. What did Estevez have in mind? Buried treasure?

'You were crouching there for some time,' Estevez said defensively.

'No,' said Caldas, 'I didn't find anything. Did you find out where that other fisherman lives? Valverde?'

'Yes.'

'Do you think you can get us there?'

'Of course, it's right nearby.'

'Come on then.'

'Have you seen the state of your shoes?' said Estevez before getting into the car.

'Yes,' Caldas replied without bothering to look.

Straight Lines

Estevez left the Playa de la Madorra behind, took the turning to Monteferro and then, a little further on, turned on to a narrow lane that descended steeply between tightly packed houses. The lane came to a dead end before a large gate.

'This must be it,' said Estevez.

They got out of the car, walked up to the dark wooden gate and rang the bell several times. There was no response. At the side, on the pillar to which the gate was hinged, there was a letterbox, but the space left for the owner's name was empty. Caldas couldn't see any letters inside.

Estevez, who had been peering through a gap between panels in the gate, grasped the top as if about to vault over.

'I don't think there's anyone here,' he said. 'Do you want me to go in?'

Caldas looked at him aghast. 'We're not here to burgle the place,' he said. He sighed, convinced he'd never understand how Estevez's mind worked, and returned to the car.

There was no room to turn the car around so Estevez had to reverse up the hill but, after a couple of minutes, despite the racket from the engine, they'd only managed to back up a few dozen metres.

'Sure we'll be able to get out?' asked the inspector.

Estevez jerked his chin towards the rear-view mirror.

'We will if that car moves.'

Caldas turned around in his seat. There was indeed a red car behind theirs. The inspector lowered the window and stuck his head out.

'There's no exit,' he shouted.

He thought he saw the driver of the red car gesturing for them to drive forward, so he told Estevez to return down the lane to the house.

As they neared the gate, it opened automatically. Estevez drove through and pulled up in the courtyard beyond.

'Is that a house?'

'What do you think?' replied Caldas, staring at the façade that gave on to the courtyard. It was a smooth, blank concrete wall.

'I don't know. It looks like a nuclear bunker,' said Estevez.

The red car drew up alongside them and a young woman in a yellow raincoat got out of the driver's seat. She came up to the inspector's lowered window. She had an angular face and dark, very short hair.

'You can turn around here,' she said. 'The council ought to put up a *No Exit* sign at the top so that people don't drive down here by mistake.'

'We're not here by mistake,' said Caldas through the open window. 'We're looking for Marcos Valverde's house. Is this it?'

'Yes. Marcos is my husband,' she said. 'Who are you?'

'I'm Inspector Caldas, from Vigo Police Headquarters.'

'From *Patrolling the Waves*?' asked the woman.

Caldas nodded.

'Has something happened to my husband?'

'No, no, everything's fine,' Caldas reassured her. 'We just need to talk to him about something.'

'Marcos isn't here at the moment,' she said hesitantly.

'In that case maybe you can help. We'll only take a few minutes of your time.'

They carried the woman's shopping bags, following her along the gravel path.

Caldas looked around. There was a small rock garden dotted with herbs and a lawn with a row of leafless fruit trees. Up ahead, he spotted lemon verbena growing at the foot of the concrete wall.

As they turned the corner, the bunker was transformed, revealing a façade made entirely of glass overlooking a sloping garden and, beyond, the sea. Caldas reflected that life hadn't treated the fisherman

101

too badly if this was his house. It looked like the seaside residence of an avant-garde architect rather than the home of a man who, only a few years earlier, had been a friend and crewmate of José Arias and Justo Castelo.

'Would you like something to drink?' she asked as they entered.

The policemen declined. While she went to put the shopping away in the kitchen, they waited in a living room that looked like a homage to straight lines and sharp edges. The wrought-iron fireplace at one end of the room was square, as were the chairs and prints on the wall. The bookcase, sofa, table and state-of-the-art sound system were all rectangular.

Estevez went to the huge window to admire a view that encompassed the entire bay, from Panxón to Baiona. Caldas went out to the garden for a moment to shake the sand from his shoes. On his return, he approached the bookcase, which was made of the same concrete as the façade giving on to the courtyard. He was looking over the classical music records when the woman returned to the living room. She had removed the yellow raincoat. She wore a white shirt with the top buttons undone, and tight trousers that showed off a shapely figure that was if anything too curvaceous for that house.

'Do you like music, Inspector?'

'Not as much as you or your husband, I suspect.'

'Me,' she said. 'But I sometimes listen to your show as well. I didn't know you were real.'

'Sorry to disappoint you,' said Caldas, and she smiled just as Alba used to, turning down the corners of her mouth.

Caldas ran his eyes over the hundreds of records ranged on the shelves, wondering whether the tune Justo Castelo had stopped whistling shortly before his death was among them.

'Do you know "Solveig's Song"?' he asked.

'Of course. It's Grieg. It's there somewhere,' she said, seating herself in one of the square armchairs. 'Please, sit down.'

'You're not from here, are you?' asked the inspector.

'No,' she said. 'I'm from Madrid. My family spent the summer here for years, but this is only my second winter in Panxón.'

'And how are you finding it?'

'I'm dying for the hot weather and crowds to arrive,' she said with a resigned smile. 'I never thought it would be so hard.'

'Tell me about it,' snorted Estevez, speaking for the first time.

'At least you live in a beautiful house,' said Caldas. 'Did you design it yourselves?'

'No. We bought it last year. The previous owner was an architect from Madrid, a friend of my family's. He was planning to retire here.'

'So how come he sold it to you?'

She looked up at the high ceiling. 'Marcos knew how much I liked the house and didn't let up until my parents' friend agreed to sell it to us. He always achieves what he sets out to do, you know. He has that gift.'

'I see. Where is he now?'

'Working, as usual. Everything he has he got through hard work.'

'And what does your husband do?'

'Too many things. He can't sit still. Construction, cars ... He's even started making wine.'

'Wine?'

'Yes. He's planning to bottle his first vintage next year. In fact, he's probably at the vineyard right now. It's what takes up most of his time these days. He likes to keep an eye on things. They're pruning the vines at the moment, so he goes there every morning.'

Caldas decided to broach the subject that had brought him there. He glanced around in search of an ashtray but couldn't see one so gave up on the idea of a cigarette.

'Has your husband ever spoken of his time as a fisherman?'

He saw in her eyes that she now understood the reason for their visit.

'You've come about the suicide of that fisherman, haven't you?'

'That's right,' replied Caldas, toying with the cigarette packet in his pocket. 'Did you know that your husband used to work with him?'

'Yes, of course.'

'Has he told you about it?'

'He doesn't need to. Marcos rarely talks about the past, but I can always find someone ready to make insinuations. Things you'd rather not hear.'

'What kind of things?'

'This is a small village, Inspector. Don't be fooled by the number of houses,' she gestured through the window towards the buildings along the beach. 'In winter they're all empty. I dislike gossip, so I

103

only go into the village when I absolutely have to. I don't want people talking about me or telling me other people's private business.'

'Did you know that the boat your husband and Castelo worked on together sank?'

'Of course I do, Inspector. And that one man died.'

'But you've never spoken to him about it?'

'Once,' she replied. 'But Marcos got angry. I suppose it's understandable that he'd want to forget something so traumatic.'

'I guess so. Did your husband keep in touch with his former crewmates?'

'Not at all, as far as I know. Not with El Rubio or that giant, Arias.'

'But they were close friends at one time.'

'I don't think they were that close, Inspector. Marcos doesn't have much in common with them.'

'Do you know them?'

Valverde's wife shook her head.

'Arias only by sight. He came back to the village not long after I moved here. I've ordered shellfish from El Rubio a couple of times, if I've been entertaining. I've had more to do with his sister, the teacher. She must be devastated.'

'Yes,' said Caldas, thinking how different the two women were.

'You know something, Inspector? I felt sorry for that man, El Rubio. He was always alone and he looked unhappy. Really unhappy. I don't think anyone was surprised that he killed himself.'

'No,' said Caldas tersely, and then pushed on. 'Has your husband seemed worried lately?'

'He's always worried about something. Marcos is like that.'

'What I mean is, has anyone tried to scare him?'

'I know what you're referring to. Surely you don't believe in village hallucinations?'

Valverde's wife and Rafael Estevez both stared at him, awaiting his response, and Caldas suddenly felt himself blushing.

'What do you mean?' he stammered, squeezing the packet of cigarettes in his pocket.

'Come now, Inspector. You know perfectly well what I'm talking about. Captain Sousa, the skipper of the shipwrecked boat. They say his ghost has been appearing and hounding El Rubio. I'm sure there are plenty of locals prepared to swear it was the skipper who drove him to suicide. You don't believe that nonsense, too, do you?'

'It's not a question of what I believe. Have you noticed your husband looking anxious, scared?'

'Of the ghost?'

'Of anything.'

'No,' she assured him. 'Marcos doesn't have time for superstition.'

Valverde's wife saw them to their car. Caldas stepped off the path a moment to run his hand over the lemon verbena.

'We'll need to talk to your husband,' he said, inhaling the fragrance on his fingers. 'Do you know if he's going to Castelo's funeral this afternoon?'

'I think so.'

Caldas gave her his card. 'This is my number,' he said. 'Call me if you need anything.'

'Anything?' she asked, and for a split second Valverde's wife disappeared and he saw Alba again, smiling at him.

Caldas blushed for a second time and lit a crumpled cigarette, trying to hide his embarrassment behind a veil of smoke.

'Nice to meet you, Inspector Caldas,' she said, and her shirt parted further as she held out her hand.

'Likewise,' he replied, taking her hand and making a superhuman effort not to stare at her breasts.

He climbed into the car, wondering how a man could have gone from working on a small fishing boat to having a house and a wife like that in so few years. He was still pondering when the high-pitched ring tone of his mobile sounded.

'I thought we were meeting for lunch,' said his father.

Caldas looked at his watch, saw that it was almost two and swore. He'd forgotten to phone and say he couldn't make it.

'I'm still in Panxón,' he said apologetically. He was still feeling guilty about his brusque exit from the car the day before, when his father had asked about Alba, and he hated letting him down like this. 'I'm sorry I didn't let you know.'

'We could meet an hour later, if you like. I've got things to do.'

So had Caldas: he wanted to go to the cemetery for the funeral and speak to the crewmembers of the *Xurelo* and the waiter of the Refugio del Pescador who'd chatted to Castelo that Saturday afternoon.

'The thing is, I need to be here early this afternoon.'

'I'll see you later at the hospital then?'

'Maybe,' he said, knowing that he almost certainly wouldn't get back to Vigo in time for visiting hours. 'Do you know how Uncle Alberto is doing today?'

'About the same as yesterday.'

'Right.'

'So you'll be having lunch in Panxón?' asked his father, without a hint of the disappointment that Caldas knew he must be feeling.

'Yes, we'll have a quick bite to eat here.'

'If you get a moment, you could drop in on Trabazo.'

Trabazo! It was a long time since Caldas had heard the name. 'Have you heard from him?'

'We spoke this morning.'

It couldn't be a coincidence. 'Today?'

'Yes. He asked about you. He always listens to your show.'

'You didn't tell him I was working in Panxón, did you?'

'No, of course not. But I know he'd love to see you.'

Speculation

Looking down at the sand darkened by the morning's rain, the police-men walked along the promenade, which ran along the top of the sea wall. The wall defended the village when, during winter storms or at spring tides, waves engulfed the Playa de Panxón.

As they neared the covered restaurant terraces where the inspec-tor had suggested they eat, Estevez asked, 'Where did you mean?'

'There,' replied his boss, pointing in the direction of two almost identical terraces.

'But which one?'

The last time Caldas had eaten there he'd been with Alba, one summer. Then there had been no screens or heaters. He couldn't remember which terrace they'd sat at, only that, though the food had been good, he'd felt uneasy. The tables couldn't be reserved and there were too many people on the promenade, a few metres away, staring at the diners, waiting for someone to vacate a table and swooping like excitable seagulls.

'That one,' he pointed to the terrace on the right, though he could just as easily have chosen the other. He was merely pleased that the promenade was empty of holidaymakers ready to pounce.

Only two other tables were occupied. Caldas and Estevez seated themselves at one a little distance from the rest and, after looking at the menu, they decided to share a potato omelette and a plate of octopus with clams.

'And two glasses of white wine,' said Caldas.

'Could you bring a salad as well?' said Estevez as the waiter was about to return to the kitchen.

Lately, his assistant always insisted on ordering salads.

'Are you taking care of yourself?'

'No,' Estevez assured him. 'It's just that the lettuce is great here.'

'Here?'

'In Galicia.'

'Oh, right.'

When the waiter had brought the wine, Caldas raised his glass to his lips and gazed at the harbour and the boats swaying on the water, moored to the buoys. He made out Justo Castelo's mooring. The rowing boat was gone. He hoped Clara Barcia would find something that would help them get this investigation going.

'Are you thinking about the ghost, or Mrs Valverde's tits?' asked Estevez, bringing the inspector back to the table.

'What was that?'

'You heard me,' smiled Estevez.

'Right,' said Caldas, taking another sip of wine.

'Can I ask you something, Inspector?'

'Of course.'

'What do you think of the Captain Sousa story?'

'I don't think anything.'

'But do you believe that Castelo's death is connected to the ship-wreck?'

'Maybe,' Caldas admitted, 'but it may also have nothing to do with it.'

Estevez snorted like a bull. 'I don't know whether to go for a piss or shoot myself. Would it kill you to be a little more specific?'

'What do you want me to say?'

'Well, what you really think about this bloody ghost business.'

'I know as much as you: Castelo received threats and, not long after, his body washed up on the beach.'

'But don't you find it odd that everyone's blaming a man who drowned over a decade ago and whenever they mention him they spit all over your shoes?'

'A little.'

'A little?'

'OK, Rafa, it seems rather strange. Is that what you want to hear?'

'Yes,' admitted Estevez. 'Why is it so difficult for you people to say things clearly?'

The waiter set the dish of octopus and clams down on the table and the delicious aroma of the seafood made them postpone their discussion. Then the freshly made omelette and salad arrived. In the local style, the salad consisted simply of lettuce, tomato and onion dressed with olive oil, white wine vinegar and coarse salt. Only once they were having their coffee did Estevez bring up the subject of the drowned skipper again.

'Have you definitely ruled out suicide?'

Caldas resisted the urge to give him a silly answer to put an end to the conversation; he knew that thinking aloud often helped him work things out.

'Yes, I think we can rule it out,' he said, lighting a cigarette.

'But, as we've heard, everyone agrees that El Rubio wasn't exactly a happy camper. The only person who doubts he committed suicide is his sister.'

'His sister, and the facts. There's the green cable tie that he couldn't have fastened himself, and the blow to his head.'

'Which blow?' asked Estevez. The day before, he'd left the autopsy room before the pathologist had shown Caldas the wound. 'His head was covered in them.'

'Yes, but almost all of them occurred post mortem,' explained Caldas. 'Only two of the blows happened while he was alive. One to the forehead, possibly from a rock. The other to the back of the head. Look at this.'

Caldas fished out of his trouser pocket the slip of paper on which the pathologist had drawn the outline of the object that had struck El Rubio from behind. He unfolded it and placed it on the table, in front of his assistant.

'I haven't shown you this, have I?'

Estevez shook his head slightly.

'He was hit on the back of the head with something this shape. Some sort of bar with a rounded end. According to the pathologist, it was a very violent blow, so violent it probably knocked him unconscious.'

'It looks like the knob of a walking stick,' said Estevez.

Caldas looked at the drawing again. 'Could be, but Dr Barrio leans towards it being the kind of spanner used for wheel nuts. In any case, it doesn't look like suicide.'

'No.'

Caldas drew on his cigarette, reflecting that placing an order for a new boat from the carpenter didn't point to suicide either, nor did the threat painted on the rowing boat, nor the anxiety that caused the abandonment of a long-held habit.

He folded the piece of paper and returned it to his back pocket.

'What about motives, Inspector?'

'Are you interrogating me?'

'No, I'm just trying to find out what the hell you think.'

'Right. And what do you think?'

Estevez gave him a hard stare and Caldas felt sure he was going to make one of his characteristically gruff remarks.

'It's strange,' he said instead. 'The bloke had no girlfriend, no enemies, and nothing worth killing him for.'

'He had a house.'

'I don't think he was killed over that.'

'People have been killed here over a lot less, Rafa. For moving a boundary stone one metre this way or that.'

'I'm not saying it's out of the question, but I doubt that nowadays anyone would be so interested in Castelo's house that they'd kill him for it.'

'Since when are you the property expert?'

'I'm not, you just have to walk around the village. There are *For Sale* signs everywhere. Developers aren't going to invest in more land when they've still got houses for sale.'

'Right,' said Caldas, who hadn't noticed this. 'Well, what then?'

Estevez took his time before replying. 'I think the most solid clue is the threat painted on the boat. Maybe that Captain Sousa has a relative ... Do you think that's possible?'

Caldas nodded.

'I don't know why you're so interested in my opinion when it's almost the same as yours.'

'Almost?'

'Yes.'

*

They paid for their meal and walked back to the car. Estevez had left it parked on the jetty, near the yacht club. They saw a few new customers in the Refugio del Pescador, but the waiter was the same one who had served them in the morning.

'Where are we going now?'

Caldas looked at his watch. There were still more than two hours until Justo Castelo's funeral.

'Do you remember the cable tie around the dead man's wrists?'

'Of course.'

'I want you to go to all the shops and department stores where you might get ties like that. Both here and in neighbouring villages. See if you can find one like it.'

Estevez nodded. 'You're not coming?'

'No. I'll tell you where to drop me. I'm going to see a friend.'

Captains Courageous

Lola was drying her hands on her apron as she opened the door and kissed him on both cheeks. She led him quickly through to the back of the house.

'He's in the garden,' she said, holding Caldas's arm. 'He'll be delighted to see you.'

He couldn't remember when he'd last walked down that hallway. It must have been twenty-five years ago, maybe more. The walls seemed lighter and the doors opening off it smaller, but he recognised the smell. It had endured intact in his memory and he could have distinguished it from a thousand others. The first whiff took him right back, to the days of his childhood, when this hallway was like a magic tunnel leading him to Manuel Trabazo.

In those days, Caldas saw Trabazo as Manuel, the Portuguese fisherman played by Spencer Tracy in the film *Captains Courageous*. Tracy was dark-haired and stocky, not lean and grizzled like Trabazo, but to Caldas they were one and the same. He'd seen the film dozens of times: a little rich boy falls overboard from an ocean liner and is rescued by a fishing boat, where one of the crew, Manuel, teaches the spoilt brat to laugh and sing. Just as Trabazo had tried to teach him so many times.

Caldas always cried in the scene where Manuel, smiling and speaking Portuguese so that the boy won't understand, orders one of his shipmates to cut the rope trapping him, knowing that he will be dragged to the bottom of the sea with the fish. The young Leo was afraid that Trabazo would end up there too one day.

*

Trabazo lay in a hammock wearing knee-high boots, dark trousers and a thick woollen jacket. A fringe of white hair partly hid his weatherbeaten forehead and closed eyes.

'Don't disturb him,' Caldas said to Lola. 'I'll come back another time.'

'If he finds out that you were here and I didn't wake him he won't speak to me for a week,' she said, adding in a whisper: 'Speak up, he can't hear too well.'

Caldas nodded. Lola approached Trabazo and grasped his arm firmly, as she'd done to the inspector a moment earlier.

'Manuel, look who's here,' she shouted.

Trabazo opened one eye, then the other, and stood up with a smile that added yet more creases to his face.

'Well, I'll be damned, Calditas. I knew you were around,' he said, patting him gently on the cheeks. 'I thought you'd forgotten your old friend.'

'My father said he spoke to you this morning.'

'Did he know you were here in Panxón?'

'Didn't he say anything?'

'That old rascal,' muttered Trabazo, still smiling. 'He asks about trivia and doesn't tell me the important stuff.'

'So how did you know I was here?'

Trabazo clicked his tongue mockingly.

'When you're a radio celebrity, you can't expect to keep a low profile. You're like a tuna in a shoal of sardines.'

'Oh, come off it,' replied the inspector laconically.

Trabazo stepped back and peered at Caldas, looking him up and down. 'Damn, Leo,' he said at last, putting his arm around the inspector. 'It's good to see you again.'

'Yes,' said Caldas. 'How are you?'

'Retired, as you probably know,' said Trabazo, heading towards the porch. 'But I'm not complaining. Since leaving the hospital I've been able to spend time on my sculptures,' he added, gesturing towards the carved stone figures on pedestals dotted around the garden. 'I can also play a game of chess after lunch without having to rush off halfway through. Though a doctor never fully retires, as you can imagine. Are you here on your own?'

'Of course.'

'I'd heard you had a thug with you.'

Caldas smiled. He was surprised how popular his assistant had become. 'He's acquired a bad reputation.'

'And a hot temper,' said Trabazo. 'He almost knocked Camilo's teeth out on the jetty.'

Caldas sighed, cursing inwardly, but decided not to enquire further.

'Do you still go fishing?' he asked instead.

'I go out every day and cast a line, unless it's raining or the sea's rough,' Trabazo said proudly. 'There's no way I'm retiring from that.'

He gestured for Caldas to sit in a wicker armchair and fetched a couple of small glasses and a bottle of coffee liqueur from a cabinet.

'How is your father?' he asked as he filled the glasses.

'I thought you spoke to him this morning?'

'As I said, he just calls about trivia,' exclaimed Trabazo. 'Today he wanted me to remind him of the name of a neighbour we used to play dominoes with. He didn't say why. Apart from the fact that the man no longer lives here, he was a half-wit. When I told your father his name, he rang off.'

So his father was still busy updating the Book of Idiots.

'He's got this notebook. He calls it the Book of Idiots.'

'So he's still making his crazy list?' asked Trabazo, puzzled. 'That was something from before your mother died.'

Apparently, Caldas had been the last to know about the notebook. 'I don't think he'd done anything with it for a while,' he said, as if excusing his father.

Trabazo smiled again and raised the glass to his lips.

'How long is it since we last saw each other – a couple of years?'

'At least,' said Caldas. 'It was at the vineyard, wasn't it?'

Trabazo nodded.

'How's Alba?'

'Not around,' said Caldas, tersely.

'Oh, dear. And your father?'

'Uncle Alberto's illness has hit him hard.'

Caldas extracted his packet of cigarettes and held it out to Trabazo. 'Want one?'

'No thanks, I'm a retired smoker as well.'

Caldas put a cigarette between his lips, held his lighter to it and

114

inhaled deeply. 'The other day, as we left the hospital, his eyes filled with tears. I'd never seen him cry before.'

'That's what happens to people with feelings,' said Trabazo. 'Their eyes fill with tears when they're upset.'

'Right,' said Caldas quietly.

'But don't let it bother you too much, Leo,' Trabazo added, seeing the face of his old friend's son darken. 'After a certain age we get more thick-skinned and things affect us less and less.'

'Right,' said the inspector again.

'Why aren't you drinking your liqueur? Your father says you've got first-rate taste.'

'Don't listen to him,' Caldas replied, taking a sip. 'Do you make it yourself?'

'No, a former patient sends me some every year,' said Trabazo, taking another drink, leaving a thick, dark coating of liqueur up the side of the glass.

'Well, it's very good,' Caldas assured him.

Trabazo leaned back in the armchair and put his feet up on the table, beside the bottle. They remained like this, in silence, as they had when Caldas was a child and he spent the night there, seeking Manuel, the Portuguese fisherman, in Trabazo.

The inspector's cigarette had almost burned out when Manuel Trabazo asked: 'You haven't come just to see me, have you?'

'No,' Caldas admitted.

The Trawler

'El Rubio was a good lad. I expect you know he had a heroin problem.'

'Yes.'

'But he got off it. He'd been clean for years.'

'Completely?'

'Completely,' affirmed Trabazo. 'You don't lie to your doctor or your priest. Why are you looking into this, Leo? I thought it was suicide?'

Caldas's reply was typically Galician: 'Did you see the body?'

'Now that I've retired they don't get me to certify deaths. Was there something strange?'

'Perhaps,' said Caldas, reluctant to reveal the details that made him sure Castelo had been murdered. 'Though no one in the village seems surprised that he should have committed suicide.'

'No, no one's surprised and, to be honest, I'm not either. El Rubio was a good man, but he was an odd sort. A loner. Addicts sometimes develop depression years later, and he always seemed like a textbook case.'

Caldas nodded.

'The method he used was one people often choose around here,' added Trabazo. 'In these villages, the sea gives and takes everything.'

'Right. Do you know if he got on badly with anyone?'

Trabazo shook his head, his white fringe flopping over his forehead. 'El Rubio never had anything to do with anyone. I never knew him to have either friends or enemies.'

'But apparently he'd received threats.'

'You mean the stuff painted on his boat?'

'So you know about it?'

'Everyone knows, Leo. But I'm not sure I'd call it a threat.'

'Do you know what it said?'

'A little,' he admitted. 'Didn't it refer to a boat that sank years ago, the *Xurelo*?'

The inspector gestured vaguely, indicating that this was more or less the case. 'There was also the word "Murderers",' he added. 'What do you make of that?'

Trabazo shrugged.

'And it happened on other occasions?' asked Caldas.

'It's what I've heard around.'

'Have you got any idea who might have done it?'

'I don't know, Leo. I suppose anyone could have. But it's odd after so many years. Though I always had the feeling there was something strange about that shipwreck.'

'What makes you say that?'

'Nothing . . .' said Trabazo. The inspector's wicker armchair creaked as he leaned forward to hear what his old friend had to say. Years of interrogations had taught him that such a 'nothing' was invariably a prelude to a revelation. Like the retreating sea that warns that a huge wave is coming, when confidences began with the word 'nothing', Caldas knew it was the moment to pay attention.

'It wasn't a night for fishing. I never understood how they were caught out at sea by the storm or why they tried to return to Panxón rather than shelter in a port that was nearer.'

'Were they fishing far from here?'

'Quite a few miles north,' said Trabazo, pointing towards the end of the garden. 'By Salvora Island.'

'Why did they go so far?'

'On the *Xurelo* they fished with a *cerquillo* net. They went out for mackerel, sardine, horse mackerel, whatever was plentiful. But it's many years since the *ria* has teemed with fish. The waters are empty now. To find big shoals you have to get away from the coast. Many boats head south, towards Portugal, but the *Xurelo* always went north. They'd spend a few nights fishing there, by the Arosa *ria*, before returning to port. They almost always came back with a full hold. Sousa had a good eye.'

'What do you think could have happened?'

'Only those who were there really know. But it's very strange. Things can change suddenly at sea. A long wave can catch you unawares or the wind can get up unexpectedly,' he said, waving his arms. 'But we all had warning of the storm that night. The *Xurelo* had left Panxón two days earlier, and there'd already been a bad weather warning. There were four men on board. The crew – Valverde, Arias and El Rubio – were young. You know all this, don't you?'

Caldas nodded.

'But the skipper of the *Xurelo* was a veteran. Older than me. His name was Antonio Sousa. He'd been at sea since he was in short trousers. He was an experienced skipper, he knew what he was doing. He wasn't rash, Leo. He'd been tested by the sea before and he had plenty of respect for it. I don't know how he could have been caught by surprise.'

'Where did they go down?'

'Right there, very near the island of Salvora. It foundered on rocks that anyone who's fished in the area is familiar with, the kind that stick out at low tide. That, too, was odd with Sousa at the helm,' he observed. 'The fact is the boat went down. The boys managed to swim ashore in their life jackets, but Sousa didn't make it.'

'What did the three of them say?'

'They were scared, too shocked to explain anything. At night and in heavy seas you can't see further than the waves washing over the deck. All they could remember was the terrific noise as the hull was torn open by the rocks, and the cold of the water. The boat took less than a minute to sink. They weren't far from the coast and they swam ashore guided by the light of a lighthouse. But it must have been horrendous.'

'I can imagine,' said Caldas, lighting a cigarette and placing the packet on the table.

'Sousa's body wasn't found until several weeks later. The boat went down a few days before Christmas and it was well into January by the time the body turned up. You have no idea the effect it has on a fishing village when a boat is lost. People walk in silence and talk in whispers. All you hear are the church bells and the sea, reminding us of its power. The storm lasted several days and the lifeboats couldn't go out. By the time divers got to examine the wreck, there was no sign of the skipper. We were all sure Sousa had drowned, but we were anxious to know if the sea would return the body to land or keep it for herself.'

Caldas thought of *Captains Courageous* and the flowers the little boy throws into the sea at the end, hoping that they'll reach Manuel the Portuguese fisherman in his underwater grave.

'I don't know if you know that lots of bodies have washed up on the beach where El Rubio was found – the Madorra,' said Trabazo. 'The current drags them ashore and they end up floating in the seaweed. Some are identified because there's news of a boat going down, but for others all we know is the date they're found. The people of the village have always buried them in the cemetery here. There's a triangular area of lawn by the entrance with anonymous graves. The unidentified corpses washed up by the sea are buried there.'

'But the *Xurelo* sank too far from Panxón for Sousa to have washed up on the same beach as Castelo,' Caldas pointed out.

'Yes, of course. Sousa's body was found caught in the nets of a trawler from Vigo, after we'd given up all hope of finding him. It was well out to sea, several miles from the wreck.'

'Did you attend the certification of the death?'

'No, no. The body was taken to Vigo and I assume a pathologist there dealt with it. But I did try to help Sousa's family. It was a long time ago but I still remember clearly the nights of waiting. After his wife hadn't slept for a week, I had to sedate her so she could get some rest.'

Caldas swallowed.

'Who identified the body?'

'His son,' whispered Trabazo. 'From the clothing. After almost a month in the water it was all he could identify.'

'Right.'

Caldas smoked, leaning back again in the wicker armchair, contemplating Trabazo's sculptures. Then, as he stubbed out his cigarette, he asked: 'What about Sousa's crew? I understand they were close.'

'Until the *Xurelo* went down, yes. But the loss of the boat tore them apart. Arias left to work on an oil rig in the North Sea a few weeks after it happened. El Rubio and Valverde stayed in the village, but never spoke again. It was as if something happened on that boat.'

'Isn't it enough that it sank?'

119

Trabazo didn't think so. 'Fishermen who survive a shipwreck become like brothers. They've faced death and escaped. It's a bond that can't be broken, like the friendship between men who've shared a trench in a war. But after the *Xurelo* foundered they no longer had anything to do with one another. They wouldn't even acknowledge each other in the street.'

Caldas nodded.

'It's also usual for the survivors to talk about their experience,' Trabazo went on. 'After all, it could happen to anyone. But none of the three ever said a word about that night. Arias left for Scotland, El Rubio withdrew into his shell and Valverde never set foot in the harbour again. They say he was scared.'

Caldas recalled that Castelo's sister had also mentioned that her brother never fished out of sight of the coast because he was afraid.

'Arias only came back to the village recently. Did they pick up their friendship?'

'No,' said Trabazo. 'Even though they were both at the fish market every morning, Arias and El Rubio barely acknowledged each other. And I don't think he had anything to do with Valverde either. Have you met them?'

'I spoke to José Arias this morning,' said Caldas. 'I haven't seen Marcos Valverde yet. I've been to his house but only his wife was there. Things don't seem to have gone too badly for him.'

'Valverde's clever and hard-working. He got out of fishing and went into construction. He must have made a lot of money.'

'His wife said he's just started a wine business.'

'So I believe, but he's not like your father, who makes wine because he loves it. He's the only person I know who chooses the wine first and then the food to go with it. He's not in it for the money or prestige, he simply wants to make good wine. That's all that matters to him. But men like Valverde see a wine label as a way to status that money alone can't buy.'

'Is he honest?'

'As much as anyone in construction can be. You've seen what they've done to the village in only a few years. There's nothing left of the dunes, nothing left of anything,' Trabazo lamented. 'Before, when master builders built houses, around here they couldn't produce something ugly even if they tried. Even the most modest houses had charm. Later on I don't know who the hell thought of using architects for building projects. Look what they've done. Rationalist buildings, they call them. But do you know what they are? Crap, Calditas, absolute crap.'

'Well, Panxón isn't as bad as some places.'

Trabazo waved his hand in disagreement. 'In photographs from thirty years ago, the only thing that's recognisable is the church. How could they have built so many houses in a fishing village like this? It's unbearable in summer now.'

Caldas thought of Valverde's wife and the months she must spend looking out of the huge window of her designer house, longing for the arrival of the hot weather and the holidaymakers.

'Did you know that people are talking about Captain Sousa?' he said, changing the subject. 'They say they've seen him, and that he's got something to do with the threats.'

Trabazo shrugged.

'Do you think the other two are scared?' asked the inspector.

'Wouldn't you be?' said Trabazo.

'I suppose I'd be concerned, at least,' admitted Caldas. 'Did you know him well?'

'Sousa? Of course. He was a close friend. Not like your father, it was different. Do you remember me talking about my time fishing off Newfoundland?'

'It rings a bell,' said Caldas, lighting another cigarette.

'I told you all about it when you were a boy, Calditas,' muttered Trabazo with a smile. 'Seems like my stories have become obsolete, like me.'

Lola arrived with a smoking earthenware dish on a tray. 'I've brought you some chestnuts, as they're in season.'

Trabazo removed his feet from the table so that his wife could set the chestnuts down. Caldas leaned towards the dish. It was an aroma he remembered well.

'Lola stews the chestnuts with rue,' said Trabazo. 'Had you forgotten about the chestnuts as well?'

'No, these I remembered,' said Caldas, breathing in the smell he would always associate with that house. 'You were telling me about Sousa and Newfoundland.'

Trabazo recounted how, after finishing his military service and

121

before going to university in Santiago, he'd spent a few months working on a cod trawler off Newfoundland.

'Do you remember or not?'

Caldas made an equivocal gesture as he slit open a chestnut. He remembered the story but he didn't want to interrupt Trabazo. He listened again to tales of cod as big as men, of nets taut to breaking point as they were hoisted from the water, and of noisy seals swimming alongside the boats.

'Do you know something, Calditas?' said Trabazo, just as he used to, to grab Caldas's attention when he was a boy. 'The seals would bark at us from the water. I was convinced they were complaining because we were taking all their fish, and my shipmates made fun of me. But you know what, Calditas? I was right. There are no more cod in Newfoundland. They've been fished out.'

Caldas remembered him describing the work on board when they were fishing on the Grand Banks. The cod were beheaded up on deck then passed to the scaler, who slit them open. Then they were boned, washed in a tank, and transferred to the hold, to be salted.

Trabazo also spoke about a storm, and a blonde in a bar in Saint Pierre. He hadn't forgotten her eyes, as blue as the sea in summer, or her giant, drunken boyfriend who had almost torn his head off.

'If one of my shipmates hadn't stood up to him, I wouldn't be here now telling you this story,' he said, dunking a freshly peeled chestnut in his liqueur and popping it into his mouth. He chewed slowly and swallowed, adding: 'That shipmate was Antonio Sousa. Nobody called him captain in those days.'

As they made their way back along the hallway, accompanied by the smell of cooked chestnuts, Caldas asked, 'Did you say Sousa had a son?'

'Yes.'

'Does he live in the village?'

'No, he left a while back to work in Barcelona. His father was buried years ago, but the rumour mill wouldn't let him forget.'

Barcelona was a long way away.

'Right.'

'He's a good lad,' added Trabazo, putting his arm around the inspector. 'I'd lay down my life for him, as I would for you.'

*

122

Opening a glass door, Trabazo beckoned to Caldas to follow.

'Remember the sitting room?' he asked, searching through a chest of drawers.

Caldas nodded. 'I remember the picture,' he said, indicating the enamel piece by Pedro Solveira that hung above the sofa. 'My father's always loved it.'

'So have I,' smiled Trabazo, taking an old photograph from a drawer. He brought it over to the inspector. 'This is me with Sousa in a bar in Newfoundland,' he said, holding out the black-and-white print.

In it, two men were raising their glasses to the camera. They wore the same expression, their eyes shining, mouths open. Caldas placed a finger on the younger of the two.

'That's you, isn't it?' he said, and Trabazo answered with a half-smile.

'I still remember the song we were singing when the photo was taken,' said the retired doctor.

Caldas now focused his attention on Sousa. He had curly hair and was slightly taller than Trabazo. Sinewy arms protruded from his rolled-up shirtsleeves. An elongated object, like a club, hung from his belt.

'We worked hard but we had a lot of fun, too,' said Trabazo, and pointed to a shadow in the background of the photograph. 'The pianist would play till dawn.'

Caldas glanced at the blurry figure of the pianist, before looking more closely at the object attached to Sousa's belt.

'What's that?' he asked, pointing.

'Sousa called it the "*macana*". It was a sort of club – a thick stick with a rounded end. I bet the blonde's boyfriend hasn't forgotten it. Sousa knocked him out with a single blow,' laughed Trabazo, and Caldas tried to smile back.

'Was it metal?'

'The *macana*? No, it was made from a very hard wood. He won it from a Mexican in a card game, or so he claimed. He always carried it, right to the end. It must have gone down with him, with the boat.'

Caldas squinted, trying without success to make out the *macana*'s exact shape.

'Have you got any other photos of him?'

'Of Sousa?'

Caldas nodded.

'No,' said Trabazo. 'But Don Fernando must have several. He used to take pictures of the fishermen in the harbour.'

'Who's Don Fernando?'

'He was the village priest until a few years ago. But even priests aren't exempt from ageing, so he's retired. These days he only says Mass occasionally, when he gets a special request.'

'Does he still live in Panxón?'

'Yes. Where else would he go after a lifetime here? He's still in the same house, behind the church.'

The Bait

Estevez was waiting outside Trabazo's house. Caldas got into the car, opened the window a crack and lay back in his seat.

'Where to?' asked Estevez.

'The harbour,' said Caldas, closing his eyes. 'How did you get on?'

'No luck, Inspector. No one in the area sells green cable ties. They say they've never even seen any. They've got black or white, but not green.'

'Right.'

'How about you?'

'I've been told about an incident involving a police officer on the jetty in the harbour. Would you mind telling me what the hell happened?'

'I told you: he spat at me, Inspector. What did you expect me to do – just go on my way?'

'You said you didn't do anything to him.'

'No, no. What I said was that I felt like throwing him into the sea but, as God is my witness, I restrained myself.'

'But you did hit him ...'

'With an open hand,' said Estevez defensively, as if the fisherman should have been grateful for being slapped rather than punched. 'They were driving me nuts, I couldn't get them to answer any questions.'

'That's no reason to beat them up.'

'I told you, he spat at me. Anyway, I only hit one of them.'

'I don't care, Rafa. I'm tired of this. If you feel jumpy and need to get it out of your system, just smash something.'

'Smash something?'

'Yes. Anything but strike someone again without good reason.'

They parked on the jetty. Justo Castelo's traps were still stacked against the wall, a few metres away. The tide was at its height. At the bottom of the slipway, by the water's edge, they saw José Arias's imposing bulk. He was no longer wearing the waterproof hat he'd sported that morning. His hair was curly and as dark as the stubble on his chin. His trailer, with the rowing boat on it, was also down by the water.

'Shall I come with you?' asked Estevez.

'Yes,' said Caldas. 'But let me do the talking.'

The policemen made their way down the slipway. A plastic bucket full of horse mackerel stood beside the fisherman.

'Are you going fishing?'

'No,' replied Arias in his deep voice. 'I'm just rowing out to the boat to bait the traps. I won't be going out until after the funeral.'

'Do you have a minute?'

'Yes, but no more.'

Caldas didn't want to waste time either.

'Did you know that Castelo found something graffitied on his boat one morning?'

Arias nodded.

'Do you know what it said?' asked the inspector.

'Pretty much.'

'You didn't see it?'

'No, I didn't.'

'It was a date,' said the inspector, though he knew he didn't need to. 'The twentieth of December 1996. Does it mean anything to you?'

Arias looked him in the eyes.

'You know it does, Inspector.'

'There was something else. A word.'

Arias raised his eyebrows questioningly.

'Beneath the date was the word "Murderers". Do you have any idea why someone should have written such a thing on Castelo's boat?'

'No,' replied the fisherman, though it sounded more like a 'yes'.

'Are you sure?' insisted Caldas.

The fisherman nodded and looked down at the fish that would serve as crab bait.

'He never mentioned it?'

'Who?'

'Castelo.'

'I told you, El Rubio and me, we didn't speak much.'

'Do you know what the people of the village think?'

'How would I know that?'

Estevez snorted and Caldas looked round. His glare was enough to stop Estevez from speaking.

'There's been talk of Captain Sousa,' said Caldas. 'I think you knew him well.'

'Years ago,' admitted Arias, again meeting the inspector's gaze.

'People claim to have seen Sousa in the village. They say he was the one threatening Justo Castelo.'

Estevez stepped back, out of range of the spitting that invariably followed any mention of the captain.

The huge fisherman, however, did not spit or touch metal. He simply said that he hadn't seen Sousa and apologised for being unable to spare any more time.

'Just one more thing,' said Caldas. 'Have you been threatened yourself?'

'Me?'

'Yes,' said Caldas.

Arias shook his head, but his eyes told a different story.

The Skipper

Four old men were playing dominoes at the table by the window. Two others were watching the game, sitting at the corners of the marble table, between players. A third man, in a fisherman's cap, stood watching, holding a glass of liqueur. They were the only customers that afternoon.

They didn't look up as Caldas and Estevez entered and crossed the bar. The policemen took stools at the end of the counter furthest from the domino players' table, and ordered coffee. The waiter was different from the one that morning. The television was switched on but muted, and the only sound was the clacking of dominoes on the marble table.

Someone had left a copy of Justo Castelo's death notice on the counter, by the cash register.

When the waiter served their coffee, they quietly introduced themselves.

'You're here about El Rubio, aren't you?' the waiter said, gesturing towards the notice.

Caldas confirmed that they were and said that someone had seen Castelo at the bar on Saturday afternoon, the day before he died.

'Yes, he was here, sitting right where you are now,' the waiter said, also keeping his voice down.

'Do you remember what time?'

The waiter was about to reply when the sound of dominoes on marble rang out, as loud as a gunshot, followed by a burst of laughter and swearing. At the only occupied table, players and spectators were all talking at once, debating the previous round. Then one of them shuffled the tiles and the voices quietened. After another slam of dominoes on the table, silence returned and the waiter said:

'At eight, as usual on a Saturday.'

'He was a regular?'

'Most of the fishermen in the village are,' he said, gesturing to a point somewhere behind the policemen. Caldas wasn't sure whether he was referring to the domino players or the boats moored on the water. 'El Rubio had coffee here every day. Always at the same time. During the week he came in for a while before going out fishing. On Saturdays he'd have a drink around eight.'

José Arias had said that the last time he'd seen Castelo alive, he'd been talking to the waiter. Caldas lit a cigarette before asking about it.

'El Rubio wasn't chatty,' said the waiter, before adding: 'But on Saturday he seemed different.'

'Different?'

The waiter nodded. 'Wouldn't you be on the day you decided to commit suicide?'

Caldas and Estevez exchanged looks.

'I realise now that he was trying to warn me, but I didn't get it then,' said the waiter.

'To warn you?'

'Yes, but I didn't see that until I found out that his body had been washed up on the beach. You don't know how sorry I am I didn't get what he was trying to tell me. He was odd, but a good guy. He didn't have an enemy in the world.'

'What was it he said to you?'

'That he was going to end it.'

'Is that how he put it?'

'Yes. He finished his drink, leaned on the bar and muttered: "I'm going to end it". Then he got up and left. How was I to know that's what he meant?' he said regretfully.

Caldas drew on his cigarette. 'Of course,' he said. 'Had he had much to drink?'

The waiter shook his head. 'The same as usual. The same drink he had every Saturday.'

'Did he seem anxious?'

129

'Maybe ... He must have been for some time. You know what they say in the village?'

'No,' Caldas lied.

'They say he was being harassed.'

'Castelo?' said Caldas, as if it was the first time he'd heard this.

The waiter nodded.

'Do they know by whom?'

'That's the weirdest part. Over ten years ago, a boat from the village, the *Xurelo*, sank. The skipper drowned, but some people are saying the boat's reappeared and that the skipper's come back to get revenge.'

'Do you think Castelo really was scared of the skipper?'

'I don't know, Inspector. It's what I've heard.'

A loud slam on the marble table signalled the end of another game of dominoes.

'Who claims to have seen the boat?' asked Caldas, raising his voice above the hubbub of the players' voices.

'No idea, Inspector,' said the waiter but, pointing at the man in the fisherman's cap approaching the counter for a refill, he added: 'But they say he knows something.'

Caldas bought the man a drink. He was getting on in years. Beneath the visor of his captain's cap, he had thick eyebrows, a hooked nose and lively eyes surrounded by lines scored by the sun and salt wind.

'We were just talking about Justo Castelo,' said Caldas.

'Terrible shame. He was so young.'

'Are you a fisherman, too?'

'I'm retired, but I still go out to sea. Fishing – well, that's another matter.'

Caldas smiled. 'Not much out there?'

'How could there be? The sea needs a rest, like all of us. If it doesn't get one, it can't reproduce. I bet you can't reproduce if you're tired, can you?'

Caldas finished his cigarette and stubbed it out in the ashtray.

'How well did you know Castelo?'

'Same as everyone else,' the fisherman replied. 'More or less.'

'Had he seemed more anxious lately?'

'Maybe.'

130

Caldas simply nodded and looked him straight in the eye, letting the seconds pass. The man in the cap, made uncomfortable by the silence, added:

'I can't say for sure whether he was or wasn't.'

'Oh, for fuck's sake,' muttered Estevez.

'Not because I don't want to,' said the old sea dog. 'It's just that I don't know. El Rubio hardly ever said a word.'

'Don't worry. That's fine,' said Caldas.

He was trying to think of how to bring up the subject of Captain Sousa, when the slamming of dominoes on the table speeded up, heralding the end of the game. Worried that the man in the cap would be drawn back to the players' table by all the shouting that would erupt at any second, he got straight to the point.

'Have you seen Captain Sousa?'

The fisherman choked on his drink.

'Touch metal,' he said, coughing, and tapping his knuckles on a metal napkin ring.

Estevez quickly tipped his stool back to get out of the fisherman's reach, only just managing not to fall over. He needn't have done so, however, as the man in the cap spat backwards, over his own shoulder. He didn't seem too concerned about his aim.

'We've heard that some fishermen here have seen him again,' Caldas went on once the man had done with hawking. 'You're one of them, aren't you?'

'Could be.'

'You've seen the skipper?'

'Not exactly.'

Caldas saw he'd have to prompt further: 'What about his boat?'

The fisherman ran his hand over the cap.

'Did you see Sousa's boat?' Caldas pressed.

'The *Xurelo*, yes,' the man replied at last.

At that moment, Caldas's phone rang. He didn't recognise the number on the display but, when the caller identified himself, the inspector withdrew and motioned to Estevez to continue the interview.

Caught a little off-guard, Estevez began, 'Was it out at sea?'

'Didn't I say it was a boat?'

'But were you at sea yourself?' Estevez insisted.

'Where else would I be?'

'Well, I don't know. You could have seen it from the harbour.'

'Could have, but didn't. I was fishing.'

'OK then. Where were you?'

'I told you,' said the man in the cap. 'I was at sea.'

Estevez took a deep breath.

'The sea's a big place,' he said. 'Could you be a little more specific?'

'Over there,' replied the fisherman, pointing towards the wall of the Refugio del Pescador as if human eyesight could pierce it. 'By Monteferro.'

'Are you sure that the vessel you saw was the *Xurelo*?'

'Yes, I think it was.'

'You think so, or you know for sure?'

The fisherman remained silent.

'Fine, it seemed to you that it was the *Xurelo*,' said Estevez.

'That's right.'

'Was there anything about the boat that helped you distinguish it from others?'

'What do you mean?'

'I don't know, you tell me. What led you to believe that it was the *Xurelo*?'

'You don't believe me?'

'I'm the policeman here and I'm the one asking the questions.'

'That's true,' said the man.

'Well?'

'Well what?'

'Could you please tell me what the fuck made you think that the boat you saw was this Captain Sousa's boat?'

'Didn't I say I saw it?'

Estevez took another deep breath. 'Didn't you think it odd to see a boat that sank years ago?'

'Wouldn't you think so?'

'Yes, I would definitely think it odd,' said Estevez, now focusing more on resisting the urge to grab the fisherman by the lapels than on getting a definitive answer out of him. 'But I'm asking you: what did you think?'

'I didn't think anything.'

'How long did you see it for?'

'Not long.'

'A minute?'

'Less than that.'

'How much less?'

'I don't know. As soon as I realised it was the *Xurelo*, I started the engine and headed out of there.'

Estevez suspected he'd paused to spit overboard. 'Which way?' he asked.

'Which way what?'

'Which way did you head out of there?'

'Back to the harbour, of course.'

'You didn't see it again?'

'The *Xurelo*?' said the fisherman, turning his finger on his temple. 'You think I was going to look back when I was scared out of my wits?'

'I don't know. You tell me.'

'I am telling you.'

'Did you or didn't you look back?'

'I thought I told you: I didn't.'

When Caldas returned, Estevez was on his feet.

'Thank God you're back, boss,' whispered Estevez, for once snorting with relief.

He told him what the man in the cap had said and Caldas took over:

'So you only saw the boat for a moment.'

The old man nodded.

'And only that one time?'

'Yes, thank God.'

'Do you know of anyone else who's seen the boat?'

The fisherman gave him a few names.

'Would you let the police know if you see it again?' Caldas asked him.

'I doubt I will,' said the fisherman with a slight smile.

'How can you be sure?'

The man slipped his hand inside his shirt and showed them the amulet hanging round his neck. 'I've got this to protect me.'

It was a fist with the thumb protruding between the index and middle fingers, like the one found in Justo Castelo's pocket.

133

'A *figa*?' said Caldas.

The old man nodded. 'Others carry horseshoes, bay leaves or little bags of salt.'

The bag of salt! Caldas hadn't thought of it since the day before.

'Salt?' he asked, surprised to hear that this was also believed to be a lucky charm.

'Yes,' replied the fisherman. 'But I prefer the *figa*. Don't you?'

Seagulls were still clustering on the slipway when they came out of the Refugio del Pescador. Arias was baiting traps on his boat. On the huge, almost deserted beach, a boy in a wheelchair was playing with a Labrador. He was throwing a ball into the sea and the dog was running after it, swimming out to retrieve it, leaping around the wheelchair, waiting for the boy to throw the ball again and bounding after it once more.

Walking to the car, Caldas thought about his father. And about the dog that greeted him excitedly and followed him among the vines.

'Where are we going?' asked Estevez.

'To Valverde's house.'

'Again?' objected Estevez.

Caldas nodded.

'That was Valverde on the phone. His wife gave him my card. I've arranged to drop in there now, before the funeral. Let's see what he knows about the skipper.'

The Shipwreck of the *Xurelo*

'It was many years ago, Inspector,' said Marcos Valverde. 'We've hardly spoken since.'

He was wearing a dark suit and tie. Caldas wondered whether it was for the funeral or he always dressed like that. Valverde was slim and not very tall. He had thick, straight, dark hair, combed back. Trabazo had said that Castelo, Arias and Valverde were the same age, but Valverde looked younger than the other two. Hours at sea had left no mark on his face and only the slightly greying hair at his temples hinted at his age.

'If you were such good friends, why did you stop seeing each other?'

'I couldn't say. These things happen. I suppose it's a defence mechanism, so as not to be constantly reminded of that dreadful night.'

'Could you tell me what happened?'

'When the boat went down?'

Caldas nodded, and Valverde took a deep breath, summoning his strength.

'It was at night,' he began. 'It was very dark and seas were very heavy. Waves were washing over the deck. We had to shout to make ourselves heard. The skipper was at the helm, struggling to maintain our course.'

'Where were you heading?' interrupted Caldas.

'We were on our way back to Panxón, near the island of Salvora.'

'That's a long way from here. Why didn't you shelter in a port that was nearer?'

'You'd have to ask the skipper,' muttered Valverde. 'But I suppose it was because we had a full hold. It was our second night and the weekend was coming up. He can't have wanted the catch to rot on board.'

'Right. So what happened?'

'It was all so fast. The skipper yelled at us to hold on. Then we heard a terrible sound, as if the hull were breaking apart. The boat stayed still for a moment on the sandbank, then it started to list. Before we knew it we were in the water and when a flash of lightning lit up the sea, the *Xurelo* had disappeared. So we started swimming like crazy. We had to get through the breakers to reach shore.'

'Were you wearing life jackets?'

'We were near the coast, but without them we wouldn't have reached shore. The skipper ordered us to put them on a few minutes before the boat went down.'

'He didn't put one on himself?'

'El Rubio handed him one, but the last I saw of him he was gripping the helm, shouting, and, no, he wasn't wearing a life jacket.'

Caldas nodded gravely.

'The skipper's only concern was to get the boat upright again, no thought for himself,' added Valverde. 'Captain Sousa was like that. A brave man, right to the very end.'

'That was the last you saw of him alive?'

Valverde clicked his tongue to confirm this.

'What happened after that?'

'We were exhausted, battered and frozen. We climbed up on to the rocks and headed towards the lights. Arias and I were quiet, but El Rubio couldn't stop crying. At daybreak we were brought back here. Captain Sousa's body didn't turn up until weeks later. It got caught up in a trawler's nets.'

'I know,' said Caldas. 'What happened after that between the three of you, the crew?'

'We went our separate ways. El Rubio carried on fishing, Arias left the village and I got by as best I could.'

Caldas glanced around, at the straight lines of the sitting room and the huge window overlooking the bay.

'You haven't done too badly.'

'Don't be fooled by what you see, Inspector. I haven't always lived in a house like this. Nothing's been handed to me on a plate.'

'I don't doubt it.'

'Can I ask you something, Inspector?'

'Go ahead.'

'Why are you looking into a fisherman's suicide?'

'Routine,' Caldas lied.

Valverde looked sceptical. 'Two policemen come all the way from Vigo on a routine investigation?'

'It's procedure,' Caldas assured him and changed the subject: 'Did you know Justo Castelo was being harassed?'

'I'd heard something like that. Someone painted the date of the sinking on his rowing boat. Is that what you mean?'

Caldas concurred.

'As you can see, it's hard to keep anything secret here,' added Valverde.

'There was a word painted on the boat as well,' said Caldas.

'What was it?'

'"Murderers".'

'What?' asked Valverde, but it was obvious from his expression that he didn't need to hear it again.

'"Murderers",' Caldas repeated anyway.

When Valverde remained silent, Caldas said, 'You didn't know?'

Valverde shook his head.

'Do you have any idea who might have done it?'

'No.'

'And you haven't seen anything similar in your own surroundings?'

'My surroundings?'

'Your house, car, your office.'

'Of course not.'

'And no one's reminded you of that night recently?'

'No one apart from you.'

'Have you felt threatened yourself?'

'In my line of work I have to be firm, Inspector. As you do in yours. I can't be popular with everyone.'

'That's not what I mean,' said Caldas. 'I expect you know that people claim to have seen Captain Sousa.'

Valverde smiled bitterly and exhaled through clenched teeth.

'Well, you can tell them I've seen him too, Inspector. Gripping the helm and shouting for us to hold on as the boat broke apart in the storm. I don't know who'd want to stir up such memories.'

'Is it possible that Justo Castelo thought otherwise?'

'El Rubio saw him go down with the boat just as Arias did. And just as I did,' said Valverde. He fell silent and looked down at his feet.

'Yet Castelo had a number of lucky charms on him, the kind used to protect oneself from . . .' said Caldas, leaving the sentence hanging.

'Protect oneself from what?' asked Valverde.

Caldas shrugged.

'Anyone's entitled to feel scared, Inspector.'

'You don't?'

'I've been very scared. So scared I haven't gone near the sea again. It's over twelve years since I even dipped a toe in. Is that scared enough for you?'

'That's not what I meant.'

'You think I should be scared of something else?'

'I suppose not.'

Valverde saw them out, along the gravel path that ran round the house. Caldas paused to run his hand over the verbena plant and breathe in the scent. Just as they were taking their leave, the wooden gate slid aside. The red car they'd seen on their last visit drove in and pulled up.

'Have you told the inspector that you know his father?' asked Valverde's wife as she got out of the car. She was wearing the same blouse as before, the one that showed off her cleavage. And again, her smile reminded Caldas of Alba.

'My father?' Caldas asked, trying not to stare.

'We've bumped into each other a couple of times. I've just started making wine,' said Valverde shyly. 'But I'm sure your father has no idea who I am.'

Eyes closed, Inspector Caldas inhaled the fragrance of the eucalyptus trees carried in on a shaft of cold air through the window.

'Still thinking of Mrs Valverde?' asked Estevez as he took the road back into the village.

'No,' replied Caldas, without opening his eyes. 'I was thinking about her husband. He's more scared than he realises.'

The *Macana*

In the early decades of the twentieth century, the priest and parishioners of Panxón decided to demolish their old church, which was too small, and build a larger one. Catching wind of this, the architect Antonio Palacios travelled to the village and convinced the locals to preserve the Visigothic arch that was contained within the old building. In return, Palacios undertook to draw up plans for a new church dedicated to seafarers.

It was built on the crest of a hill close to the arch, to serve as a landmark to fishermen, with walls of rough stone topped with an octagonal cupola. Abutting a square, crenellated belfry, Palacios designed a circular tower enclosing a staircase leading to the top of the belfry.

Around the upper, conical section of this tower, painted red and white like a lighthouse, he placed four human figures, holding hands, each looking out at a compass point.

Estevez parked at the foot of the hill and Caldas got out of the car. He told his assistant to wait there and set off up the steep path to the Templo Votivo del Mar. The paving was decorated with a pattern of black and white stones. On reaching the entrance, Caldas walked round the church and looked out over the deserted village. It appeared lifeless beneath the grey sky. Even the eight plane trees on the slope, their branches now bare, seemed to be waiting for spring, when they would once again provide shade.

Caldas went up to the back door of the building that adjoined the church and rang the bell. He called out that he was there to see Don Fernando and a voice told him to wait inside the church.

*

The interior, as deserted as the rest of the village, reminded him of the upturned hull of a ship.

He sat waiting for the priest in a pew up by the altar, admiring the mosaics on the vaults and upper chancel. There were images of saints appearing before shipwrecked sailors, and other religious and seafaring scenes. The only one Caldas recognised was the arrival of the caravel *Pinta* in Baiona with news of the discovery of America.

In an aisle, in the dim light coming through the windows, he made out the Virgin of El Carmen with the baby Jesus in her arms, rising above a raging sea. The figure was on a bier, as if to be carried in a procession. At the feet of the Virgin, among the crests of the waves, three sailors clung to the wreckage of a ship.

Caldas went to look more closely at the anguished faces of the three fishermen beseeching the Virgin to intercede. He was struck by their waterproofs, which were just like those of the fishermen in the harbour, and he pictured Arias, Valverde and Castelo battling the storm. He couldn't help looking for Captain Sousa, but there was no fourth man in the waves.

Caldas thought of the medallion of the Virgin of El Carmen around El Rubio's neck. He wondered if he'd had it with him the night the *Xurelo* sank, or if he'd only started wearing it later, in gratitude for a favour like the one sought by the three carved wooden figures.

He had just sat down in the pew again when the elderly priest entered through the vestry door, walking with a cane.

Caldas rose.

'Please, no need to get up,' said the priest, motioning with his left hand. 'I'm not going to say Mass.'

This made the policeman smile, but he remained on his feet as the old priest approached, black cassock trailing on the ground.

'Are you Don Fernando?' asked the inspector.

'What's left of him,' replied the priest, looking through thick lenses that made his eyes appear huge. 'And you are?'

'Inspector Caldas,' he said. 'From Vigo Police Headquarters.'

'Please, sit,' insisted the priest, sinking into a pew himself. 'Do you know the church?'

'Only from the outside,' admitted Caldas.

'It's beautiful, isn't it? But the years have passed and it's in need of repair. See that?' he said, pointing his cane at the plastic buckets placed beneath one of the windows. 'A few joints leak when it rains, and some of the mosaics have fallen off. But you can't get just anyone to repair pieces like these. You need experts and money. Sometimes faith alone is not enough.'

'No, of course not.'

'What brings you here, Inspector?'

'I've heard that you used to be keen on photographing the fishermen in the harbour.'

'I still am,' said the priest. 'I'm not quite dead yet.'

Caldas smiled. The priest got up, leaning on his cane with both hands, and beckoned Caldas to follow him to the door through which he'd just come.

'It's been a long time since anyone took an interest in my photographs,' said the priest over his shoulder as he headed along the corridor, his cassock sweeping the floor.

He stopped in front of a door, opened it and stood aside to allow the inspector to enter first. Caldas found himself in a room with a coffered ceiling. Through the window opposite, the sea was visible beyond the rooftops of the village.

The bookcases, in the same dark wood as the ceiling, were crammed with books and papers. There was a large desk and a studded, leather-backed chair.

'Most of the photographs are in those binders over there,' said the priest, indicating thick leather binders lined up on shelves. 'Which ones are you interested in?'

Caldas cleared his throat: 'Have you any of Captain Sousa?'

Behind the strong lenses, Don Fernando fixed his huge eyes on the inspector.

'A few,' he said, sitting down in the chair. 'Would you mind handing me that binder down there?'

Caldas did so, and the priest opened it out on the desk and began slowly turning the self-adhesive pages covered in neat rows of black-and-white photos. Now and then, a larger picture occupied almost an entire page.

'You're not convinced that El Rubio's death was suicide, are you?' asked the priest.

'You aren't either?'

'I have absolutely no idea, Inspector. But unfortunately I know how far a desperate man can go,' said the old man. 'I went to see the family this morning. His sister believes that someone threw him into the sea.'

'I know,' said Caldas.

'So the police are after the late Captain Sousa,' murmured Don Fernando, still turning pages, leaning so close he might almost have been trying to identify them by smell.

'Well, as I'm sure you know, some people are claiming to have seen him around.'

'We have to believe in something. God willed it so,' mumbled the priest. Then, placing a finger on one of the photos, he said: 'This is Sousa here.'

Caldas leaned over the priest's shoulder. The picture must have been taken around the same time as the one Trabazo had shown him. Sousa was too far away and the *macana* was a blurry line hanging from his belt.

'Are there any more?' asked Caldas.

The priest turned another page and slid the open album towards the inspector. A large photograph filled the entire page. It showed a seaman of advanced years wearing a woollen hat and rubber boots. He was smiling, sitting on the jetty on a bollard to which a thick rope was tied. His legs were crossed so his belt was not visible.

'Is this the captain?'

Don Fernando nodded. 'And this is him, too,' he said, pointing at the page opposite.

Caldas held his breath when he saw the two pictures on that page. They were much more recent. Antonio Sousa's face was deeply lined beneath the familiar woollen hat. He was on the deck of a fishing boat, staring straight at the camera. On the bridge, beneath the window, the name *Xurelo* was painted in dark letters.

In both photos the *macana* on the captain's belt was so clearly visible that Caldas felt he could have reached in for it. It was just as Trabazo had described it: a thick wooden club with a rounded end.

'Could I borrow one of these photos? I'll bring it back tomorrow.'

'If you think it might help ...' said the priest.

'Many of your neighbours believe that Sousa has something to do with Castelo's death.'

'Blaming a ghost is reassuring. It gives a name to uncertainty. That's what faith is. It's preferable to thinking that someone has chosen to kill himself rather than go on living, or that we have a murderer in our midst, don't you think?'

Caldas concurred, not taking his eyes off the wooden club in the photograph.

'Do you remember the sinking of the *Xurelo*?' he asked.

'As if it were yesterday.'

'Did you see the captain's body?'

Don Fernando shook his head. 'The coffin was closed when it was sent from Vigo. Why would I want to see my friend's body?'

Caldas didn't know what to say.

'Poor Gerardo, Sousa's son, saw it,' said the priest. 'That was his last memory of his father. Isn't that a shame?'

'Yes,' said the inspector. 'I suppose it is.'

'The *Xurelo* isn't the only boat from the village to have foundered, Inspector. You can't fight against the rocks, the wind and the waves,' said Don Fernando, looking out of the window. 'Out there, sandbanks lie in wait for sailors. Like a snake stalking a rabbit, they lurk, quite still, waiting for a moment's inattention. We have to live with it.'

The priest tapped some blue folders on one of the top shelves with the tip of his cane.

'One of them is marked *Xurelo*. Would you mind getting it down for me?' he asked the inspector.

When the folder was on the desk before him, Don Fernando removed the rubber bands securing it. Inside were several folded yellowed newspaper cuttings.

'This is what was reported about the sinking of the *Xurelo* from the time it went down to the day the captain's body was found,' he said.

He slid the photo of Sousa inside the folder and handed it to the inspector.

'As long as you don't lose it, you can take this, too.'

They chatted in the study for a few more minutes. Don Fernando recounted tales of other men drowned in the bay in such detail that it seemed he himself had been at the mercy of the waves.

'Do you go out fishing yourself?' asked Caldas.

The old man's eyes widened behind his thick lenses.

'We priests don't go out in boats, Inspector,' he said, with a wink like the flutter of a bird's wings. Then he added: 'It brings bad luck.'

Caldas returned to the car at the foot of the hill. Estevez had reclined the seat and was dozing with his hands behind his head.

Caldas got in and closed the door gently but woke up his assistant nonetheless.

'How did it go, boss?' asked Estevez, setting the seat upright.

'Well, I think,' replied Caldas, opening the folder and glancing at the photo of the captain again.

'There's still an hour till Castelo's funeral,' remarked Estevez. 'Where shall we go in the meantime?'

Caldas didn't want to wait. 'Back to Vigo,' he said, lowering the window slightly, just enough to let in some fresh air.

He wanted to show Barrio the picture of the *macana*, to see if it could be the object with which Castelo had been struck before he was thrown into the water. He took his cigarettes from his pocket and placed one between his lips but didn't light it, playing instead with the lighter.

'What's in the folder?' asked Estevez as they drove off.

'Cuttings about the sinking of the *Xurelo* and a photo of Antonio Sousa taken a few days before he drowned,' replied Caldas, removing the elastic bands and showing him the photograph. 'Look at the club he's got on his belt. Incredible, isn't it?'

'What's incredible is that you believe this ghost story, too,' replied Estevez.

'I don't know what to believe,' said Caldas, taking the unlit cigarette from his mouth and drumming on his lighter.

Estevez gave him a sidelong glance. 'Inspector,' he warned, 'if you're about to spit, do me a favour and open the window a little wider.'

Spiral

Caldas called the pathologist from the car. More than a decade had passed, but Barrio still remembered the recovery of the veteran seaman's body caught up in the nets of a trawler from Vigo. It had been one of his first cases.

'The body had been in the water almost a month,' he said. 'You don't easily forget a case like that, Leo.'

'I can imagine,' said Caldas. 'Do you remember how it was identified?'

'No, but I always keep a copy of the report I send to the judge.'

'Could you get hold of it?'

'Is it urgent?' asked the pathologist, and Caldas detected a hint of annoyance in his voice.

'Were you about to leave?'

'In a little while,' he replied, but he sounded as if he already had his coat on. 'Unless you need me to stay ...'

'Would you mind hanging on for twenty minutes or so?' asked the inspector. 'I've got something important to show you.'

When he hung up, Caldas opened the folder again, set aside Sousa's photograph and unfolded the first cutting. Beneath the headline 'Fishing Boat from Panxón Sinks near Salvora' ran a half-page article about the shipwreck, including a photograph of rough seas at the scene of the accident and another of the boat's port of origin. The news that the skipper of the boat was missing was emphasised in bold type.

Caldas started reading the article but by the third line he was feeling carsick. He placed the cutting back in the folder and opened the window a little wider. Breathing deeply, he leaned back and closed his eyes.

Guzman Barrio sat in his office waiting for the inspector. He'd hung his coat back on the rack.

'Let's see whatever it is that's so important it couldn't wait till tomorrow,' he grumbled as they entered.

Caldas set the priest's photograph of Captain Sousa down on the desk.

'I wanted you to see this,' he said, placing the slip of paper with the outline of the blow to Justo Castelo's head beside the photograph. 'Look at the club on the man's belt. It's narrow with a rounded end, like your drawing here, see?'

The pathologist looked closely at the *macana*.

'Yes, they are similar.'

'So do you think Castelo could have been hit with this?' pressed Caldas.

'Maybe,' replied Barrio after a moment's thought.

'Any way to confirm it?'

'We could try,' said the pathologist. 'You haven't got the club itself, of course ...'

Caldas shook his head.

'Any more photos?' asked Barrio.

'None as clear as this one.'

The pathologist looked at the picture again and smoothed his hair with his hand.

'Give us a couple of days, let's see what we can do,' he said at last, before asking, 'Who's the man in the photo?'

'That's why I called you, Guzman. It's that fisherman whose body was found years ago in the nets of the trawler.'

'Antonio Sousa?'

Caldas nodded.

'What's he got to do with all of this?'

'He was from Panxón. Castelo was on his boat the day it sank. It's not clear what happened.'

'And?'

'He's been seen again in the village.'

'Who?'

'Sousa.'

'Sousa?' echoed the pathologist, puzzled.

'That's why I asked you to find the report.'

'They think it's his ghost,' added Estevez, with a mocking smile quickly erased by Caldas's reproving glance.

There was a moment's silence, then Barrio asked Caldas, 'Surely you don't think so, too, do you?'

'It doesn't matter what I think,' replied Caldas. 'I just want to know how the body was identified. Just in case.'

'It's absurd.'

'Absolutely. Have you got the report or not?'

Barrio motioned to a spiral-bound document.

'Any photos?' asked the inspector.

'At the end.'

Caldas flicked through the pages until he found the photos taken during the recovery and autopsy of Sousa's body. Seeing them alongside the one taken by the priest, it was hard to believe they showed the same person.

'The face is completely decomposed,' he said, holding a photo out to his assistant.

'Bloody hell,' cried Estevez in alarm. 'Don't show me that.'

'Did you confirm that it was him?' asked Caldas.

Barrio motioned towards the report.

'So it states in there.'

'Oh, stop it, Guzman. I'm not trying to catch you out. I just want you to tell me how you knew it was Antonio Sousa. I need to be certain that there was no mistake, that's all.'

The pathologist took the report from him and, after leafing through it, said:

'His own son identified the body. Is that certain enough for you?'

'You know better than I do that you can't rely on the relatives. His son probably could hardly look. He'd have identified anything just so as to be able to bury the body,' said Caldas and, pointing at Sousa's face, he added: 'I mean, look at the state it was in.'

'It had been in the sea for weeks. What would you expect?'

Estevez smiled, but the inspector wouldn't give up.

148

'Was a DNA test carried out?'

'Of course not, Leo. We're talking about more than twelve years ago.'

'How about dental records?'

'We didn't check them either,' replied Barrio. 'We'd been waiting for the body to turn up, you know. The search had been on for weeks. Anyway, we had enough to make an identification.' He turned the pages of the report again. 'The clothing was what Sousa had been wearing when the boat went down, and the medallion of the Virgin of El Carmen was the same.'

'There are thousands of fishermen with one of those around their neck.'

'I told you, his son identified the body,' said the pathologist, laying the report on the desk open at the page with the photos.

The inspector looked at Sousa's decomposed face once again. 'Just tell me one thing, Guzman. Could it have been someone else?'

'Of course not,' said Estevez, but Caldas ignored him. He wanted to hear it from the pathologist.

'Could it?' he repeated.

'What do you want me to say, Leo?'

'Just tell me if it's possible.'

'If what's possible? That another drowned man was wearing Sousa's clothes and his medallion and looked like him?'

'Is it possible or not?'

'Bloody hell, Leo ...'

'Yes or no,' said Caldas.

Estevez reflected that even under torture the pathologist would be unable to give a definite answer.

He was proved right.

Cold Water

Caldas took refuge behind the glass door of his office. He dropped the folder of cuttings about the sinking of the *Xurelo* and the report on the recovery of Antonio Sousa's body on the desk, and sank into the black desk chair. He needed to recharge his batteries after an almost sleepless night and a day in Panxón. He rubbed his eyes hard and kept them closed, but the thoughts churning in his head prevented him from resting. He knew that the information gathered in the first few hours of an investigation was always the most useful. After that, instead of solidifying, traces became blurred and disappeared, and details merged into a thick fog that hid the truth and made solving a case not a matter of time, but of chance.

This was why, at the very start, he liked to enter the crime scene and examine it, trying to find the essence of the criminal that pervaded it. But in this case Caldas had nowhere to search. The clock was ticking and Justo Castelo's boat still hadn't turned up.

A few old fishermen had been frightened by the spectre of Captain Sousa but, judging by the lucky charms in Castelo's pockets, they weren't the only ones to be afraid of ghosts. And, though they denied it, El Rubio's crewmates were frightened, too. Caldas had seen it in their eyes.

He thought of the date of the sinking daubed on El Rubio's rowing boat and the word painted on the hull: 'Murderers'. Murderers. Castelo hadn't simply dismissed it as a sick joke, Caldas was sure of that. He'd immediately removed all trace of it from the boat but hadn't been able to erase it from his mind. This was why his family had sensed that something was worrying him. Worrying him so much that he'd stopped whistling a tune he'd been whistling for years.

The *macana* also pointed that way. The club that Sousa had won in a card game was similar in shape to the mark on Castelo's head. Caldas didn't believe in coincidences. And Trabazo had spoken of Sousa's skill in handling the weapon. The pathologist thought the impact to Castelo's head had been violent enough to knock him out and, long ago, in Newfoundland, Sousa had felled a much bigger man than Castelo with a single blow.

Caldas took another look at the photo of Sousa's putrefied face in the pathologist's report, and an inner voice told him that things were usually what they seemed.

If Sousa was alive, if he hadn't drowned when the boat sank, why had he waited so long to settle scores? If, as the report stated, he'd died over a decade ago, was it possible that someone was avenging the death of the skipper of the *Xurelo*? And, if so, what had prompted it now, when time should have healed the wounds?

Trabazo had jotted down the telephone number of Sousa's son – who'd left Panxón because of all the rumours – on a slip of paper. Caldas took it from his pocket and picked up the phone, but hung up again almost immediately. He had no idea how to handle the call. What could he say? Was he going to make an accusation, or ask a son who had seen what he believed to be his father's corpse whether the man was still alive?

Caldas thought of his own father. He'd missed their lunch and hadn't managed to get to the hospital that afternoon either. He looked at his watch and wondered if his father was still in town. He dialled his mobile number – if he hadn't gone back to the estate yet, maybe they could meet for a drink.

'You're back in Vigo?' said his father when he answered.

'I've just got here,' Caldas lied. 'Are you still around?'

'No, no, I'm back home. There's more pruning to do tomorrow so I want an early start. And I needed to breathe. I'd been in town since late morning.'

First one to the chin.

'Sorry about that.'

'Don't worry. I know you saw Trabazo. How did you find him?'

'Not bad. How's Uncle Alberto doing?'

'He's OK . . .'

'Right,' said Caldas tersely. 'Will you be visiting him tomorrow?'

'I go in every day.'

Second one to the cheek.

'So maybe I'll see you tomorrow,' he said, about to hang up.

'Just one thing, Leo.'

'What's that?'

Caldas prepared himself for a third blow.

'Do you remember what the brother of Basilio, who ran the drug-store, was called?'

'The one who was a bit dim?'

'That's the one. I've been trying to think of his name all day.'

'No idea.'

After speaking to his father, he called Clara Barcia. She told him they'd started examining Justo Castelo's auxiliary boat that afternoon.

'They didn't lie to you, Inspector. It's very faint, but there does seem to be a date on there.'

'Do you know what it is?'

'The day is 20 December,' said Barcia. 'But we still can't make out if the year is 1995 or 1996.'

'Ninety-six,' said Caldas, recalling the year of the sinking of the *Xurelo*. 'Anything else?'

'Nothing legible. It's a really old boat and it's been repainted quite a few times. There were lots of marks but they could have been anything.'

'What about the cable ties?'

'Inspector, I left you a summary of all the information. Haven't you read it?'

'In my office?' he asked, looking around.

'On your desk,' said Barcia, before continuing: 'We couldn't find green ties anywhere. They may be available abroad but they don't ever seem to have been sold here.'

Caldas rummaged among the papers on his desk. He could find any document in the apparent chaos with his eyes closed, but only if he'd put it there himself.

'Got it, Clara,' he said, retrieving the report from a pile.

He glanced through it. She'd been as thorough as ever.

He left his office, with the folder of press cuttings collected by Don Fernando under his arm, together with the report on Sousa's corpse and the summary drawn up by Clara Barcia.

He found Estevez in the toilets. He had his coat on and was leaning over the basin washing his face.

Caldas thought he could probably do with a splash of cold water himself to clear his head.

'How about a glass of wine at the Eligio?' he said from the door. It had been a long day. They deserved a drink.

'Not today, boss.'

'Not even one? It's only eight o'clock.'

'Give me a break, boss,' said Estevez, smoothing his hair with dampened hands. 'I'm meeting someone.'

'Meeting someone?'

'That's what I said.'

'Right.'

Estevez glanced at him in the mirror. 'Got a problem with that?'

'No, no, fine,' stammered Caldas and closed the door behind him.

The Promenade

It had rained heavily again by the time he got to the Eligio. The cast-iron stove was lit and several tables were occupied. Caldas hung his raincoat on the rack and went over to the empty bar. Behind him he could hear the academics, in their usual place, and Carlos's deep voice at a table at the back.

'Hey, Leo!' one of the academics called out. 'We were just talking about your show yesterday.'

Caldas didn't try to set them right – they thought *Patrolling the Waves* was his show and that was that.

'What's that tune you play while you're thinking?'

He nearly turned around and left.

'What was that?'

The man who'd asked about the tune must have noticed his annoyance because he added, raising both hands, 'We think it's great. If music helps you concentrate ...'

'What piece is it?' asked another.

'We know it's Gershwin,' said a third. 'But we're not sure about the title.'

'Well ...' said Caldas, scratching his head.

'It's "Promenade", isn't it?' said the first.

'What are you talking about?' said another, looking at the inspector rather than the man he was disagreeing with. 'It's "Walking the Dog", for God's sake.'

Caldas felt like saying that he didn't know the title, hadn't chosen the damn tune and, far from helping him think, it completely put

154

him off, but he simply shrugged and promised to find out the name the next day at the radio station. He turned and waited for Carlos to serve him. Leaning on the marble counter with his chin in his hands, he stared at a small picture on the wall opposite, by the newspaper rack. It was an oil painting of the head and shoulders of a woman, by Pousa, one of the many local artists who'd found refuge in that enlightened bar. Caldas had seen the picture hundreds of times. The woman was dressed in yellow and turned to the side with a sad look. She reminded him of Alicia Castelo, with her only brother dead and her husband away at sea. The model who had posed for Pousa had dark hair and wore yellow, while the dead man's sister was blonde and dressed in mourning, yet both women had the same sorrow in their eyes.

'It's for breaking a *meigallo*, a spell,' said Carlos, setting two glasses on the counter.

'What?'

'The little bag of salt. Didn't you want to know what it was for?' said Carlos, filling the glasses with white wine. 'It protects against *meigallos*, wards off evil spirits. Same as the *figa* really,' he finished, placing his thumb between his index and middle fingers.

Caldas took a sip of wine, savouring it for a moment before swallowing. Then he said, 'Yes, a fisherman in Panxón told me this afternoon.'

Carlos drank from his glass and indicated the academics behind the inspector. 'They knew,' he said. 'But I had no idea.'

'Nor me,' said Caldas.

Once Carlos had returned to the kitchen, the inspector opened the folder, pulled out the report the pathologist had written more than twelve years earlier, and placed it on the bar.

'Wouldn't you rather sit at a table?' asked Carlos a moment later. 'The small one at the back's empty.'

'Actually, I would.'

'More wine?'

Caldas nodded.

'How about something to eat?' Carlos asked as he refilled his glass. 'We've still got some veal with chickpeas. Tastes even better today.'

155

Caldas shook his head and mumbled an almost inaudible 'No, thanks'. He didn't want a heavy meal that would have him tossing and turning in bed. He needed a good night's sleep.

On the tiny table, beneath an orange sunset by Lodeiro, the open folder hardly left room for his glass of wine. Caldas turned his attention to the pathologist's report. He read it twice, the first time straight through quickly, the second looking at the photos alongside the pathologist's comments. There was nothing to make one think that the body found entangled in the nets of the trawler might not be Antonio Sousa's, but there was no real proof either. The lengthy spell in the water had made the nails and skin on the fingers begin to decompose, so it hadn't been possible to take fingerprints and compare them with the missing man's.

The pathologist hadn't even been able to confirm that the corpse's eyes were the same colour as Sousa's. The dark eyelids were closed in the photos, but they had probably been shut by the fishermen who found him, as the autopsy stated that the skipper's eyes had been partially eaten away by fish.

Identification, as Dr Barrio had told him, had been based on the clothes and medallion, and the son's statement. The clothes, however, were waterproofs like those worn by any fisherman, and there was nothing especially distinctive about the medallion. As for the son, Caldas felt sure he'd only cast a quick glance at the body in the morgue. The pictures in the report showed a corpse with greenish eyelids and lips, standing out in a livid, pulpy face. Even for someone like Caldas who was used to dealing with dead bodies, it was difficult to look at such a disfigured face.

He'd known Barrio for years. He was sure the pathologist wouldn't have wanted to prolong the family's and the village's pain unnecessarily. They had endured weeks of anguish and uncertainty over the skipper's fate. On hearing that a body had been recovered, they must have been keen to have it released to them, so that they could bury it and start the healing process. Caldas could imagine the family's distress. Without an identified body, there could be no death certificate, no payout from the insurers, no widow's pension. If the corpse wasn't found, hardship was joined to grief in the missing man's home.

Caldas could understand why the pathologist had not investigated further when everything pointed towards the body being that of Captain Sousa. He was sure there had been no bad faith or negligence. He had the feeling that, had he been present at the recovery of the body, he himself would have urged the pathologist to speed things up so that the body could be returned to the family as soon as possible. The business with the ghost seemed ridiculous but, as he discovered more of the circumstances of Justo Castelo's murder, he was prodded by increasingly sharp doubts.

The third time Carlos came to refill Caldas's glass, he brought a plate of fried sardines that the inspector hadn't ordered.

'You shouldn't drink on an empty stomach,' said Carlos.

'True.'

Caldas put the report away in its folder, which he placed on the floor leaning against the leg of his stool. But once Carlos had gone he pushed the plate to the corner of the table, picked up the folder and took out Clara Barcia's summary.

It didn't include details of the examination of Justo Castelo's rowing boat, though on the phone Clara had corroborated what the carpenter in Panxón had said: the date of the sinking of the *Xurelo* had been painted on the dead man's rowing boat and subsequently erased. The Forensics team hadn't been able to decipher the word that accompanied the date, but Caldas didn't need to wait to be told – he already knew what it was.

He started reading Barcia's report. Justo Castelo, known locally as El Rubio, was forty-two and single. He was from Panxón, where he worked as a fisherman. He lived alone and didn't have a girlfriend as far as anyone knew. His widowed mother lived with his sister and her husband in a house in the same village. The dead man's brother-in-law had been on a trawler off the west coast of Africa for the past two months.

The man's body had been found floating in the surf at the Playa de la Madorra on Monday morning. When he was pulled from the water he was wearing a thick jumper over a white shirt, corduroy trousers and rubber boots. Around his neck he had a gold medallion of the Virgin of El Carmen. In his pocket he had a *figa*, a little bag of salt, some half-disintegrated banknotes and two keys on a ring.

The summary included a statement from the man who had spotted the body from the road and that of others who had been present at the recovery. Everyone agreed that Castelo had gone out fishing in his boat first thing on Sunday morning, though Barcia stressed that none of them had actually seen him set off, and she doubted that he was intending to do any fishing as the market was closed that day.

Caldas smiled. Barcia was not only extremely thorough, she was also intuitive and had plenty of common sense. He was glad to be working with her.

She had included the most relevant details of El Rubio's autopsy. She confirmed that he had drowned, and distinguished between the two blows to his head – one to the back caused by a long object and the other, more unevenly shaped, to the forehead, probably a result of being dashed against rocks.

As for the wrists, she echoed the pathologist's opinion: since the fastening was round by the little fingers, she didn't think it possible that Castelo had tied his own hands.

The main suppliers of cable ties in the area had been contacted. They were only supplied in an unusual colour by special order, and there had been no orders for green ones.

At the end of the summary came the list of calls made from the deceased's phone during the past week. There were only three, all local. Two to his mother's house, and a third, on Saturday afternoon, was a very short call to a neighbour whose name meant nothing to Barcia. Caldas, however, had to read it twice. Justo Castelo had spoken on the phone to José Arias, his crewmate on the shipwrecked boat.

'Damn,' muttered Caldas.

He looked at his watch. It was almost ten at night. He took out his mobile and dialled his assistant's number. Estevez answered with a grunt.

'Are you busy?' asked Caldas.

'A little.'

'Right.'

'Are you calling just to piss me off?'

'No, no. It was just to say that we have to go back to Panxón. Pick me up at the same time.'

'At seven in the morning?' complained Estevez. 'Can you tell me why we always have to get up so bloody early?'

'Castelo phoned José Arias the afternoon before he died. Arias lied to us and I want to know why.'

'Does it have to be at seven in the morning?'

'I don't want him to be asleep when we get there.'

'Don't worry, boss. If need be, I'll wake him for you.'

Caldas put everything back in the folder and stood up. The plate of sardines sat untouched. He took his raincoat from the rack, paid and said goodbye to Carlos. The academics were still discussing music as he opened the door to leave the Eligio. He closed it and headed over to their table.

'Have you heard of "Solveig's Song"?' he asked.

All four men nodded.

'It's by Grieg,' said one.

'One of the movements from *Peer Gynt*,' added another.

Apparently Caldas was the only person not to know the piece. 'Do you know how it goes?'

The academics looked at each other and one of them began to hum. Soon all four of them were humming the tune that Justo Castelo had whistled until not long before his death.

Caldas didn't recognise it.

He left the bar. In the street, the rain was beating its own rhythm.

Underwater

Caldas hung his wet raincoat on a hanger over the bath and, in the sitting room, switched on the radio almost automatically. At home, where others found a haven, he found only loneliness.

He looked at the shelves of records and wondered whether 'Solveig's Song' was among those that Alba had left him.

For a long time their relationship had seemed like a candle burning down. Only by extinguishing it could something be preserved, but he had preferred to let it burn to the end. It was Alba who had snuffed it out.

The next day, her wardrobe had been empty, but many of her books and records remained on the shelves. For weeks, Caldas had wondered whether she'd forgotten them, or if it meant that she'd left the door ajar behind her. One day, as he put on a record, he recalled a conversation they had had. And then he realised: Alba had left behind everything in which he'd ever shown an interest.

He couldn't find the song El Rubio had whistled every afternoon at his mother's, so he picked something by Louis Armstrong and put it on the record player.

He was still thinking about El Rubio's phone calls. The list of numbers confirmed that José Arias had been lying when he said they never spoke. They had kept in contact. At the least, they'd had one conversation. They'd spoken on Saturday afternoon, the day before Castelo died. Had that been the last time?

Estevez had persuaded him that they didn't need to get to Panxón first thing. And if he was honest Caldas thought he'd rather their visit caught Arias by surprise. Still, he was keen to know what the phone call had been about, to scrutinise the big man's face when he found out that they knew he'd lied.

The inner voice in which Caldas had such faith told him he was on the right path. It was whispering that he should seek the solution to Castelo's murder in the night of the sinking of the *Xurelo* and Captain Sousa's supposed death. Caldas was determined to listen.

He lay down on the sofa, opened the blue folder and took out the cuttings the old priest had given him.

The first was from Sunday 22 December 1996, two days after the boat sank. Above a photo of the rocks, and another of the *Xurelo*'s port of origin, ran the headline: 'Panxón Fishing Boat Sinks Near Salvora'.

Caldas read the article closely. It contained a lengthy account of how the *Xurelo* had foundered on rocks off the island of Salvora and how the three crewmembers had swum ashore and been taken to hospital, to be discharged soon after.

One of the men who had led the rescue team complained that bad weather was hampering the search for the missing man, and believed it foolhardiness unworthy of an experienced seaman to have ignored advice to return to port. By contrast, the skipper of another fishing boat in the area claimed that Sousa had informed him by radio of his intention to take shelter, and couldn't understand why he had changed his mind.

News of the sinking featured in other papers that day. All the articles contained the same account of events and description of the adverse weather conditions. Some included comments from local people who had come to the aid of the crew, but Caldas could only find a statement from one of the survivors in one paper: Marcos Valverde explained how, despite the skipper's efforts to steer the boat, the storm had driven them on to the rocks. The boat had gone down in seconds. 'Where were you headed?' the reporter had asked. Valverde's reply was short: 'Home.'

The next cutting Caldas unfolded was from the following day, Monday the 23rd. There were three articles with accompanying pictures. One showed the latest petrol station held up by a couple of motorcyclists who'd been eluding the police since the previous summer. Another showed people searching for a woman who had disappeared in Aguiño three days earlier. In the third picture, much larger than the others, Captain Sousa's weather-beaten face looked out from beneath a woollen cap.

Beside this photograph, in bold type, it read: 'Search for *Xurelo* Skipper Resumed'. The article recounted how the search for the skipper of the shipwrecked vessel had been delayed until the afternoon. Only two Sea Rescue Service helicopters were involved, as bad weather had so far prevented lifeboats from putting out to sea.

On subsequent days the newspapers only ran brief items on the search for the skipper. A week after the sinking, by which time the search had been called off, a life jacket from the *Xurelo* had been found out at sea. After that, there was nothing more until 28 January, when Antonio Sousa's body, after more than a month in the water, had been found tangled in the nets of a Vigo trawler.

Caldas started reading the article but soon fell asleep, overcome with exhaustion.

He dreamed he was swimming in a storm and in the waves, a few metres away, he could see a fisherman in yellow waterproofs. 'Help,' shouted the man, eyes wide with terror, 'my hands are tied, I can't swim.' Caldas struggled towards the fisherman, but by the time he reached him he had disappeared underwater.

He awoke with a start, covered in sweat, just as he had as a boy when he dreamed that he was swimming beside the drowned pharmacist. He opened his eyes and stared at the ceiling. It sounded as if there was an elephant trumpeting inside the flat.

It took him a couple of seconds to recognise the solo. He had the feeling Louis Armstrong was laughing at him as he sang huskily: *Exactly like you.*

162

Unspoken Questions

On Thursday, Caldas woke early, showered and set out for the station with his hands in his pockets and the blue folder under his arm. The streetlights were still on and, though the rain had stopped, they shone down on a city drenched by the night's downpour.

In his office, he reviewed Clara Barcia's notes again. At nine thirty he went out for coffee and his first cigarette of the day. When he got back, between glancing at the clock and wondering when Estevez would deign to turn up, he photocopied the cuttings about the sinking of the *Xurelo* so that he could return the originals to the priest in Panxón, and reread the report on the recovery of Sousa's body.

Almost without thinking, he took the slip of paper Trabazo had given him from his pocket and dialled the number on it. Then he lit another cigarette and took two deep drags.

'Gerardo Sousa?'

'Yes?'

'I'm Inspector Caldas, from Vigo Police Headquarters.'

'So you've decided to call.'

'I'm sorry?'

'Dr Trabazo said he'd given you my number.'

'Right.'

'He asked me to be friendly.'

Thank goodness. 'Have you got five minutes?' asked Caldas.

'Yes, of course.'

'Did Dr Trabazo say why I wanted to speak to you?'

'No,' said Antonio Sousa's son.

163

'Did you know that Justo Castelo's body was found washed up on the beach on Monday morning?'

'Yes.'

'Has anyone told you the circumstances of his death?'

'No,' he replied. Caldas thought he sounded resigned, rather than curt.

'His hands were tied.'

'Right.'

'You knew?'

'I heard something like that, yes. He committed suicide, didn't he?'

'He may not have.'

'So you're looking into who . . .'

'That's right,' said Caldas with relief, thinking that Sousa's son was going to make things easy for him. But he was wrong.

'That's why you're calling?'

'Well . . .' said Caldas, drawing on his cigarette for strength to continue the conversation. 'Castelo had received threats recently. Did you know?'

'No.'

'Someone painted a date on his rowing boat. The date of the sinking of your father's boat,' he said, sure that Sousa's son already knew. 'Beside it was the word "Murderers". Do you know who might have done it?'

'No idea.'

'I'm sorry if this is stirring up painful memories.'

Sousa's son cleared his throat.

'How did you get on with Castelo?' asked Caldas.

'Me?'

'Yes.'

'From the day my father died, he never looked me in the eye again. Nor did the other two. They stared at the ground as they gave us their condolences.'

'They never told you what happened that night?'

'They didn't have the guts to. Arias even left the village.'

'Why do you think they behaved like that?'

'I'm not the one to ask, Inspector. You should be talking to Arias or Valverde. They're still alive, aren't they?'

Caldas took a drag of his cigarette to stop himself saying, 'For now.'

'So what do you think happened?'

'All I know is that none of them lifted a finger to pull my father from the water. They were close to the coast and wearing life jackets. They could have saved him, but they escaped like rats. They were cowards.'

Caldas dragged again on his cigarette.

'Are you aware that some people in Panxón claim to have seen your father alive?'

'I left the village so I wouldn't have to listen to that kind of thing any more, Inspector. I was suffocating. I realise now that I didn't get far enough away.'

Hunched in his chair, Caldas listened to the rest of Gerardo Sousa's story. Two years after the sinking, a fisherman had arrived in port claiming to have seen his father out at sea on his boat. Since then, not a year went by without someone reporting a sighting of the *Xurelo*.

'What do you make of it?'

'I don't know what they're seeing, Inspector. But the *Xurelo* was dynamited and removed from the water in pieces years ago. You can check.'

The man did not mention his father's fate again and Caldas decided not to press him. He didn't ask about the *macana* or get him to say how he'd identified the body in the autopsy room. But there was one question that Sousa's son had to answer.

'Just one more thing, Mr Sousa,' said Caldas, stubbing out his cigarette. 'Could you tell me where you were last weekend?'

'Here, in Barcelona. I was working.'

'May I ask where?'

'I'm a sound technician. I work in radio,' he said. 'Like you.'

Estevez arrived at ten. He looked as cheerful as he did when Superintendent Soto told him to subdue unruly detainees down in the cells.

'I thought we were going to Panxón?' he said.

Caldas nodded and took his raincoat from the rack.

He climbed into the car, opened the window a crack and closed his eyes. He thought of Sousa's son, his grief, the stifling atmosphere of the village that had driven him away, and his job as a sound technician that meant he had been a long way from Panxón at the time of the murder.

An Empty Niche

The smell of low tide pervaded the village as they got out of the car. After asking around, they found José Arias's house, a two-storey building at the end of a narrow street. Caldas rang the bell several times but no one came to the door.

'You see! We should have got here earlier,' he complained. 'After a night's fishing there's no way he's going to get up.'

'Let me have a go,' said Estevez, elbowing the inspector out of the way and ringing the bell insistently.

Getting no reply, he placed an ear against the door, listening for movement inside. He must not have heard anything as he started beating on the door, first with his knuckles then with open palms.

It was Estevez's fault they had got to Panxón late. Had they arrived early, as Caldas originally wanted, they would have found Arias selling his catch at the market. A guilty conscience was making Estevez strike the door ever harder.

'Stop it, Rafa,' said Caldas, remembering Castelo's shattered shed door. 'We'll come back later.'

Estevez stopped and went to stand beside the inspector, swearing under his breath. Suddenly, as if propelled by a spring, he rushed at the door, giving it a kick that almost tore it from its hinges.

'Arias, open up, police!' he yelled, furious, hammering on the door with his fist.

The inspector pulled him away with difficulty.

'What's the matter with you?'

He saw with relief that the door was still in place, though a crack in the wood revealed where Estevez had kicked it.

'You don't want to wake him up any more?'

Caldas wondered what the hell Estevez was on – LSD? Not knowing what to reply, the inspector threw up his arms and looked upwards. A woman was standing on the balcony of the house opposite. Her hair was full of curlers and she was staring fixedly at Estevez.

Caldas glanced round at the other windows, but the woman in the curlers was the only person looking out. With all the commotion, he was surprised there weren't more people on their balconies.

'Does José Arias live here?' he asked the woman, pointing at the front door.

'He does,' she replied, her curlers shaking slightly.

'Do you know if he's in?'

'I assume he isn't,' she said, adding before she disappeared inside: 'He's not deaf.'

Caldas decided to pay Alicia Castelo a visit. Maybe she knew why her brother had phoned Arias the afternoon before he died.

They rang the bell and an elderly woman came to the door. She was too sprightly to be the dead fisherman's invalid mother.

'We'd like to speak to Alicia Castelo.'

'Alicia's not in,' said the woman. 'It's just her mother and me here.'

'Do you know where we might find her?'

The woman nodded gravely. 'At the cemetery.'

Estevez drew up beside the railings, through which they could see walls topped by rows of dark stone crosses.

'The graveyards here are so pretty,' murmured Estevez, and Caldas agreed. It wasn't the first time he'd heard his assistant admire Galician cemeteries.

At the entrance, Caldas paused to contemplate the ranks of houses stretching from the foot of the promontory down to the sea.

It was hard to imagine that the area had once been sand, with the Gaifar dunes extending inland for several hundred metres. This was how it had been for centuries, until developers were given the go-ahead and the dunes were buried beneath holiday homes, reduced to a tongue of sand so narrow that in winter it disappeared at high tide.

In the cemetery at Panxón a narrow alley led off either side of the central avenue. The wealthiest families had vaults decorated with sculptures, but mostly the dead lay in niches set into the stone walls, one on top of the other in groups of five, each covered by a small roof with the name of the family engraved beneath. The roofs were surmounted with crosses.

Fallen flowers marked the path taken by the cortège the previous afternoon, and Caldas and Estevez followed it down one of the side alleys. Some graves bore photographs of the dead together with their names and dates. Almost all showed pictures of elderly men and women, and Caldas felt sure that none would have wanted to be remembered in this way.

Further on, on a name plaque beneath a cross, Caldas read: TRABAZO FAMILY. One of the niches was empty, and he frowned as he thought of *Captains Courageous* and Manuel the Portuguese fisherman.

Following the trail of flowers, before they reached the steps that led to the lower part of the cemetery, they passed a small area dotted with simple crosses.

'The unknown fishermen who've been washed up on the beach lie beneath those crosses,' said the inspector. 'The people of the village gather the bodies of the drowned and bury them here.'

'How do you know?'

'A friend told me.'

Alicia Castelo was crouching, placing flowers in a niche without a plaque. She wore black and her hair was tied back in a ponytail, like the day before.

They greeted her and she explained that, though the plaque wouldn't be in place until the following day, her mother had asked her to tend her brother's grave.

'We've ordered white stone, like our father's,' she whispered, indicating the niche above, also decorated with fresh flowers.

She said that her husband was still in Namibia. He'd been away for three months but his stint was coming to an end the following week. He'd be returning home and staying for at least a month.

169

'There's not much he could have done even if he'd been here,' she said.

'Right.'

'Have you come to talk to me?' she asked.

'Yes.'

Her blue eyes lit up. 'Have you found out who killed him?'

'Not yet,' said Caldas. 'Do you remember telling us that he had nothing to do with the other crewmembers of the *Xurelo*?'

'Yes, of course.'

'Well, your brother phoned one of them the day before he died. In fact, it was the last call he made.'

'One of his crewmates on the *Xurelo*?' she said with surprise. 'Which one?'

'José Arias.'

'My brother called him?' she said, her face incredulous.

'Yes. We've checked all the calls made from his phone. The last one was to Arias's house. We thought you might know why he called him.'

Alicia Castelo covered her mouth with her hand. 'No, I don't know,' she faltered. 'Have you spoken to him?'

Caldas glanced at Estevez. 'No,' he said. 'We haven't been able to, yet.'

As they walked back to the car, Estevez stopped and pointed to one of the name plaques.

Caldas read the inscription, in white letters on dark marble: 'Antonio Sousa Castro, boat captain, 4/7/1933–20/12/1996'. There was no photograph, and only a rusty container of flowers.

'There's your skipper,' said Estevez.

'Yeah,' said Caldas. 'Maybe.'

Dominoes

In the Refugio del Pescador, four fishermen sat playing dominoes at one of the marble tables by the window. They'd seen José Arias first thing at the fish market, but not since. As his boat was still moored in the harbour, they assumed he was at home sleeping.

After a coffee, the two policemen left the bar. The calm sea reflected the grey sky and Justo Castelo's traps stranded on the jetty. There was still no news of his boat.

They made their way through the village to the narrow street where Arias lived. From a distance they could see the mark left by Estevez's kick on the solid wooden door. They rang the bell several times but there was no answer.

They were about to leave when the door of the house next door opened and a woman came out.

'We're looking for your neighbour, José Arias,' said Caldas as she passed.

'I know,' she said, and Caldas recognised the woman who'd looked down from her balcony earlier. She was no longer in curlers but still stared at Estevez with distrust. 'He went out early,' she added.

'Do you know where he was going?'

The woman said she didn't and asked, 'Are you really from the police?'

Caldas showed her his badge.

'I'm Inspector Caldas.'

'The one on the radio?' she said. 'Dr Trabazo's friend?'

Caldas was amazed at how fast news travelled.

'We're all very fond of the doctor,' she said. 'No one can under-stand why they made him retire. You should see his replacement.'

'You're not happy with him?'

'He's nice enough,' she said. 'But God help anyone who falls into his hands.'

'Right,' smiled Caldas. 'I believe Arias hasn't been back in the vil-lage long?'

The woman's expression changed. 'I'm not one to talk.'

'I'm sure you're not,' said Caldas, knowing that the time had come to listen.

The woman told them that her neighbour had come back from Scotland, where he'd lived for a time after the sinking of the boat. It was rumoured that he'd left a wife and children behind there, but nobody knew for sure. Arias was a quiet man, which was fine by her. He didn't disturb her even though he came in from work so early, and he didn't drink any more. The Scottish woman must have domesticated him. On his days off he went to a bar in the harbour for a game of dominoes or stayed at home and watched TV.

'Did he ever have guests?' asked Caldas.

'More lately,' said the woman enigmatically, before falling silent.

'More?'

'I'm not saying anything,' she said self-importantly. 'But some-times he had people back.'

'Who?'

'You know . . .'

'El Rubio?' asked Caldas.

'I'm sorry?' Startled, the woman glanced at Arias's front door and then at the other end of the narrow street. It seemed that this wasn't a question she'd been expecting.

'Did Justo Castelo come round here?' asked Caldas.

José Arias's neighbour knew she'd said too much. She'd walked into a trap of her own making and now tried to extricate herself. 'I don't remember.'

'When was he here?' asked Caldas, blocking her retreat.

The woman glanced again at the end of the street and then at Estevez. He was standing back but she obviously still found his pres-ence intimidating.

'No one will know you've spoken to us,' said Caldas.

'I don't like to meddle . . .' she said apologetically.

'I know. Please don't worry,' said the inspector gently before continuing to press her: 'You saw Justo Castelo?'

'Once,' she said eventually.

'When was that?'

'Friday or Saturday, I'm not too sure.'

'Last week?'

'Yes.'

'He came to Arias's house?'

The woman nodded. 'They talked for a while, not long. Then El Rubio left.'

'Could you hear what they were talking about?'

'When El Rubio arrived he was saying, over and over, "I can't take it any more".'

'What about Arias? What did he say?'

The woman shrugged. 'They closed the door.'

'How long were they inside for?'

'I don't know,' she said hesitantly. 'Five, maybe ten minutes.'

'Right,' said Caldas pensively.

'I felt sorry for him, you know,' the woman added.

'Who?'

'El Rubio. He was a good lad. You've got to be pretty desperate to do something like that.'

Caldas agreed.

'He must be scared, too,' the woman said, gesturing towards her neighbour's house. 'I expect you know what people are saying: El Rubio was being threatened.'

'Yes.'

'God forbid, but maybe Arias is next.'

The woman's expression again changed. She repeated that she wasn't one to gossip, and hurried away down the street. She looked up to greet José Arias as she passed him.

The Lost Fender

'I don't know what you're talking about,' said Arias in his deep, deep voice. He was carrying several bags of shopping in each huge hand.

'You lied,' said Caldas. 'You said you hadn't spoken to Castelo in years.'

'Because it's true,' growled Arias, dropping the bags to the ground.

Caldas was glad Estevez was there. This narrow little street was no place to annoy someone of Arias's size.

'We know you spoke to him.'

Arias turned to glare after his neighbour and Caldas thought that if she hadn't already departed the woman would have been struck dead.

'It's in Castelo's phone records. Do you know who he called last?'

'How should I know?'

'He called you,' said Caldas, looking him in the eye. 'On Saturday afternoon, the day before he died.'

'Me?'

Caldas had expected him, caught in a lie, to avoid his gaze or look furtive in some other way. But Arias simply seemed surprised.

'Isn't this your number?' asked Caldas, and he read out the number in case there was some mistake.

Arias confirmed that it was and Caldas went on, 'Now do you remember the call on Saturday afternoon?'

Arias lowered his head.

'Why did he call you, may I ask? If you never spoke face to face, how do you explain the phone call?'

Arias kept his eyes lowered, and Caldas thought of the radio show and the tune that moron Losada played while he was thinking.

'El Rubio had lost a rubber fender out at sea,' the fisherman said at last. 'He called to ask if I'd found it.'

'A what?'

'A fender,' said the fisherman. 'To protect the boat. Sometimes they fall off.'

'Why didn't you tell me when I asked if you'd spoken to him?'

Arias gathered up his shopping bags. 'I'd forgotten.'

As they left Monteferro behind, rain started to spatter the windscreen. At first it was gentle, but soon it became a downpour. Drops got in through the inspector's open window.

'He lied to us,' said Estevez.

'I know.'

'Why didn't you mention Castelo's visit?'

'And give away his neighbour?' said Caldas, and tutted. 'Anyway, he'd just have come up with an excuse, like he did about the phone call.'

'That's true.'

The inspector leaned back and recalled the words Arias's nosy neighbour had overheard: 'I can't take it any more.' Castelo had said it repeatedly as he went inside the house. The waiter at the Refugio del Pescador had heard him say something similar on Saturday afternoon: 'I'm going to end it', Castelo had murmured as he finished his drink. These phrases now reverberated in the inspector's mind. What had caused Castelo such anguish?

The things painted on his rowing boat, the good-luck charms found among his belongings and the desperate visit to his fellow shipwreck survivor pointed in just one direction, as did the blow to his head and the fear on the faces of José Arias and Marcos Valverde.

The shower had passed and the windscreen wipers now could be set to intermittent. When Caldas opened his eyes he saw, to their left, the dark grey sea topped with white-crested waves. He wondered where Castelo's fishing boat was. Someone had had to approach it from another boat in order to kill him. What the hell had happened to it?

175

He stared straight ahead, at the city of Vigo spreading like a stain around the *ria*. First low houses, then the tall blocks of the district of Coia and, further on, the rest of the city spilling untidily over the hillsides, with the hospital rising above it all near the Monte del Castro.

Caldas closed his eyes and his mind travelled from Justo Castelo's boat to room 211 in the hospital, his Uncle Alberto's emaciated arm and the green mask through which he breathed.

A Truce

Estevez had gone out for lunch. After half an hour in his chair trying to order his thoughts, Caldas picked up the black notebook and rose to his feet. He knew his mind worked better when he was wandering among people than sitting alone in his office.

The inspector made his way from the police station down to the Montero Rios Gardens. He walked along the seafront to the end of the jetty that sheltered the boats in the harbour. The wind had swept the sky above the *ria* clear of clouds and a couple of sailing boats were putting out to sea. Caldas thought of Valverde's wife. Behind the huge window of her designer home, she must have been relishing the first sunny afternoon in days.

He lit a cigarette and leaned on the wall overlooking the *ria*, beside an angler with a line cast out into the water. Caldas looked down at the foam formed by the sea beating against the concrete jetty. He pictured Castelo trying to swim with his hands tied, like the man in yellow waterproofs who had called out to him in his dream, and he wondered if the green cable tie served any other purpose than to make swimming impossible and the death look like suicide. In that case, anyone involved in the murder would have displayed their distress. But José Arias had tried to hide his. What could have instilled such fear in such a big man?

Caldas walked back along the jetty. A merchant ship passed, its foghorn as monotonous as Justo Castelo's existence. The only discordant note in the lonely fisherman's life had been the graffiti on his rowing boat, but this referred to an event that had occurred many years before – the sinking of the *Xurelo*. Caldas didn't believe in coincidences. He was convinced that the two things were linked. The fear that had driven Castelo to fill his pockets with lucky charms also showed in the faces of his former crewmates. Why were they refusing to talk? Could Antonio Sousa really have returned? Maybe someone was avenging the skipper's death. But who? And why now, so long afterwards? Caldas felt he was still very far from finding answers. It had been five days since El Rubio's death. If he didn't make progress soon, maybe he'd never discover the truth.

The inspector was still pondering this when he got to the Calle Canovas del Castillo and passed dozens of tourists who'd just disembarked from a cruise liner. Some were heading for the oyster stalls at La Piedra market, others for the new shopping centre that sat like a black patch over the city's eye as it looked out to sea.

Before he reached the arcades of Ribeira, he turned into the Calle Real and walked up into the old town. Manuel Trabazo was right: in the past there had rarely been any ugly buildings.

He looked at his watch. The walk had left him little time for lunch. He went into a bar and ordered a ham sandwich and a glass of white wine. He sat at the counter and thought about Estevez. He pictured him wolfing a salad in some nearby bar.

He left after his coffee and walked along the Calle de la Palma past the cathedral. Down a side street he caught sight of waiters in the Plaza de la Constitución setting out tables on the bar terraces. Like an animal stretching after a long sleep, the city was coming to life in the sun.

At the entrance to the radio station, Caldas greeted the doorman. He didn't want to get to the studio any earlier than necessary, so he lit a cigarette as a pretext for staying out in the street till the last minute.

When the bells started to strike the hour, he stubbed out his cigarette and went upstairs. As he walked down the corridor, he heard the theme tune to *Patrolling the Waves*. He peered into the control room and waved at Rebeca and the sound technician.

'The caller from Monday hasn't turned up,' Rebeca informed him.

'Who?'

'The breathalyser man, remember? He was going to stop by today so you could both go and see the local police.'

He'd forgotten all about it.

'Oh, right.'

On the other side of the glass, Losada was at the microphone, gesturing frantically towards the clock.

'You're late,' he said as Caldas entered the studio.

'As usual,' replied Caldas, sitting down by the window. He switched off his mobile phone and put in on the desk beside his open notebook.

In a familiar ritual, the theme tune faded, the red studio light came on and Losada announced sonorously, 'Welcome to *Patrolling the Waves*, where the ordinary citizen enters into a dialogue with the police, with the aim of improving community relations in our city.'

Caldas knew by heart the string of inanities with which Losada introduced him.

'We have with us the implacable defender of upright citizens, the fearsome guardian of our streets, the scourge of hooligans, Patrolman Inspector Leo Caldas. Welcome to the show, Inspector.'

'Thank you.'

'In today's edition of *Patrolling the Waves,* the inspector is here at Radio Vigo to answer you the listeners' questions.'

Caldas turned to the window. Children were chasing pigeons and street cleaners were making the most of the break in the rain to sweep up dead leaves along the Alameda. He only put on his headphones when Rebeca held up the sign with the name of the first caller and Losada handed over with the words, 'Ricardo, good afternoon. You're through to Leo Caldas, patrolman of the waves.'

Ricardo got straight to the point: 'I'm calling because my upstairs neighbours are disturbing me at night and I'm wondering if there's anything I can do about it.'

'How are they disturbing you?' asked Losada.

'You know ...'

'No, we don't know, the listeners don't know,' said the presenter in his affected voice. 'Please tell the city of Vigo what kind of disturbance your neighbours are causing.'

'Well, you know ... noise.'

179

'What kind of noise?' persisted Losada. Caldas wondered why they needed him there at all when he hardly got a chance to say anything.

'They're very passionate,' said the caller.

'Sorry?'

'They haven't been together long so, well, it's understandable, they want to get to know each other. But it's one thing to get to know each other, and another to scream all night long. It's been going on for almost three weeks.'

'An ideal subject for a man like Leo Caldas,' said Losada with a smile. 'Let's see what our patrolman has to say.'

'Prurient moron,' Caldas said to himself.

He was about to answer the caller when Losada raised a hand and the tune from the previous show started playing in his headphones. He held up his arms. How did they expect him to think with that bloody music playing? Losada leaned towards the microphone and lowered his hand slowly.

'Well, Inspector?'

'I don't think there's anything that can be done,' said Caldas.

But Losada wasn't about to let a call like this one get away.

'Isn't there some bylaw restricting noise levels?' he asked.

Caldas had no idea. 'Not for that kind of noise. Your neighbours are in their own home, aren't they, Ricardo?'

'In hers, yes,' said Ricardo.

'Then there's very little you can do.'

'But they're doing it on purpose,' said Ricardo.

'That may make a difference,' said Losada, raising a hand for the technician to play the jaunty tune.

Caldas gestured energetically for him to turn it off but Losada kept his hand up for a moment longer.

'Does it make any difference, Inspector?' Losada asked.

What did the fool expect him to say? Did he think he could send a couple of officers round to the couple's bedroom to measure the decibel level?

'I was a newly-wed myself once, Inspector Caldas,' said Ricardo, reluctant to give up. 'And I'm telling you, that girl screams just to annoy me. It can't be anything else.'

'Right.'

To put an end to the call, Caldas asked the man to give his details off air and promised to take the matter up with the City Police.

In his black notebook he wrote: *City Police one, Leo nil.*

The next three calls were all about traffic. The fifth caller complained about the poor street lighting near his home, the sixth was a football fan angry about Celta's recent results. Then a man who'd lost his dog called in.

City Police eleven, Celta one, Leo nil, read the entry in his notebook by the end of the show. Caldas hadn't been able to help a single caller but, since every time he fell silent Losada raised his hand and the damn tune played, he'd spoken more than usual.

'What's that music called that you play before I answer?' he asked, removing his headphones.

'It's called "Promenade" or "Walking the Dog".'

'Both?'

'Yes. It's by Gershwin,' said Losada.

'Don't you remember, I asked you not to play it any more?'

'I think it works really well.'

Caldas took his phone from the desk and stood up. 'I don't.'

'Well, everyone says they love it.'

'Who's everyone?'

'I don't know, Leo,' said the presenter, gesturing towards the window overlooking the Alameda. 'Everyone. Don't you get out?'

Caldas didn't reply. He shut his notebook and headed for the studio door.

'Anyway, the tune fits in perfectly with what we're after, Leo.'

The inspector turned round. 'What we're after? Would you mind telling me exactly what the hell we're after? Anyway, I don't care. Please don't play it any more. Not while I'm on air.'

'May I remind you that this is my show.'

'You're an idiot.'

Caldas left the studio, waving goodbye to Rebeca. Downstairs, the doorman came to meet him.

'There was a man here to see you, Inspector.'

'Damn! The breathalyser man. Where is he?'

'He left.'

'Where did he go?'

'I don't know. When I told him he couldn't go upstairs, he left.'

'You didn't allow him upstairs?'

'Of course not,' said the doorman. 'He was drunk.'

The sun was setting behind the buildings of the old town, colouring the sky orange, like the Lodeiro that hung on the wall of the Eligio. Caldas set off back to the police station, switching on his mobile phone. The display lit up to show he'd missed a call.

He read the name twice: Alba. Alba? Why would she be calling after all this time? He stood in the middle of the pavement staring at the phone in his hand. He didn't dare dial. He told himself she'd call back if it was something important, and walked on, cursing Losada and his stupid show. Why did he have to have his phone switched off when Alba called?

A few steps further on, he stopped and dialled.

'Hello?'

'Have you put Santiago Losada in your Book of Idiots?' said Caldas.

'The presenter?' asked his father, adding before Caldas had a chance to answer: 'Of course I have.'

With a sigh of relief, Caldas put his phone in his trouser pocket and set off again for the police station, thinking of Alba.

The Lighthouse at Punta Lameda

He spent the rest of the afternoon in his office, with the glass door closed and his phone in front of him on the desk. He spoke to his father again and promised he'd go to the hospital the following day. He also opened the blue folder containing all the information on the Castelo case several times, but couldn't concentrate on what he was reading. It occurred to him that they could get a court order to have Sousa exhumed. It was the only way of checking that it really had been Sousa's body tangled in the nets of the trawler.

A late visit from Superintendent Soto made him change his mind.

'Any suspects?' he asked after Caldas had filled him in on some of the details of the case.

'No.'

'Nothing?'

'Well . . .'

'Well what?'

'There's someone called Antonio Sousa who might have something to do with it,' he said, and instantly regretted it.

'Where is he?' asked Soto.

Silence.

The door opened and Estevez came in.

'Do you know where this Sousa is?' the superintendent asked him.

'In a wooden box for the past twelve years.'

'And he's the suspect?'

'Not exactly,' said Estevez with a smile.

Soto turned towards the inspector.

183

'What the hell are you up to, Leo?' he said as he made his way out. 'Even Estevez can see it's nonsense.'

Once they were alone, the inspector asked, 'Did you drop by just to make me look stupid?'

'I'm sorry, boss.'

'Never mind,' muttered Caldas, turning back to the contents of the folder. 'What's up?'

'While you were on the radio I called Clara Barcia. A couple of hours ago a scuba diver found a sunken boat. It might be Castelo's. They're going to try and raise it this afternoon.'

'Where is it?'

'I'm not sure. Do you want us to drive over there?'

Caldas dialled Barcia's number. She didn't reply, so he left a message. When he hung up, Estevez was whistling the Gershwin tune.

'What are you whistling?'

'Sorry, it's really catchy.'

'You listened to the show?' asked Caldas, aghast.

'Never miss it.'

Estevez was crazier than he thought. Wasn't it enough to see the boss all day at work?

'You tune in to *Patrolling the Waves*?'

'No need, boss. Olga puts it on the loudspeaker.'

'What?'

'Didn't you know?'

Caldas sank back into his chair, looking up at the ceiling. He needed a rest.

'So are we going to have a look at that boat or not?' said Estevez impatiently.

'Better to go tomorrow.'

Estevez dropped him off at the Town Hall and Caldas handed the list of complaints collected during the show to the City Police. Then he walked down to the Eligio and, placing his phone on the bar in front of him, ordered a glass of white wine. With his second glass, Carlos brought him a plate of ham croquettes.

The academics knew all about the Gershwin tune having two names.

184

When Caldas left the bar about an hour later, someone there was still whistling the damn thing.

At home, he switched on the radio and flopped on to the sofa. He was dozing when his phone caused him to sit up with a start.

'Hello?'

'I've only just got your message, Inspector. Is this too late?'

Caldas wanted to hang up.

'Don't worry, Clara. Has your team got the boat out of the water?'

'Yes, but I don't think we'll find anything useful,' Clara said apologetically.

Caldas hadn't been expecting to find fingerprints on a boat that had been on the seabed for several days.

'Are you absolutely sure that it is Castelo's boat?'

'Yes, of course.'

'Where was it?'

'It was off Punta Lameda by the lighthouse, in Monteferro. Do you know it?'

'Is it near the beach where the body was found?'

'No, no. The boat was round the other side of the mountain, by the shore,' said Barcia. 'There was a hole in the hull and it was weighted down with rocks. Whoever scuttled it wanted to make sure it wouldn't float back up again.'

After hanging up, Caldas stretched out on the sofa again. Something about Barcia's assumption didn't make sense. Why sink the boat so near the coast if you didn't want it to turn up? Why not sink it in the open sea?

Still turning this over in his mind, he fell asleep, staring at the mobile phone on the table as if that would make it ring.

A Wake

Next morning, he took a shower. Eyes closed under the stream of water, he leaned down to grab the razor from the shelf. He liked to shave in the shower, without foam or mirror. He simply ran his hand over his chin to check if he'd missed anything. He'd only ever stopped shaving this way for a few weeks, when Alba had given him an electric shaver, which he never got used to.

When he'd finished, he put the razor back and soaped himself thoroughly. He was covered in suds when he heard the phone ring.

Only one person could be calling this early.

He hurried out of the shower, leaving a white trail on the floor from the bathroom to the coffee table in the sitting room.

'Hello?'

'Leo, it's me.'

'Who?' he asked, feeling silly for asking.

'Me, Alba,' she replied, as if it were necessary.

'Oh. Hello.'

'Sorry to call so early.'

They both knew it wasn't early for him.

'Don't worry.'

'I just heard about your Uncle Alberto. How is he?'

It was as if he'd heard her voice only yesterday.

'So-so.'

'What about your father?'

'Well . . .'

'Give him my love, won't you?'

'Of course,' he whispered.

'And how are you, Leo?'

Not good, he thought. Not good at all.

'I'm fine,' he said. 'How about you?'

'I'm fine, too.'

When he'd rung off, he shook the water from the phone and left it face down on a newspaper. Then he returned to the shower feeling that Alba had slipped away for ever, like the foam that had slid from his body to form a puddle on the floor.

The Rock Pool

Monteferro was the last stretch of untouched coast south of Vigo. Miraculously it had withstood the relentless advance of urban development and, though the isthmus that joined it to the mainland was dotted with houses, the cliff-edged promontory was still covered with green. At its summit stood a twenty-five-metre-high memorial to sailors drowned at sea.

For the third time in a few days they took the road from Panxón to Monteferro. This time they didn't turn left down the narrow street that led to Marcos Valverde's house, but continued straight on, between the pale trunks of eucalyptuses whose intense fragrance filtered in through Caldas's open window.

Behind closed eyelids, he could see Alba.

'That way?' asked Estevez, stopping the car by an unpaved road leading off to the right, like a tunnel through the trees.

The inspector opened his eyes and looked around. Barcia had said that a forest track led to the lighthouse at Punta Lameda.

'Yes, I think so.'

Estevez turned and nosed the car down the potholed track beneath a vault of branches. Further on, they emerged from the forest and skirted the mountain, while below the sea sparkled in the morning sun.

The last hundred metres were paved and led to a small lighthouse perched on rocks at the western end of Monteferro. The Forensics van was parked outside.

Queasily, the inspector climbed out of the car. He breathed in some fresh sea air before following Estevez to the lighthouse railing. Officer Ferro waved from a nearby rock and came towards them. He said they had been searching the area where the boat had been found, but the rain of the past few days had erased all clues.

'Where was the boat?' asked Caldas.

'Down there,' said Ferro, pointing. 'Sunk in a deep rock pool. Shall I show you?'

'Can we get to it?'

'Yes,' Ferro assured him. 'But watch your step. Some of the rocks are treacherous.'

Ferro was enjoying his day by the sea. It was like an early start to the weekend when he'd go fishing in his boat. They followed him from rock to rock, with Caldas behind Ferro and Estevez behind the inspector. The sea was almost dead calm but waves still struck the shore with a splash.

'They chose the only sheltered spot. There are rocks just out there forming a barrier,' explained Ferro, stopping at the water's edge to point at a small reef further out.

'I can't see them,' said Estevez.

'That's because the tide's coming in, but an hour ago they showed above the surface. Can't you see the foam?'

'Yes, I can see that.'

'Well, that's where the waves break. Anything nearer than that is sheltered. At low tide it's almost like a swimming pool and at high tide only the water on the surface moves.'

Caldas looked around. As Ferro had said, the water was calmest here.

'So Castelo's boat was on the bottom?' he asked.

'Just there,' indicated Ferro. 'There was a hole in the hull and it was weighted with rocks. They wanted to make sure it went down.'

'Was the hole made deliberately?'

'And how. It was made from the inside. Then the boat was filled with rocks and allowed to sink.'

'How could someone have negotiated the rock barrier to get the boat in?' asked Estevez.

'There's a gap over there,' said the Forensics officer. 'But not just anyone could do it. You'd need to know the coastline.'

'Who found it?' asked Caldas.

189

'A boy scuba fishing. He followed a conger eel into the pool and saw the boat on the bottom. It was pure chance.'

'One thing's for sure,' said Estevez. 'A boat couldn't just get dragged in here by the tide.'

'Definitely not,' Ferro agreed. 'It was brought here on purpose. This was an ideal spot to sink it. They didn't want it to be found.'

'But if they'd sunk it out at sea wouldn't it have been even harder to find?' asked Caldas.

'If they'd taken it way out, yes, of course. But there's always a chance it would be dashed against rocks by the current, breaking up and floating to the surface. Down here the water's still. If the ballast does its job, the boat should stay put. The only risk was what actually happened – it was spotted by a diver. But at this time of year it's unusual for anyone to go out. Normally it would have stayed at the bottom all winter and got covered in seaweed.'

They drove back along the track to the road but, instead of heading to Panxón, Caldas told Estevez to turn the other way, towards the top of the promontory. The road grew steeper, passing through an acacia grove that had not yet been invaded by eucalyptus. Then the pines began, covering the slopes down to the sea and filling the air with their sharp fragrance.

They parked on the esplanade by the memorial, and made their way to the lookout point.

'Damn, this is pretty,' exclaimed Estevez when he saw the view. Caldas agreed.

To the south, Panxón was hidden by trees, but they could see Mount Lourido at the end of Playa America and, further on, the Playa de la Ladeira beneath the La Groba mountains. Baiona, with its medieval fortress, marked the limit of the bay. Beyond, they could just make out Cabo Silleiro, the final swerve of the coast before it headed south in an almost straight line for 400 kilometres to Cabo da Roca near Lisbon.

To the north rose the Cíes Islands with their mother-of-pearl beaches and, further on, the point of Cabo Home, the tip of the north shore of the Vigo estuary, like an animal lying beside the sea. It was a clear day so the outline of the island of Ons was visible beyond that, facing the next estuary along, that of Pontevedra.

They could even distinguish the faint silhouette of another hump of land in the background, and Caldas wondered if it was the island of Salvora where the *Xurelo* had foundered so many years before.

'Those small islands, the nearest ones, what are they?' asked Estevez.

'The Estelas,' said Caldas.

'Why haven't you brought me here before?'

Caldas shrugged. He still found it surprising that a man who could break someone's jaw without batting an eyelid could appreciate a view.

'Do you mind if I go and take a look at the memorial?' said Estevez. The inspector went with him.

On the stone monument, the Virgin of El Carmen looked out to sea with the baby Jesus in her arms. Above her was hung a bronze garland of flowers and, beneath, an inscription: *Salve Regina Marium*. A plaque on the side asked that prayers be said for drowned sailors.

While Estevez went round the back of the monument Caldas took out his mobile phone. Alba's voice had been echoing in his head all day. He dialled Manuel Trabazo's number and told him that El Rubio's boat had been found by the lighthouse at Punta Lameda. Trabazo knew the spot.

'Do you think it's where Castelo drowned?'

'No,' said Trabazo without hesitation.

'How can you be so sure?'

'Punta Lameda is on the north side of Monteferro. The beach where his body was washed up is on the south side. If he'd fallen into the water at Punta Lameda, his body wouldn't have turned up where it did, on the Madorra. The current would have dragged it inland up the *ria*.'

'I thought you said anyone drowned in the area washed up on the Madorra?'

'Those who drown nearby or right out at sea,' said Trabazo. 'But if a body falls into the water close to the rocks on one side of Monteferro, it doesn't turn back and head round to the other side. Test it out. Throw a piece of wood into the water at Punta Lameda and see where it ends up. I bet you a bottle of wine it doesn't go round the mountain.'

191

'Right,' murmured Caldas. So El Rubio had been killed elsewhere and his boat towed to the lighthouse and sunk.

'Where are you?' asked Trabazo.

'Here, in Monteferro. By the monument. Trying to make sense of it all.'

'I'm going out fishing. Why don't you come with me?'

Caldas hadn't been on a boat in years.

'Out to sea?'

'You'll see it more clearly out there, Leo,' insisted Trabazo. 'How about we meet at the harbour in half an hour?'

As they drove down the hill, Caldas leaned back, with his eyes closed and the window open.

'Shall we stop off for another look at Mrs Valverde's tits?' asked Estevez as the trees of Monteferro gave way to the first houses.

Caldas tutted. He had no interest in Mrs Valverde's breasts. It was her smile that fascinated him.

The Sky-blue Boat

When Estevez dropped him off in Panxón, the village seemed quite different. There were people on the promenade and, on the beach, some brave souls were walking along the shore, feet in the water. On the terrace of the Refugio del Pescador, a few old fishermen sat in the sun.

Caldas looked at his watch. The fish market had been closed for hours. At the end of the jetty a couple of anglers were casting their lines out over the water, and the inspector headed towards them.

As he passed the yacht club he breathed in an acrid odour that mingled with the smell of the sea. He saw the carpenter through the railing. He'd moved the boat he'd been caulking when they'd interviewed him out into the sun, and he was applying a coat of tar to the hull.

The grey cat was at his feet, watching his maimed hand move back and forth as he applied the tar.

Caldas made his way along the jetty towards Justo Castelo's traps, which were still stacked against the whitewashed wall. He sat down on a bollard and lit a cigarette.

Arias's boat, the *Aileen*, was moored to a buoy, its traps piled up on deck. Caldas assumed that Castelo's boat was a similar size, and he wondered if it was possible to tow such a boat in past the rocks at Punta Lameda. He'd ask Trabazo.

Until now Caldas had imagined one person approaching El

Rubio from another vessel. But if Castelo's boat was too big to tow, at least two people must have been involved. One would have remained on their boat while the second sailed El Rubio's boat to the lighthouse.

Caldas stubbed out his cigarette and walked back along the jetty. He leaned on the wall of the yacht club and watched the carpenter dip his brush into the tar and let the excess drip off before spreading it over the wood.

The cat was still watching the carpenter's hand move back and forth.

Trabazo came up beside him, dropping a plastic box full of fishing lines, floats and hooks on the ground, and slapped the inspector on the back.

'Watching the craftsman at work?' said Trabazo, indicating the carpenter with a nod of the head. 'He may have a few fingers missing, but that lad's got a gift. The wood seems to obey him.'

'Do you know, I didn't think they made boats out of wood any more.'

'It's obvious you don't fish, Calditas! The only reason people don't use wood is because it needs maintenance, but a true fisherman will always choose it. In a wooden boat you're really in the ocean, embedded in it. You can feel it in the small of your back,' said Trabazo. 'Boats made of plastic or fibreglass just slide over the water. They're quite different.'

The carpenter looked up. He laid his brush down on top of the tin of tar and waved at the doctor.

'Charlie not getting dizzy today?' asked Trabazo, pointing at the cat.

'He must be about to, Doctor,' said the carpenter, smiling through his ginger beard. 'He's been watching me for about half an hour. I'm expecting him to keel over any minute.'

They carried the rowing boat down the slipway, placed Trabazo's box inside and climbed aboard. The boat rocked and Caldas had a feeling he shouldn't have accepted his friend's invitation. He became sure of it when he saw Trabazo glance disapprovingly at his shoes. Some shoes, Calditas, he seemed to be thinking. What did they all have against his shoes?

194

Trabazo began rowing out to the buoy and Caldas gripped the gunwale of the small boat with both hands.

'How's your father?' asked the doctor.

'Backwards and forwards between the vineyard and the hospital.'

'But he's OK?'

'Yes, he's OK,' said Caldas. Then he asked, 'Did you know he had a dog?'

'Your father?'

'A big brown one,' said Caldas. 'He claims it isn't his, but it follows him around everywhere.'

'Well, you did have a little dog once ... What was its name?'

'Cabola,' said Caldas.

'That's right. Cabola.'

'But it was my mother's dog. It died soon after she did.'

'I remember,' said Trabazo, and put down an oar to feel in his pocket. 'I'll show you something when we get to the boat.'

They reached the buoy, tied up the rowing boat and climbed aboard Trabazo's main boat, a *gamela* almost five metres long with a small outboard motor. It was sky-blue and looked in need of a fresh coat of paint. A rock on the end of a chain served as its anchor. It wasn't a doctor's boat; it was a true fisherman's boat.

'The other day, after I gave you that photo of Sousa, I went through the chest of drawers and found this,' said Trabazo, taking an old photograph from his pocket and handing it to the inspector. 'Your parents and me. I thought you'd like to have it.'

They looked as if they were in their twenties. They were sitting on some steps, his mother, smiling, between the two friends.

Trabazo bent down to connect the fuel tank and pulled on the starter cord several times until the motor came to life.

Caldas, still staring at the photo, steadied himself as the boat started to vibrate.

'You know, sometimes I forget her face,' he said, sitting down on the middle bench. 'Some nights I dream about her, I know it's my mother, but the face I see isn't hers.'

Trabazo released the mooring rope, sat down in the stern holding the tiller, and said, 'In time everything goes, you forget the face, you forget the voice.'

'What?' said Caldas, and the doctor began to sing quietly, '*Avec le temps, avec le temps, va, tout s'en va . . .*'

'Who sang that?'

Trabazo steered the boat between buoys. 'Léo Ferré,' he replied. 'Your mother adored him.'

Sea Bass Rock

As they doubled the jetty Trabazo steered towards Monteferro. The boat moved through the water with its bow raised.

Some of the houses that were scattered over the strip of land between the mountain and the mainland appeared to be clinging to the rocks, but most were squeezed among the trees, vying for views of the bay. Caldas searched unsuccessfully for the glass façade of the Valverdes' house.

'They were planning to develop the whole mountain,' said Trabazo, with a sweep of his free hand. 'Can you believe it? They'd even started laying out streets.'

'So what happened?' Caldas was making sure not to look to either side. He held his head up and stared straight ahead, concentrating on exposing his face to the cold sea air.

'The entire village rose up and a judge ordered the tree felling to be halted. Precautionary suspension, I think the term is. We'll see how long that lasts.'

As he spoke, Trabazo backed off the throttle so that the inspector could hear him.

'Did you go to see Don Fernando?'

'Yes,' said Caldas.

'Any help?'

'Yes, definitely.'

'He spent years photographing the fishermen.'

This was not what had most impressed the inspector. 'Did you know that he's got an archive of cuttings about shipwrecks?'

'Not just shipwrecks,' said Trabazo. 'He keeps anything to do with the village. It's his way of experiencing the thrill of the sea, through the adventures of others.'

'Right.'

They left the houses behind and sailed past the pine-clad slopes of Monteferro stretching above the cliffs. At the summit stood the monument to the memory of drowned sailors.

'We'll head that way later,' said Trabazo, pointing at a spot along the coast. 'Now I'm going to show you a place no one else knows. Sea Bass Rock, I call it. I've been fishing there for over thirty years.'

'You only fish for sea bass?'

'There I do. Only lovely bass,' said Trabazo. 'Though you never really know what you're going to get nowadays. Did you hear about El Rubio landing a sunfish a few months ago? TV reporters even came to interview him.'

'Yes, I read the newspaper cutting,' said Caldas.

'Did Don Fernando show it to you?'

'No,' said Caldas. 'It was framed on Castelo's sitting-room wall.'

As the boat skirted around Monteferro the Cíes Islands appeared ahead. They looked further away now than they had from the top of the mountain.

'El Rubio can't have drowned beyond that point,' said Trabazo, slowing the boat and indicating a rounded rock. 'Look at the waves. See how they split apart? If he'd drowned beyond that rock, the current wouldn't have dragged him to the Madorra on this side of the mountain, but to somewhere round the other side. His boat may have been found round there but Castelo can't have fallen into the sea beyond that rock.'

'I see.'

'It couldn't have been suicide.'

'I know,' said Caldas, still staring straight ahead.

Trabazo looked at the inspector expectantly but Caldas said nothing more.

'Do you have any idea who might have done it?' Trabazo pressed.

'You know what they're saying in the village, don't you?' said Caldas.

'What they're saying?'

'Do you know or not, Manuel?'

'Just about.'

'And what do you think?'

'What do you mean, what do I think?'

Caldas decided to get straight to the point. 'Do you believe in ghosts, apparitions?'

'Bloody hell, Leo!' muttered Trabazo. 'You don't mention things like that on a boat.'

'Well, do you believe in them or not?'

Trabazo turned the tiller abruptly and the boat reared up. 'No,' he said firmly. Then he knocked on the motor and spat over the side.

They continued in silence until the lighthouse at Punta Lameda appeared among the rocks a few minutes later. The Forensics van was parked in the same place, on the paved stretch of road. Trabazo brought the boat up close to the cliff and let it bob on the water with the motor in neutral.

'Over there,' he said, pointing. 'The perfect place to hide something. I'd never have thought of it.'

Caldas nodded.

'You can't see it from here,' the doctor went on, 'but there's a rock barrier a few metres from the shore. At high tide waves wash over it, but at the bottom of the pool the water's always still.'

Caldas peered over the gunwale. Dark seaweed swayed beneath the boat, looking like the antlers of a rhythmically moving herd of moose.

'Can we get any closer?'

'We'd run the risk of hitting a rock, but for two hours before or after low tide you can get in OK. It's not that difficult,' said Trabazo. 'You just have to play with the throttle. And once you're in past the barrier you're safe. It's like a swimming pool.'

'Only at low tide?'

'It's the only time that all the rocks are visible and the surface of the water is calm.'

'Do you think you could get in if you were towing another boat?'

'A boat like El Rubio's?' Trabazo shook his head. 'No, no room to manoeuvre.'

'That's what I was afraid of,' sighed Caldas.

'He was alone on his boat when he left port, wasn't he?'

The inspector nodded.

'That means there were two of them,' said Trabazo, as if reading Caldas's mind.

'At least,' whispered Caldas, before asking: 'Doesn't it seem rather risky bringing it here?'

'If you don't know the coast it's more than risky, it's suicide.'

'That's not what I mean,' said Caldas. 'Somebody on shore or on another boat could have seen it all.'

'I doubt it. On a Sunday morning no professional fishermen would be out. And the rest of us aren't up that early,' smiled Trabazo. 'Especially when it's raining.'

'Do you know what time low tide was on Sunday?'

The doctor squinted as he did the mental calculation.

'The first low tide was around five thirty in the morning and the second about twelve hours later, around six in the evening.'

Caldas clicked his tongue.

'It had to be the morning,' he mumbled, looking up at the cliffs merging into the green slopes of Monteferro.

There were no houses there, no window behind which to look for a witness.

'Can you jump ashore from there?' he asked, indicating the rock pool.

'As I said, it's as still as a swimming pool. You can climb up and down without any problem as long as the tide's not covering the barrier. Years ago fishermen from the village used to set traps here.'

There were plenty of rocks below the lighthouse. Caldas thought of the stones used to weight the boat down at the bottom of the pool. There was no need to look for those elsewhere.

He tried to spot Officer Ferro. He must be up there somewhere, hunting on amid the boulders on the slope. Caldas stopped looking when the rocking of the boat began to play havoc with his insides.

'Shall we go?'

'Yes, of course,' said Trabazo, moving the throttle lever. 'We came out for some fishing.'

The boat reared up and Caldas was relieved to feel the sea breeze on his face.

They sailed back round Monteferro towards Panxón.

'Change places with me,' said Trabazo, suddenly switching off the engine.

Caldas took a couple of unsteady steps and collapsed on to the bench in the stern. The smell of petrol was much stronger there. Trabazo reached down for the oars and fitted them into the rowlocks. Then he sat down on the bench Caldas had vacated and, facing the inspector, began to row.

'You're lucky, Calditas,' he said. 'No one apart from me knows about Sea Bass Rock.'

Caldas craved the fresh air that had blown in his face when they'd been using the motor.

'Do we have to row there?' he asked.

'We don't want the fish to know we're here.'

The inspector swallowed. 'No, of course not,' he said.

Trabazo started whistling the Léo Ferré song that he'd sung back at the harbour. In a boat he was a happy man.

Unlike Caldas.

'Is it far?' Caldas asked again a few minutes later.

Trabazo shook his head. 'Up ahead.'

Caldas leaned across and looked out over the surface of the water that stretched ahead. There were no rocks between them and the shore, several hundred metres away.

'Are you sure? I can't see anything.'

'Well, of course you can't, Calditas. Do you think it would be anything to boast about if it had been in plain view? Sea Bass Rock is twenty fathoms down.'

'Ah.'

'You'll see. I bet you a glass of wine at the Refugio del Pescador that at least five bass bite in the next two hours.'

Caldas was in no state to think about wine. Two hours? But he didn't have the heart to ask Trabazo to cut short the fishing trip. The bass were his white whale.

Caldas stood up and took his mobile phone from his pocket. He needed to tell Estevez to pick him up a little later than planned.

'You're not thinking of using that contraption near my fish, are you?' Trabazo hissed.

The sun was starting to bother Caldas as much as the sound of the oars and movement of the boat.

'What?'

201

'We're almost above the rock. If they hear your voice, what do you think my fish will do? Hang around to be caught? Come on, switch that thing off.'

Caldas sat down again, feeling sick. He turned off his phone and closed his eyes, taking deep breaths.

Trabazo pushed the plastic box towards him. 'Instead of sitting there sunbathing, why don't you bait the hooks?'

Caldas opened his eyes. 'Bait them?'

'There are several spools in the box. Take out two that have got a hook on the end of the line. That'll save some time.'

Trabazo was right – the sooner this trip was over the better.

'The worms are in the little tin,' said the doctor. 'Pick two and thread them on the hooks.'

'Two what?'

Caldas prised open the tin. In it worms wriggled on damp sand. 'They're alive,' he said.

'Of course they're alive. Say a prayer and on to the hooks with them.'

'Bloody hell,' muttered Caldas.

'I thought you were a policeman?'

Caldas took hold of one of the worms, but before he could get it anywhere near the hook he was overcome by a wave of nausea.

The inspector stared up at the blue sky. He had thrown up so many times that Trabazo had decided to cut short his suffering and get him back to dry land. The closest place was a cove at the foot of Monteferro where Caldas now lay on the sand, trying to recuperate.

'Some shipmate you turned out to be,' said Trabazo, getting up and heading for the boat, which was beached on the shore. 'You should be ashamed of yourself, ruining an old man's fishing trip!'

Caldas didn't have the strength to smile.

'At least my sea bass will be happy,' the inspector heard him say. 'You left them enough food for a fortnight.'

Caldas lay there, feeling his temples throb. His stomach was gradually recovering but the dizzy spell had given him a severe headache. He thought of his conversation with Alba. At first she had seemed close, but when she hung up she had sounded distant. He sighed and raised himself on his elbows. His head and his heart ached.

He watched Trabazo pick his way through the rocks, carrying a bag. Was he looking for crabs? He must be at least seventy. Where did he get the energy?

Caldas waited, motionless, for Trabazo to return.

'How are you feeling?'

'As if I've been beaten up.'

'Do you think you're strong enough to get back on the boat?'

'What are my chances of feeling sick again?'

'Truthfully?'

'Yes.'

'Pretty high.'

Caldas looked around. 'Then I'll just stay here for ever.'

Trabazo smiled. 'There's a track up there. You can reach it by car.'

Caldas looked at his watch and turned on his phone. Estevez would be back in Panxón by now. He was glad he hadn't told him to pick him up later.

'Do you think you can explain to my assistant how to get here?'

'Does he have a good sense of direction?'

'Like a homing pigeon,' said Caldas, dialling Estevez's number.

Trabazo gave Estevez directions, and then sat down beside the inspector.

'Find anything?' asked Caldas, motioning towards Trabazo's bag.

'Horrors,' said the doctor. 'Why are people such pigs?' He held up the bag. 'Look at what I picked up in just a couple of minutes: tins, plastic bottles, bits of glass. And this place is pretty inaccessible. Someone had even thrown a ring spanner onto the rocks.'

'A what?'

'A ring spanner,' Trabazo repeated, taking it out of the bag and handing it to Caldas. 'For tightening wheel nuts. And it's pretty new. It was in a gap between rocks. One of these days they'll chuck out a steering wheel.'

The inspector looked at the spanner. It was a metal bar with a rounded end. 'Where did you find it?' he asked, getting to his feet.

Estevez drew up at the end of the track and honked the horn several times.

'You won't be stopping off in Panxón now, will you?' asked Trabazo before heading back to his boat.

'No,' Caldas replied, 'I'm going straight back to Vigo.' He wanted to show the spanner to the pathologist as soon as possible.

'Oh well . . .'

'Why?' asked the inspector.

'I wanted to tell you something.'

'Can't you tell me now?'

The doctor shrugged. 'Earlier, I mentioned that some of the fishermen set their traps where El Rubio's boat was found. Do you remember?'

The inspector didn't. 'Yes,' he said anyway.

'Well, I've only known one man fish there. Guess who?'

How should he know? 'Who?' asked Caldas.

'Antonio Sousa. The skipper.'

The inspector climbed up to where Estevez was waiting and turned to look back down at the small cove. Out at sea, the sky-blue boat was heading for the harbour in Panxón, bow raised. Trabazo was Manuel the Portuguese fisherman once more.

Caldas greeted his assistant. He got into the car, wound down the window and closed his eyes. He had the spanner in a bag.

He wasn't sure he believed in ghosts any more.

The Spanner

'Feeling better?' asked Estevez as he entered the inspector's office.

Reclining in his black chair, Caldas nodded. 'Did you take it to Dr Barrio?' he asked.

'That's where I've just been.'

'So what did he say?'

'That he'd call if he found something,' said Estevez.

'Did he think it might match the mark on Castelo's skull?'

'How should I know?'

'Didn't he say anything?'

'That he'd call if he found something.'

'All right,' said Caldas, sighing and stretching his legs.

Estevez looked down. 'Have you seen the state of your shoes?' he said.

Caldas lifted a leg and saw that, as well as a headache, the trip on Trabazo's boat had left him with stains all over his shoes as a memento.

'Right,' he said. 'Thanks for that, Rafa.'

Estevez didn't move.

'I don't think he could have been hit with that spanner,' he said.

'Care to elaborate?' asked the inspector.

'Where was it?'

'You want me to go over it again? Trabazo found it in a shallow rock pool in the cove where you came to collect me.'

'And a metal object like that can't be dragged in by the tide, can it?'

'No, I don't think so.'

'Well, there you go, Inspector. Think about it. It can't be.'

'Why not?'

'Because it would be ridiculous for someone to throw the murder weapon on to the rocks when they've got the whole sea at their disposal, don't you think? As silly as sinking the boat in that pool right at the foot of Monteferro instead of taking it out to sea.'

'No, that does make sense,' said the inspector. 'Remember what Ferro said: in that pool the boat stays put. But if they'd scuttled it round the other side of the mountain, the current would eventually smash it against rocks and the pieces would float to the surface.'

'Well, that only strengthens my case. If they took so much trouble hiding the boat, why didn't they do the same with the weapon they used to kill El Rubio?'

'He wasn't killed with the spanner, Rafa. Justo Castelo drowned.'

'Makes no difference, Inspector. If you were in a boat, would you throw the incriminating item on to the rocks or to the bottom of the sea?'

'Depends.'

'What do you mean? It doesn't depend on anything, Inspector. Would you get rid of the evidence or would you go sprinkling it like breadcrumbs in a fairy tale to show us the way?'

'That's if you expect an investigation into Castelo's death, but I'm not so sure,' said Caldas, taking his cigarettes from the drawer. He hadn't had one since he'd sat waiting for Trabazo on a bollard in the harbour.

'Why not?'

Caldas pulled out a cigarette, sniffed it and put it back. He still didn't feel up to smoking.

'Because no one investigates a suicide.'

Estevez was about to say something but held back.

'Try to see it from that angle,' the inspector continued. 'We've got a depressive fisherman who puts out to sea on a rest day. He sails first thing in the morning, so he doesn't bump into any neighbours and have to answer awkward questions. A few hours later his body washes up on the beach, hands tied like lots of other suicides. Why would the police look into the death? It's a textbook suicide. If the cable tie had been fastened round by his thumbs rather than his little fingers, that's what we would have thought, too. We'd have asked

206

around and everyone would have confirmed that Castelo was a strange loner. The lucky charms would have pointed to someone who was superstitious. There would have been no investigation, Rafa. I'm sure of it. El Rubio would have been buried, prayers said, and that's that.'

'What about the blow to the head?'.

'Barrio only paid attention to it because the cable tie had alerted him. Otherwise he'd have attributed it to the fall. It was just one more injury, one of many.'

Estevez looked sceptical. 'That all makes sense,' he said, 'but it still doesn't explain why they threw the spanner on to the rocks.'

'Don't you see, it didn't matter where the spanner ended up if nobody was going to be looking for it. Castelo's body washed up on the Madorra. Where was the spanner? One, two kilometres away. Who would have made the connection? If nobody knew he'd been hit on the head, what did it matter if someone found the object he'd been hit with?'

'I agree, but why get rid of the weapon on the shore if it was just as easy to chuck it out at sea?'

Caldas shrugged. 'Who knows?' he said. 'At seven in the morning it's still pretty dark. Maybe they threw the spanner into the darkness on their way to the lighthouse. As I say, they thought the death would look like suicide, so they didn't care if anyone found it.'

'You're sure there were several of them?'

'There had to be more than one,' replied Caldas. 'Do you remember Hermida's wife saying that Castelo was alone on his boat when he left port?'

Estevez nodded.

'In which case they could only have approached him by sea,' said Caldas, pushing the pack of cigarettes across his desk as if it were the fisherman's boat. 'One person on his own would have had to leave his own boat adrift while he took Castelo's to the lighthouse. That's why there had to be at least two of them.'

'He could have towed it.'

'I don't think so. Trabazo claims it would be impossible to get past the rock barrier towing a boat like El Rubio's. Anyway one person on his own would have had trouble subduing him in such a small space,' Caldas added, toying with the cigarette packet, increasingly confident of his argument. 'And remember that the blow that knocked him unconscious was to the back of the head. Someone probably distracted him while someone else came up behind him and whacked him with the spanner.'

'That's if we can confirm that he was hit with the spanner.'

'I'm right, you'll see,' said Caldas.

He picked up his office phone, dialled Dr Barrio's number and switched to speakerphone so that Estevez could hear.

'How did you get on with the spanner, Guzmán?' Caldas asked, after exchanging greetings.

'I'm still working on it.'

'You can't give me anything now?'

'It could be the murder weapon, Leo,' said Dr Barrio. 'The shape's right.'

'Any prints?'

'It's been in contact with sea water,' replied the pathologist. 'It's clean.'

'Do you know how long it's been underwater?'

'When was the fisherman killed?'

'Sunday.'

'That's five days, isn't it?' said the pathologist. 'It could be, yes. The steel hasn't begun to rust yet.'

When he rang off, Caldas tapped the desk with his cigarettes. 'There you are: confirmed.'

'Confirmed?' asked Estevez, astonished. 'Really?'

'Didn't you hear what the doctor said?'

'He said it could be. Is that what you call confirmed?'

'What did you want, a sworn statement?' replied Caldas. 'It'll do me.'

Estevez shrugged. 'All right. Let's take it he was hit with the spanner. There aren't any fingerprints or clues of any kind, so what good does it do us?'

The inspector rubbed his eyes. Estevez was right. It was five days since Castelo's murder and they'd hardly progressed at all.

'What do we really know?' said his assistant.

Caldas considered telling Estevez to go to hell. Couldn't he see his boss was in no fit state to think? The boat trip had left him feeling quite ragged.

'You start,' he muttered.

'Well, we don't know a thing,' said Estevez, spreading his arms. 'We've got no suspect, no motive, nothing.'

'We know he'd been threatened.'

'What if the graffiti on his boat was part of the set-up?' asked Estevez. 'Everyone believing that Castelo was scared made it even more likely that we'd think he committed suicide.'

Why was Estevez insisting on making him think?

'On the contrary, Rafa. By scaring him they'd only put him on his guard. Anyway, it's not just the graffiti. There's what Arias's neighbour overheard. Remember that Castelo went into Arias's house saying he couldn't take it any more,' said Caldas, drumming his fingers on his cigarette packet. 'And the waiter at the Refugio del Pescador said something similar. And there are all the lucky charms. Castelo really was scared.'

'You're not still thinking of Captain Sousa, are you? If you take what Barrio said as definitive, Sousa's *macana* didn't have anything to do with it.'

Caldas wondered how he'd ever get rid of his headache if Estevez kept pestering him.

'No, it didn't, Rafa. But there's the stuff painted on the boat, the lucky charms, and the calls between the fishermen after all those years. You saw the look on the faces of José Arias and Marcos Valverde as well as I did. What are those two scared of? On top of all that, guess who used to go fishing in the pool where El Rubio's boat was found?'

'Captain Sousa?'

'Correct.'

'How do you know?'

'Trabazo told me. Sousa sometimes set his traps there.'

Estevez placed his palms together and Caldas thought he was going to kneel and recite a Hail Mary.

'Please,' said his assistant, 'would you mind not doing that with the cigarettes? If you need something to help you think, I can whistle the tune they play for you on the radio.'

Caldas flushed and put down the cigarette packet. Who the hell did Estevez think he was?

'Surely you don't still believe that Castelo was murdered by a ghost?' Estevez went on.

'No, not by a ghost,' sighed Caldas.

'Well?'

Would he never leave?

'Well what?' asked Caldas.

'Do you still think that Captain Sousa has something to do with all of this?'

'I don't know how, but I think he has. It can't be a coincidence. Did you call the radio station in Barcelona?'

Estevez nodded. 'Sousa's son was working last weekend,' he said. 'There are more than twenty witnesses corroborating it. He didn't kill Castelo.'

It was what Caldas had expected.

'Right,' he said and, picking up a document at random from his desk, he pretended to start reading. But Estevez went on, 'Here's a thought.'

Caldas put the document down.

'Let's hear it.'

'Maybe Arias and Valverde are scared of us.'

'Us?'

'Of us nosing around knowing it wasn't suicide. Didn't you say that there had to be at least two people involved?'

'I don't think it was them,' said the inspector, restraining the urge to toy with the cigarette packet.

'Why not?'

'You saw for yourself, things are going pretty well for Valverde these days, and Arias doesn't seem like the kind of man who goes looking for trouble. They haven't spoken to each other in more than twelve years. What would they gain from El Rubio's death? Anyway, both Arias and Valverde said they didn't believe it was suicide. Would you say that if you were the murderer? No, those two are scared of something else.'

Estevez nodded. 'There's one more thing I don't understand,' he said after a moment. 'How did the murderers know that Castelo would be out in his boat early on Sunday morning?'

Caldas had also wondered about this.

'I don't know,' he whispered.

Estevez looked down, maybe to stare at Caldas's dirty shoes, or to avoid watching him play with his cigarettes again.

'What's on your mind?'

'Nothing,' replied Estevez.

Caldas leaned back expecting more questions, but Estevez turned and left the office. When Rafael Estevez said 'Nothing' he meant exactly that: nothing.

The Blue Folder

That lunchtime Caldas only left his office to go to the toilets to wipe his shoes with toilet paper. The rest of the time he lay back in his black chair, going over the details of the investigation, wondering if he'd missed something.

He opened the blue folder yet again. It now contained Barcia's report on the preliminary inspection of the boat found by the lighthouse at Punta Lameda. This maintained that the hull had been breached from the inside. Unfortunately, its time underwater had wiped the boat clean of traces.

He called Forensics. Back from a morning searching at Punta Lameda, Ferro confirmed that the rocks used to weigh down the boat had been collected from near the pool. Ferro had found tyre marks on the track nearby, but no prints of any kind around the rock pool. The rain that week had washed them away.

Caldas reread Barcia's report and all the newspaper cuttings about the sinking of the *Xurelo*. He thought of El Rubio's phone call to José Arias. The shipwrecked boat was the only link between the two fishermen. Something had caused them to get in touch again after all these years, but what?

He also glanced at the report on the recovery of Captain Sousa's body. At one stage he'd doubted that the corpse found in the nets of the trawler really was that of the skipper of the *Xurelo*. Now he believed it made no sense for Sousa to have hidden for so long. In addition, the pathologist had determined that Castelo hadn't been struck by the wooden cudgel Sousa carried on his belt, but with the spanner found among the rocks. And, anyway, ghosts didn't act in pairs.

Caldas had thought that the murder might be part of a plot for revenge, retribution for a wrong inflicted many years before, but the skipper's only son had a solid alibi: he'd been over a thousand kilometres away on the day of El Rubio's murder.

But if Sousa wasn't involved in Castelo's death, why the hell had the date of the sinking been daubed on the rowing boat? Why was somebody stirring all that up again?

After four days' investigation, they had found neither motive nor a single suspect. They had no idea why the murder had been committed or by whom. Estevez was right. They had nothing.

In the middle of the afternoon he glanced at his watch. If he hurried he could still get to the hospital in time. He put the papers back in the folder and returned it to the pile it had come from.

After taking his leave of Estevez until the following Monday, he went outside and lit a cigarette. His headache had abated.

Old Sea Dogs

The door to room 211 was ajar. Caldas knocked before stepping inside. Two nurses were busying themselves around Uncle Alberto's bed.

'Shall I wait outside?' asked Caldas.

'Probably best,' said one of the nurses.

Caldas went out and walked down the corridor to the waiting room. His father was sitting there, chatting to a young woman.

'Leo!' he smiled.

'Is he all right?' asked the inspector, gesturing towards his uncle's room.

'They're changing him,' his father said, seeking to reassure him before introducing the young woman: 'Silvia's mother is in 208,' he said. 'This is my son Leo. He works in radio, you know.'

Caldas smiled stiffly at the woman.

'I'd better get back to her,' she said, standing up.

'So I work in radio, do I?' he asked, once the woman had disappeared down the corridor. 'Is that how you're introducing me now?'

'Would you rather I said you're an old sea dog?'

'So you've spoken to Trabazo?'

'What do you think?' said his father with a smile.

Caldas sat down beside him.

'He was worried about you,' added his father.

'I'm not surprised. I felt bloody awful.'

'He, on the other hand, is still in great shape, isn't he?'

214

'Yes, he is.'

A nurse came out of Uncle Alberto's room. The inspector's father got to his feet but sat down again when he saw her go back inside.

'By the way, do you know someone called Marcos Valverde?' asked Caldas.

'Should I?' asked his father.

'He's a developer in Panxón and he's just started making wine. He knows you. He sends his regards.'

His father raised his eyes, trying to remember. 'What's his wine called?'

'I don't think he's bottled his first vintage yet.'

'The name doesn't ring a bell,' he said. 'But send him my regards anyway.'

Caldas smiled.

'Alba called me.'

'Alba?' said his father, not looking at him.

'Yes. This morning.'

'I was only going to ask about her if you mentioned me retiring again.'

Caldas wondered if he really did only talk about Alba to get back at him.

'I'm joking,' said his father, pulling a face. 'What did she say?'

'She'd heard Alberto was in hospital and wanted to know how he was.'

'She asked about Alberto?'

'Yes, and you.'

'She must have wanted something else ...'

Caldas shrugged. 'No, she was just calling to tell me to give you her love.'

'And that's all?'

'That's all,' said Caldas.

His father looked into his eyes. 'How did she sound?'

'OK, I suppose.'

'You suppose?'

'We only spoke for a minute,' said the inspector. He looked down at a point between his feet on the white hospital floor, as Alicia Castelo had done the day he had met her outside the pathologist's lab. He was beginning to think it had been a bad idea to tell his

215

father about the call. When the subject of Alba came up the conversation always ended badly.

'The police must be in dire straits if you've reached the rank of inspector, son.'

'What?'

'You're going to earn a top spot in my Book of Idiots.'

'Me?' said Caldas. They'd been talking about Alba for a minute, maybe two, and his father was already insulting him.

'Don't you see, if she'd only called to send me her love, she'd have called me herself?' said his father.

'She'd have called you?'

'It wouldn't be the first time.'

'You speak to Alba?'

'That's not OK?'

Caldas shrugged. 'I don't know . . .'

'Anyway, never mind. I'm sorry. The fact is she called you and told you to give me her love, didn't she?'

'That's right.'

They sat in silence until his father asked, 'Do you want me to listen or to give you my advice?'

Caldas looked up. 'You know I don't like talking,' he said.

'I know,' said his father.

A nurse looked in and said they'd finished changing the patient. Caldas's father thanked her and stood up.

'Coming?' he said, and the inspector followed him down the corridor.

They entered the room. The television was on, muted: Uncle Alberto's window on to the world.

'Look who's here,' said the inspector's father. The patient's face wrinkled into a smile behind the green respiratory mask.

Caldas told him about his trip in Manuel Trabazo's boat that morning.

'Speaking of boats,' interjected the inspector's father, indicating the television.

A news bulletin was showing aerial shots of the crew of a boat being rescued in a storm. They were being hoisted, one by one, from the deck up to a helicopter. A caption at the bottom of the screen

216

read: 'All eleven crewmembers of Galician trawler wrecked on Great Sole Bank rescued alive.'

The item ended with pictures of the listing boat, now crewless, being swallowed by the waves. Caldas thought of the *Xurelo*, and the nightmare Captain Sousa and his crew had gone through. And of the case that was getting away from him.

They continued watching the bulletin, and Caldas observed his father and uncle discussing each story in their wordless language.

He recalled a film he'd seen with Alba some time ago. The central character was an old man who travelled hundreds of kilometres on a lawnmower to visit his sick brother, from whom he'd been estranged for years. At the end of the journey, at the brother's house, they'd hardly said anything. They'd sat together on the porch, settling their differences with no need for words.

It was dark by the time they left the hospital. Caldas walked his father to the car.

'You're not coming, are you?' his father asked, opening the door.

Caldas shook his head. 'I've got to work,' he apologised.

'It's Friday.'

'I know,' said Caldas.

'I'll be getting here around one tomorrow,' said his father, gesturing towards the hospital building. 'On Saturdays visiting hours start before lunch.'

'I'll try to drop by.'

His father nodded, then said: 'About what you said earlier ...'

'What?'

'About Alba.'

'Ah.'

'Be brave, Leo.'

'Brave?'

'Yes. Call her,' said his father. 'Get back together. Have a family, children, whatever she wants.'

'Children?'

'Why not? It's a question of priorities. Do you think I liked you?'

The inspector glanced sideways at his father, who was smiling.

'Before I got to know you, I mean.'

'I don't know if I could do it,' mused Caldas. 'I wouldn't want them to grow up without a father.'

'Bloody hell, don't exaggerate. Being a policeman isn't like going to war.'

'I'm not talking about dying,' said Caldas. 'I'm talking about not being there.'

His father got into the car. He turned the key in the ignition, switched on the lights and lowered the window.

'We do the best we can, Leo.'

'I know,' said Caldas, and he tapped on the hood a couple of times. 'See you tomorrow. Don't worry about me. I'll grow up.'

'We don't grow up, Leo,' said his father before driving away, leaving Caldas standing in the car park. 'We just grow old.'

The Map

After leaving the hospital Caldas walked down the Calle Mexico. Opposite the railway station he turned down the Calle Urzaiz, crossed the Gran Via and continued downhill along the crowded pavement until he reached the cast-iron streetlight designed by the Galician modernist architect Jenaro de la Fuente. Then he made his way along the Calle del Principe accompanied by the smell of roasting chestnuts and buskers' music. Just before the Puerta del Sol, at a corner where an Andean Indian stood playing panpipes, he turned left into a small side street, the Travesia de la Aurora, and arrived at the Eligio.

Inside he went up to the bar, greeted Carlos and inhaled the delicious aromas coming from the kitchen.

'Pasta with clams, isn't it?'

'Bloody hell, Leo,' exclaimed Carlos. 'That's some sense of smell you've got.'

'I haven't eaten all day.'

'How come?' asked Carlos, setting a glass before the inspector and filling it with white wine.

'I went out on a friend's boat this morning and got seasick,' Caldas confessed. 'I haven't felt like eating.'

Beneath his thick moustache, Carlos gave a small smile and disappeared into the kitchen to place the inspector's order.

Caldas went over to the academics' table with his glass of wine and sat down. A moment later, Carlos emerged from the kitchen and returned to his post behind the bar.

'So the patrolman of the waves gets sick on boats,' he said with amusement.

'I wish it was only boats,' said Caldas wryly.

'You weren't on that trawler that sank on the Great Sole Bank, were you?' teased one of the academics. 'Did you see the rescue on the news?'

Everyone had.

'They only just saved the crew before the ship went down,' added another.

'Where is the Great Sole?' asked Caldas, who'd heard the name hundreds of times but couldn't have located it on a map.

'To the south-west of the British Isles,' said one academic.

'Yes,' said another. 'Off the coast of Cornwall.'

There was praise for the helicopter pilots who risked their lives flying in terrible storms.

'Well, when I was at sea I always looked forward to a storm,' said Carlos. Before running the bar opened by his father-in-law, he had been a merchant seaman.

'Why was that?' someone asked.

'Because we'd have to shelter in port,' Carlos explained. 'We knew we'd be getting off the ship and having a walk, so when a storm was forecast we were delighted.'

Caldas recalled one of the cuttings about the sinking of the *Xurelo* that he'd read that afternoon. A skipper fishing in the area had expressed surprise that the boat had gone down. He claimed that Sousa had told him over the radio that he was intending to haul in all the gear and return to port.

'Is it the same for fishing boats?' asked Caldas.

'Just the same,' said Carlos with a deep laugh. 'In bad weather, everyone heads back to port for a drink and to hell with fishing until the storm eases.'

Carlos's words echoed in Caldas's head. Suddenly he was alert. 'In bad weather, everyone heads back to port,' he repeated to himself.

He went up to the bar. 'Hey, Carlos, if you were sailing near Salvora and a storm broke, where would you shelter?' he asked quietly.

'I'm not sure,' said Carlos. 'Why?'

'I need to know.'

'Wait there.'

Carlos went to the bookcase by the door and returned with an atlas. He set it down on the bar and opened it at the page for the Rias Baixas, the southerly estuaries of the Galician coast.

'This is Salvora here,' he said, placing a finger on the island at the mouth of the Ria de Arousa.

'So where would you shelter?' pressed the inspector.

'I suppose I'd head for Ribeira or Villagarcia,' said Carlos, stroking his moustache. 'They're deep enough for merchant ships.'

'What if you were in a small fishing boat?'

'What size?'

'The kind that goes out for a couple of nights.'

'Ah, then I'd head for Aguiño.'

'Aguiño?' asked Caldas. 'Sure?'

'I think so,' said Carlos, taking another look at the map. 'Yes, I'm sure. What's up?'

'I've got to check something,' muttered the inspector, setting off back to the police station. He still hadn't had anything to eat.

Cuttings

Caldas greeted the officers chatting together on duty at the entrance and went straight to his office. There he lit a cigarette, opened the blue folder and took out the newspaper cuttings that the priest of Panxón had kept for over a decade. He unfolded them one by one, certain he'd seen the name Aguiño somewhere.

He found what he was looking for in an article from a local newspaper dated Monday 23 December 1996, three days after the sinking of the *Xurelo*. Beneath an account of the resumption of the search for Sousa's body were two shorter items. The first noted that two hooded motorcyclists had held up a petrol station. The second briefly reported the disappearance of a woman from Aguiño.

AGUIÑO WOMAN MISSING

A resident of Aguiño, Rebeca Neira, aged thirty-two, has been missing from her home since last Friday night.

Her disappearance was reported by her son yesterday morning, Sunday 22 December. During the afternoon, groups of neighbours and members of the Civil Protection Force searched for the young woman in the vicinity of her home. The search was halted without success as darkness fell.

Police sources told this newspaper that they consider the most likely explanation for her disappearance to be that she left home of her own free will, but they are not ruling out other possibilities.

Caldas read the article twice. The woman had last been seen on the evening of Friday 20 December, the night of the sinking of the *Xurelo*.

There was a small photograph with the article. It showed a man searching a ditch at the side of a road. The inspector looked through the other cuttings, hoping to find more about the disappearance but there was nothing else about the Aguiño woman.

Maybe it had nothing to do with the sinking of the *Xurelo*, but the two incidents had occurred on the same date, and the port of Aguiño was the closest to where the boat had been fishing when the storm broke.

Caldas slumped in the black chair, stomach rumbling. He took a drag of his cigarette to quell the hunger pangs and picked up the newspaper cutting again. He stared at the photo of Captain Sousa, whose wrinkled face stared back at him from the top of the page. Then he read the article about the disappearance of Rebeca Neira once again. This time his attention was drawn to the fact that her son had reported her missing. A copy of the missing person report must have been forwarded to Galicia Police Headquarters for its records.

Caldas picked up the phone. The officer who answered at Police Headquarters said that Nieves Ortiz did indeed still work the night shift.

'Would you put me through to her, please?' Caldas asked. 'I'm Inspector Caldas, from Vigo.'

A moment later Nieves's high-pitched voice came on the line. 'It's been a long time, Patrolman,' she said. Caldas pictured her broad grin and tiny eyes.

It was over a year since she'd requested a transfer to the Headquarters in La Coruña, but at the station in Vigo they still missed the way she roared with laughter.

'What can I do for you?' she said, after asking after former colleagues.

'I need to check a report.'

'Fire away.'

'See if you can find a missing persons report on a woman called Rebeca Neira,' said the inspector.

'Where from?'

'Aguiño.'

'Do you know the date?'

'Between 20 and 22 December 1996.'

'Ninety-six?'

'That's right.'

'I'll have to go to the archives,' said Nieves. 'Do you want to wait or shall I call you back in a minute?'

'If it's only a minute I think I'll wait,' said Caldas, lighting another cigarette.

'I've got the report,' she said when she came back on the line.

'Anything else in the file?'

'Nothing,' replied Nieves. 'There's a handwritten note in the margin of the report that says: "Enquiries are being made which will duly be recorded". But there are no more documents.'

The inspector tutted.

'Maybe it was a false alarm,' said Nieves.

'Maybe,' said Caldas, annoyed that another line of enquiry had come to nothing.

'Shall I send you this anyway?' she asked.

'Would you mind?'

'Shall I fax it to you at the station?'

After the inspector had thanked her and hung up, he sat smoking at his desk. If there were no more documents in the file, it must be because the woman had turned up safe and well soon afterwards. He looked again at the yellowed newspaper article. It stated that the most likely explanation for Rebeca Neira's disappearance was that she had left home of her own free will. Caldas knew that things were usually as they seemed.

He stubbed out his cigarette and left his office carrying the ashtray. He emptied it in the waste bin in the toilets and rinsed it under the tap. Back in his office he put the ashtray in a drawer. Then he looked at his watch.

It was gone ten thirty at night when Caldas left the police station. He was hungry and felt as if he'd spent all week going round in circles investigating Justo Castelo's murder, ending up right back where he started.

An Old Report

He was tired and, though tempted by the pasta with clams at the Eligio, decided not to go back there. He just wanted to have a quick snack and go home, so he walked round the corner to the Rosalia de Castro café. He went up to the bar and ordered a cup of broth, an omelette and a glass of wine, and then sat at a table in the window to wait for his meal.

On a TV up on the wall they were replaying aerial shots of the boat listing in heavy seas on the Great Sole Bank. The sight of the waves reminded him of the attack of seasickness that had forced him ashore at the cove in Monteferro. He tried to console himself with the thought that, thanks to that, Trabazo had found the spanner among the rocks. Caldas was convinced it had been used to strike Castelo on the head. Why else would someone throw away a new spanner like that if not to get rid of evidence?

It was eleven fifteen by the time he finished his meal. He asked for the bill, lit a cigarette, paid and left. He felt the wind that had chilled the night air and heard the young people partying in the Montero Rios Gardens, by the marina. Every Friday, they came from all over the city to celebrate the end of another week.

He rubbed his hands vigorously and set off home. As he passed the police station, he stubbed out his cigarette and went in to see if Nieves Ortiz had sent the missing persons report on the Aguiño woman.

He found the report in the fax in-tray, and sat down to read it at one of the empty desks. Thirteen years earlier Diego Neira Diez, aged fifteen, had reported the disappearance of his mother, Rebeca Neira Diez, aged thirty-two. He had contacted the police at eleven in the morning on Sunday 22 December 1996, stating that he hadn't seen his mother, with whom he lived in the parish of Aguiño, since the night of Friday 20 December.

According to the statement, at around eleven on the Friday night, Rebeca Neira told her son that she'd run out of cigarettes and left the house. She returned over an hour later, and Diego heard her talking to someone under the small porch at the front door. A man burst out laughing and his mother asked him to be quiet, reminding him that her son was in the house. This made Diego Neira uncomfortable. Opening the front door, he found his mother there with two men. He muttered that he was going to spend the night at a friend's house and ran off.

It was pouring with rain, so he stopped to shelter in a nearby shack. From there he saw one of the men enter the house with his mother while the other man headed back towards the port. Once the rain subsided, Diego Neira set off once more for his friend's house.

He returned home the following day, the Saturday, at around one o'clock. He found the house empty, clean and tidy. He remained there, and when it got dark he went to bed.

He didn't get worried until the Sunday morning when he saw that his mother hadn't slept in her bed. He then phoned Irene Vazquez, a close friend of his mother's. She, too, had not heard from Rebeca since the Friday afternoon and, after hearing the boy's account, went with him to the police.

Diego Neira stated that he didn't know who the two men were and hadn't even seen one of them properly, only silhouetted in the darkness. But he'd got a good look at the other one, who'd headed back to the port. He'd passed very close to the shack where Diego was sheltering from the rain and the road was well lit.

He was wearing waterproofs and rubber boots, like those used by fishermen. He looked about thirty, and was slim with a shock of very fair hair. Diego Neira had never seen him before.

Caldas reread the boy's description of the stranger. It couldn't be a coincidence.

He got up and went to his office. There, at his desk, he read through the report once again. Then he dialled the number of Galicia Police Headquarters and, for the second time that evening, asked to be put through to Nieves Ortiz.

'Did you get the report?'

'Yes. Thanks,' said Caldas. 'Are you sure there's nothing else in the file?'

'Absolutely, Leo.'

The inspector sighed. 'Could there be a more comprehensive report somewhere else?'

'There shouldn't be,' said Nieves.

'Could you check?'

'Now?'

'Do you mind?'

'I can try. But why the rush? It was over twelve years ago, wasn't it?'

'It may have something to do with the case I'm working on.'

'What was the missing woman's name again?'

Caldas read out the name on the report. 'Rebeca Neira,' he said. 'Rebeca Neira Diez.'

The inspector took his ashtray from the drawer and lit a cigarette, as Nieves tapped away on her keyboard at Police Headquarters.

'I can't find anything else on the computer, Leo,' she said a moment later. 'But let me have another look in the archives. Give me three minutes and I'll call you back.'

Caldas thanked her and hung up. If the missing persons report was the only document in the file, perhaps the woman had turned up. But he was sure the fair-haired man the boy had seen was the fisherman who had been found floating in the seaweed on the beach in Panxón thirteen years later.

Caldas wondered why José Arias and Marcos Valverde had lied, why neither of them had mentioned that they'd sheltered from the storm in the port of Aguiño. He wanted to hear their answers and watch their faces, and find out why they had set sail again despite the storm, in seas so heavy that their boat had foundered.

He picked up the phone again and called Estevez.

'Do you know what time it is?' said his assistant.

Caldas looked at his watch: it was twelve thirty.

'Were you asleep?'

'No,' muttered Estevez.

'I don't think the *Xurelo* was on its way back from fishing when it sank.'

'It happened over twelve years ago,' groaned Estevez. 'Couldn't you have waited till Monday to tell me?'

'I need to speak to José Arias and Marcos Valverde. I want to know why they hid this from us. Will you come and pick me up at seven? I'd like to be in Panxón when Arias gets back from fishing.'

'When?'

'Tomorrow.'

'When you say tomorrow you mean in seven hours' time?'

'That's right.'

Estevez gave a deafening snort. 'Tomorrow's Saturday, Inspector.'

'I know.'

'Couldn't we ask him about it on Monday?'

'The fish market's closed on Mondays, Rafa,' replied Caldas. 'Will you pick me up at seven? I'll wait downstairs.'

He extinguished his cigarette and went to the toilets to empty the ashtray. As he was rinsing it, it slipped from his fingers and broke in half in the washbasin.

Holding a piece in each hand, Caldas approached the woman who cleaned the police station.

'You don't have some glue by any chance, do you?' he asked, motioning towards the trolley loaded with containers that the woman was pushing with her foot.

'No,' she replied, staring at the two halves of the ashtray. 'Anyway, even if you stick it back together, it'll never be the same.'

Five minutes later Nieves Ortiz called him back.

'I've had a look, Leo, but I can't find anything other than the report I sent you. That must have been it.'

'Do you know if they still live in Aguiño?'

'There's no record of a change of address,' she said after checking.

Caldas read the police identification number on the report. 'Would you be able to tell me whose badge this is?' he asked, and read out the number.

'Let's see,' said Nieves, tapping on the keyboard at the other end of the line. 'It was Deputy Inspector Somoza's.'

'Was?'

'He's no longer with the police,' she said. 'He retired eight years ago. Do you need anything else?'

'No, that's all, Nieves. Thanks so much. Sorry to have bothered you.'

'Don't worry,' she said, and then asked: 'How's Alba?'

'Fine,' replied Caldas tersely.

'Say hello to her from me.'

'Yes.'

'Tell her to look after you,' she added. 'And not let you work so late.'

The inspector swallowed hard. 'I will.'

He hung up and rose from his desk. He took his raincoat and the copy of the missing persons report and threw the pieces of ashtray into the wastepaper basket. The cleaner was right: once something had been broken, it could never go back to the way it was.

Fresh Air

At seven in the morning it was still pitch-black. The inspector stood waiting in the lobby of his building. After a few minutes, headlights drew up outside and he hurried out. He climbed into the car, leaned back in the passenger seat and opened the window a crack to let in fresh air.

'Morning,' he said. Estevez's only response was to press his foot down on the accelerator.

They drove down the Avenida de Orillamar and continued beside the sea until they reached Bouzas. In the shipyards there were no lights or any trace of the glow of welding that lit up the skeletons of half-built ships during the week. The only illumination was the neon sign of a nightclub across the street, throwing light on the young people queuing to get in, determined to extract a few more hours of fun from their Friday night.

As they turned off the ring road and on to the coast road, Caldas filled Estevez in. He told him about Captain Sousa's intention, relayed by radio to another skipper, to shelter in port when the storm broke and that the nearest port was Aguiño. He said he'd found a reference to the disappearance of a woman from the village in one of the newspaper cuttings given to him by the priest of Panxón. He added that he'd got hold of the missing persons report filed by the woman's son, in which the boy described one of the men he'd seen talking to his mother on the night of the storm.

'Listen to this,' said Caldas, unfolding the report. 'He says the man was about thirty, wearing waterproofs and rubber boots. He was slim with very fair hair.' He put the report away. 'Justo Castelo was twenty-nine. How many fair-haired fishermen that age could have landed in a small fishing village like that one?'

Estevez shrugged.

'I'm sure it was him,' Caldas went on. 'Don't you see? The night the *Xurelo* sank it had been in Aguiño, and they weren't simply fishing, as they claimed.'

'Do you really think it's significant?'

'I don't know. But this is all we've got to go on and I want to see if it leads anywhere.'

'So what happened to the woman?' asked Estevez, drumming his fingers on the steering wheel.

'Rebeca Neira? I don't know – the missing persons report is all I found.'

Estevez gave him a hard stare. 'That's it?'

'Yes.'

'Bloody hell, Inspector. In that case, nothing happened.'

'I know,' said Caldas. 'But if the boat was in Aguiño, I want to know why neither Arias nor Valverde mentioned it. When I asked Valverde why they hadn't sheltered in a port, do you know what he said? "You'd have to ask the skipper." Well, now I want them to tell me. I want to know why they hid it from everyone, I want them to tell me what happened that night, to explain again exactly how Antonio Sousa drowned.'

Estevez shook his head doubtfully. 'Do you still think Sousa has something to do with Castelo's death?'

'Don't forget the things painted on the rowing boat: the word "Murderers" and the date of Sousa's death, 20 December 1996. It can't be a coincidence. There has to be a link between Sousa's death and Castelo's, and I think the other two know what it is. Otherwise why would they be so evasive when I mentioned the captain's name?'

'Maybe it's just a painful memory.'

'Maybe,' said Caldas, closing his eyes again and craning towards the open window. 'But in that case they needn't have lied.'

As they arrived in Panxón, with Monteferro a vague, dark shape against the sky, Estevez said, 'One thing, Inspector.'

'What's that?'

231

'Today's Saturday. I shouldn't be here.'

'Nor should I,' said Caldas.

'Are you taking the piss?' snorted Estevez. 'We're here because of you.'

'This isn't just a whim of mine, Rafa.'

'Well, it certainly seems like it. Couldn't we have waited till Monday?'

'I told you, there's no fish market on a Monday.'

'So what?'

'What do you mean, so what?'

'That fisherman doesn't dematerialise on days when there's no market. It wouldn't make any difference if we waited till Monday and questioned him at his house.'

'One man's already dead, Rafa, and there could be more. Time is important. You know that.'

'Of course I do. But time's important for the living as well,' snapped Estevez. 'You can do what you like with your own weekend, but it's not fair to take other people's free time as you please.'

'As I please?'

'Yes. It seems to bother you that other people have a life outside work.'

'What?'

'You heard me. It doesn't matter to you whether you phone at night or during the day. To you it makes no difference if it's a Tuesday, Friday or Sunday. All days are the same. You pick up the phone and off you go without even bothering to ask if someone's busy or not.'

'If this is because of yesterday, I didn't realise how late it was when I called,' said Caldas apologetically.

'Because of yesterday, and the day before, and today ...' Estevez, who'd spoken in bursts, now paused, as if taking aim before delivering the *coup de grâce*. 'It's not my fault if you don't have a life,' he said, 'but you have to understand, not everyone's like you.'

Caldas hunched in the passenger seat, not knowing what to say, and Estevez added, 'You know I like to talk straight.'

'Right,' the inspector replied, closing his eyes again.

The Rustling Bag

They arrived in Panxón at seven thirty. They parked under a street lamp, near the slipway, and waited in the car with the heating on and headlights off. On the water, they could see the lights of Arias's and Hermida's boats. The two fishermen were emptying the contents of their traps into black baskets, which they would later unload on land.

'Can I take a look at that report?' asked Estevez.

Caldas handed it to him, and his assistant held it up to the light from the street lamp.

'Did you notice the surname, Inspector?' said Estevez after a moment.

'Whose?'

'Mother's and son's,' said Estevez. 'They've both got exactly the same surname: Neira Diez.'

'She was a single mother. Look at their ages.'

'The boy fifteen, the mother thirty-two,' read Estevez.

'She was only a kid when she had him.'

At a quarter to eight the auctioneer arrived in his van. He parked outside the fish market, opened the metal shutters and switched on the lights.

Soon afterwards, Ernesto Hermida's wife in her white apron made her way between boats down to the water's edge to wait for her husband. The old fisherman drew up at the bottom of the slipway in his rowing boat and handed her the baskets, which she dropped to the ground. Then, each holding a handle, they lugged the baskets one at a time up to the fish market.

Arias was in his orange waterproofs. He, too, had filled two baskets, but he carried them easily up the slipway, watched greedily by several seagulls.

At two minutes to eight, Caldas and Estevez got out of the car and headed towards the market. Hermida's catch was already set out on the long metal table – shrimp on the right and crabs on the left – beneath the sign cautioning against eating, drinking, smoking and spitting inside the building. It smelled more strongly of the sea inside than out.

From the entrance, the policemen could make out José Arias's dark hair and orange waterproofs. He was crouching, sorting his catch. He handed each tray to the auctioneer as he filled it, to be weighed and set on the table.

There were almost a dozen people waiting for the auction to begin. Caldas recognised the two women and the man with grey sideburns who'd divided the catch between them the last time. They were circling the table, like wolves around a flock of sheep. The other buyers showed less interest.

The auctioneer finished weighing the catch, checked that all the trays were marked with their weights and positioned himself behind the table. Then he puffed out his top lip and blew out the air suddenly.

'Let's begin, it's five past eight,' he said, rubbing his hands. Then he called out, 'I'm selling shrimp! I'm selling shrimp!'

The buyers moved up to the table, as if drawn by a magnet. Hermida and his wife also stepped forward to follow the progress of the auction. Arias, however, went on cleaning out his baskets, as though it had nothing to do with him.

'We'll start at forty-five euros,' the auctioneer announced, indicating the trays of shrimp wriggling in the cold blue light of the fluorescent tubes.

Then he took a deep breath and began calling out prices as if reciting the letters of the alphabet: 'Forty-five, forty-four and a half, forty-four, forty-three and a half, forty-three, forty-two and a half, forty-two ...'

One of the women halted the bidding and selected the best items. José Arias meanwhile headed towards the entrance, carrying his empty baskets in one hand and a blue plastic bag in the other. If he was surprised to see the policemen there, he didn't show it.

'Good morning, Inspector Caldas.'

'Do you have a moment?' asked Caldas.

'You're here to speak to me?'

Caldas nodded, and lit his first cigarette of the weekend. 'But we're not in a hurry,' he said and, gesturing towards the plastic bag that contained several wriggling crabs, added: 'Go ahead and finish what you're doing.'

Arias glanced back inside the fish market. The auctioneer's chant floated out through the open door.

'Now's fine,' said the fisherman in his deep voice. Caldas realised that Arias would rather talk there in the empty street than later when the auction was over. 'Is it about El Rubio's phone call?'

'You tell me,' replied Caldas and motioned towards the spot where the fisherman had released the female crabs the previous Tuesday.

Arias crossed the road and went down the slipway. The policemen followed, making their way between rowing boats lit up by nearby street lamps.

'You don't know?'

'I don't like being lied to,' said the inspector.

The fisherman halted. 'I told you, I'd forgotten about the call.'

'I know.'

'So what do you want?'

Caldas drew on his cigarette before answering, 'The truth.'

'I told you the truth, Inspector. El Rubio lost one of his fenders out at sea and ...'

'Do you expect us to believe that?' Caldas interrupted.

'I don't expect anything,' said Arias slowly. The plastic bag rustled in his hands.

'Do you remember the date painted on Castelo's rowing boat?'

The fisherman nodded.

'There was the word "Murderers" as well,' said the inspector.

'I know. You said.'

'What happened that night?'

'The boat went down. You already know.'

235

'Apart from that.'

'Isn't that enough?'

'What happened to Captain Sousa?'

'He drowned,' said the fisherman gravely.

'Why was the boat out at sea instead of sheltering in port like all the other fishing boats?'

'It was the skipper's call.'

'So you didn't put in to port?'

The tip of the inspector's cigarette glowed.

'No.'

'You're sure?'

The fisherman nodded.

'You're lying to me again,' said Caldas.

'What did you say?'

The plastic bag rustled again as Arias gripped it more tightly. Caldas was glad Estevez was with him.

'Did you put in at a port?' Caldas pressed.

'No,' replied the fisherman, but then corrected himself: 'I don't remember.'

'You stopped in Aguiño, didn't you?' asked Caldas.

'Where?'

'Aguiño,' repeated Caldas. Arias said nothing, simply looking towards the beach.

'What happened that night?'

'It was a long time ago, Inspector,' said Arias, dodging the question. 'I'm telling you, I don't remember.'

'You can't have forgotten.'

'Well, I have.'

In the dawn hush, the plastic bag rustled again.

'What really happened to Captain Sousa?' asked the inspector. 'Why did someone daub "Murderers" on Castelo's boat? Why was El Rubio killed?'

Arias opened his trembling hands and the baskets and plastic bag fell to the ground. Caldas shrank. Had Estevez not been there, he would have backed away.

'Didn't you hear the inspector?' interjected his assistant, not looking in the least bit intimidated.

'I can't remember anything,' Arias whispered, eyes cast down.

They questioned him a little longer, but his answer remained the same.

'He remembers the whole thing,' said Estevez, opening the car door.

Caldas stubbed out his cigarette on the ground. 'I know.'

The inspector had seen the fear in the fisherman's eyes and he wondered what had really happened on the *Xurelo*. Why was Arias so afraid of someone finding out the truth?

'Aren't we going to arrest him?' asked Estevez.

'And charge him with what?'

Estevez shrugged, started the car and reversed. As Caldas lowered the window he saw the fisherman on the slipway. He was sitting on one of the boats, like a felled colossus. His orange waterproofs glowed in the early-morning light. On the stone slipway, the crabs had found their way out of the plastic bag and were scuttling down to the sea.

The Fortress

They stopped for breakfast at a bar facing the Playa de la Madorra. Estevez leafed through the newspaper. The sinking of the Galician trawler on the Great Sole Bank filled the front page.

'Did you see the rescue on TV?'

Caldas said he had. Through the window he contemplated the fortress at Baiona, which was still lit up, across the bay, and the waves breaking on the seaweed-strewn shore.

As they returned to the car the bells of the Templo Votivo del Mar struck nine o'clock. They took the road to Monteferro and turned off to the left, down the narrow street that led to the large wooden gate.

They got out of the car and pressed the buzzer. Marcos Valverde's wife answered.

'Hello, this is Inspector Caldas,' said Caldas.

The gate slid open, revealing the grey concrete bunker-like façade.

There were two cars, wet with dew, parked in the courtyard. One was Mrs Valverde's red SUV. The other was a black sports car. In the gravel garden, pansies were beginning to open in the first rays of the sun.

Caldas was hoping Mrs Valverde's smile would greet him, but it was her husband who came out. His hair was wet and combed back as if he'd just got out of the shower. He was wearing a dark green polo-neck and beige corduroy trousers.

'Is something the matter?' he asked.

238

'No,' said Caldas, thinking how different Valverde looked without his suit and tie. 'I apologise for coming so early.'

'Please don't worry. I've been awake for hours.'

'Could we speak to you for a few minutes?'

'Of course,' said Valverde, but didn't invite them in.

Caldas saw the verbena growing against the house and was tempted to go and inhale its fragrance. Instead he took his packet of cigarettes from his pocket.

'Do you smoke?'

Valverde shook his head. The inspector placed a cigarette between his lips and held the lighter to it.

'My father remembers you,' he lied. 'He sends his regards.'

'Thank you,' said Valverde. 'But I'm sure you didn't come here just to tell me that.'

'No, of course not,' said Caldas gesturing towards the house full of sharp edges. 'Do you recall our conversation the other day?'

The former crewmate of Arias and Castelo nodded.

'Do you remember that I asked why you didn't shelter in port the night of the wreck?'

'Yes, of course. I told you, we had a full hold. I assume that's why the skipper decided to return to Panxón.'

'Would you mind if I repeat the question?' said Caldas, drawing on his cigarette.

Valverde looked at him, then at Estevez, then at the inspector again.

'I don't understand.'

'It's very simple. Did you put in somewhere the night the *Xurelo* sank?'

'I already said we didn't.'

'Are you sure?'

Valverde opened out his arms and smiled. 'Of course I am.'

'You haven't forgotten anything?'

'Of course not.'

Caldas spoke very slowly: 'In that case, I can only think that you were lying before and are lying again today.'

'What?' said Valverde, no longer smiling.

'You know that things didn't happen as you've said. I'm giving you a chance to tell me the truth now.'

'I have no idea what you mean.'

Caldas unfolded the missing persons report. 'I know that you and your shipmates spent a few hours in Aguiño.'

Valverde turned back towards the house for a moment before replying, 'Who told you that?'

'Is it true?'

This only drew a snort from Valverde.

'Is it true or not?'

'It was a long time ago,' said Valverde. 'I don't remember clearly.'

'Don't give us that. Is it true or isn't it?' said Estevez, taking a step forward.

'What do you want me to tell you?'

Caldas gave him the same answer he had given Arias a little earlier: 'The truth.'

Valverde stared at the ground, shaking his head.

'I can't.'

'One man has already died,' said the inspector. 'Two if you count Sousa.'

Valverde now met his gaze. 'I know.'

'Yet you still won't say what happened on the boat that night?'

Valverde said nothing.

'You won't tell us what happened to Captain Sousa?' the inspector persisted.

'I can't,' repeated Valverde.

'What are you afraid of?'

'As I said to you before, anyone can feel afraid.'

'What are you and Arias so scared of?' continued Caldas. 'What happened that night?'

Just as Arias had done earlier on the slipway in the harbour, Valverde took refuge in his failure to remember, like a tortoise retreating into its shell.

'Would you like me to jog his memory?' Estevez whispered in the inspector's ear. Caldas knew just how his assistant would accomplish this.

'No,' he said quietly, and then warned Valverde: 'Maybe a judge can make you talk.'

'Maybe, Inspector Caldas,' said Valverde. 'Maybe.'

*

Estevez turned the car around in the courtyard and set off up the hill between the closely packed houses. The large wooden gate closed behind them.

'He's scared shitless,' said Estevez. 'They both are.'

'I know,' said Caldas.

'Why didn't you let me have a go?'

'A go?'

'You know . . .'

'Right.'

Caldas opened the window slightly and closed his eyes, but Captain Sousa's weather-beaten face appeared behind his eyelids so he opened them again.

A Catch at the Lighthouse

'I'll be five minutes,' said the inspector, opening the car door. He walked up the hill to the Templo Votivo del Mar and went inside. He soon returned, holding an envelope.

'What have you got there?' Estevez asked as Caldas climbed into the passenger seat.

'A photo of the crew of the *Xurelo*. We'll go to Aguiño on Monday. I want to see if anyone recognises them.'

Estevez glanced at the photograph. In the foreground, Captain Sousa was sitting on a stool, his woollen cap pulled down to his eyebrows. The three younger men stood smiling behind him, in their waterproofs.

'Are we going back to Vigo?' asked Estevez.

'Would you mind if we stopped off at the lighthouse?' said Caldas.

Estevez sighed and set off for Monteferro, but instead of taking the paved road to the summit, he turned right, along the track leading to Punta Lameda, driving through the eucalyptus woods and skirting around the mountain.

There was a yellow car parked by the lighthouse and Estevez pulled up behind it. The sky was blue and waves crashed against the rocks with great surges of foam. The Cies Islands rose straight ahead, their white sandy beaches gleaming in the morning sun. There was no one around.

They made their way to the place where Castelo's boat had been found. The rock barrier that sheltered the pool was partly visible.

The air smelled of forest and sea, and screeching seagulls could be heard above the roar of the waves.

Caldas went to stand on a smooth rock, close to the water's edge but beyond the reach of splashing waves. Out at sea, he glimpsed the triangular white sails of racing yachts. Two huge freighters from Vigo were heading for the mouth of the *ria*. Caldas could make out the containers on the deck of the nearest one. He could also see the lifeboats beneath blue covers, beside the gunwale. He reflected that he wouldn't have been able to see it all so clearly on the morning of Castelo's death, when sheets of rain would have obscured the view.

As he watched the wake fade behind the freighter, Caldas thought of the previous night. While tossing and turning in bed longing for the sound of Alba's pendant jingling, he had found a small space in his mind for Justo Castelo's murder. If no boats had set out that morning from the ports close to Panxón, maybe the murderers had come from a larger vessel. Caldas lit a cigarette, cupping the lighter with his hand to shield it from the wind, and looked out at the freighter again. He wondered if the skipper of a ship would allow one of its dinghies to be lowered without good reason.

Caldas stood leaning over the pool, reflecting that only someone who plied the coast regularly would know about the small reef that protected it from the waves. Only someone familiar with the shoreline of Monteferro would know that the pool was sheltered by a rock barrier and that at low tide the water there was quite still.

As he took another drag on his cigarette, the wind blew the smoke in his eyes. When he opened them again the freighter had grown smaller on the horizon. The ship was moving out to sea, and the idea of a murderer from elsewhere receded with it.

'I still think it's stupid sinking the boat right next to the shore when you could do it out at sea,' said Estevez, coming to stand beside him.

'We went over all that yesterday.'

'Yes, I know,' said Estevez. 'And you convinced me about the spanner. They can't have cared where it landed. Like you said, no one investigates a suicide.'

'That's what I think.'

'But this is different,' said Estevez.

'This?'

243

'The sunken boat. No one would look for a weapon if they believed El Rubio had thrown himself into the sea, agreed, but they'd still look for the boat. So why leave it here?'

'Because the water at the bottom of the pool is quite still and the boat would stay down there much longer.'

'But why did they want to hide it?'

'So that prints would be washed away, I assume.'

'What prints?' asked Estevez. 'If they attacked him from another boat, they can't have left many. Anyway, this pool doesn't have special cleansing properties. I don't see any difference between sinking the boat here and doing it elsewhere.'

Caldas saw this was true. In any case, the boat wouldn't have needed to be underwater too long before all clues were erased.

'If I was faking that fisherman's suicide,' Estevez continued, 'I'd have left the boat adrift for the current to dash it against rocks. I wouldn't have brought it round this side of the mountain.'

'But what if someone had found it before it sank?'

'They couldn't have,' replied Estevez. 'I'd have made a hole in the hull to make sure it went down before I jumped back to the other boat. All they've achieved by sinking it in here is letting us know for sure that it wasn't El Rubio who brought it here, don't you think?'

'Perhaps,' said Caldas. He remained on the rock, smoking, while Estevez went down the slope away from the lighthouse.

'There are two guys down there,' said Estevez when he returned.

'Where?'

'One in a boat and one on the rocks.'

Caldas followed him, first down the slope, then from rock to rock. When his assistant leaned to peer over the cliff edge, the inspector did likewise.

As Estevez had said, there was a man in a dinghy and another perched on a rock surrounded by sea spray, tethered to the boat by a harness he wore over his wetsuit. He was gripping a scraper in one hand and a couple of plastic bags hung from his belt. The other man was keeping the dinghy a few metres away. He was holding on to the end of the rope and adjusting the throttle to keep from being dashed against the rocks.

'They're collecting *percebes* – gooseneck barnacles,' said Caldas.

When the sea withdrew, the man on the rock climbed down to the dark exposed strip and scraped barnacles off the rock with his spatula. Then, when his companion in the boat warned him of the next incoming wave, he scrambled back up to safety. Sometimes he got away with bags full of *percebes*, but at others he barely escaped with his life.

'Is that how they're always collected?' asked Estevez, sounding surprised.

'Yes,' said Caldas. 'They form colonies on the rocks, in places where the sea beats against them. You've got to look for them there.'

Estevez whistled. 'Now I know why they're so expensive.'

'And so delicious,' added Caldas, who could think of no better company at table than a plate of *percebes*. He loved nothing more than shelling one of the barnacles and savouring the intense briny taste of its flesh.

'How do they get them when the weather's bad?' asked Estevez.

'You don't get *percebes* when the weather's bad,' replied Caldas, who hadn't seen any in the display cabinet at the Bar Puerto for weeks.

'I don't understand it,' said Estevez as the man scrambled out of the way of another wave.

'What don't you understand?'

'Why they risk their lives like that.'

Caldas shrugged. 'They need to eat.'

'Well, they should eat something else,' said Estevez gravely.

The inspector looked at him out of the corner of his eye and Estevez burst out laughing.

A little later, his bags full, the man on the rocks jumped into the water and the other man hauled him to the dinghy by the rope. Once he was aboard, they sailed away from the coast.

'Are we heading back, Inspector?' asked Estevez, still slightly flushed from laughing.

They were almost back at the car when they heard the drone of a boat engine nearby. They peered over the lighthouse wall and saw the *percebes* collectors in their dinghy. They were approaching the pool where Castelo's boat had been found. The policemen watched as the pilot steered the craft between the rocky shoreline and the reef protecting the pool. Caldas thought of the bad weather the previous Sunday. The murderers would have had to perform the same manoeuvre in much heavier seas. Only someone with great experience would have dared attempt it.

The man in the wetsuit climbed out of the dinghy with the bags of barnacles, and waved goodbye to his companion.

'Now we know who the yellow car belongs to,' murmured Caldas.

Estevez nodded. 'Why have they landed here?'

'Because they're doing this illegally,' said Caldas quietly. 'They must have over twenty kilos of *percebes* there. If they came ashore in a harbour they might be reported, or worse.'

The dinghy sailed away and the policemen waited by the lighthouse while the fisherman climbed the hill. He looked about twenty. He was slim, of medium height, and the sea water had made his hair curl.

He looked surprised when he saw another car parked near his at that early hour, and even more so when the two men leaning on the lighthouse wall headed towards him.

'Good morning,' said Caldas.

The man raised his eyebrows in response and continued on his way.

'You've done pretty well there,' the inspector continued, pointing at the bags of *percebes*.

'Well . . .'

'Could we have a word?'

'You're from the police, aren't you?'

'That obvious, is it?'

The young man nodded.

'It's not about the catch,' Caldas reassured him. 'We just want to ask you a few questions.'

The man put the bags down, as if lowering weapons. He said he was from Panxón but worked in Vigo. At weekends, if the weather was good, he and his brother got to Monteferro at dawn, supplementing their income with what they found on the rocks.

'Were you here last weekend?' asked Caldas.

The boy shook his head. 'Seas have been too heavy for the past fortnight,' he said. 'That's why there are so many *percebes* today.'

'Can you still get here by boat in bad weather?' asked Caldas, glancing at the spot where the dinghy had dropped the boy off.

'Yes, of course you can,' he replied. He explained that steering a boat into the pool wasn't difficult for an experienced pilot.

'Anyone who's sailed around here can get in, even in rough seas. You just have to go easy on the throttle,' he said, moving his hand as if accelerating on a motorbike. 'And make sure the tide's out so you can see the rocks and don't get any nasty surprises.'

When they asked why he'd picked that spot to unload the catch, the young man replied, 'When the tide's out, it's like a pier. It's the only place you can land without being seen. Anywhere else the rocks are too dangerous or you're overlooked by houses.'

In Caldas's mind the boy's words caused an instant reaction, like precipitation in a test tube. How had it not occurred to him earlier?

'Do many people know this place?' he asked.

'The lighthouse?' said the boy.

'The place you landed,' clarified Caldas.

'The fishermen from the village know it.'

'Right.'

'But others know about it as well,' added the young man, jerking his head in the direction of the two parked cars. 'You can get here by car.'

Caldas rubbed his face and rummaged in his jacket for his cigarettes. He lit one and said, 'I think I now know why they sank it here.'

'Why?' asked Estevez.

'I'll tell you later,' he said. Then, addressing the young man, 'You can go.'

'What about the *percebes*?' he asked hesitantly.

'Take them,' replied Caldas. 'You collected them.'

The man thanked him and hurried away with a bag in each hand and a smile on his face.

'One more thing,' called out the inspector.

The young man turned around. He'd stopped smiling, but he grinned when Caldas asked:

'How much do you want for a couple of kilos?'

Once the clandestine fisherman had driven off, Caldas set out his theory for Estevez.

'I don't think they came to the pool to dispose of the boat. I think they left it here because it was the only place they could land where they were safe from prying eyes.'

'Say that again?' said Estevez.

'I'm saying that while one of the killers left in his boat – the one they boarded El Rubio's from – the other one brought Castelo's boat here. But not to sink it, just to land without being seen.'

Estevez looked around. He could see nothing but water, rocks and trees.

'Why didn't they both leave in the other boat after throwing Castelo into the sea?'

'Maybe they didn't want to be seen together,' suggested Caldas.

'Maybe,' agreed Estevez. 'But why did they sink the boat?'

'You said it yourself: because El Rubio's body was round the other side of the mountain. That's why they didn't simply want to leave his boat adrift. It would have seemed odd for the body to turn up on one side of Monteferro and the boat on the other. They needed to land here, so they had to sink the boat here, too.'

The inspector climbed back down to the edge of the pool and Estevez followed.

'See the rocks piled up by the wall?' asked Caldas. 'They're like the ones found in Castelo's boat. I think that after jumping ashore they threw the rocks down from up there to make a hole in the hull to make sure the boat stayed on the bottom.'

'But if things happened like that, if one of them landed here, where's the other boat?' asked Estevez. 'No boats went in or out of any of the local harbours last Sunday.'

'We'll have to ask further afield.'

Estevez snorted. 'Has it occurred to you that maybe the other boat doesn't exist, Inspector?'

'So how did they reach Castelo?'

'Maybe someone was hiding on his boat, waiting for him.'

'We've already been over this: Castelo was the only one aboard when he left the harbour. Hermida's wife saw him from her window.'

'That woman's getting on a bit,' said Estevez. 'And it was dark. She could have got it wrong.'

'She could,' said Caldas. 'But Castelo would have spotted if anyone was on board. The wheelhouse of his boat has windows, like Arias's

248

and Hermida's, and his traps were piled up on the jetty. He'd have known if there was someone else on his boat.'

'It was dark,' Estevez repeated.

'But the woman saw him turn on his light. I'm telling you, there was nowhere for anyone to hide. They had to get to him by sea, and there had to be more than one of them.'

Caldas set off back up the hill to the car.

'So how do you explain that they knew El Rubio was putting out to sea that morning?' asked Estevez, walking along beside the inspector.

Caldas stopped and threw open his arms. It was the second time in two days that his assistant had asked him the same question.

Security Systems

Leaving the lighthouse behind, they drove along the potholed track that ran first beside the sea, then through the pale trunks of the eucalyptus grove. The trees' sharp fragrance blew in through the car window on chill air that gusted over the inspector's face.

When they reached the road, Caldas looked out and asked his assistant to slow down as they drew near to the first few houses.

'What are you looking for?' asked Estevez, surprised to see the inspector peering like a bird of prey, instead of sitting with his eyes closed as he usually did in the car.

'I want to see if any of these houses have security cameras,' said Caldas. 'You check on that side, will you?'

The number of burglaries in the area had increased over the past few years and many homeowners had installed alarms and other security devices. The inspector was hoping that a CCTV camera outside one of the houses had caught someone heading along the road the previous Sunday. It was the only road leading away from the lighthouse. After landing at the pool and making their way down the track, they would have had to pass along that stretch of road.

'There!' said Estevez soon afterwards, pulling the car up alongside one of the first houses.

It was a modern house with a garden surrounded by a high stone wall. The camera was on the second floor, directed at the entrance, the most vulnerable point of the perimeter. Any car driving along the road would be caught on camera.

250

Caldas rang the doorbell but there was no answer. The blinds were drawn and the letterbox was overflowing with rain-dampened junk mail. He assumed it was a holiday home, so he simply noted down the name of the security firm that had supplied the alarm, prominently displayed on the wall as a deterrent. He also took down the house number on the stone wall and returned to the car.

They drove on slowly, scanning every wall, door and window. They saw several security firm signs, but no more cameras.

At the crossroads, Estevez asked, 'Are we going back to Vigo?'

Caldas nodded and they turned left, away from Panxón.

They stopped for petrol.

'I'm going for a piss,' said Estevez, after he'd filled the tank.

'Try to get another bag,' said Caldas. 'We need to divide up the *percebes*.'

Estevez nodded and headed towards the toilets. While he waited, the inspector called Clara Barcia and gave her the name of the security firm and the house number.

'Do you think there'll be any footage from last Sunday?' he asked.

'Depends on the equipment, Inspector.'

'The equipment?'

'The recording equipment,' said Barcia. 'If it stores images on disk there'll be several weeks' worth but if it's the kind that uses a tape you can forget about Sunday. There'll only be a couple of days' footage.'

'Right,' said Caldas. 'Thanks, Clara.'

Estevez had got back by the time the inspector hung up.

'You shouldn't have called her, Inspector.'

'Why not?'

'Because it's Saturday.'

'She didn't complain.'

'No,' said Estevez. 'Not to you.'

Estevez drew up outside Caldas's apartment building, exactly where he'd picked him up earlier that morning. The inspector climbed out of the car, stretched and looked at his watch. It was eleven thirty. They got the two kilos of *percebes* out of the boot and divided them up.

'I've never tried them,' said Estevez.

'Well, a kilo isn't a bad start,' said Caldas. 'Shall I tell you how to cook them?'

'If you don't mind,' replied Estevez.

'It's easy. Set a pan of sea water on to boil, with a bay leaf . . .'

'Does it really have to be sea water?' interrupted Estevez.

'You can use tap water with salt added,' said the inspector. 'When it comes to a rolling boil, add the *percebes* and wait for it to come back to the boil. Count to fifty, drain, serve and enjoy.'

'Do I eat them hot?'

'Yes,' said Caldas. 'Cover them with a cloth so they don't get cold.'

'OK,' said Estevez. 'See you Monday then.'

'Get in early on Monday, Rafa,' said the inspector, holding up the envelope containing the photo the priest of Panxón had given him. 'We need to go to Aguiño. Let's see if they remember that woman and her son.'

'Do you still believe that Sousa . . .' said Estevez. Caldas made a face that Estevez was at a loss to interpret.

Estevez opened the car door and, before seating himself behind the wheel, pointed at the bag in the inspector's hand.

'Do you think she'll like them?'

'Who?'

'You know.'

Caldas glanced at the *percebes*. 'I think so,' he replied. 'Better than salad anyway.'

The Crew

Inside his apartment, Caldas put the envelope containing the photo of the *Xurelo*'s crew down on the table and switched on the television with the remote. Then he went to the kitchen, placed the bag of *percebes* in the bottom of the fridge and had a swig of water straight from the bottle. Back in the sitting room, he picked up the photograph and went to lie on the sofa.

Captain Sousa, in his woollen cap, was seated in front of the others, staring straight at the camera. Caldas thought he looked proud of his boat and his crew. The three younger men stood behind him. They were in yellow waterproofs almost identical to the ones worn by the fishermen pleading for mercy from the Virgin of El Carmen in the Templo Votivo del Mar.

José Arias was in the middle. He was several inches taller than the other two. Then as now he had stubble on his chin, but his smile and his youth made him look much less fierce than the man the inspector had met in Panxón. To his right stood Justo Castelo, the unmistakable blond hair flopping over his eyes. On the other side was Marcos Valverde who didn't yet slick his hair back. Even in those days he looked the youngest of the three. Behind them the word *Xurelo* was partly visible.

Caldas slid the photo back into the envelope and put it on the table. Like a boat stranded at low tide, the investigation had come to a standstill. Caldas wondered when the tide would turn.

He looked at his watch: it was just after one. Remembering that his father had said he'd be getting to the hospital before lunch, he picked up his mobile phone.

'Are you at the hospital?'

'I've been here since one o'clock,' said his father. 'Are you going to drop by?'

'Yes,' said Caldas. 'Why don't you come here for lunch afterwards? I've got a kilo of fresh *percebes* in the fridge.'

'I have a better idea,' said his father. 'We've got something to celebrate.'

Caldas listened, then said, 'It's not allowed.'

'Bloody hell, Leo. Aren't you ever off duty?'

The inspector cooked the *percebes*, drained them and placed them, wrapped in a damp cloth, in an insulated plastic container. Then he hurried out, hailed a taxi and told the driver to take him to the hospital.

'Have you brought them?' asked his father as he entered room 211. His uncle smiled behind the mask.

Caldas held up the bag and went to the high table. He moved the radio and newspapers to the floor, took out the plastic container, opened it and placed the cloth filled with *percebes* straight on to the table.

'Leave the box there for the shells,' said his father, turning the handle that raised the head of his brother's bed.

'Are you going to tell me what we're celebrating?' asked the inspector.

'Alberto can go home.'

He looked at his uncle. He was still smiling.

'When?'

'This week,' said his father. 'He's been seen by a new doctor. He doesn't think Alberto needs to stay here, as long as he's got oxygen. How about that?'

Caldas wasn't sure it was good news.

'That's great,' he said, smiling back at his uncle.

'He's going to come and stay with me,' said his father. 'At least until he's a bit better and can manage on his own.'

Caldas nodded.

'I'll let you know when he's being discharged and you can help move him, Leo.'

'Of course,' said the inspector, laying a hand on his uncle's wrist.

He could feel every bone in the emaciated arm, but behind the smiling eyes was a happy man.

'You can meet the dog.'

The patient frowned, clearly not knowing what Caldas was talking about.

Caldas turned to his father. 'Haven't you told him you've got a dog?'

'Me?'

Caldas tutted and looked at his uncle.

'He's got a dog,' he said, pointing at his father. 'A brown one. Quite big.'

'It's not mine.'

'Of course it is,' said Caldas. 'It lives on the estate and it won't let him out of its sight.'

'Well, there are birds on the estate, and moles, and flies,' said his father. 'And it would never occur to me to consider them mine.'

Caldas and his uncle were still smiling as the inspector opened out the cloth. He shelled the first *percebe* and handed it to his uncle. Alberto took it with a bony hand and raised it to his lips, the mask hissing as he removed it.

'Where's the wine?' asked his father, peering under the table.

'What?'

'You don't expect us to eat all these *percebes* without wine, do you?'

Caldas smiled. He thought his father was joking. But he wasn't.

The Threshold

On Monday morning the city was cold and hazy, as if covered in a cloud of ash. Caldas shaved in the shower, dressed and walked to the police station. When he got there Estevez was standing by Olga's desk, in his coat, looking at a map of Galicia on the computer screen.

'Where is it we're going?' he asked.

'Aguiño,' replied Caldas, placing his finger on the screen at the tip of the Barbanza peninsula, between the *rias* of Arousa and Muros.

'Have you got the exact address?'

'I think so,' said Caldas, taking from his jacket pocket the copy of the missing persons report he'd put there with the photo of the boat's crew. Rebeca Neira's address was written in pencil in the margin. Olga keyed in the address and a map of the area appeared on screen.

'Off we go then,' said Estevez, grabbing the map as it emerged from the printer.

They drove down the Calle del Arenal and took the motorway out of Vigo. Caldas had his eyes closed so, when they crossed the Rande Bridge, he didn't see the flat-bottomed boats lined up in the *ria* or the Cies Islands in the misty distance.

'Doesn't the noise bother you?' asked Estevez, with a sideways glance at the slightly open window.

'Yes, it does,' said Caldas but didn't close it. He would rather let in the fresh morning air even if it meant enduring the noise.

*

After another fifty kilometres they left the motorway and crossed the River Ulla. Mist hung over the treetops as they drove along the Barbanza peninsula to Aguiño.

It was a small village – a few hundred houses built around a harbour and beach.

'There's no police station here, is there?'

'No, of course not,' said Caldas. 'Any problems are handled at Ribeira.'

Glancing at the map, Estevez turned off to the right. The road led uphill away from the sea, with small houses dotted among fields on either side.

'It must be one of these,' said Estevez.

'There are some people over there,' said Caldas, indicating a white two-storey house. Thick smoke, paler than the day, rose from the stone chimney. Beside the house grew a gnarled chestnut tree, missing half its leaves.

Estevez pulled up outside and Caldas wound the window right down to call out to a woman sweeping the front steps. She was so small that the broom in her hands looked like a gondolier's pole.

'Hello,' said Caldas. 'Could you tell me where Rebeca Neira lives?'

The woman stopped sweeping. She looked no more than thirty – too young to be the woman they were looking for.

'Who?'

'Rebeca Neira,' repeated the inspector.

She looked at them in silence, as if trying to work out why they wanted to know.

'Who's asking after her?'

'We're police officers,' said Caldas. 'From Vigo.'

'One moment.'

She propped the broom against the wall and went inside the house.

'Mother,' they heard her say. 'Some policemen are asking about Rebeca the First.'

She returned with an older woman who put a coat around her shoulders as she came outside. Her grey hair was held up by dozens of black pins. She was even smaller than her daughter.

'You're looking for someone?' she said.

'We're looking for the house where Rebeca Neira lives,' said Caldas. 'Can you help?'

The woman approached the car and, with no need to bend down, peered through the open window just as her daughter had done a moment earlier.

'It's that one,' she replied, pointing across the road.

The policemen looked in the direction she'd indicated and saw a stone house, almost completely hidden by the morning mist and rampant vegetation. The blinds were dirty and falling apart, the windows broken, and brambles climbed all over the railings that surrounded the property, stretching thorny branches towards the road. The house had obviously been empty for years.

They got out of the car. Caldas inhaled deeply – the air smelled of the sea, of damp earth and wood smoke.

'How long since she moved out?' he asked.

'You can see for yourself the state it's in.'

The inspector glanced again at the dilapidated house. The garden was so overgrown a rhino could have been hiding in there.

'But she still lives in the village?'

'Who?'

'Rebeca Neira.'

The woman shook her head. 'She left years ago.'

'Do you know where she went?'

'She didn't say goodbye,' the woman said, brusquely.

Caldas nodded. 'She lived with her son, didn't she?'

'Yes, just the two of them,' she replied, emphasising the words.

'He no longer lives in Aguiño either?'

'No.'

'How long ago did they leave?' asked Estevez.

Mother and daughter looked up as if scanning the sky for a plane they'd just heard. Estevez seemed like a giant beside the two tiny women.

'Ten or twelve years ago,' said the one with the hairpins. 'Maybe longer.'

'You haven't seen them since?'

'I haven't,' she said firmly.

The inspector looked at her daughter and she shook her head: she hadn't had any news about Diego and Rebeca either.

258

Caldas unfolded the missing persons report, which gave the name and identity number of the police officer who'd dealt with the case: 'Somoza', Caldas read. Nieves Ortiz had said he was from Aguiño. Maybe he knew where Rebeca Neira and her son had moved to.

'Does Deputy Inspector Somoza still live in the village?'

'The policeman?' said the mother. 'He retired some time ago.'

'But does he still live here?'

'Yes,' said the woman. 'Next to the church.'

They got back into the car and, before closing his eyes, Caldas had another look at the ruins of the Neiras' house.

'Are we going to the deputy inspector's house?' asked Estevez.

Caldas nodded and leaned back, wondering again when the tide of the investigation would turn.

A Former Policeman

Deputy Inspector Somoza was a tall man in a grey woollen jumper who stooped as he walked. He had a big nose, thick lips and sparse white hair that was combed back. Though he wore glasses he squinted myopically, causing his face to furrow.

'I'm no one's colleague nowadays,' he said when they'd identified themselves. 'I'm retired.'

Caldas smiled. 'We wanted to ask you something.'

The man invited them in and they followed him down a narrow hallway. Shuffling in his felt slippers, he showed them into a tiny sitting room that was overflowing with furniture. They sat down at a *mesa camilla*, a small table with a heater beneath it, facing the television which was switched on. On a low table, beside a ceramic lamp, Caldas saw an old photograph of Somoza in uniform. He had thick, dark hair and wasn't wearing glasses but he was already squinting at the camera, mouth gaping.

The deputy inspector switched off the television with the remote control. 'What can I do for you?'

'We're investigating the murder of a fisherman.'

'In Aguiño?'

'No,' replied Caldas. 'In a village on the Vigo estuary. But it may have something to do with a boat that sank near here, and with this,' he said, handing Somoza the missing persons report.

Somoza glanced at the document. 'This happened a long time ago.'

Caldas nodded and showed him the photograph of the crew of the *Xurelo*. 'In the report the boy mentioned a fisherman with very fair

260

hair,' he said, pointing first at the relevant section of the document, then at Justo Castelo in the photograph. 'We think this may be him.'

Breathing noisily through his mouth, Deputy Inspector Somoza looked at the report and photograph.

'The boat went down on the same night in shallows off Salvora. The skipper drowned,' said Caldas. 'We're trying to find out what happened just before.'

The retired policeman shrugged. 'I don't see how I can help.'

'We're trying to track down Rebeca Neira or her son.'

'They left the village.'

'So we've been told. Do you know where they moved to?'

Somoza shook his head and pushed the report and photograph across the table towards the inspector. 'I know as much as anyone else. They left.'

'Did Rebeca Neira ever tell you what happened that night?'

Somoza took a deep breath before answering, 'Rebeca never came back to the village.'

Had Caldas been a dog he would have pricked up his ears.

'What?'

'Everyone called her Rebeca the First. She was always ahead of the rest. In everything. She became a mother when she was still a child herself.'

'What's that got to do with it?'

'She must have gone off with some man,' said Somoza contemptuously. 'It wouldn't have been the first time that going out for a beer turned into several nights of bingeing.'

'You didn't investigate her disappearance?'

'Of course we did,' he said. 'We looked for her until we found out she'd left.'

'How did you find out?'

'I don't recall the details,' he replied. 'It was years ago.'

'But you saw her again?' asked Caldas.

'I didn't. But that doesn't mean anything.'

'What about the boy?'

'He left, too, a few days later. She must have come to get him or called to tell him to meet her somewhere.'

'Did the boy withdraw the report?' asked Estevez. Caldas knew the answer – there was no subsequent statement in the file.

261

'He never returned,' said Somoza. 'Either to withdraw it or enquire about the investigation. He came to us that first time but that was all.'

'Weren't you surprised?' pressed Estevez.

Somoza shook his head and screwed up his face even further. 'Rebeca the First liked to go out in the evening. She was always a bit wild. She had that reputation. I expect the boy was ashamed to admit that it was another one of his mother's escapades.'

'So you never found out what happened?'

'You know what police work is like,' said Somoza defensively, raising his palms and then slapping them down on the table. 'Before you've closed one case you get caught up in the next. It's hard to find time for anything else.'

Caldas nodded.

'Where did she work?'

'I don't remember,' the old man replied. 'Not in the village.'

'Wasn't she missed at work?'

'No one apart from her son reported her missing.'

Caldas looked at the photo. The departure of mother and son provided no new clues about the hours leading up to Captain Sousa's death.

'Do any relatives of the Neiras live in the village?'

'No,' said the retired policeman, breathing hard through his mouth. 'Her parents weren't from Aguiño. Her father got a job here on a hake trawler when Rebeca was small. In those days there was plenty of work, lots of people came from elsewhere. By the time she disappeared, it was years since her parents had moved away.'

'Do you know where they went?'

Somoza shrugged. 'They must have gone to find work in another port, or maybe they went back to their village. They were getting on.'

'Do you remember where they came from?'

'I don't think I ever knew.'

Somoza could tell them nothing more. Caldas returned the missing persons report and photo of the crew of the *Xurelo* to his jacket pocket. He stood up and quickly took his leave. He needed a cigarette.

Rebeca the First

While they had coffee at a nearby bar Caldas reread the report. The waiter confirmed that Irene Vazquez, the friend who had accompanied Rebeca Neira's son to the police station, still lived in Aguiño. She worked in a pharmacy near the harbour.

They parked the car by the church and walked down to the harbour. Dozens of small boats were moored on the still water. By the fish market, they could make out a larger fishing boat tied to bollards on the jetty, surrounded by a cloud of seagulls. Caldas was sorry that the view was shrouded in thick mist.

They walked past the fishermen's association. On the canteen door a poster was still up for the *Fiesta del Percebe* held in the village the previous summer.

'By the way,' said Estevez when he saw the poster, 'thanks for the *percebes*. They were quite a revelation.'

'Did you get through them all?'

'I could have eaten twice as many,' said Estevez.

'You did remove the shells, didn't you?' joked the inspector.

'Of course I did,' said Estevez. 'After the first one anyway.'

The sign on the glass door of the pharmacy read *Open*. Above, a light shone in a green halo of mist. Behind the counter stood a tall woman with a fringe of dark hair falling over brown eyes. The name Caldas sought was embroidered on the pocket of her white coat.

'Irene Vazquez?' he asked anyway.

She looked from one policeman to the other before answering in the affirmative.

'I'm Inspector Caldas,' he said, confident that his name would mean nothing to anyone here – Aguiño was definitely too far from Vigo to receive *Patrolling the Waves*. 'This is Officer Estevez. We're from Vigo Police.'

'Is it about the burglary?' she asked.

'No,' said Caldas. 'We're looking for a woman called Rebeca Neira.'

Again she looked at both of them in turn before replying, 'Rather late for that, isn't it?'

'We know she left the village,' said Caldas. 'We were wondering if you might know where we can find her.'

'Rebeca didn't go anywhere,' she said drily.

'We've just spoken to Deputy Inspector Somoza,' said Caldas. 'He claims that she left.'

'Somoza is a pig and a liar. Always has been.'

Caldas took out his cigarettes.

'If you want to smoke, we can go through to the back,' said Irene Vazquez, coming out from behind the counter.

She went to the glass door, turned the sign so that the word 'open' faced inwards, and locked the door. 'This way we won't be interrupted,' she said.

She led them through to a room at the back of the pharmacy lined with shelves of medicines. There was a table and two chairs and, on the table, a television so small it looked like a toy. On a separate shelf stood an electric coffee machine, and the smell of coffee mingled with that of the medicines' plastic packaging.

'This is where I spend my night shifts,' she said. 'Reading or watching TV.' She set an ashtray on the table beside the television.

'Would you like one?' said Caldas, offering her a cigarette.

'I'd rather have one of mine, thanks,' she said.

Once the cigarettes were lit, she asked, 'So what is it you want to know?'

'As I said, we're trying to track down Rebeca Neira.'

'Or her son,' added Estevez, leaning against the wall behind the inspector's chair.

'Yes, or her son,' said Caldas. 'We need one of them to identify someone for us.'

'Diego doesn't live in Aguiño any more.'

'What about Rebeca?'

Irene Vazquez took a drag of her cigarette and watched the smoke she blew out rise to the ceiling.

'Rebeca's dead,' she said.

'Dead? We were told she'd left the village.'

'Somoza will never admit it. If he had any conscience he'd be eaten up with guilt,' she said, smiling bitterly. 'But I know Rebeca's dead.'

'When did she die?' asked the inspector.

'The twentieth of December 1996,' she said. 'She was murdered that night.'

Caldas drew on his cigarette and she did the same.

'Are you sure?'

'As sure as I am that you and I are sitting here smoking.'

Irene Vazquez clearly remembered the Sunday morning of Diego Neira's call.

'He asked if I'd seen Rebeca. I said I hadn't. Diego was no longer a child. He understood that his mother was young and liked to go out and have fun sometimes. It wasn't the first time she'd stayed out all night. But he sounded pretty low. He said he wasn't feeling well. I was sure Rebeca would get back any time, but I felt sorry for him. After I rang off, I got dressed and went over there. They lived in the upper part of the village. I live here on the first floor,' she said, pointing upwards. 'It was a short walk to theirs – five, maybe ten minutes. When I arrived Diego was lying under a blanket on the sofa watching TV. He was disappointed when he saw it wasn't his mother. He wasn't very talkative, but in his own way he was a nice boy. And affectionate. Very affectionate. He got up to give me a kiss and then went back to the sofa. He didn't say anything, just stared at the TV. He was coughing. I felt his forehead and he had a slight temperature. I remember that the sitting room was very tidy. There was a sliding door to the kitchen. I looked in. It was just as neat, and I said so. I thought he'd cleaned up and I said his mother would be pleased when she got home. Rebeca was very organised. She liked everything to be in its place. You should have seen her exercise books at school,' she said with a smile. 'Her notes were perfect. She was very bright, you know. Top of the class. Ever since she was little. That's why we called her Rebeca the First. No one else came close. But she wasn't just good at her schoolwork. She was the best at everything. All the boys were crazy about her, she had a lovely figure, and the brains to go as far as she wanted. It's such a shame she got pregnant so young. It put an end to everything. We all tried to convince her not to keep it. One of the teachers spoke to her. But Rebeca was stubborn. She always did what she wanted. When she made up her mind, no one could stop her,' said Irene. 'She went ahead and had the baby. We all adored little Diego, but he changed her life.' She paused a moment and opened the window to let out the smoke. 'She managed all on her own. She never said who the father was. At first we'd ask. After a few drinks we'd go through the names of boys in the village, one after the other, but she'd just smile and wouldn't say a word. She never said who the father was,' Irene repeated. 'I'm not sure even he knew.'

She looked at the policemen. 'I'm sorry, I'm digressing,' she said.

'Please, don't worry,' said Caldas, encouraging her to continue.

'Anyway, the house was neat and tidy, so I praised Diego. But he said he hadn't touched a thing, it must have been his mother who'd tidied up. He'd seen her the last time on Friday evening when he left for his friend's house and, when he got back early on Saturday morning, he'd found the place like that. She wasn't there and he assumed she'd popped out for something, so he lay down on the sofa. He spent all day there, coughing and dozing. He got up some time in the afternoon to make himself a sandwich then went back to the sofa. On Sunday morning, when she still wasn't back, he called me and I went over there again. We talked for a while and I asked if he'd had breakfast. He said no so I offered to make him something, but he wouldn't let me. He said I was the guest, and went to the kitchen. He opened the cupboard where they kept the cups and was surprised to see that his own cup was missing. He searched the cupboard, and looked in the bin, but there was only the stuff he'd thrown away himself the day before. He was a bit finicky, like Rebeca, and he looked everywhere until eventually he settled for a different cup. I was going to make the coffee,' said Irene, taking a drag of her cigarette. 'Rebeca's coffee-maker wasn't like this one,' she said, gesturing at the shelf. 'It was one of those Italian ones that everyone's got – the kind you screw together and put on the hob.'

The policemen said they knew the type, and she went on:

'I'd hurt my hand so I got Diego to open the coffee pot for me.' She mimed the action. 'He did, and went quiet. He'd turned pale, as white as this table. I asked him what was wrong, and he came over, holding a part of the coffee pot in each hand. I didn't understand. He dropped the coffee pot on the table and looked around. Then he sat down and started crying. He kept saying: "They've hurt her." I held him for a few minutes and when he pulled himself together I got him to explain. He showed me the coffee pot again: the grounds were still in the filter. It hadn't been cleaned out.'

She finished her cigarette, stubbing it out in the ashtray, before continuing.

'Diego knew what his mother was like – obsessively clean and tidy. She'd never have wiped the pot and left old coffee grounds inside,' said Irene. Caldas held his lighter to the new cigarette she had placed between her lips. 'Diego started prowling around the kitchen, opening drawers, checking inside the oven and the fridge. He got more and more agitated. I asked what was wrong, and he said plates and glasses were missing, and the serving dishes from supper on Friday. The cloths weren't on their hooks and the big knife Rebeca always kept by the sink had gone. Everything that had been on the cooker when he'd left for his friend's house on Friday night had disappeared. He also said that, when he got back on Saturday morning, there was something strange about the way the sitting-room chairs were arranged. He hadn't thought it significant at the time, but now he did. He started crying again and saying that something bad had happened to his mother. He said he'd seen her with two fishermen on Friday night. She'd gone out for cigarettes,' she said, holding up her own, 'and when she came back, she was with those two men. It was pouring with rain, and they stood under the porch talking. Diego could hear them from inside the house, he could make out the voices of the two men and his mother. One of the men hardly spoke but the other one was talking very loudly, insisting she let them in for another drink. Rebeca said she'd rather postpone the partying to another day when her son was out. They asked how old her son was. When she said fifteen, they burst out laughing. They couldn't believe she had a son that age. She asked them to keep their voices down, and laughed, too. She promised she'd invite them in another day when Diego wasn't at home.'

Caldas nodded as he listened to Irene's account, familiar with some of it already from the missing persons report. He felt that the tide he'd been awaiting for days was now rolling in with Irene's words.

'You know how teenage boys are. As soon as he heard his mother imply he was in the way, he stormed out. He didn't want to cramp her style. He insisted that it all sounded friendly. Otherwise he wouldn't have left her alone with them. He'd never have gone out if she'd seemed uneasy,' said Irene. 'Diego ran off, only stopping to say he was going to stay at a friend's.'

Irene paused again to smoke. Her eyes were dry, but she was grieving.

'Did he recognise the men?' asked the inspector.

'He said he didn't even look at them as he left. But he saw one later,' she replied, and went on to tell them what they'd already read in the report. 'Diego stopped to shelter from the downpour. Now I think he did it not just to get out of the rain, but to see what his mother was doing. He saw her go inside with one of the men. The other one headed back to the harbour. He passed very close, so Diego got a good look at him. He had fair hair and was wearing fishermen's waterproofs. Diego had never seen him before. He wasn't from the village.'

'What about the other one?' asked Estevez.

Irene looked up and peered at Estevez from under her dark fringe. 'He didn't see him,' she said quietly.

'Was he in waterproofs, too?'

'I don't know,' she whispered.

Caldas nodded and she went on with her story.

'Diego went to his friend's house and came back on Saturday morning. You know the rest. He found everything clean and tidy,' she repeated. 'It wasn't until the next day, when he saw the coffee grounds, that he realised it hadn't been his mother who'd cleared up, and we went to report her missing.'

The report didn't include all the information the woman had just provided.

'Did you tell Somoza all this?'

She said no.

'The pig questioned everything Diego said. He was sure Rebeca

268

was off having fun. "You know your mother," he said. Instead of helping a worried kid, that policeman made fun of him. I can't bear to think about it. He claimed he was really busy, and told us not to bother him with nonsense. When Diego said there were two men, do you know what he answered? "Two? Rebeca's in fine form." That's what he spat out in front of the boy. Can you believe it? Diego wanted to leave. He'd rather not file a report than have to endure humiliation at the hands of that old bastard.'

'But he did file one,' said Caldas, holding out the document.

'Because I insisted. I forced him to make a statement. He hardly spoke. I had to drag the words out of him. I don't know why I bothered. It didn't do any good. Somoza said he'd be in touch if anything came up, but we never heard a word. I went to see him a few days later. He was busy trying to catch two guys who'd held up a petrol station. They turned out to be a couple of boys from Corrubedo – junkies. But Somoza made them sound like Bonnie and Clyde. But about Rebeca's disappearance he didn't lift a finger. He claimed no one had heard of the fair-haired fisherman or his friend, and that searching the area had come to nothing. He still thought Rebeca must have taken a fancy to one of the men and would be back any day, when she got fed up. I insisted that she would never have abandoned her son like that. I said maybe she'd been hurt or even killed. "If she's dead, her body'll turn up," he said with a filthy smile. He didn't bother to look for her. He didn't do a thing.'

'How did Diego react?'

'How do you think? He was devastated. When we got home, he lay down on the sofa again. He cried for days. I didn't know what to do, who to go to. Some bastard had left him without a mother, and the police had simply made fun of him. He was fifteen,' said Irene with a sigh. 'I stayed at the house for over a week. We spent Christmas together, with the table set for three. I gave him sleeping pills every night, so he'd get some sleep. It was me who didn't sleep,' she smiled. 'He was such a lovely boy. They destroyed his life, just as they destroyed his mother's. What happened to them wasn't fair. We spoke to the Civil Protection Force. They organised searches for Rebeca in the area that night and for a few days afterwards.'

'But they didn't find her,' said Caldas.

'No,' she said, her fringe parting like curtains as she shook her

269

head. 'But I'm sure someone killed her. Why else would they have bothered to clean up the house?'

'Did the police ever identify the men she was with?'

'No.'

'They never found out who they were?'

'No, never,' she replied. 'Diego believed they were fishermen. But it was a stormy night. No one could put to sea. Any boats in harbour that Saturday stayed there until Monday or Tuesday. There wasn't a single boat from elsewhere.'

'What did you do after that, over the following days?'

'We waited.'

'In case she came back ...'

'No,' she said, her hands trembling as she took another cigarette from the packet. 'I no longer believed she'd come back. Nor did Diego. He was just waiting for someone to come and tell us that ... you know.'

'Right,' mumbled Caldas. 'Why didn't you go back to the police? Why didn't you go directly to the police station?'

Irene shook her head. 'Diego couldn't face Somoza again. So I said I'd go to the police station, but he begged me not to. He was scared, and resigned to letting things take their course. He said there was no point in my going. Somoza was telling anyone looking into Rebeca's disappearance that he had reasonable grounds to believe that she'd run off with some man. Reasonable grounds. He hadn't lifted a finger and then he spoke of reasonable grounds to believe. Diego thought other policemen would treat him the same. He didn't think it was personal.'

'But you did?'

'Somoza is a pig, and always has been,' she said. 'Now you see an old man with a sour face, glasses and gaping mouth, but for years he believed his police badge gave him the right to trample over people. The worst of it is that most people let themselves be intimidated. But not Rebeca. She was a one! There was one time she really put him in his place. She stood up to him.'

'What happened?'

Irene drew on her cigarette before replying. 'Somoza was always leering at her. He wouldn't leave her alone. He thought that because she'd had a kid in her teens ...'

270

'Right.'

'Rebeca was young but she told him where to go. It was one summer during the village *fiesta*, in front of everyone. I'm sure he never forgave her,' she said. 'And in the time after her disappearance he got his own back. He humiliated Diego because his mother had once humiliated him.'

'When did the boy leave the village?'

'A few weeks later. At the beginning of the new year. He'd had enough of not hearing anything and enduring the village gossip. Everyone believed Rebeca had gone off with a man. They still do,' she said. 'One afternoon, Diego came and told me he was leaving. We both knew he'd never see his mother again even if he stayed in Aguiño. He left the next morning.'

'Do you know where he went?'

'To his grandparents' village. I don't remember the name. It was up north, near Ferrol. They went back there when they retired. Diego went to live with his grandmother. The grandfather had died not long before. Neda!' she said suddenly. 'That was the name of the village.'

'Does he still live there?' asked Caldas.

She took another drag.

'No. The grandmother died and he moved on.'

'Where to?'

'I don't know.'

'You didn't keep in touch?'

'At first we spoke often on the phone. He'd call to find out if there was any news. He said he dreamed about his mother and the fair-haired fisherman. He couldn't get the man's face out of his head. I felt so sorry for him. I'd tell him to forget about the man, it wasn't worth it, but he said he didn't want to forget, and he'd cry. I couldn't see his face but I knew he was crying. So was I. I felt terrible for not being able to do anything to comfort him. I just said I was thinking of him and that I loved him,' she whispered, staring down at the table. After a moment's silence, broken only by the screeching of seagulls in the harbour, she went on: 'He called less and less. First it was once a week, then once a month, until eventually he stopped.'

'When did you speak for the last time?'

'It must have been six or seven years ago. He called me on my saint's day, to congratulate me. He said his grandmother had died and he was leaving Neda.'

'Did he say where he was thinking of going?'

'I suggested he come back to Aguiño. I said their house was falling into ruins. But he didn't want anything to do with either the house or the village. He felt stifled here. He felt stifled just thinking about coming back. He said he'd go wherever he could find work.'

'What did he do?'

'I don't know. He didn't talk about his life. He just called to let me know he hadn't forgotten,' she said, stubbing out her cigarette. 'Poor Diego,' she murmured. 'Poor boy.'

'Have you got a picture of him?' asked the inspector.

'I've got some upstairs. From when he was a baby.'

'No later ones?' asked Caldas.

Irene looked at Caldas, then at Estevez, then back at Caldas.

'It's Diego you're interested in, isn't it?' she said. 'Has he got himself into some sort of trouble?'

'He may have done,' said Caldas, taking from his pocket the photograph of the crew of the *Xurelo*.

He placed it on the table beside the ashtray, which was now full of cigarette butts.

'This is the crew of a boat that sank near here, on rocks near Salvora,' he explained. 'They foundered the night Rebeca Neira disappeared. They may have put in at Aguiño, at least for a few hours.'

Irene placed a finger on the fair hair of Justo Castelo in the photograph. 'Is that him?'

'It could be,' replied the inspector.

Holding back her hair, the woman leaned over the photograph and peered at each of the faces.

'Which one went inside Rebeca's house?'

'It could have been any of the others.'

'Do you think she was on the boat, too?'

Caldas shrugged.

'Did they survive?'

'The three younger men did. They managed to swim ashore. But the skipper drowned.'

Irene looked at the photograph again and Caldas told her what had brought them to Aguiño. 'The fair-haired one was called Justo

Castelo. Last week his body washed up on the beach at Panxón. He'd been murdered. We're investigating his death.'

The woman looked up from the photograph. 'You think Diego had something to do with it?'

Caldas decided not to tell her that a few weeks earlier the word 'Murderers' had been daubed on Castelo's boat. Nor that the date of the sinking, of Rebeca Neira's disappearance, had been inscribed beneath it.

'I don't know,' he said. 'That's what we're trying to find out.'

A Packet of Cigarettes

'We've just come from the canteen at the fishermen's association,' said Caldas after giving his name. 'The waiter there said that the Aduana was the only bar in the harbour that was open in the evenings in 1996.'

'That's right,' replied the man, staring wistfully at the floor. 'I closed up in 1998, after thirty-five years. Now the canteen's the only place for fishermen to go. But it closes in the evening. And why not? Boats stopped going out fishing at night a long time ago.'

Caldas nodded and the man went on, 'Don't be fooled by the empty harbour – this place was one of Galicia's most important fishing ports once. They caught a lot of sardine, a lot of hake. A major port,' he said. 'Did you see the boat that's a bit bigger than the others?'

The policemen nodded, recalling the trawler half-glimpsed through the mist.

'It's the *Narija*,' said the man. 'There used to be dozens like it here. The market was overflowing with fish. Crates of hake coming out of the door. But then stocks started to go down. You think it'll never happen, but it does. Of course it does. The only boats left now go out for octopus,' he said contemptuously. 'At the market you can buy *percebes*, clams, roughy ... But hardly any fish – real fish, that is.'

'Of course,' said the inspector, encouraging him to continue. He was happy to let the old man talk, granting him the time that death would soon deny him.

'People came from all over,' said the former owner of the Bar Aduana and listed the towns that had supplied the Aguiño fleet with crew. He went on: 'We made a living from the harbour. Our children expect to make theirs from the beach.'

'Things change,' murmured Caldas.

'Some,' said the man. 'Not others.' Then he asked, 'Why are you here?'

'We want to know if you remember any of these men,' said Caldas, showing him the photograph. 'They were the crew of a boat from Panxón that used to come and fish in this area.'

The man peered at the picture. 'I remember the older one,' he said, placing his little finger on Antonio Sousa's woollen cap. 'Everyone referred to him as Captain Sousa. He sometimes moored in the harbour and came into the bar for water or a meal.' He looked up at the policemen. 'But I thought he was dead. Didn't his boat founder by the Asadoiros islets near Salvora?'

'That's right.'

The man looked at the photograph again. 'You know I saw him the night his boat went down?'

Caldas and Estevez exchanged glances.

'He came into the bar?'

'That very night,' he said, going on unprompted. 'There was a storm. The fleet was in harbour and the local fishermen were all at home, enjoying a night off with their families. I was about to head home myself. I'd already turned out all the lights when the skipper arrived. He asked if I could get him and his crew something to eat. The stove was off so I made them some sandwiches and left them water and wine on a table in the gallery. The Aduana had a glassed-in gallery at the front, so people could sit and look out at the sea even when the weather was bad.'

The policemen nodded.

'I went home. I'd locked up the bar itself but left the gallery open so they could eat in there, and the skipper went back to get the crew. The next time I saw him was in the papers. He drowned that night.'

He looked at the faces in the photograph. 'The boys survived, didn't they?'

'Yes, all three of them,' said Caldas.

'I don't know what they were thinking, putting out to sea. The skipper seemed like the cautious type.'

Caldas had his own ideas about why they'd set sail despite the storm.

'Do you remember a woman who was known as Rebeca the First?' he asked, putting away the photograph.

'Rebeca the First,' said the man quietly. 'Of course I remember her. She lived in a stone house about five minutes away. She left the village years ago.'

He fell silent, smiling as if at a pleasant memory.

'Rebeca the First,' he said again. 'What became of her?'

Caldas shrugged. 'Was she a customer of yours?'

'In a way,' replied the man, still smiling. 'We didn't get many pretty girls at the Aduana. They preferred a different kind of bar. Rebeca the First only ever came in for cigarettes.'

'She got her cigarettes at your bar?'

'Nearly always,' he said. 'She'd come in, put coins in the machine, bend down for the pack of cigarettes and leave, with us all staring after her.'

'At one stage, she went missing and the area was searched . . .' said Caldas, leaving his sentence hanging in the hope that the man would say more.

He did. 'Yes, I remember. For the first few days it caused quite a stir. Later we heard she'd run off with a man.'

'The night she disappeared she went out for cigarettes,' said Caldas, again encouraging him to continue.

'That's right. I was asked if she'd been into the Aduana. But the bar was closed that evening. There was a storm,' he said and fell silent, as if listening to the echo of his own words, looking Caldas straight in the eye.

So now you see it, too, the inspector said inwardly, and asked the man: 'Anything wrong?'

'No, nothing,' he said, signalling to Caldas that it was time to listen carefully. 'Would you mind showing me that photo again, Inspector?'

Caldas put it on the table and the man placed a finger on Justo Castelo's fair hair.

'I was asked if I'd seen a fisherman with very fair hair in the harbour that weekend.'

'Who asked you?'

'Irene, from the pharmacy,' he said, staring at the photo.

'No one else?'

'No,' he said. 'I told her I hadn't. I never saw the skipper's crew. Do you think Irene was referring to this lad?'

'Maybe.'

Outside Caldas lit a cigarette and put his hands in his pockets. Pale mist still lay over the village, shrouding it in damp.

Caldas and Estevez walked in silence, towards the church tower that loomed above the other buildings. As they passed the canteen of the fishermen's association, they heard laughter. By contrast, the seagulls had ceased their screeching and alighted mutely on the ground.

As they got back to the car, Estevez jerked his head towards Somoza's front door. The former deputy inspector was shuffling out in his slippers.

'Aren't we going to talk to him again?' asked Estevez.

Caldas watched Somoza, trying to picture him as the arrogant policeman who had humiliated Diego Neira. All he could see was a defeated, stooping old man with a short-sighted squint and gaping mouth. 'What for?' he replied. 'There's no point.'

At the quay, they glimpsed the *Narija* between houses. It was fading into the mist like the ghost of Captain Sousa that had brought them to Aguiño that morning.

The Man on the Billboard

At eleven thirty, as the last of the village houses receded behind them, Estevez asked, 'So, what do you think?'

'About what?'

'Do you think they murdered that woman, Rebeca Neira?'

'Don't you?' said Caldas.

'Please don't start!' muttered Estevez. 'I'm asking you.'

'Why else would they set sail in a storm? And, anyway, even if they didn't do it, her son's convinced they did.'

'You think it was him who killed Castelo?'

Caldas nodded.

'How did he track them down after all this time?' asked Estevez. 'Panxón is south, and Diego Neira went to live a long way north.'

'I don't know,' said Caldas, looking out of the window.

The sea was still hidden by a mantle of mist, but a strong smell of brine revealed its proximity.

Caldas took out his mobile phone and called Olga to get the number of the police station in Ferrol. When he got through there he asked for Quintans.

'Could you do me a favour?' he asked, once they'd exchanged greetings.

'Hit me,' said Quintans.

'I'm looking for a twenty-eight-year-old man who lived in Neda for a time from the start of 1997. His name's Diego Neira Diez,' said Caldas, looking at the missing persons report.

'Have you got a recent address?'

'All I know is that he lived at his grandparents' house in Neda at least until six or seven years ago. Then he moved away, but he may have come back. I need any information that might help me find him: where he lives, if he has a partner or friends, what he does for a living – anything.'

'I'll call you back tomorrow.'

'Don't make it any later than that,' said Caldas. 'It's urgent.'

'Don't worry, I won't,' said Quintans. Before hanging up, he asked, 'How are you doing?'

'Fine.'

'And Alba?'

'She's fine, too,' replied Caldas, his voice so steady it sounded sincere even to him.

Then he closed his eyes, but it wasn't Alba he saw behind his eyelids, it was a mother torn from her home one rainy night. As the Léo Ferré song Trabazo had quoted on the boat went, time makes you forget the face and voice of those who are no longer here. His thoughts travelled back to the harbour in Aguiño, the fishermen hastily setting sail so that no one could place them there that night, the *Xurelo* foundering on rocks, the men in their waterproofs calling out, terrified, in the storm.

'Who do you think went inside Rebeca Neira's house?' he asked.

'There are only two possible candidates,' replied Estevez.

'Three,' said Caldas.

'You think the skipper …'

'Why not?' replied the inspector. 'It must have been someone with authority over the others. If not, how do you explain them agreeing to set sail in those conditions?'

'That hadn't occurred to me,' admitted Estevez. 'Do you think they were all in on what happened to the woman?'

'I wouldn't be surprised. You saw how Arias and Valverde reacted when we mentioned Aguiño,' said Caldas. 'Let's see what they have to say now.'

A little later he made another call, this time to Clara Barcia's mobile. He asked about the footage from the security camera on the house in Monteferro.

'We were going to go through it this afternoon,' she said. 'Would you like us to do it sooner?'

Caldas glanced at his watch: it was a quarter to twelve.

'This afternoon's fine,' he said, and leaned back in his seat. He wanted to hum 'Solveig's Song', which Justo Castelo used to whistle in his mother's house. But though the academics at the Eligio had sung it to him, he couldn't remember the tune. He clicked his tongue and looked out of the window. On a billboard an advertisement for a fishing tackle shop showed a man proudly holding up a fish that dangled from a fishing line.

'I know how he tracked down El Rubio,' he said suddenly.

'How?' asked Estevez.

'It was around this time last year.'

'How do you know?'

'You went to Castelo's house?'

'Yes, with you.'

'Did you notice the photos in the sitting room?'

His snort conveyed that he hadn't.

'About a year ago, Justo Castelo caught a sunfish,' said Caldas. 'It's a big round tropical fish, as rare off the coast of Galicia as a great white shark. Several newspapers ran features about it, with a photo of Castelo holding up the fish. There was a framed copy in his living room. He was even interviewed on TV.'

'Bloody hell,' muttered Estevez, raising his eyebrows. 'Since last year ... Why has he waited until now?'

The inspector had a question of his own: 'How long since his mother went missing? Twelve, thirteen years?'

'About that.'

'I don't think he was in any hurry. The murder wasn't committed on an impulse. He was patient,' said Caldas, recalling the graffiti that had so disturbed Castelo a few weeks before his death. 'He planned it well.'

Caldas closed his eyes again.

He wondered how many tunes Diego Neira had stopped whistling.

An Empty Window

When the motorway forked, instead of turning off into Vigo, they drove on, up and around the city that spread out over the slopes, above the sea.

'What a great view,' said Estevez as they reached the top. Caldas opened his eyes.

The mist had retreated out to sea, revealing the mouth of the estuary and the Cíes Islands. An ocean liner was heading towards the port, to release its cargo of tourists equipped with their maps, raincoats and cameras on to the streets of Vigo.

Caldas caught sight of the green hospital building at the foot of Monte del Castro, and pictured Uncle Alberto counting the hours, happy to relinquish his room to another patient. When had his father said they were discharging him?

He gazed at the landscape – the gentle curve of the coast broken only by the tower block on the island of Toralla and the dark shape of the headland at Monteferro – before closing his eyes again.

The motorway ended a kilometre from Panxón, and they drove the rest of the way past empty holiday homes. The sky, like the sea, was grey.

They parked by the promenade and got out of the car. They were greeted by the same smell they had left behind in Aguiño. Caldas looked around.

The promenade was almost deserted. A group of elderly people was seated at a terrace table enjoying a rain-free morning. On the

281

beach, two women walked at the water's edge with their trousers rolled up and shoes in their hands. Near the slipway, the boy in the wheelchair was throwing a ball for his Labrador. Beyond it, on Playa America, waves broke with great jets of spray. On the Panxón side, by contrast, they seemed to caress the sand as they rolled in and, in the shelter of the harbour, the boats hardly swayed on the water.

Justo Castelo's traps were still stacked against the white wall of the jetty. At its tip, the same anglers held their fishing rods out over the water.

In the streets of the village, a woman was sluicing down the pavement outside her house, and a few people walked by, plastic bags in hand.

Caldas and Estevez made their way to the narrow street where José Arias lived. They rang his doorbell several times but there was no answer.

Glancing at his watch Caldas saw that it was ten past one – the fisherman would have been asleep for about four hours.

'Shall I open it?' said Estevez. 'I'll just give it another little nudge ...'

Caldas looked at the mark on the door caused by Estevez's last 'little nudge'. 'That won't be necessary,' he said, turning at the sound of footsteps behind him.

He recognised Alicia Castelo's fair hair and swallowed hard. She was wearing a black dress and her arms were crossed to protect herself against the cold. As she drew nearer, she looked up at Arias's neighbour's window. Caldas glanced up, too. The net curtains did not move.

'I saw you as you passed my house, Inspector,' she said. 'Could I speak to you for a moment?'

'Yes, of course.'

Taking out his cigarettes, Caldas said to his assistant, 'Keep ringing the bell.'

'No one's going to answer, Inspector,' said the drowned man's sister. 'He's not there.'

'Do you know where he is?'

'He's left.'

'Left?' said Caldas. 'The village?'

'Yes,' she said. 'On Saturday afternoon. A few hours after he spoke to you.'

'Damn,' muttered Caldas. He should have listened to Estevez and arrested Arias at the time, holding him in custody until they returned from Aguiño. It had been foolish to put him on his guard and leave him unwatched. He could be anywhere by now. He might even have gone back to Scotland. It was where he'd taken refuge after the sinking of the *Xurelo*, and he had a daughter there.

'José Arias has done nothing wrong,' murmured Alicia Castelo. 'That's what I wanted to speak to you about.'

'Hasn't he?'

'You remember the call made from Justo's house?'

'Yes, of course.'

Caldas glanced up at the neighbour's window again, to check they were not being overheard.

'It wasn't my brother who called him.'

Caldas understood immediately, unlike his assistant.

'Then who did?' asked Estevez.

Alicia glanced up again, then down at the ground.

'Me,' she whispered. 'I called José from my brother's house.'

'José,' Caldas repeated to himself. It was the first time he'd heard anyone refer to the hulking fisherman like that.

'It wasn't him. You've got it wrong. He hasn't spoken to Justo for years.'

'So why has he run away?' asked Caldas. He decided not to tell her that the nosy neighbour had seen her brother enter Arias's house the day before he died.

'To protect me,' she said. 'My husband is coming back from Namibia this week. José didn't want to put me in an awkward position, where I'd have to testify. I was with him the morning my brother was murdered,' she said glancing up again. 'It's a small village, as you've seen. My mother couldn't take it.'

'I understand.'

'But I don't care what people say,' she went on, trying to hold back the sobs. 'I already lost him once, a long time ago. I don't want to lose him again now.'

Caldas looked into her blue eyes. They had filled with tears as they had every time he'd seen her.

'Do you know where he is?' he asked, resisting the urge to put his arms around her.

'No,' she said, wiping her eyes. Her voice sounded like a lament from the sea. 'I don't know. I just hope it doesn't take him another twelve years to come back.'

The Song

Estevez waited at the bottom of the hill with the engine running while Caldas made his way up to the Templo Votivo del Mar to return the photographs of Sousa and the crew of the *Xurelo* to the priest. When he got back to the car, they set off for Marcos Valverde's house.

The large wooden gate was closed so Caldas climbed out and rang the bell. He gave his name and the gate slid aside revealing the house's concrete façade. The inspector walked into the courtyard and waited while Estevez parked beside the red car. The air smelled of freshly mown grass.

'Do you think he's got away, too?' asked Estevez, gesturing towards the space where Valverde's black sports car had been on Saturday morning.

'Let's hope not,' said Caldas, stepping off the gravel path to go and breathe in the fragrance of the verbena for a moment before continuing round the house to the front door.

In the sitting room two large logs were burning in the square cast-iron fireplace and a clarinet concerto was playing. On the other side of the room the table was set for two.

'My husband will be home any minute,' said Valverde's wife, going over to the sound system and turning the volume right down. She selected another disc from the shelves, inserted it into the CD player and invited them to sit on the sofa.

'May I ask why you're here?' she said, sitting in an armchair as angular as everything else in the room, except herself.

'We'd like to speak to your husband.'

'I'm a grown-up, Inspector,' she said, her eyes shining. 'What's going on?'

'You already know. We're investigating Justo Castelo's murder.'

'What's Marcos got to do with it?'

'He and Castelo used to work together—'

'Over ten years ago, Inspector,' she interrupted, her voice even. 'Since I've known Marcos he hasn't set foot in the harbour once. He has no interest in what goes on there. He has nothing to do with any of the fishermen.'

'We know.'

'So how is he connected with that man's death?'

Caldas sidestepped the question. 'It's our duty to check everything out.'

'You're trying to protect him, aren't you?'

'I'm sorry?'

'The other day you asked if I thought my husband had seemed worried lately, or if anyone had tried to scare him. That's it, isn't it? Is someone trying to hurt Marcos?'

'Has he seemed more anxious?' asked Caldas.

'Please don't be so Galician, Inspector. Can't you be more direct? He is my husband. Is there something I should be concerned about?'

'Have you asked him that question?'

'You don't know Marcos,' she sighed. 'I think he may be even worse than you.'

'Don't you believe it,' muttered Estevez. 'They're all the same.'

Valverde's wife was about to say something when they heard the sound of a car in the courtyard.

'That's him,' she said, rising to her feet. The two policemen stood as well.

'Have you still got my number?' asked Caldas.

'Yes,' she whispered.

'Please don't hesitate to call me,' he said, and she turned down the corners of her mouth in the beginnings of a smile.

She went to the sound system and turned up the music. Caldas didn't take his eyes off her.

'This is the song, Inspector,' she said, gesturing towards one of the speakers.

'The song?'

'"Solveig's Song",' she said, as if no explanation were needed. 'You asked about it the other day.'

Caldas nodded. Valverde's wife smiled, and he glimpsed Alba's smile briefly before it disappeared.

The inspector turned to look out of the huge window. While they waited for the former member of the *Xurelo*'s crew, he watched the waves with their crests of foam, looking like lambs on the water.

Justo Castelo's sister was right. 'Solveig's Song' did sound like a Galician tune.

A Conjuror

'What are you doing here? Why have you come back to my home?' hissed Valverde. A dark tie and the lapels of a grey suit were just visible beneath the property developer's open overcoat. 'My wife was worried enough by your visit the other day.'

'We need to speak to you.'

Valverde glanced around the empty sitting room.

'I told you everything I remembered on Saturday.'

'I don't believe you,' retorted Caldas. 'Are you going to tell us what happened in Aguiño?'

'I told you, I don't remember.'

'You're lying. No one forgets a night like that, no matter how long ago it was.'

'Maybe I've got a poor memory,' said Valverde quietly.

Estevez came up behind the inspector and whispered in his ear, 'I know a cure for that.'

Caldas tutted disapprovingly. Estevez was quite capable of shoving Valverde's head into the fireplace to jog his memory.

He said to Valverde, 'Would you mind if I tell you a story?'

'My wife has supper waiting,' said the developer, gesturing towards the dining table.

'It won't take five minutes.'

Valverde hesitated. He glanced at the closed door through which his wife had departed and motioned to the policemen to follow him back out to the garden. He headed away from the house along the

288

gravel path, stopping once they were far enough away not to be over-heard from the house.

'So what's this story you want to tell me?' he asked, turning towards the policemen.

Caldas took out his cigarettes and pulled one from the packet. He lit it and drew on it a couple of times before speaking.

'It's about a fishing boat. The skipper was a veteran and he had a crew of three younger men, all friends. One wet, windy evening, when they were quite a distance from their home port, they heard a forecast of worsening weather,' he began, and Valverde averted his gaze towards a corner of the garden. 'Despite the warning, they continued fishing until they were forced to shelter in a nearby port. It was late. The harbour was deserted. From the boat they saw the lights go out in the only bar that was open in the evening. The skipper knew the owner and thought he could get him to give them something to eat before closing. The owner not only agreed to serve them wine and sandwiches but when he went home he left the gallery at the entrance open so they could sit inside.'

Caldas drew on his cigarette. Valverde was rubbing his hands on his legs. He took the pause as an invitation to confirm the account and was about to speak when the inspector continued:

'At around eleven, as the four men sat chatting in the gallery, a young woman came in. She'd come to buy cigarettes,' said Caldas, holding up his own cigarette. 'No ordinary girl, but a real head-turner. Are you following me?'

Valverde nodded, his mouth half-open like a small boy watching a conjuror. Caldas went on.

'She couldn't get cigarettes because the bar was closed, so the fish-ermen offered her some of theirs. She was friendly as well as pretty. She sat down for a drink but after a while she said she had to get home. The weather was terrible and two of the men offered to walk her back. She didn't refuse. She was enjoying their company and was happy to prolong the encounter a little while longer. But the men weren't content to leave her at her front door. They wanted to come inside, the girl said no. She claimed that if things had been different she'd have let them in but that she couldn't that night because her son would still be up. The fishermen insisted – they didn't believe she had a son, they thought she was just making excuses. But, still friendly, she stood her ground,' said the inspector, raising his cigarette to his lips. 'They were about to give up when the front door opened. In the darkness, the fishermen caught a glimpse of her son. He was a teenager, and they couldn't believe she had a son that age. He mumbled something about spending the night at a friend's and rushed off.'

Caldas exchanged a look with Estevez. He swallowed as his mouth was dry from talking and smoking. Valverde shoved his hands into his coat pockets but still couldn't stop fidgeting.

'One of the fishermen decided to return to the boat but, now that the son was out of the way, the other one persuaded the woman to let him in. Once inside, he was determined to overcome every obstacle she put in his way. But then something went wrong. He went too far. He had to clean up the house and dispose of the woman's body. He went back to the boat and tried to convince the other three that they had to set sail before morning. His powers of persuasion worked once more. They put out to sea in the early hours but they didn't get far. The storm was too severe. They were driven towards shallows and the boat started to take on water. In under a minute, the *Xurelo* had gone down.'

The developer raised a hand to his forehead, covering his eyes.

'The three younger men managed to swim ashore in their life jackets, but the skipper drowned trying to save the boat. Weeks later, his decomposing body was found in the nets of a trawler miles away. The woman was never seen again. Maybe she disappeared out at sea like the skipper.'

Caldas paused to draw on his cigarette again, watching Valverde, who was still shielding his eyes with his hand.

'The three fishermen returned to their village, but their friendship, like the boat, had foundered in the shallows. They broke off all contact and never spoke of what happened that night. They hoped that it would all disappear in the mists of time,' he continued. 'But then, years later, when they thought everything had been forgotten, graffiti appeared on the boat of one of the men who had walked the woman home. "Murderers", it read, together with the date of the sinking and of the woman's disappearance. The people of the village attributed it to the ghost of the drowned skipper. They had never understood why the crew had put out to sea in a storm, and had always suspected that something murky lay behind the sinking of the *Xurelo*. The three fishermen, however, feared something else. They were scared, bewildered at having been found. They wondered how they'd been tracked down after all that time.'

Caldas finished his cigarette and bent to stub it out on the ground.

'One morning, weeks later, the body of the fisherman who was threatened washed up on the shore,' he said, pointing towards the sea.

Valverde took his hand away from his eyes, then touched it to his tie knot before thrusting it into his coat pocket again. 'Who told you all this?'

'The man who returned to the boat was Justo Castelo,' said Caldas, ignoring Valverde's question. 'Which of the others went inside the woman's house?'

'It wasn't me,' said Valverde.

'That's not what I asked.'

Valverde glanced at Estevez and then said, 'I don't know. I don't know who went in.'

'You were there. You must know,' said the inspector.

'It was a long time ago.'

'We just need a name.'

'I can't give you a name, Inspector.'

'Was it you?' asked Caldas, looking Valverde straight in the eye.

'No.'

'Then tell me who was with the woman,' he pressed. 'Or was it more than one of you?'

'No.'

'Was it Arias?'

'I don't remember,' said Valverde, covering his eyes again.

'Have you been threatened?'

'No, I haven't,' he said, his voice barely audible.

He was cornered. Caldas tried to offer him a way out. 'Did you know that José Arias has left the village?'

'When?'

'On Saturday,' replied Caldas. 'Did you know?'

'No,' said Valverde. 'I haven't spoken to him for years.'

'Since that night?'

'Since the days that followed.'

'Was it him?'

'I don't remember,' he said yet again, and his reply never changed after that. He continued to claim that he couldn't remember until the policemen left.

Shuffling, eyes fixed on the dead leaves on the path, Valverde saw them back to their car. He leaned on his black sports car as Estevez manoeuvred out of the courtyard.

Caldas lowered the window and made one last try. 'You still don't remember who went inside the house?'

Valverde shook his head.

'If you do happen to remember, give me a call.'

'I will,' he said, but his tone suggested the opposite.

'Why are you afraid?' asked the inspector.

'Haven't I got reason to be?'

'Not if you have a clear conscience,' said Caldas. But he wasn't sure he was right.

As they drove up the hill back to the main road, Estevez complained, 'Why don't you ever let me have a go?'

'How would you get him to talk?'

'I don't know,' said Estevez, scratching his chin. 'String him up by that tie of his, maybe?'

Caldas's eyes widened. 'You're not serious?'

'No,' smiled Estevez.

The Hunt

'Shall we get something to eat?' Estevez asked, getting out of the car 'It's almost three.'

'You go,' said Caldas, though his stomach had been rumbling on the journey back from Panxón. 'I need to speak to the superintendent.'

He made his way through the police station and opened the glass door to his office. He was relieved to see that there were no Post-it notes with urgent messages stuck to his desk. He hung up his raincoat and left the room.

Superintendent Soto was on the phone but gestured for him to enter. The inspector sat down opposite him.

When the superintendent hung up, Caldas felt like asking how he managed to keep his desk so clear when Caldas's own was a vast array of papers. Instead he said, 'We know who killed the fisherman in Panxón.'

'A neighbour?' asked the superintendent.

'No,' Caldas replied, and went on to summarise the new developments in the case.

When he'd finished, he explained what had brought him to the superintendent's office. 'I'd like there to be an investigation into the disappearance of Rebeca Neira, Superintendent.'

'Aguiño is outside our jurisdiction.'

'Couldn't you have a word with Headquarters?' asked Caldas. 'That boy isn't a simple executioner. He ended up alone at fifteen. He came to us and, instead of helping him, we destroyed him.'

Soto sighed. 'Would you mind explaining the whole thing again? But slowly this time,' he said. 'Let me see if I can understand.'

'Where do you want me to start?'

'At the beginning.'

'The business in Aguiño?'

'Yes, and the business in Panxón, Leo. From the beginning,' said the superintendent.

Caldas explained how Castelo's body had been found. He described the blows to his head and the green cable tie binding his wrists.

'Sounds like suicide,' said the superintendent.

'That's what everyone in the village believes. The man was a depressive and former drug addict. But the cable tie was fastened round by his little fingers. According to the pathologist, he couldn't have done it himself.'

Soto nodded, and the inspector went on to say that, though fishing was prohibited on a Sunday, Castelo had put out to sea at six thirty that morning.

'Was he alone?' interrupted Superintendent Soto.

'Yes,' replied Caldas. 'We have a witness who saw him set sail. The deck was empty. There was nowhere for anyone to hide.'

'So how did they get to him?'

'From another vessel,' said Caldas, and he described the spot where the dead man's boat had been found a few days later, by the lighthouse at Punta Lameda, on the other side of Monteferro.

Caldas explained that a boat couldn't be towed to the rock pool there, meaning that at least two people had to have been involved in the murder.

'One of them must have remained on his own boat while the other one took Castelo's boat to Punta Lameda.'

'Why didn't they sink the boat out at sea?' asked the superintendent, just as Caldas had.

'Because they needed to land without being seen,' said Caldas. 'The pool is like a natural harbour. It's a spot illegal fishermen use to land their catches.'

'I see.'

The inspector described the graffiti that the fisherman had removed from his boat. He explained that the date daubed on the hull was the date of the sinking of the *Xurelo*, and he told Soto about Arias and Valverde, the crewmates Castelo had fallen out with, and Captain Sousa, the skipper drowned when the boat foundered, whose ghost several village fishermen claimed to have seen in the mist on board his fishing boat.

'Wasn't he your suspect?' asked the superintendent with a smile.

'He was,' said Caldas, and described the *macana*, the club the skipper wore on his belt, whose shape corresponded to the mark on the dead man's head.

'He was struck with the skipper's club?'

'No,' said Caldas. 'We found a spanner in among the rocks at Monteferro. The kind used on wheel nuts. It's with the pathologist. He thinks it may have been that.'

Then he told the superintendent about Rebeca Neira again, about the article in the newspaper that had aroused his suspicions, and the missing persons report filed by Diego, the woman's teenage son. He showed him the place in the report where the boy stated that he'd seen two men with his mother, one of them with very fair hair.

'And you say you went there?' asked Superintendent Soto.

'This morning,' said Caldas. 'As I said, the woman never turned up. Her closest friend is convinced that she was murdered that night. When the son got home the next morning he found the house spick and span, and, though he noticed that things had been slightly rearranged, he didn't pay much attention. The following day, when his mother's friend was at the house, he was alarmed when he found grounds in a coffee pot, which had only been cleaned on the outside. His mother was very fussy and would never have left it like that. Then he realised that everything that had been on the table and worktop had disappeared.'

Superintendent Soto looked through the report.

'None of that information is in here,' he said. So Caldas told him about Deputy Inspector Somoza, of his humiliation of Diego Neira in the days following his mother's disappearance, of the boy's dejected departure from the village and his phone calls to the pharmacist assuring her that he hadn't forgotten the fair-haired fisherman.

'There was no investigation?'

'No, none,' replied Caldas. 'Searches were conducted in the area, but then it was all forgotten. The son left the village and everyone assumed he'd gone to join his mother.'

Now Caldas told him about the Bar Aduana:

'The missing woman often bought cigarettes there,' he said. 'The bar closed years ago but the owner still remembers that night.'

Soto listened carefully as the inspector recounted how the owner had left the gallery open so that the fishermen could eat out of the rain.

'He didn't see the crew,' said Caldas. 'But he recognised the captain. The man still can't understand what possessed them to set sail in such a terrible storm.'

'They didn't want anyone to place them in Aguiño in the morning,' said the superintendent.

'Exactly.'

'Do you think they were all in on what happened to the woman?'

'Maybe.'

'And that policeman? What was his name?'

'Somoza,' said Caldas. 'He had a score to settle with Rebeca Neira and didn't do a thing to try to find her or shed light on her disappearance. He didn't even go and interview the bar owner.'

'What about the neighbours?'

'They assumed she'd gone off with someone of her own free will.'

Raising his eyebrows, Soto handed back the report. 'Have you tracked down the son?'

'Not yet. All we know is that until six or seven years ago he was living in Neda, near Ferrol. That's it.'

'Have you contacted the police station there?'

'Yes, I had a word with Inspector Quintans,' said Caldas. 'He agreed to get back to me this afternoon or tomorrow.'

Soto nodded. 'You talked about two people in the boat. Do you know who his accomplice was?'

'Not yet. But we've got footage from a security camera on a house near the turning that leads to the lighthouse,' continued Caldas. 'Barcia should be going through it right now.'

After a silence, the superintendent asked, 'How the hell did he find them?'

'The news,' said Caldas. 'Justo Castelo caught a rare tropical fish. It was all over the news. He was even interviewed on TV.'

'When was that?'

'Last year. He had all the time he needed to check out the area and make his move. Diego Neira must be about twenty-eight or -nine by now. Do you know how many men that age there are on the beach in summer? He could have watched El Rubio for weeks without arousing any suspicion, waiting to be led to his mother's killer.'

'Do you think he'll go after the others?'

'I don't know. Anyway, only one of the two fishermen is still in the village.'

'Who?'

'Valverde.'

'Have you questioned him?'

'Yes, but he's scared. He won't say a thing.'

'What about the other one?'

'Arias? He's vanished. I'm afraid it was my fault,' said Caldas. 'On Saturday morning we went to Panxón and asked him if they'd put in to port in Aguiño the night of the wreck. He was evasive and claimed not to be able to remember exactly what happened, but a few hours later he disappeared.'

'Is he the one who lived in Scotland?'

'That's him,' said Caldas. 'He claimed that he and Castelo hadn't spoken since they stopped working together on the boat, but a neighbour saw Castelo go into his house on Saturday afternoon, the day before he was murdered, and he seemed pretty jumpy.'

'Maybe he was afraid of something.'

'Maybe,' said Caldas with a shrug. 'We only know about that one lot of graffiti, but there must have been more. I think the boy spent months tormenting them before he acted.'

'Well, all his games have got him into quite a bit of trouble.'

'Yes.'

Rubbing his eyes, the superintendent asked, 'Do you think that man, Arias, has gone back to Scotland?'

'It's possible. He lived there, he knows the place.'

'Have you checked flights?'

'Not yet,' said Caldas.

'Do you think he killed the woman?'

'I think this is the second time he's disappeared.'

Soto nodded. 'The son will go after him.'

'I expect so,' said the inspector, adding quietly: 'I would.'

'Just in case, keep an eye on the developer.'

Caldas said he would.

He was getting to his feet when Soto asked, 'Why did he kill him like that?'

'Like what?'

The superintendent put his wrists together. 'Throwing him into the sea with his hands tied, as if it were suicide.'

'I don't know,' said Caldas, standing. 'Will you have a word with the judge about the woman's disappearance?'

'I will,' said Soto, 'but first find the son.'

Patrolling the Waves

Caldas looked at his watch and cursed under his breath. He went to his office to get his raincoat and headed out with the black notebook under his arm. At the entrance to the building he bumped into Estevez.

'Where are you off to?'

'The radio station,' replied Caldas, showing him the notebook. 'It's Monday.'

'Have you had lunch?'

'No.'

He turned into the Calle Castelar, lighting a cigarette to take the edge off his hunger, and crossed the Alameda, dodging the children running about under the watchful eyes of their mothers. By the statue of Mendez Nuñez, a couple of white-haired tourists were peering at a map of the city. Caldas assumed they'd come from the liner he and Estevez had seen sailing into the estuary that morning.

By the stone fountain, a puppy was chasing pigeons, which flew up into the air repeatedly to get out of its way. The puppy's owner was holding a plastic bag scrunched up in his hand and Caldas smiled at the thought of his father crouching to scoop the large brown dog's excrement into a similar little bag.

He took two quick drags on his cigarette before stubbing it out and going inside the modernist building. After greeting the doorman, he took the stairs to the first floor, made his way down the radio station corridor and looked in at the control-room door to say hello to the technician and Rebeca.

Through the glass he saw the fool Losada sitting at the microphone.

He pushed open the heavy studio door and slipped inside. The theme tune was already playing.

'You're late,' muttered Losada.

The inspector did not reply. He sat down by the window, switched off his mobile phone and set it on the desk beside the black notebook. Looking at Rebeca, Losada's producer, in the control room, he wondered what the other Rebeca had been like, the one who had been missing since that night in 1996. Then he looked out at the people walking along the Alameda.

The presenter signalled to the technician and opened the programme intoning the usual string of nonsense with false gravitas: '... scourge of hooligans, implacable defender of upright citizens, fearsome guardian of our streets, Inspector Leo Caldas. Good afternoon, Inspector.'

'Hello.'

He didn't put on his headphones until Rebeca held up a sign with the name of the first caller.

'Welcome to *Patrolling the Waves*, Laura,' said Losada, as if receiving her at court.

The woman explained that she'd been penalised for driving without wearing a seat belt.

'I've been fined for not being tied into my seat,' she complained, 'but in buses people are standing up, packed in, some even carrying small children. It's just a money-making scheme – fines, tickets ...'

Many listeners rang in to report crimes. Others, like this woman, simply wanted to get something off their chest. All Caldas could do was offer them a sympathetic ear.

'Right,' he murmured.

Instead of ending the call and moving on, the presenter leaned in to the microphone and said in his pompous voice, 'Laura, let's hear the patrolman's response.'

The inspector spread his arms in exasperation, looking at Losada in disbelief. Response? What was the idiot on about? Did he think Caldas could change the traffic laws?

But Losada just carried on, raising a hand to signal for the Gershwin tune.

Caldas told him to switch off the microphones, and when the red light went out he demanded an explanation.

'Just say anything,' replied Losada.

'And I thought I asked you not to play that music any more. I find it too distracting.'

'I'm not going to get rid of it just because of that,' said Losada superciliously.

'What do you mean, "just because of that"?'

The red light came on again as Losada took his finger off the button.

'Well, Inspector?' he said, lowering his hand so that 'Promenade' faded out. 'What do you have to say to our caller?'

Caldas resorted to the first bromide that came to mind. 'The law isn't perfect but it's what we've got. I'll have a word with the City Police anyway and pass on your comment.' Then he wrote in his notebook: *City Police one, Leo nil.*

The next caller was the chairman of a residents' association in the district of Teis. Seagulls were nesting on the roof of their building and they attacked anyone who tried to remove them.

City Police two, Leo nil.

Then came a couple of complaints about noise at night, three about traffic, and one man called in angry about the paint on zebra crossings becoming slippery in the rain.

'How many days a year does it rain here in Vigo?' he asked. 'A hundred and twenty? Wouldn't it make sense to use non-slip paint?'

As before, the damned tune started playing before Caldas had a chance to respond.

He couldn't be bothered to complain to Losada again. He gave in. With the sound of the clarinet and piano in his headphones, he turned to the window. A girl was crossing the Alameda, feet splayed and pregnant belly showing beneath her clothes. Caldas calculated that Rebeca Neira must have been even younger when she became pregnant. Still a child herself, she'd had to be both mother and father to the newborn. Too difficult. Caldas sighed, imagining how scared

Diego must have felt, how upset when he saw Somoza do nothing and the law appear to mock him. He couldn't blame him for taking action.

'Well?' said Losada in his affected voice, staring straight at Caldas. 'Huh?'

'Zebra crossings ... slippery paint ...'

'Oh, right,' said the inspector. 'I'll pass on the complaint to the City Police.'

City Police nine, Leo nil.

During the ad break that followed the call, Losada berated Caldas. 'Could you please pay a bit more attention?'

'I've told you, that tune puts me off,' Caldas mumbled. But he wasn't thinking about the music any more. Or the gardens outside the window. The only thing on his mind was Diego Neira, Rebeca Neira's disappearance and Justo Castelo's death.

He thought of Superintendent Soto's words: 'Why did he tie his hands?' he'd asked. The inspector had not been able to come up with an answer.

The eleventh caller was a woman on the verge of tears. She'd lost her dog during their morning walk and was offering a generous reward to anyone who found it. Then a man called in about the unpleasant smells coming from a restaurant that had just opened next door.

'Good afternoon, Eva,' Losada said to the next caller with feigned warmth.

'I'm calling because my son and his friends are being bullied by a group of boys in the park.'

'How old is your son?' asked Caldas.

'Eleven.'

'And the other boys?'

'I don't know,' said Eva. 'My son and his friends won't say who they are.'

'That's understandable.'

'I know it's only kids' stuff – I mean, they've just had a bit of a scare and a few coins stolen – but they won't go to the park any more and I'm worried it's going to get worse. Do you think we should get our son to report them to the police, Inspector?' the woman asked and, on Losada's signal, the music started.

While he waited for the Gershwin to end, Caldas's thoughts returned to Panxón and El Rubio's final hours. He thought of the superintendent's question, and reflected that the fisherman must have been as scared as the caller's son. What if Diego Neira had tied his hands to force him to reveal who'd gone inside the house with his mother? The day of the autopsy, Guzman Barrio had said that the blow to the head might have happened by chance. It seemed unlikely but the pathologist never ruled anything out. What if he was right? What if El Rubio had banged his head on some part of the boat while trying to get away? Maybe the spanner hadn't played a part at all.

The music was still playing and thoughts were still swirling in the inspector's head. Diego Neira had to get Justo Castelo to say who had gone into the house. Could it be that he hadn't intended to drown the fisherman? That he'd only wanted to scare him, to make him reveal the murderer's name? Why not? Caldas reflected.

The graffiti proved that Diego Neira had been near the fishermen on other occasions. He could have spent months going to Panxón without arousing suspicion. If he'd wanted to kill them he could simply have shot them and gone home. Nobody would have made a connection between him and the crew of the *Xurelo*.

The thought that Diego Neira might be innocent made him feel better. Maybe the fisherman had jumped overboard out of fear. Maybe, when he'd jumped, he'd been tied to a buoy or a float that had later disappeared beneath the waves.

Caldas looked at his watch, longing for the show to end so that he could go and see the pathologist again.

Losada pressed the button turning off the red light and microphones.

'What the hell are you doing, Leo?' he asked.

'Huh?' said Caldas. Then he smiled. He was whistling the tune.

Resistance

As he descended the stairs at the radio station he felt convinced that the graffiti and cable tie had had the same aim: to scare El Rubio and force him to reveal the name of his crewmate.

By the time he reached the lobby, he was determined to find Diego Neira and stop him blighting his life even further in his desire for revenge. There would be time later to find his mother's killer.

Out in the street, he phoned the pathologist.

'Could the fisherman have hit his head jumping from the boat?' he asked without even saying hello.

'Jumping?'

'Throwing himself into the water. Maybe he struck a handrail or something else on the boat.'

'What do you mean "throwing himself from the boat", Leo? His hands were tied.'

'Even so,' said Caldas. 'I think he may have jumped.'

'To commit suicide?'

'To escape.'

'From whom?'

'It's a bit of a long story, Guzman,' said Caldas. 'Is it possible?'

'Is what possible?'

'The blow to the head,' he said. 'Could he have hit his head on some part of the boat?'

'No,' replied the pathologist firmly.

'No?'

'No, Leo. He was hit with the spanner you brought in the other day.'

'Are you sure?'

'Absolutely. I compared it to the marks on the corpse and there's no doubt. It's what he was hit with.'

It didn't change things all that much. Maybe Neira had struck the fisherman with the spanner to subdue him, so he could tie him up without a struggle.

'The spanner's from a large car,' added Barrio. 'A 4x4. They have bigger wheel nuts than ordinary cars.'

'Right.'

After a silence, the pathologist asked, 'Have you spoken to Barcia? She called you a little while ago.'

Caldas had seen he'd missed two calls, but hadn't had time to check who they were from. 'No,' he said. 'I've only just come off air. Do you know if she's looked at the security camera video?'

'That's why she wanted to speak to you.'

'Has she found something?'

The pathologist replied with a question. 'Can you drop by here?'

Caldas checked his two missed calls, in case Inspector Quintans had left a message that would help him track down Diego Neira, but both were from Barcia.

He crossed the Alameda and walked back to the police station along the Calle Luis Taboada. Instead of heading for his office, he went straight to see Estevez.

'Coming?'

Estevez rose to his feet. 'Where to?'

'To Forensics. They've got the footage from the house in Monteferro.'

'Anything there?'

'Seems like it.'

They got into the car and the inspector opened the window slightly before closing his eyes.

'Diego Neira may not have killed El Rubio,' he said, eyes still closed.

'What?'

'He tied him up to get him to talk, but he didn't throw him into the sea.'

'So who did?'

'Castelo himself.'

'You think he committed suicide?'

'I think that when he found out who the boy was, he thought he'd rather jump than stay on the boat.'

'Because of what Neira might do to him?'

'Or because of what might happen if he talked.'

They were heading up the Calle Colon when Estevez asked, 'Is that what really happened, or what you'd like to have happened?'

'Can't it be both?'

Night Vision

'It's not exactly a tape,' explained Barcia as she switched on a monitor on the wall. 'It's a bit more sophisticated than that: the camera's got a motion sensor and night vision. It stores everything it records on a hard drive.'

Caldas and Estevez listened, sitting at the desk.

'So it only records when something moves?'

'That's right,' said Barcia, then she pointed at the lower right-hand corner of the screen. 'It shows the date and time of recording here.'

The policemen nodded.

'For instance, this is from 3.05, a few hours before Justo Castelo put out to sea.'

Suddenly a black-and-white image of a house and garden appeared on screen. In the foreground there were some bushes and a path leading to the front gate. The wall on either side of the gate was so high that almost nothing beyond it was visible. But above the gate they could see a section of the road leading to Monteferro and the pavement on the other side. That was where the dog that had triggered the recording was walking.

'It's really clear,' said Estevez.

Caldas was also impressed with the quality of the picture.

'You can play around with the picture. See?' said Barcia, zooming in on the dog.

The animal became more distorted as its image grew on the screen. Once it moved out of camera range, the screen went black again.

'The next recording is from 5.40.'

The fixed shot of the garden reappeared and a light-coloured car drove past, crossing the screen from left to right.

Barcia wound back the recording and paused it when the car was level with the front gate. They could see the driver.

'It's not the man we're looking for,' said the inspector. 'Castelo didn't set sail from Panxón until six thirty. And, anyway, this car's heading towards the lighthouse and we're interested in what's going the other way.'

The door of the viewing room opened suddenly.

'Have you shown it to them?' asked Guzman Barrio, sitting down beside the policemen.

'We've only just started,' said Barcia.

The pathologist glanced at the paused image of the car on screen. 'That's the first one, isn't it?' he said, and Barcia nodded.

'The first one?' said Caldas.

'Wait and see.'

'So, as I was saying, this was taken at 5.40,' said Barcia. 'The next one is from 6.05.'

Again, the fixed shot of the garden. This time it wasn't a car that passed but the head of someone walking along the pavement closest to the house, wearing a light-coloured hood. Barcia forwarded and reversed the footage in slow motion.

'This guy's definitely coming from the lighthouse,' said Estevez.

'It's still too early,' the inspector pointed out.

'Be patient,' the pathologist said with a smile.

'The next shot is at 7.03,' said Barcia. Estevez turned round in his chair, alert. Caldas didn't move.

But this was still too early. Ernesto Hermida's wife had maintained that El Rubio had left port only half an hour earlier. You could get from Panxón to the lighthouse by boat in fifteen minutes but, if Caldas was right, Neira would have had to knock out El Rubio and wait for him to come round before trying to get him to confess. And, anyway, it would have taken him some time at the rock pool to make a hole in the hull and collect rocks to weight the boat. You couldn't do all of that in half an hour.

'Pay attention now,' Dr Barrio murmured.

A car drove past the gate of the house, a light-coloured 4x4 in the lane furthest from the entrance. The passenger seat was empty, and the driver's face was obscured by the roof of the vehicle.

'Did you notice?' asked the pathologist.

'I noticed that seven is too early if the fisherman was still alive at six thirty,' said Caldas.

'Well, that's all there is,' said Barcia.

'There must be something.'

'No, nothing,' she said. 'The next bit of footage is at 11.08. A family driving past towards the mountain. They come back soon afterwards. Do you want to see it?'

Eleven was too late. The tide would have made it impossible to get into the pool at that hour.

'There's no car heading towards the lighthouse with one person in it and returning with two?' asked Caldas. 'Or anyone heading back from the lighthouse around seven thirty or eight?'

'You've seen all there is, Inspector.'

'But didn't you notice?' insisted Barrio.

'Didn't I notice what?'

'You explain,' said the pathologist. Barcia zoomed in on the image of the car driver, but it became distorted. She zoomed out gradually and paused it when she thought it sharp enough.

'Look at the anorak of the 7.03 driver,' she said, placing a finger on the screen. 'The sleeve's got two dark stripes down it.' Then she rewound the recording. 'This is the car that went past at 5.40,' she said, again zooming in on the driver. 'See the same stripes on the sleeve?'

'Yes,' said Caldas and Estevez together.

'Now look at the driver's head.'

When the head filled the screen, Estevez asked, 'What's he wearing – a hat?'

'A hood.'

'In the car?'

Barcia nodded. 'And there are two dark stripes around the edge.'

'It's the same guy,' said Estevez. 'He drove to the mountain and back again. There's nothing odd about that.'

'Let's see if you find this odd,' said the pathologist, as Barcia fast-forwarded the recording and paused it at the person who walked past the house.

She didn't need to zoom in – the stripes on the hood were clearly visible.

'Is it the same man again?'

'Strange, isn't it?'

'Let's see if I can get this clear,' said Caldas. 'A car goes past at 5.40 and the driver returns from the mountain on foot. At what time?'

'At 6.05.'

Twenty-five minutes was enough time to park the car at the light-house and walk back.

'Then, an hour later, he goes past again in the car. Is that right?'

'That's it: at 7.03.'

'But he didn't walk back to his car . . .'

'Maybe he went cross-country. Otherwise the camera would have caught it.'

Caldas stared at the picture on the screen, seeking an explanation.

'Sure it's the same car?' asked Estevez.

'Certain,' said Barcia, rewinding the recording and stopping it at the car heading towards the mountain. 'Look at the aerial. It's bent. And the paintwork is scratched at the back there.'

Then she wound forward, and Caldas saw that the car driving back also had a bent aerial and scratched paint. There could be no doubt: it was the same car.

'And remember the spanner, Leo,' said the pathologist. 'It's from a big car like this one.'

Caldas did not reply. He was resting his elbows on the desk, cupping his face in his hands. He clicked his tongue.

'What's up, Inspector?' asked Estevez.

'Nothing,' he said, then added: 'He's fooled me. He's fooled us all.'

The Tangle

'Clara, I need you to do me a couple of favours,' said Caldas. 'First, get hold of the telephone number of a man from Panxón called Ernesto Hermida, and a bar in the village called the Refugio del Pescador.'

'And the second favour?'

'Let me see the report on the recovery of Justo Castelo's body.'

She found him the report first.

'Thanks, Clara,' said Caldas, starting to leaf through it. When he found what he was looking for, he sighed and leaned back, fingers laced behind his head. He had the feeling that a huge wave had, at last, set the investigation moving, dragging it towards its final destination. Unfortunately that wasn't where he'd expected it to end up.

'Are you going to tell us what's going on?' asked Estevez impatiently.

'Yes,' said Caldas, looking at the frozen image of the 4x4 driver on the screen.

He rummaged in his pocket for his cigarettes and turned towards the pathologist. 'Mind if I smoke? I'll open the window.'

Dr Barrio shrugged. 'Go ahead – no need to open it. My patients won't complain.'

Caldas smiled and held the lighter flame up to a cigarette.

A moment later, Barcia returned with the telephone numbers jotted down on a Post-it note like the ones Olga left all over his desk.

Caldas picked up the phone. The cable was all tangled up. 'Could you put it on speaker phone?' he asked Barcia before dialling.

A woman's voice answered.

'Hello?'

'Is that the home of Ernesto Hermida?'

'Who's calling?'

'It's Inspector Caldas of Vigo Police. Do you remember me?'

'From *Patrolling the Waves*?' asked the fisherman's wife.

Dr Barrio, Barcia and Estevez smiled as the inspector confirmed that it was indeed him.

'My husband's out at the moment, setting the traps.'

'That's fine. It's actually you I wanted to speak to.'

'To me?'

'It's about Justo Castelo. Do you remember telling me you saw him from your window, rowing out to his boat?'

'The day he died?'

'Do you remember?'

'More or less.'

'Can you tell me what he was wearing?'

'What they all wear.'

'And what's that?'

'Waterproofs.'

'Do you remember what colour El Rubio's were?'

'Yellow, maybe?'

Caldas was sure that was the colour.

'You don't by any chance remember if he had his hood on?'

'Of course he did,' the old woman replied without hesitation. 'He was well wrapped up. It was pouring.'

'What the hell is going on, Inspector?' asked Estevez when Caldas hung up.

The inspector slid the report towards him across the desk, open at the page with the description of Castelo's clothing.

'Read this,' he said. 'Justo Castelo wasn't wearing yellow waterproofs when his body was found. They were navy blue.'

'That's right,' said Barcia. 'Very lightweight ones.'

Caldas took a couple of drags of his cigarette before dialling the number of the Refugio del Pescador. Over the loudspeaker, the waiter's voice rose above the din of the television and customers.

'Hello, it's Inspector Caldas. We spoke last week.'

312

'Good afternoon, Inspector.'

'I wanted to check something with you. Do you remember the last time you saw El Rubio? He was there in the bar and you thought he seemed worried.'

'Yes, of course.'

'Do you remember what he was wearing?'

'No.'

'Was he wearing waterproofs?'

'No, I'm sure he wasn't. It was a Saturday, Inspector. The fishermen don't work on a Saturday night. They never come to the bar in their rain gear.'

'Even if it's raining?'

'Even if it's pouring, Inspector. They might wear rubber boots, but the waterproofs are for work only.' He paused for a moment before adding, 'El Rubio was wearing a black or navy cagoule.'

'Are you sure?'

'No,' admitted the waiter, 'but it's what he usually wore.'

When he hung up, Caldas saw that Barrio, Estevez and Barcia were all staring at him expectantly.

'It wasn't Castelo,' he said, cigarette dangling from his lips.

'Who?' asked Estevez.

'The man on the boat. The one the old woman saw. It wasn't Justo Castelo. It was him,' he said, pointing at the screen at the man hiding beneath his hood.

'What about Castelo then?'

'He was at the Refugio del Pescador on Saturday evening, chatting to the waiter at the bar. He had a bit more to drink than usual and left, saying he was going to end it. He was determined to settle a situation that had been disturbing him for weeks. It didn't work. I think that on Sunday morning, when his fishing boat left the harbour, Justo Castelo was already floating in the sea with his head gashed open and hands bound with a green cable tie.'

Caldas looked at the pathologist. 'Could he have been in the water since Saturday night?'

'As I said, a day or two. I can't be any more accurate when it comes to the sea.'

Caldas nodded. 'In that case it's clear.'

Estevez was still mystified. 'What's clear?'

'Don't you see?'

All three looked blank.

'Castelo was killed on Saturday night. He was struck on the head, tied up to make it look like suicide and thrown into the sea,' said Caldas. 'To complete the deception, the killer had to make sure the boat wasn't moored to the buoy at daybreak. He had to get it out of the harbour so that everyone would think that, like many before him, El Rubio had decided to go fishing for the last time. To set sail and jump into the sea. Do you follow now?'

They did.

'The man who murdered him had been biding his time for months. He knew what he had to do. Before heaving Castelo over the side, he took the float with the keys to his fishing boat and to the padlock for his rowing boat. The next day was a Sunday. A Sunday in winter. The streets would be deserted, the harbour empty. Castelo's killer drove his car to the natural harbour by the lighthouse at Punta Lameda. There he'd be able to get rid of the boat and come ashore without being seen. He could sink the boat in the pool where it would remain until the following summer, when El Rubio's death would have been forgotten.'

He paused to draw on his cigarette before continuing.

'He left his car there and, in the dark and wearing waterproofs like the dead man's, he walked to Panxón. When he got to the quayside, he dragged Castelo's rowing boat into the water, rowed out to his fishing boat and then headed as fast as possible for the lighthouse. There he came ashore, scuttled the boat in the pool, got into his car and left the scene.'

Estevez was amazed.

'So it was only one man.'

'Yes, just one.'

Diego Neira had acted alone, and had turned out to be more of a cold-blooded killer than Caldas had hoped.

'I thought it was strange someone knowing El Rubio was going to set sail on a Sunday,' Estevez murmured.

Caldas agreed.

'What about the good luck charms – were they part of the set-up too?' asked the pathologist.

The inspector shrugged. 'Maybe,' he said. 'But knowing how superstitious fishermen are . . .'

They were silent for a moment, then Dr Barrio pointed at the screen and said, 'So that's the man who killed him.'

'I think so.'

'Do you have any idea who he is?'

'His name's Diego Neira.'

'Who's he?' asked the pathologist.

Caldas stood up. 'You explain it to him, will you?' he asked Estevez. 'I'm going to get rid of this cigarette butt in the toilets.'

Little by Little

It was dark by the time they left the Forensics offices. Estevez drove the inspector to City Hall so that he could pass on the callers' complaints to the City Police.

'So he didn't tie him up just to make him talk,' Estevez remarked.

'No,' Caldas murmured, not opening his eyes. 'He didn't settle for simply scaring him into talking. It's not what I thought.'

'Do you think Castelo told Neira the name of his mother's killer?'

'Quite likely.'

'Then he'll kill again.'

'If he can, yes,' the inspector mumbled.

Estevez pulled up outside City Hall. Caldas thanked him for the lift and got out.

'Do you want me to wait?'

'No need, Rafa. I'll walk back.'

As his assistant drove off, Caldas tore a page from his black notebook and went in to hand it to the duty officer.

Instead of heading straight back to the Puerta del Sol, Caldas walked from City Hall to the Falperra fountain and then down the Calle Romil. He looked up at the sky. A strong wind had blown all afternoon, pushing the clouds inland. Nothing remained of the cold of previous nights.

As he reached the Paseo de Alfonso XII, a huge, almost full moon appeared above the estuary and, across the still water, the Morrazo peninsula and Cies Islands were silhouetted.

As he walked, Caldas thought of Justo Castelo, of his sister Alicia, of Rebeca and Diego Neira. He'd solved the mystery of the fisherman's death, though they still hadn't caught Neira. Caldas was never interested in the culprits. To him, the main thing was knowing the motives, the reasons. Yet, on discovering the truth, he hadn't felt the relief of other occasions. This time it all seemed clouded with bitterness.

At the Puerta del Sol the scales of the merman's tail gleamed in the moonlight. Caldas continued along the Calle del Principe, almost immediately turning right into the Travesia de la Aurora.

It was almost eight when he pushed open the wooden door of the Eligio.

'Good evening, Leo,' chorused the academics as he entered.

Caldas went up to the bar and Carlos greeted him with a glass of white wine. Soon the academics were talking about seagulls nesting on roofs throughout the city. A little later, someone at the back started whistling 'Promenade'.

Caldas turned round. Could it be that his mere presence now triggered a Pavlovian response in people so that, upon seeing him, some began discussing the show and others hummed the Gershwin tune?

Carlos brought him a second glass of wine and a plate of steamed cockles.

'How's your father doing?' he asked.

Caldas suddenly remembered that his uncle was being discharged any day. He took his mobile from his pocket and, chewing his first cockle, went out into the street in search of better reception.

'Leo, well, well!' said his father on answering the phone.

'When's Uncle Alberto being let out?'

'Tomorrow afternoon at five. Can you be there? To help me get him into the car mainly.'

'Of course,' said Caldas. 'How is he?'

'Dying to be here.'

'Do you think you'll be OK with him?'

'Well, at least here he'll get proper food and fresh air.'

'True.'

'And wine.'

'Is he allowed to drink?'

317

'Yes, but I don't think he feels like it.'

'Little by little,' said Caldas.

'That's right – little by little.'

The inspector promised to be at the hospital at five and went back to his plate of cockles.

Tyre Tracks

In the morning the inspector shaved in the shower, had breakfast in a bar reading the paper and walked to the police station. It was a beautiful day. Clear, without a single cloud. Another cruise liner was entering the port. The tourists would be able to leave their raincoats behind.

'Has Quintans called from Ferrol?' he asked Olga as he arrived.

'This morning?'

'Or yesterday.'

'Not this morning. I left you a couple of messages yesterday.'

Among the piles of papers, he found two little yellow Post-it notes stuck to his desk, but neither bore the name he was looking for. Sinking into his black chair, he picked up the phone and called the station in Ferrol.

'Hi, it's Leo,' he said when he got through to Quintans.

'I'm sorry I haven't called back,' said Quintans. 'But that man you're after is as slippery as an eel.'

'You can't find him?' asked Caldas, already knowing the answer.

'No way. He lived in Neda until six years ago, but you already knew that.'

'What about friends, girlfriends, jobs?'

'Nothing. Diego Neira's like a ghost. He's got no remaining family and the few people who knew him can't give a precise description. They remember him as an ordinary guy. You know – medium height, medium build, brownish hair .... And definitely a bit of a loner.'

'Any photos?'

'None,' said Quintans. 'And he never went to school in the village.

319

At least the secondary school has no record of his ever enrolling there.'

'Damn.'

'Give me a few more hours. I'll try to have something for you this afternoon or tomorrow.'

Afterwards he called Barcia to ask if they'd identified the 4x4 on the security camera recording.

'It's a fairly old model Land Rover. It could be white, beige, sky-blue, yellow – any light colour.'

'We may as well check if there's a car in Panxón like it, just in case.'

Barcia had already thought of this. 'There are two,' she said. 'And another six in nearby areas. I was going to ask the local police to see if any of them has a broken aerial and scratched paintwork.'

'We were thinking of passing by there late morning,' said Caldas. 'If you send the list of addresses we can check out the cars ourselves.'

'OK, Inspector. Shall I send it straight to you?'

'Better send it to Olga.'

He was about to hang up when he remembered something that had occurred to him in a wakeful moment during the night.

'Something else, Clara. Around the lighthouse at Punta Lameda there were tyre tracks. Ferro photographed them. I think it would be a good idea to check if any belong to a 4x4 like the one we're looking for.'

'Will do, Inspector.'

'One last thing. Neira was living in Neda, near Ferrol, until a few years ago. It would be good to know how many Land Rovers like that there are there.'

Caldas put the phone down and surveyed his desk. Piles of papers stood like a barricade before him. He glanced at his watch. Estevez wouldn't arrive until eleven. Taking a deep breath as if about to dive into a swimming pool, he reached for a document.

By the time his assistant appeared in his doorway an hour later, many of the documents were crammed into Caldas's wastepaper basket. Others had simply moved, becoming the foundations upon which new piles would soon rise.

'Are we going?' asked Estevez.

'Yes,' said the inspector with a sigh of relief.

The flags of the boats in the fishing port were fluttering in the breeze. Beyond, in Bouzas, the frames of ships under construction gleamed in the autumn sunshine.

They took the ring road and then the road laid on an old tramline that led to Panxón. Monteferro was no longer a dark shape in the mist, but a green forest rising above the blue sea.

As they drove, Caldas showed Estevez the list of owners of 4x4s similar to the one they'd seen on the security camera recording.

'Let's see if there's a light-coloured one.'

'Do you think he'll be in Panxón?'

'No,' said Caldas. 'But we may as well check.'

'I bet Neira's gone after Arias to Scotland.'

'We don't know for sure that Arias is there.'

'Makes no difference. Diego Neira will be on that fisherman's trail like a bloodhound. There's nothing like running away to make someone chase you.'

There were two Land Rovers of the model they were looking for in Panxón. They drove to the first address but didn't even need to get out of the car to rule that one out: it was parked outside, and it was dark green, dirty and rather dilapidated.

The second 4x4 on the list belonged to a retired fisherman, who'd bought it second-hand several years earlier. He kept it safely in his garage. He showed it to them. It was white but completely unscratched and the aerial was intact.

'Now what?' asked Estevez as they were leaving.

'There are six more in the area. Why don't you drop me off at the harbour and go and take a look at them?' suggested Caldas, handing him the list. 'I don't like cars.'

Medication

Panxón looked quite different in the sun. There were more fishing rods at the end of the jetty than at other times, and more people on the beach, walking from one sea wall to the other along the water's edge. Many tables on the terraces displayed *Reserved* signs.

Caldas passed several young men on the promenade, some on foot, others on bicycles, alone or in pairs. He could tell nothing from their faces, but he wasn't really expecting to see anything there. He'd looked into the eyes of killers many times and knew that they looked just like anyone else. Murder was human. Anyone could kill.

He took off his sweater, rolled up his shirtsleeves and made his way to the narrow street where José Arias lived. Judging by the amount of junk mail in the letterbox, he hadn't returned, but Caldas rang the bell anyway.

'He's gone away, Inspector,' said a woman's voice from above.

'How do you know?' Caldas asked the woman with the curlers leaning out of her window.

'He left on Saturday evening. He was carrying a suitcase.'

'Did he say where he was going?'

'I didn't ask,' replied the neighbour with sudden dignity. 'I don't pry into other people's business.'

Caldas walked back to the harbour. The market had been closed for hours but the air still smelled strongly of fish. He passed the Refugio del Pescador. Inside, at one of the marble tables a game of dominoes was in progress.

Crossing the road towards the slipway, he saw the *Aileen* loaded with traps, moored to its buoy. He looked at the jetty and wondered how long Justo Castelo's traps would remain there, stacked against the white wall.

'Would you like to come fishing, Inspector?' said a voice behind him.

He turned round. The old salt who claimed to have seen the *Xurelo* in the mist was peering at him from beneath his captain's cap.

'I'm sorry?'

'I asked if you'd like to come fishing,' the man said with a smile.

Caldas tutted and made his way to the jetty. Outside the yacht club, two freshly painted wooden boats were drying in the sun. Passing El Rubio's traps, he approached the anglers. In a metal bucket, a fish he didn't recognise was flapping about.

At the end of the jetty, he looked out, letting the breeze blow sea spray into his face. On the side facing the open sea there were great concrete blocks that had been blunted by the wind and waves.

A small boat was entering the harbour and Caldas recognised Manuel Trabazo's sky-blue *gamela*.

When he reached his buoy, the doctor leaned over the side to retrieve the mooring line with a hook. He tied up the fishing boat, jumped into his small rowing boat and began rowing towards the stone slipway.

Caldas stood waiting for him down by the water's edge.

On the beach, the boy in the wheelchair was throwing a ball for his dog.

'Look what you missed, Calditas,' said Trabazo, holding up a plastic bag. He was grinning beneath his white fringe.

Caldas opened the bag. Inside were half a dozen sea bass. The gills of one or two were still fluttering feebly.

'They're from my rock,' said Trabazo with a wink. 'All six in under an hour.'

The inspector helped him haul his boat on to the trailer and then pull the trailer up to the level section of the slipway.

'Doctor!' the old sea dog called out from the door of the Refugio del Pescador.

Trabazo looked up and the man said mockingly, 'Your friend doesn't want to come fishing.'

'Don't be mean, Pepe,' Trabazo shouted back.

'Why did you tell him?' asked Caldas in a whisper.

'They saw me set sail with you and come back on my own,' said Trabazo, laying the oars inside the boat and winding a chain around them. 'What could I say – that I'd thrown you overboard?' He pulled the chain tight and secured it with a small padlock. 'I hear they're letting your uncle out.'

'Yes, he's being discharged this afternoon.'

'Will he be better off at your father's than in hospital?'

Caldas shrugged. 'At least he'll have company.'

'That's something.'

'Yes.'

Trabazo looked round and wiped the sweat from his forehead with his sleeve. 'Lovely day, isn't it?' he said. 'What's the time?'

Caldas looked at his watch. 'One o'clock.'

'Already?' said Trabazo with a whistle. 'Time for my medicine. Why don't you come along?'

The inspector followed his old friend to the bar of the Refugio del Pescador. Trabazo ordered a glass of white wine. So did Caldas.

The Message

Half an hour later, Estevez collected the inspector and they drove back to Vigo. Estevez had found all the Land Rovers. None was the one caught on the security camera in Monteferro.

At a quarter past two they drew up outside the police station. Caldas went in to see if there was a message from Quintans.

'Nothing,' said Olga, and the inspector left again.

'Coming for lunch?' he said to his assistant.

'I'm meeting someone.'

'Right.'

By the time he got to the Bar Puerto he was too late for *percebes*. The display cabinet was empty, and Cristina confirmed that the few that had come in that morning had already been shared out among the customers.

He sat at the back at a table with two dockworkers he'd seen there before. He ordered scallops and fried sardines and, in honour of his assistant, a salad.

Cristina brought an earthenware jug of chilled white wine, and Caldas poured himself a glass while he waited for his meal and thought again of Diego Neira. He now knew the essentials – who he was and what his motives were, even the make of his car. It was only a matter of time before they tracked him down, but the sooner the better if they wanted to stop him killing again. Caldas was hoping that the superintendent would then agree to persuade a judge to reopen the case of Rebeca Neira's murder. However much harm the son had caused, he had a right to know what had happened to his mother, to bury her remains and lay his own grief to rest.

It was frustrating that Quintans was taking so long to come up with a photograph. Diego Neira wasn't from Panxón but he was familiar with the area, the rock pool and the habits of the fishermen. Caldas was sure he'd spent time near the harbour, probably in July or August, blending in with the other tourists, staying in a rented house, at a campsite or hotel.

The scallops arrived and Caldas didn't so much devour as inhale them. Meanwhile, he told himself that if he hadn't received any useful information from Quintans by the following day he'd go to Neda himself to find something.

Cristina brought the sardines and the salad, humming 'Promenade'.

'What's that you're humming?' asked Caldas.

'No idea,' she said, removing the plate of empty scallop shells and gesturing towards the other side of the restaurant. 'They were singing it over there.'

He finished his meal with coffee. Then he paid, and walked back to the station smoking a cigarette. He looked into his office: no Post-it notes on the desk. He closed the door and went to see Soto to fill him in on the latest developments. He told him about the video and explained that it wasn't Castelo that Hermida's wife had seen setting out in the boat.

'I still don't understand why he bound Castelo's wrists,' said the superintendent once Caldas had finished.

'Because it was perfect. On one hand, it meant he could make it look like suicide and finish Castelo off quietly, without arousing suspicion. Nobody would look into the suicide of a depressive. On the other hand, I'm sure being tied up made El Rubio tell him what happened in Aguiño that night in the hope that he'd let him go.'

'Nice guy that Neira.'

Caldas clicked his tongue. 'It's not all his fault.'

Soto assented. 'Do you think he'll go after the others?'

'I'm sure of it. If he planned all this to kill the accomplice, he's hardly going to leave the killer alive.'

'Do you reckon he's gone after Arias in Scotland?'

'If Castelo talked, I think it's very likely.'

'And if he didn't?'

'In that case Valverde's got a problem,' said Caldas. 'Neira may want to get rid of both of them.'

'To make sure he hits his target?'

'Exactly.'

Open Doors

Estevez dropped him off outside the hospital. Caldas crossed the lobby and took the stairs to the second floor. He walked down the corridor of closed doors and opened the one numbered 211.

Uncle Alberto smiled behind the green mask. He was sitting on the bed, now stripped, in trousers and a sweater that were too loose for him. The table where the radio and newspapers had been was empty and a leather holdall sat, packed, on the floor.

'Hello, Leo,' said his father, looking out of the window at the city.

'Shall we head downstairs?'

'We've got to wait for the ambulance.'

'I thought you were going in the car.'

'So did I, but the doctor thought it better to have an ambulance. For the oxygen,' he added.

A male nurse entered pushing a wheelchair with an oxygen cylinder on the back. He disconnected the breathing mask from the wall and attached it to the cylinder. Then he helped Alberto into the chair.

They proceeded down the corridor in single file, Uncle Alberto with his green mask leading in the wheelchair and, behind him, the nurse, the inspector's father and, finally, Caldas carrying the leather holdall.

As the ambulance door closed, the inspector asked his father, 'What about you?'

'I'll take the car.'

Caldas saw his father's car a short distance away and nodded. He felt bad about not going with them, but he had too much to do.

'Will you both be all right?'

'Sure.'

'I was planning to come and see you this weekend.'

'OK,' said his father, heading towards the car. 'If you get a free moment.'

Caldas stood at the kerb waving as they drove off. Once they'd disappeared from sight, he walked back to the police station and shut himself in his office. He made a few calls and went through the papers that he'd moved from one pile to another that morning. At seven his mobile rang.

He didn't recognise the number.

'Inspector Caldas?'

'Yes.'

'This is Ana Valdés.'

The name meant nothing to him but the voice was familiar.

'Do I know you?'

'I'm Marcos Valverde's wife, from Panxón. Don't you remember me?'

He may not have known her name but he hadn't forgotten her smile.

'Yes, of course. What can I do for you?'

'I'm sorry to bother you,' she said, 'but as you gave me your number . . .'

Caldas cut short her apology. 'Has something happened?'

'Our front gate has been damaged.'

'What?'

'The garden gate. Several panels have been torn off.'

'When?'

'This afternoon. I found it like that when I got home.'

'Was the house broken into?'

'I don't think so.'

'Did you see anyone?'

'No, no one.'

'What about your husband?'

'Marcos was in the house. He didn't hear anything.'

'But you're both OK? Your husband's OK?'

'Yes, we're fine, but pretty worried.'

With good reason, thought the inspector. 'Where are you calling from?'

'I'm in the car on my way to Vigo. I'm not spending the night in that house.'

'Have you got somewhere to stay?' he said, and immediately regretted it.

'Yes, we've got a flat in the centre. I often stay there on Saturday nights after a concert. But I'm concerned about my husband.'

'Is he still at the house?'

'Yes,' she whispered. 'He's trying to get hold of a carpenter. He's going to meet me in town once the gate's fixed.'

'Have you reported it to the police?'

'No.'

'Why not?'

'Marcos was adamant that we shouldn't.'

'I assume he doesn't know you're calling me?'

'No. Please don't tell him.'

'Fine,' said Caldas. 'But we'll have to go over there.'

He heard a sigh of relief. 'I'd be very grateful, Inspector.'

'No need to thank me. I'm just doing my job.'

He expected her to end the call but she asked, 'Do you think this has something to do with what they're saying in the village?'

'I don't know, but please don't worry about that now.'

'I can't help it,' said Valverde's wife. 'I'm scared.'

When he hung up, Caldas went to the superintendent's office, collecting Estevez en route.

'Someone's tried to get into Valverde's house.'

The superintendent looked up from the document he was reading. 'When?'

'This afternoon. His wife got home to find the front gate smashed up. She's just phoned to tell me.'

Soto asked the same question as Caldas himself earlier: 'Is the husband all right?'

'Yes. He was in the house but didn't hear anything.'

The superintendent rubbed his forehead. 'Do you think it was Diego Neira?'

'I'm not certain,' replied Caldas. 'But Valverde is.'

'Did he say so?'

'No, but he didn't want to call the police, and they're not staying at the house tonight. He's trying to find someone to fix the gate as soon as possible and then he's leaving.'

'Do you know where they intend to go?'

'They're coming to Vigo. Apparently they've got a flat here. She's already on her way.'

'Are you going out to Panxón?'

'Yes, if only to have a look.'

Soto rubbed his forehead again. 'If Neira was there this afternoon, his car can't be far away.'

'That's what I thought.'

'It's a 4x4, isn't it?'

'Yes, a Land Rover. Light-coloured and rather old. Clara Barcia has the details,' said Caldas.

'OK then,' said Soto, picking up the phone. 'You two head over there. I'll make sure the car's found.'

The Wooden Gate

The inspector urged Estevez to drive faster and, a little more than fifteen minutes later, they caught sight of the Templo Votivo del Mar by the light of a moon still as full as the night before. They'd travelled in silence, Estevez concentrating on the road and Caldas leaning back, eyes closed and window open a crack.

He opened his eyes as Estevez stopped the car at the bottom of the steep hill, headlights pointing at the gate of the Valverdes' house. There was a large hole in the bottom corner by the pillar on which the gate was hinged. Leaving the lights on, they got out of the car to inspect the damage.

The gate was made up of four horizontal panels each about half a metre wide held together with iron fittings. The two lower panels had been partly pulled aside, leaving a gap big enough for even Estevez to crawl through.

'They prised them off from the pillar side,' said Estevez.

Caldas agreed and peered through the gap. Valverde's black sports car was parked in the courtyard.

He couldn't see the huge sitting-room window from there but he could tell from the brightness of the garden that there were lights on inside the house.

He straightened up and rang the bell.

'Who is it?' said a man's voice.

'Inspector Caldas.'

'Who?'

'Inspector Caldas. The police,' he added.

'I'll be right out, Inspector,' said the voice. Caldas assumed that the automatic gate mechanism must have been damaged as well.

While Valverde made his way out, Estevez went to turn off the car headlights. When he got back he raised his arms and rested his hands on the top of the gate. 'If he wanted to get in, he could just have jumped over. It's not very high,' he said, saying what Caldas had been thinking since seeing the damage.

'He probably didn't want to get in,' said the inspector.

'You think it was just a warning, like the graffiti?'

'Could be.'

They heard Valverde's footsteps on the gravel. Then the gate opened inwards with a creak.

'What brings you here?'

'This,' said Caldas gesturing at the gate.

'It's just a bit of damage to a couple of the panels. I've already called a carpenter to come out and patch it up,' said Valverde, dismissively. 'I'm having an alarm installed tomorrow. It's not as safe round here as it used to be.'

'Do you really think whoever did this wanted to get in to rob you?'

'You don't?'

'I don't know,' replied Caldas. 'Why would someone bother to break down the gate when it would be less effort to climb over?'

Valverde stared at the damaged panels.

'I hadn't thought of that,' he said, but his tone suggested otherwise.

'Will you be staying here tonight?'

'No,' said Valverde. 'My wife is scared. We're going to spend a night, maybe two in town, until we get the alarm fitted.'

'You don't believe it was a burglary either, do you?'

'What?'

'I meant that you know this wasn't done by a burglar.'

'I don't understand why you think I—'

'Nobody would leave their house if they thought someone was going to try to break in,' interrupted Caldas.

Valverde snorted. 'We're leaving because of my wife—'

Caldas cut in again: 'Who are you afraid of?'

'Please don't push me, Inspector. We've been over this already.'

'I'm just trying to protect you. I don't understand why you won't let us help.'

Valverde was silent and Caldas knew he wouldn't get any answers this time either.

'Fine,' said Caldas. 'If you decide you want to speak to us, you know where to find us. Think about it, before it's too late.'

They went back to the car and heard the gate creak shut and the sound of Valverde's footsteps receding on the gravel path.

'If you wanted to scare him, you succeeded,' said Estevez.

'Yes.'

With the gate closed and no room to turn the car around, Estevez started reversing up the hill but stopped a few seconds later.

'What's the matter?' said Caldas.

'There's a motorbike coming.'

Turning, Caldas saw a headlight a couple of metres away from the car.

'It can only be going to Valverde's house,' murmured Estevez.

'Well, let it pass,' said Caldas.

Estevez edged the car up close to the wall on one side of the street and the motorbike slipped past on the other.

The rider was wearing a dark helmet. He stopped at the gate, turned off the engine and dismounted. He raised the seat and pulled out a metal box, placing his helmet in the empty compartment. Then he turned towards them.

The policemen recognised the red beard of the carpenter they'd seen working on boats at the yacht club. He, however, dazzled by their headlights, did not recognise them.

'Is this where they need a carpenter?' he asked, shielding his eyes with his maimed hand.

'Yes,' said Caldas, leaning out of the window. 'You have to ring the bell.'

Estevez pressed down on the accelerator and the car reversed up the hill, the engine revving so loudly that Caldas only just heard his mobile phone ring. It was Olga.

'Are you still at the station?'

'I'm going to be here for a good while longer,' she sighed, and

334

went on to explain why she'd called: 'The superintendent wants to know if you want the search for the Land Rover extended to Portugal.'

'In theory, no,' said Caldas. 'Let's wait until we hear from Quintans.'

'He just called, actually.'

'Quintans?'

'Yes,' said Olga. Caldas wondered why she hadn't told him at the start.

'Did you give him my mobile number?'

'No. He said he'd call back in the morning.'

'He didn't tell you anything?'

'Yes, he said he'd found the son. Neira.'

'Where?'

'I don't know. He just said he'd found him. Apparently he had an accident a few years ago.'

'The son?'

'Yes, of course, I suppose so.'

'Have you got his mobile number?'

'Whose?'

Caldas sighed. It was this sort of thing that made him sympathise with Estevez. 'Quintans'.'

'No, but I can get it from Ferrol,' she said. 'I'll call you right back.'

Caldas hung up and clicked his tongue. 'Damn, it can't be,' he muttered.

'What's up?' asked Estevez.

'I think the gap was for someone to get into the house,' said the inspector. 'We need to go to the harbour.'

'Are you going to tell me what's going on?'

'Yes, but let's get back on the road first,' urged Caldas.

In his mind's eye he could see the ball, the black dog and the boy in the wheelchair.

Once Estevez had manoeuvred the car out of the narrow street, Caldas repeated what Olga had just told him.

'Apparently Diego Neira had an accident a few years ago.'

His phone rang. It was Olga again.

'Did you get the number?'

'Yes, of course,' she said. 'Have you got something to write it down on?'

Caldas jotted Quintans' phone number on his cigarette packet.

'An accident?' asked Estevez once the inspector had hung up.

Caldas responded with a question. 'Have you noticed a boy in a wheelchair on the beach these past few days?'

Estevez stared at him in disbelief.

'So that's why he had to make a hole in the gate: he can't jump over,' he said.

Caldas nodded and dialled the number Olga has just given him. It was engaged.

'Bloody hell,' muttered Estevez, and accelerated hard.

The Wheelchair

Caldas still hadn't got through to Quintans when Estevez drew up at the harbour. They got out of the car and headed towards the Refugio del Pescador. Games of dominoes were in progress at all the tables by the window. The waiter who had described what Castelo was wearing on his last evening there was at the back, behind the bar.

'Good evening, Inspector.'

Caldas asked him if he knew the young man in the wheelchair.

'I know who you mean, Inspector. He's not from the village. He's only been around for a few weeks.'

Caldas went over to one of the tables. The old sea dog was playing with three other fishermen. He gave the inspector a sidelong glance, as if he feared retaliation for his teasing that morning. The captain's cap lay on a corner of the table.

Caldas waited as the clacking of dominoes on marble speeded up and then subsided before asking, 'Do you know where I might find a boy who goes down to the beach in a wheelchair?'

'With a dog?' they all asked, as if the inspector's description had not been precise enough. Caldas wondered how many other boys in wheelchairs there were on the beach at that time of year.

'Yes,' he replied.

'He's not from around here,' they chorused.

'But do you know where I can find him?'

They looked at one another.

'He was around just now,' said one, waving towards the window.

Another one turned and interrupted the game at the next table.

'Do you know where the disabled lad lives, the one on the beach in a wheelchair?'

The four men at the other table also required greater precision. 'The one with the dog?'

'That's the one.'

One of the men scratched his chin with a domino. 'I think he's renting one of Pepe O Bravo's houses,' he said, slamming a double-four down on the table.

'And where's that?' asked Caldas.

They all replied together, 'Do you know the cemetery?'

The policemen went back to the car.

'Do you know how to get there?'

'Yes, of course,' said Estevez. The inspector tried Quintans' number again. It was no longer engaged.

'It's Leo.'

'I called you at the station a little while ago.'

'I know,' said Caldas.

'Diego Neira was working in Ares until three years ago. Did Olga tell you?'

'She didn't say anything about the name of the village, but she mentioned he'd had an accident,' said the inspector. 'I think we've found him. I was just calling to say thanks.'

'You've got him?'

'Yes,' said Caldas. 'We're on our way there now. Do you know, earlier this evening he prised open part of a front gate so he could break in in his chair.'

'What do you mean, chair?'

'Isn't he in a wheelchair?'

'I don't know,' said Quintans. 'At any rate, he didn't need one three years ago.'

'I thought you told Olga he'd had an accident?'

'Yes, but it was just to his hand, Leo. He lost a couple of fingers using a circular saw.'

Caldas felt the blood pounding at his temples. 'What?' he stammered.

'He lost several fingers,' repeated Quintans. 'He was working in a carpenter's workshop, building wooden boats. From what I've heard, he's quite a craftsman.'

Diego Neira

The tyres screeched at every bend, but Caldas didn't complain. 'Hurry,' he kept saying, face raised towards the partly open window, gripping the door handle with both hands. 'Hurry until we get to the turn-off.'

Estevez braked suddenly, making the car skid, before turning down the narrow street that led down to the gate.

Caldas opened his eyes.

'Take it slowly now.'

As they came round the bend, their headlights lit up the motorbike, parked where its owner had left it. The carpenter was crouched, with his back to them, as if he really were inspecting the damaged gate. He held a torch in one hand and a tool they didn't recognise in the other.

For a moment he froze like a cat in the glare of the headlights. Then he stood up and turned round.

The inspector looked at his bearded face and swallowed hard. He wasn't as he'd imagined, but it was definitely Rebeca Neira's son, the man he was looking for.

Estevez stopped the car. 'Are we going?' he asked, flicking the safety catch on his automatic pistol.

'You don't need that,' said Caldas.

'Are you sure?'

'Yes, Rafa, I'm sure. We're not going to hurt him.'

They opened their doors and got out slowly. The headlights were still on.

'Diego Neira?' Caldas called out.

The carpenter looked up, trying to see who had called his name, and Caldas saw his neck muscles tense.

'Diego,' he repeated. 'I'm Inspector Caldas, of the police. We're here to arrest you.'

The man did not reply or shield his eyes from the lights, which must have been dazzling him. He stood before the gate, face blank, arms slightly bent in a defensive position.

The policemen both moved forward until they were standing in front of the car.

'Put what you're holding down on the ground, Diego,' said the inspector, but the carpenter remained motionless.

'Didn't you hear the inspector, son?'

Neira slowly lowered his arms, but at the last moment he jerked his arm forward and flung the torch into the air. In an instant, while the policemen had their eyes on the torch, Neira had rolled on the ground and disappeared through the gap towards the house.

They went after him. Caldas followed Neira through the hole while Estevez vaulted over the gate.

By the time the inspector had crawled through, Neira was on the ground gasping for air, pinned beneath Estevez's bulk.

'Don't hurt him,' said Caldas.

While Estevez handcuffed Neira and took him to the car, Caldas approached Valverde. The developer had watched the carpenter's arrest from a distance.

'Who is that?' he asked.

'His name's Diego Neira.'

Valverde shook his head, as if the name meant nothing.

'He used to live with his mother in Aguiño,' said Caldas.

They watched the man being led away, head bowed and hands cuffed behind his back.

'Is he that girl's son?' said Valverde at last.

'Yes.'

'Why me?' he whispered. 'I had nothing to do with it.'

'That's not quite true, you did have something to do with it.'

'Nothing,' he said adamantly.

'Sometimes that's not enough,' said Caldas. 'You knew what

340

happened that night. You could have confronted the killer, turned him in to the police.'

Valverde looked up and gave a long snort, trying to release some of his tension.

'Confront him?' he said. 'And end up at the bottom of the sea like Captain Sousa?'

Caldas reflected that he himself had floundered in this case just as Sousa must have done in the waves all those years ago.

'We're going to look into the events of that night,' said Caldas. 'But there's still time for you to speak to us voluntarily.'

The developer gave such an extended snort that this time he almost winded himself.

'I'll be going to see my lawyer tomorrow,' he said at last. 'Maybe I'll call in at the police station afterwards.'

Face to Face

The next morning, Caldas sat facing the carpenter, still trying to extract a confession. He hadn't managed to get a single word from him the night before. He'd mentioned Panxón, the graffiti and Justo Castelo's death before moving on to the subject of Aguiño. The response had always been silence.

The inspector had hoped that a few hours in a cell would make him more willing to talk, but the man continued to stare at the white wall ahead of him almost without blinking.

'I'm not like Somoza,' said Caldas. 'I'm certain your mother didn't leave you. The men you saw at your front door were at the Bar Aduana the night she disappeared. She met them there.'

Still Neira said nothing. But the look in his eyes seemed to convey that thirteen years was too long.

Caldas tried again. 'We're determined to get to the bottom of things, but we need your help. You came to us once and we failed you,' said Caldas. 'Give us a chance to put things right.'

Neira spoke for the first time, 'So you're saying that for you to charge my mother's killer I've got to confess to murder? And you claim you're not like Somoza? You're all the same.'

Caldas reflected that at least the silence had ended.

'You smoke?'

'No,' muttered Neira.

Caldas lit a cigarette.

'I'm not asking you to admit to anything you haven't done.'

'Well, I haven't killed anyone.'

'So tell me what happened. I'm prepared to listen.'

'Are you? I'm honoured.'

'And to believe you if what you say is credible,' added Caldas.

Neira looked him in the eyes. 'I had nothing to do with El Rubio's death.'

'You didn't throw him into the sea?'

'No.'

'And you didn't bind his wrists with that cable tie? Where did you get it?'

'I don't know what you're talking about.'

'So it wasn't you who daubed his boat with graffiti?'

'Of course it was me. I'd been doing it for months. But that doesn't mean I killed him.'

'You'd been painting graffiti on the boat for months?'

'I graffitied his rowing boat, left notes at his house, on his boat, in his traps. I wanted to get him off balance so he'd lead me to the man who killed my mother.'

'Did you succeed?'

'Almost.'

'Almost?'

'He was about to crack when he died.'

'How do you know?'

'You should have seen him. He can't have been getting more than a couple of hours sleep a day. Until yesterday I was convinced he'd killed himself.'

'Until yesterday?'

'When you told me in the car how the cable tie was fastened.'

The day before, during the drive back to Vigo, Caldas had explained how they'd tracked Neira down, assuming that he'd confess when faced with the evidence. He'd been wrong.

'Did you ever speak to El Rubio face to face?'

'Face to face?'

'Did you ever tell Castelo who you were?'

'Of course I didn't.'

'Why not?'

'I was scared of ending up like my mother.'

'What were you going to do when you found the man who was with her?'

Neira looked Caldas in the eyes. 'I wanted to ask him why,' he whispered. 'I wanted to ask him why he had to kill her.'

Caldas swallowed. 'And then?'

Neira shrugged. 'I'd have thought of something.'

He'd waited over thirteen years. He was in no hurry.

'You should have come to us,' said Caldas.

Neira smiled contemptuously.

The carpenter admitted what Caldas had guessed: he'd seen El Rubio on the news. Over a decade later, he'd found the fair-haired man of his nightmares staring at the camera self-consciously, holding up a tropical fish on a hook. He was a little heavier, but it was the same man who'd passed Neira as he sheltered from the rain on that night long ago. By the time he switched off the television, he'd decided to go and find work in Panxón.

'Do you have a car?'

'No, a motorbike.'

'The one you were riding yesterday?

'Yes.'

Caldas didn't press him further. Ferro was in Panxón searching Neira's house. If he had a car, Ferro would find it.

'What were you doing the evening of the Saturday before last?'

'I was at home. I never go out in the evening,' said Neira without hesitation.

'Were you alone?'

'With Charlie,' he replied, and the inspector remembered the grey cat at the workshop.

'Right.'

'Could you do something for me?' said the carpenter.

'Of course.'

'Would you have a word with Dr Trabazo and ask him to look after Charlie?'

Drawing on his cigarette Caldas assured him that he would, before continuing the interrogation. 'When did you break down Valverde's gate?'

'What?'

'You didn't pull off those panels?'

'My job is to fix things, Inspector, not break them.'

'But damaging the gate gave you the perfect excuse to be alone with Valverde, one of the *Xurelo*'s crew.'

'That's true. But I didn't do it.'

'Were you intending to kill them all?'

'I wasn't intending to kill anyone,' he said. 'It was them who killed my mother.'

'I can understand how you feel—'

'How can you understand?' Neira interrupted scornfully.

'I assure you I understand better than you think,' said Caldas quietly. He didn't say that he, too, sometimes got up in the middle of the night to look at a photograph because he'd forgotten someone's smile.

Neira lowered his eyes.

'Tell me what happened with Castelo,' said the inspector and, deciding to offer him a way out, he added: 'Was it an accident?'

'I can't tell you,' whispered Neira. 'Because I don't know.'

Caldas was about to start all over again when there was a knock at the door and he was handed a yellow Post-it note: Marcos Valverde had arrived.

The inspector left the interrogation room and went to get his assistant.

'You carry on,' he told Estevez. 'See if you can get him to tell you any more.'

Nodding, Estevez headed towards the closed door.

'Hey!' the inspector called just as Estevez was about to go in.

'What?'

'Go gently.'

The Way Back

'José Arias was a heavy drinker. He had a more or less official girl-friend – Alicia, the teacher. El Rubio's sister,' said Valverde. Caldas nodded. 'But by the third drink he'd forget all about her.'

'Didn't Castelo ever say anything?'

'El Rubio had enough to deal with, coming off heroin. He was getting better, but wasn't all the way there yet. We had some terrible times with him on the boat. Sousa was like a father to him. He forgave him everything.'

Keen to keep him to the subject of the shipwreck, Caldas asked, 'So what happened at the bar?'

'We sat outside, on a covered terrace where the owner had left our meal. The woman arrived just as we were finishing. She wanted to buy cigarettes, but the bar was closed. We offered her ours and she came to sit with us. Arias and El Rubio started making her laugh. Sober they were pretty quiet, but with a couple of drinks inside them they were funny. You'd never guess it, would you?'

Caldas shook his head. He hadn't known Castelo, but Arias didn't seem like much of a joker.

'The girl was enjoying herself, but after a little while she said she had to leave. Arias and Castelo offered to walk her home. "We'll make sure you don't drown," I remember them saying. Because it was pouring with rain.'

'What was Captain Sousa doing?'

'He'd gone back to the boat to sleep as soon as we finished eating.

He was in his sixties. He always liked to turn in early when we put in to port.'

Inspector Caldas gestured for him to get back to the night in Aguiño.

'They went off with the girl, but El Rubio came back pretty soon after. He couldn't really compete with Arias when it came to women,' smiled Valverde. 'We finished the wine and left.'

'Back to the boat?'

'Yes. We sat in the cabin, resting. The skipper was already snoring in his bunk.'

'When did Arias get back?'

'He turned up about an hour or so later. He woke El Rubio and asked him to go ashore. I was half asleep, but I saw them leave.'

'Didn't you think it odd?'

'No,' he said firmly. 'They were close. I thought they were going to carry on partying, like other times.'

'When did they return?'

'I don't know how much time passed, Inspector. Around dawn, I was woken by the skipper yelling so I went up on deck. Sousa was furious, saying who did they think they were, casting off without his permission.'

'How did they respond?'

'El Rubio told him to keep quiet, but Arias didn't say a thing. He just carried on unmooring the boat, ignoring Sousa. You've seen him,' said Valverde, raising his arms. 'Well, fifteen years ago, he was even scarier.'

'I can imagine.'

'But Captain Sousa didn't scare easily. He stood up to them. He insisted that the *Xurelo* wasn't leaving port unless he said so, and he tried to retie one of the loose mooring lines, but Arias pushed him aside. The skipper fell over but he still wouldn't be intimidated. He got to his feet and faced Arias. He asked what had happened with the girl to make them want to get away. Then Arias hit him – several times on the head with a bottle. We threw ourselves at him, but by the time we stopped him the skipper was unconscious. Arias took him aft while El Rubio cast off.'

'And what were you doing meanwhile?'

'Surviving,' he murmured. 'I thought we were going to head into

347

the estuary, to shelter from the storm. But El Rubio set a course south. Arias handed me a life jacket and told me to get ready to swim. I asked what they were going to do. He just told me to put on the life jacket and go into the cabin. He went aft along the gunwale.'

Valverde paused and snorted as he had the night before outside his house. Then he went on, 'There was a bundle on the floor, wrapped in a dark polka-dot blanket. He tied it up with a rope at either end and wrapped a chain around it. As we rounded the jetty, he threw it overboard. I thought it must be the skipper's body and I started crying. The waves were getting really big. Arias went back to the cabin and took the helm, steering towards Salvora. When we were only a few dozen metres from land, he yelled to us to get ready. A few seconds later the three of us jumped into the water and started swimming for shore. As we reached it we saw the *Xurelo* hit the rocks. It sank soon after.'

Valverde snorted again.

'Before we set off towards the village to report the sinking, Arias made us rehearse the story I told you the other day: that we were heading back with a full hold on the skipper's orders and were caught in the storm, and that the boat hit rocks and went down before Sousa had even had time to put on his life jacket.'

'Right,' murmured Caldas. 'Rebeca Neira, the woman in the bar – was she on board?'

Valverde nodded. 'I didn't see her. But when the skipper's body turned up in the nets of that trawler I realised it was her that had been in the blanket that Arias dumped overboard.'

Caldas got to his feet. 'You'll have to repeat all this in front of a judge.'

'I know,' replied Valverde, looking at him with shining eyes.

Caldas wasn't sure whether it was remorse, fear or a sense of deliverance he could see in them.

The Blanket

Caldas went to see Superintendent Soto and filled him in on what Valverde had just said.

'How did you get him to talk?'

'He realised he'd have to sooner or later,' said Caldas. 'He knows we're going to reopen the investigation and he chose to make a statement without Arias being there. I don't think he could have done it otherwise. He's terrified of him.'

Soto nodded.

'Will you speak to the judge?' asked Caldas.

'I'll do it today,' said Soto. 'Did you record Valverde's statement?'

'Yes, of course,' replied Caldas with a tight-lipped smile.

'How's it going with Neira?' asked the superintendent.

Caldas shrugged.

'Estevez is trying to get something out of him, but so far he hasn't let down his guard. He admits to the graffiti, but still claims he had nothing to do with Castelo's murder.'

'Do you believe him?'

'No.'

Caldas went to his office. He slumped into his desk chair and rubbed his eyes. A moment later Ferro dropped by.

'Any luck finding the car?'

'No,' said Ferro. 'We're still looking. I'm here about something else.'

'Go on.'

'José Arias has got a police record.'

'Has he?'

'For criminal damage,' said Ferro. 'He was arrested in 1995. He wrecked a bar in Baiona. It took two whole squads to overpower him.'

Caldas went back to the interrogation room and found Diego Neira with a red mark on his left cheek.

He approached Estevez and hissed in his ear, 'I told you not to hit him.'

'But he refuses to talk,' muttered Estevez.

Caldas ordered his assistant out and sat down opposite Neira.

'I've just seen Marcos Valverde,' he said. 'He's told me about the night your mother disappeared.'

Neira looked into his eyes. 'Who was it?'

'They were all involved.'

'Was it him?'

'No, it was Arias.'

'And you believe him?'

'Yes. I think he's telling the truth.'

The young man went back to staring at the wall, as if trying to bore through it. 'Will you catch him?'

'Yes, of course we will.'

'Do you know where he is?'

'We think he's gone back to Scotland. The judge is willing to issue a warrant to get him back. Then he'll pay for what he did.'

'Did Valverde tell you where my mother is?'

'He thinks she's at the entrance to the harbour at Aguiño.'

'In the sea?'

'Yes.'

Neira looked at him. He seemed calmer now. 'Will you look for her?'

'We'll try,' said Caldas. 'But we can't give any guarantees. It's been a long time.' Then he asked: 'Did you used to have a polka-dot blanket?'

'Yes, it was mine,' said Neira. 'It disappeared the same night as my mother. Why?'

The inspector did not reply.

350

'Do you know, I even got to the point where I prayed she was dead?' Neira confessed. 'Anything was better than thinking she'd abandoned me.'

Caldas looked down and leafed through some documents to delay returning to the subject of Castelo's murder.

'If you're innocent, why did you try to run away yesterday at Valverde's house?'

'I've told you, I'm not too fond of the police.'

Caldas moved his chair closer to the table.

'Here's what I think happened: you met up with Castelo on Saturday night. You'd arranged it in one of the notes you left him. You thought he needed to talk, to unburden himself, but he refused to tell you what happened to your mother. You made some excuse and went to your car. You took a spanner from the boot – the kind you use on wheel nuts – and you hit him on the head. Then you bound his wrists and went through his pockets, where you found the keys to his boat. You waited for him to come round and threatened to throw him into the sea unless he talked. Where did this happen?'

Neira remained silent.

Caldas offered him a way out: 'Did he fall?'

'You've got the wrong man, Inspector,' muttered Neira, still staring at the wall.

'You were afraid that Castelo had warned the other two, and thought you'd make it look like suicide so they wouldn't be suspicious, didn't you? At dawn the next day you drove to the lighthouse at Punta Lameda. You knew the spot. You knew you'd be able to land there without being seen. You walked back to Panxón wearing waterproofs like Castelo's. You sailed his boat to the lighthouse, jumped ashore and sank it, covering your tracks. Then you got into the car and disappeared. That's it, isn't it?'

Silence.

'Whose car is it?' Caldas pressed, trying to catch him out. 'Who was helping you?'

Caldas went on questioning Neira until mid-morning. Then he was taken before the judge for more questions.

The response was always the same: a fixed stare and sealed lips.

Solid Proof

Caldas had lunch alone at the Bar Puerto and spent all afternoon in his office. He was just about to start writing his report when Ferro rapped on the glass door. He'd come from searching Neira's house and the workshop at the yacht club.

'You wanted to see me, Inspector?' he said from the door.

'Did you find the car?'

'No, nothing: no documents, keys or garage at the house. The neighbours have only ever seen him on a motorbike.'

'What about the cable ties?'

'We didn't find any of those either,' said Ferro.

Caldas went back to his papers.

'Was there anything else?' asked Ferro.

'What about Valverde's gate?'

'There must have been twenty tools in the workshop that Neira could have used to prise off the panels.'

'Right.'

Ferro was about to leave when Superintendent Soto came to say that the judge had remanded Neira in custody, awaiting trial, but had also called to urge them to find the 4x4.

'Without the car, I think a conviction's unlikely,' said Soto. 'We've got no solid proof.'

'Do you really believe that?' asked Caldas.

'The fact is, everything we've got is circumstantial. No confession, no witnesses, not even a fingerprint.'

Caldas looked at Ferro.

352

'Check all the Land Rovers registered in Neda and Ares,' he said. 'They're the places Neira lived before he moved to Panxón. Maybe the car belongs to someone he knows.'

'What about checking the ones in Aguiño?' asked Ferro.

'Yes, them, too.'

When Ferro had left Caldas asked the superintendent, 'Does the judge know we arrested Neira at Valverde's house?'

'Yes, of course.'

'And?'

'That's why he hasn't let him go,' said Soto. 'But he wants the car.'

It wasn't his last conversation with the superintendent that day. Around six in the evening, Soto summoned him to his office.

'José Arias has been found in Scotland,' he said. 'He was caught this morning at the home of his former partner. He'd gone to collect his daughter.'

'Has he made a statement?'

'Yes,' said Soto. 'He admits he was in Aguiño and that he'd had a bit too much to drink, but he claims all he can remember is the freezing water. It seems he's going to accuse Valverde of murdering all three: Rebeca Neira, Antonio Sousa, even Justo Castelo.'

Caldas reflected that, having fled twice, the fisherman would have trouble convincing a judge of his innocence.

'When is he being brought back?'

'I'm not sure,' answered Soto. 'Soon.'

The Woman in the Yellow Dress

At nine o'clock, when he'd written his report, Caldas walked up the Calle de la Reconquista, crossed the Calle Policarpo Sanz, and went a little way along the Calle del Principe before turning into the Travesia de la Aurora. He pushed open the wooden door of the Eligio, greeted the academics and went up to the bar.

He really needed the glass of white wine that Carlos poured him.

'Tired?'

'A little.'

'How's your uncle?'

Caldas clicked his tongue and headed outside to make a call. At a table at the back, one of Pavlov's dogs had started whistling 'Promenade'.

'He's doing OK,' said his father.

'Sorry I haven't called. Things have been hectic.'

'Don't worry about it. How are you?'

'Tired,' he said, then added quickly: 'Fine.'

'I'll be going into Vigo tomorrow around midday,' said his father. 'I've got to buy a pulse oximeter.'

'A what?'

'It's for measuring how much oxygen Alberto needs.'

'Right.'

'If you like you could come back here with me afterwards.'

'Tomorrow?'

'It's Friday,' said his father. 'I thought you said you'd be coming here on Friday?'

The inspector suddenly felt overwhelmed. He decided to put off making a decision for a few hours. 'I'll call you tomorrow morning to confirm.'

'You won't forget?'

'Of course not,' he said, knowing that he probably would.

He went back inside the Eligio. He leaned on the marble bar and stared at the small painting by Pousa of the woman in the yellow dress with the same sad eyes as Alicia Castelo. The fisherman's sister had called that afternoon: there was a rumour going around the village that a man had been arrested for Justo's murder.

'He's only a suspect,' said Caldas.

'It isn't José, is it?' she asked and held her breath. When Caldas didn't reply she pressed him: 'Did he kill my brother?'

Caldas couldn't bring himself to tell her that she'd have to get used to living without Arias, that although he hadn't killed her brother she'd lost him again.

'No.'

'Thank God,' murmured Alicia Castelo before hanging up.

Taking his glass, he went to sit at a small table at the back. In the corner, the poet Oroza was chatting with two young women.

Carlos brought him another glass of wine and a plate of octopus with potatoes.

'Take a seat?' said Caldas.

Carlos fetched a bottle from the bar and went round refilling glasses.

'So they won't keep pestering me,' he said, sitting on a stool opposite the inspector.

They sat, drinking, conversing in silence. Like Uncle Alberto and his father. Like the two old men in the film he'd seen with Alba.

The Driver

When he entered his office the next morning, Caldas found a yellow Post-it note stuck to his desk.

He picked up the phone.

'What's up?'

'I think you need to see something, Inspector,' said Barcia.

'What's it about?'

'The security camera video. Can you come by?'

'Now?'

Caldas and Estevez went into the Forensics viewing room. They sat on the chairs closest to the monitor.

Once again they saw the black-and-white image of the garden, the shrubs and winding path leading to the front gate. Barcia paused the recording at the shot of the Land Rover, visible above the gate, on its way back from the lighthouse.

'Look closely,' she said, zooming in on the driver.

'At what exactly?'

'The driver's hands,' she whispered.

She didn't need to say more.

The image was blurry but they could still make out five fingers on the hand holding the steering wheel.

'Are you sure that's the right hand?'

'It makes no difference,' she said, rewinding the recording until they saw the 4x4 drive past in the opposite direction.

The driver's other hand also had all five fingers.

'That's not Diego Neira,' said Barcia.

'Clearly not,' said Caldas, sighing.

He didn't open his eyes until Estevez parked outside the police station. He was wondering whose hands they'd seen on the recording.

Neira hadn't taken the Land Rover or Castelo's boat to the lighthouse, but that didn't mean he wasn't guilty of El Rubio's murder. Someone had helped him to dispose of the boat, but Caldas couldn't work out who. He swallowed. He wasn't sure he wanted to find out. He knew that he himself would have helped a friend who had no one else to turn to.

He went to Superintendent Soto's office and told him what Barcia had shown them.

'So who the hell is it then?'

'We don't know,' said Caldas. 'But it definitely isn't Neira.'

'What do I say to the judge now? He's fixated on the Land Rover.'

Soto was starting to have doubts so Caldas tried to reassure him. 'Don't say anything, Superintendent. At least, not until we find the car. The driver has to be someone close to Neira.'

'You think so?'

'Definitely,' said the inspector. 'It has to be.'

The Winemakers

At one o'clock his father drew up outside the police station. Caldas had told Superintendent Soto that he'd be leaving for the weekend a few hours early. He needed to distance himself from the case, to get some perspective.

'You can get hold of me on the mobile if anything crops up,' he'd said. 'Though I don't think we'll get much further today unless the Land Rover turns up.'

His father smiled as Caldas got into the passenger seat and lowered the window a fraction. He'd been expecting him to cancel at the last minute.

'Alberto's really looking forward to seeing you.'

Caldas nodded and closed his eyes.

Twenty minutes later he opened them when his father asked, 'Have you spoken to Alba?'

'No.'

'When are you going to?'

The inspector sighed and opened the window a little wider. If they hadn't been driving on a motorway at over a hundred kilometres an hour, he'd have thrown himself out of the car.

'I don't know. I don't even know if I'm going to call her.'

'Can you open the glove compartment?' asked his father.

'What?'

Caldas's father pointed.

'That's the glove compartment.'

358

'I know.'

'Well, open it,' said his father. 'Inside there's a blue notebook. Would you mind entering a name on the last page where you see writing?'

Caldas smiled. 'You keep the Book of Idiots in here?'

'Only when I'm going somewhere.'

The inspector opened the glove compartment and took out the notebook. His father called it blue, but the covers were so worn it was impossible to tell the original colour.

He placed it on his knees. There were notes explaining why each person had been included in the Book of Idiots. As Caldas flicked through the pages the names became more familiar.

He had to shut it quickly as he felt the first waves of nausea. He was about to put it back in the glove compartment when he saw, among all the papers his father kept there, a small sealed transparent plastic bag.

'If you don't write your name in there, I will,' said his father, but Caldas wasn't listening.

He was holding up the bag, unable to take his eyes off the plastic cable ties inside.

'What's this?' he asked.

'They're ties. You fasten them like this,' said his father, taking his hands off the steering wheel momentarily and miming the action.

'Where did you get them?'

'We were given a sample a couple of weeks ago before the start of pruning, at a winemakers' meeting. To see if they were any good for tying vines. They're meant to show less if they're green. I'd forgotten they were there.'

'All the winemakers got a bag like this?'

'All the ones at the meeting.'

'Damn,' muttered the inspector. 'Can you turn round?'

'What?'

'I have to get back to Vigo,' said Caldas.

He didn't need to add that it was important.

He called Superintendent Soto from the car. 'I think I know where the 4x4 is,' he said. 'We're going to need a search warrant. Can you have a word with the judge?'

The Tie

They took the turn-off to Monteferro and then the narrow lane leading down to the Valverdes' house. A couple of workmen were
installing a new gate, identical to the damaged one, which now lay
on the ground. A van bearing the logo of Valverde's construction
company was parked to one side.

They rang the bell and Valverde's wife came out. She was wearing
a leather jacket and jeans tucked into high boots.

'Good afternoon,' said Caldas. As always, her smile reminded him
of Alba.

Between the lapels of her jacket, the top buttons of her black shirt
were straining.

'I'm so glad to see you. I was going to call to thank you. Marcos
told me about the other night. If you hadn't been there, God knows
what would have happened.'

Caldas shrugged.

'Would you like to come in?'

'Yes,' said the inspector, glancing at Valverde's black sports car
parked beside his wife's red SUV. 'Is your husband in?'

She gestured towards the other side of the house.

'He's out the back with one of his men. We're having an alarm put
in. We're also going to get a dog,' she said resignedly. 'Even though
you've arrested that man, I'm still going to have trouble sleeping here.'

'Did you stay in Vigo last night?'

'Yes,' she said. 'And we're driving back there as soon as the gate's
fitted.'

*

She led them round the house, stopping before the large window that overlooked the garden and the bay. A leafless chestnut tree stood in the middle of the lawn and, beneath it, a metal bench. The air smelled of damp earth and the sea.

Marcos Valverde, in a grey suit and tie, was talking to a young man by the wall that surrounded the property. Catching sight of the policemen, he motioned to his employee and they both started back towards the house.

As the two men made their way across the lawn, Caldas said to Valverde's wife,

'How long will you be staying in town?'

'Until the alarm's ready,' she sighed. 'Though if it were up to me I'd never come back.'

Caldas nodded. 'You said you go to Vigo every week, didn't you? To concerts.'

'Yes, on Saturdays,' she said.

Caldas tried to keep his voice even as he asked, 'Were you there the Saturday before last?'

'I haven't missed a concert in months, Inspector,' she replied. 'They're therapeutic.'

'Right.'

Valverde shook hands firmly with them both, while his workman disappeared down the path towards the entrance. There was little sign of the frightened man who had made a statement at the police station the day before.

'Have you found Arias?' he asked.

'That's what we want to talk to you about.'

'Would you like a glass of wine?' asked Valverde's wife.

'No, thank you,' mumbled Caldas, though he could have done with one.

'I'm sure I can change your mind,' she said, turning down the corners of her mouth. Then she headed inside with Estevez's eyes pinned to her behind.

Instead of following Mrs Valverde into the house, Caldas set off across the lawn with Valverde. Estevez followed a few paces behind.

'Have you found him or not?' asked Valverde.

'Yes, we have.'

361

Valverde gave a sigh of relief. 'Where?'

'In Scotland,' said the inspector quietly as he walked. 'He was going to collect his daughter when they arrested him.'

'Well . . . Has he been questioned?'

'Yes, by the British police. We'll have to wait until they hand him over to us.'

Caldas stopped beside the tree stripped of its leaves by autumn. He took out his cigarettes and sat down on the bench. Valverde sat down beside him.

The inspector lit a cigarette and contemplated the castle at Baiona and the waves breaking at the foot of the lighthouse at Cabo Silleiro, their foam hiding the horizon.

'Beautiful view, isn't it?' said Valverde proudly.

Caldas agreed.

'Your wife once said that you have a gift for getting what you want. You've made money, married a glamorous woman from Madrid, got the owner of your dream house to sell it to you,' said Caldas, motioning towards the glass façade behind him. 'Does your wife know that you once failed to get what you wanted from a young woman called Rebeca Neira? You've never told her about that, have you?'

'What?'

Valverde turned to look at him, but Caldas kept staring straight ahead at the sea.

'That woman was only the beginning,' he said. 'Then came Captain Sousa. He stood up to you, too.'

'I hope you have proof to back up all your accusations, Inspector.'

'We've got Arias's statement.'

'Arias? Please! I saw him hit the skipper and throw the bundle into the water before leaving the boat to founder on the rocks.'

'That's not how he remembers it.'

'Is Arias really trying to pin those deaths on me? He's the one who ran away after the sinking of the *Xurelo* and ran away again from that man Neira.'

'No,' said Caldas. 'It's you that Arias has always been running from.'

'From me?' said Valverde with a forced smile. 'A man like him, run away from me?'

'He knew what you were like. So did El Rubio. That night on the

362

deck of the *Xurelo* they both saw how far you were prepared to go when something got in your way. That's why they've kept quiet all these years.'

'That's nonsense. Arias would say anything to avoid going to prison. Even a child could tell he's lying.'

'I believe him,' said the inspector. 'And I also believe that you killed Justo Castelo.'

'Did Arias say that, too?'

'No. That's my own opinion.'

'Well, you have a lively imagination, Inspector.'

Caldas was still staring straight ahead.

'El Rubio was going to talk, but you weren't about to let him ruin your life. You hit him on the head and threw him into the sea with his hands tied.'

'You're out of your mind, Caldas,' said Valverde, getting to his feet. 'I'm going to call my lawyer.'

'As you please.'

Valverde looked first at the inspector, then at Estevez, who was listening, leaning against the trunk of the chestnut tree. Estevez tensed visibly as Valverde put his hand in his pocket to take out his mobile phone.

'How dare you come to my home and accuse me of murder without a shred of evidence?'

'Who says we don't have evidence?' said the inspector softly, aware that Valverde found his quiet tone exasperating. 'We have the object you struck Castelo with – a spanner of the sort used to tighten nuts on car wheels. It was found among the rocks, at the foot of a cliff,' he said, waving his hand towards the west. 'You didn't even bother to throw it out to sea. After all, who was going to investigate a suicide?'

'That spanner isn't mine,' said Valverde. 'My car's out there in the courtyard. Why don't you go and check before making more slanderous accusations?'

'Don't worry, we'll be checking everything,' said Caldas. 'But first, tell me something: did Justo Castelo come to see you on the Saturday night?'

Valverde made an effort to calm down. He wanted to avoid any false moves. 'Even if he did, that doesn't mean—'

'Did he or didn't he?' the inspector cut in.

'He was here at around eight,' admitted Valverde. 'To talk to my wife. She sometimes bought seafood from him directly, you know ...'

'Right,' said Caldas. 'But your wife was in Vigo, at a concert.'

Valverde looked him in the eye, then nodded. 'It's true. That's why El Rubio didn't come into the house. He left, and that was the last time I ever saw him. Later I heard that he'd been seen on his boat early on Sunday morning and that his body was found on the beach the next day.'

'No,' said Caldas. 'It wasn't him who was seen in the harbour on the Sunday. It was you.'

'I was at the vineyard first thing in the morning,' insisted Valverde. 'There were people working there. They can tell you.'

'No, I'll tell you what happened: on the Saturday night, before throwing El Rubio into the sea, you searched his pockets and found the keys to his boat. The next morning, by which time Castelo had been in the water for hours, you drove to the lighthouse at Punta Lameda. You knew the place because the skipper used to set his traps there. You knew it was the perfect spot. You parked by the lighthouse and walked back to the harbour, with your face hidden beneath your hood. Then you sailed El Rubio's boat to the pool and sank it, to cover your tracks and make sure the boat wasn't found on one side of the mountain while the body was found on the other side. Then you got back into your car and drove to the vineyard, so that the workers there could provide you with an alibi.'

'Do you really think anyone's going to believe such a story?'

'I think they will,' replied Caldas. 'It was all recorded by a security camera on a house near the turn-off leading to Punta Lameda. The footage shows a car heading towards the lighthouse. Soon after it shows the driver walking back to the village,' he said, simulating the action of walking with two fingers. 'And an hour later, though he seemingly hasn't returned to the lighthouse, the driver is once again at the wheel of the car driving away from it. The car is a light-coloured 4x4. An old Land Rover with a bent aerial and scratched paintwork at the back.'

Just as Caldas finished speaking, Valverde's mobile phone rang.

'Aren't you going to get that?' asked Caldas when it had rung for what felt like an eternity. 'It'll be your winery. To say that some of our

364

colleagues have arrived with a search warrant. As I said, we're checking everything.'

Valverde stared at the phone display in bemusement – he wasn't used to losing.

Caldas leaned back and lit another cigarette.

'When did you come up with the idea of faking Castelo's suicide?' he asked. 'Was it at that winemakers' meeting, when you were given the green cable ties?'

Valverde did not reply. The inspector continued, 'How did you find out that the carpenter was Rebeca Neira's son?'

Silence.

'How many carpenters have you got on your payroll?' asked Caldas, knowing he'd get no answer. 'I don't know why I didn't realise that you didn't need to call in a carpenter who repaired boats to fix your gate.'

Still Valverde said nothing.

Caldas went on, 'Your wife got scared when she saw the damaged gate. You should have got her away from the house on some pretext, before prying apart the gate panels and calling the carpenter. Pretty funny, don't you think? We came here to protect you, but we saved Neira from ending up like his mother.'

Caldas's phone rang and he answered.

'We've got it, Inspector,' said Ferro at the other end of the line. 'You were right. The car was here. It's the one on the video recording. The spanner's missing. And you'll never guess what was in the glove compartment.'

'A bag of green cable ties?'

'How did you know?'

While Estevez handcuffed Valverde, Caldas took a last drag on his cigarette and stubbed it out on the ground.

'Is this really necessary?' asked Valverde, raising his handcuffed wrists.

'Absolutely,' said Caldas.

As they walked back across the lawn, the inspector turned towards the prisoner.

365

'Why did you do it?' he asked quietly.

Valverde shook his head and looked down at the ground.

'Why did you have to kill that boy's mother?' the inspector pressed him.

'It was an accident,' mumbled Valverde.

'What about the others?' asked Caldas. He wondered if it was possible to kill in cold blood in order to cover up an accidental death. 'Were they accidents, too?'

'No,' whispered Valverde. 'The others weren't. I told you before: anyone can feel afraid.'

As they passed the huge windows, they saw glasses set out on the table and a bottle cooling in the ice bucket. Valverde's wife came out to meet them, but her smile disappeared when she saw the handcuffs on her husband's wrists.

On the sound system, 'Solveig's Song' was playing.

It sounded like a Galician song.

Murmurs

On Wednesday, just after eight in the morning, Estevez parked opposite the stone slipway. Justo Castelo's traps were no longer on the jetty.

They got out of the car and went across the road to the fish market. After greeting the two retired fishermen at the entrance they peered inside. Hermida and his wife were standing with their backs to them, listening to the auctioneer call out prices on the other side of the table and, in his orange waterproofs, the huge fisherman was leaning against the wall at the back of the hall. He raised his eyebrows when he caught sight of the policemen and came towards them. He was carrying a plastic bag full of crabs.

The man with the grey sideburns halted the bidding and Arias stopped and waited while the buyer selected two trays of crabs. The man then handed the labels with the weights of each tray to the auctioneer, for his name to be noted on them.

When the auctioneer gestured towards the remaining crabs and prepared to restart the auction, Arias joined the policemen.

'I was going to drop by the police station this morning.'

'Well, we've saved you the trip.'

'Care to come along?' said the fisherman, holding up the plastic bag.

'Yes, of course.'

From the slipway, among the trailers and rowing boats, they could still hear the sound of the auction, now reduced to a murmur.

'El Rubio came to see me on the Saturday,' said Arias, crouching at the water's edge. 'He said he hadn't slept for weeks. It wasn't just the graffiti on his boat. He was finding notes in his traps almost every day. He knew it wouldn't stop until he revealed the name, so he went to Valverde's office.'

'Did he tell you this?'

Arias nodded. 'Valverde offered him money, but El Rubio said all he wanted was his peace of mind back. So Valverde kicked him out. He said he couldn't waste any more time, he had to get on with his work, and told him to come to his house on Saturday night.'

'Why did Castelo come to see you?'

'I don't know,' replied Arias. 'To tell me he'd decided to talk, or to get things off his chest maybe. He was scared. Scared of confessing and scared of keeping quiet. We'd hardly spoken since the *Xurelo*, but he knew I'd understand. He'd helped Valverde clean up the house in Aguiño and take the girl's body back to the *Xurelo*, but he wasn't a murderer.'

'You knew he hadn't committed suicide, didn't you?'

'I suspected it, yes.'

The fisherman waited until the plastic bag was empty and stood up.

'Why did you take off?' asked Caldas.

Arias shrugged.

'With El Rubio dead I wouldn't have been able to defend myself. Valverde had threatened to pin the girl's murder on me if I talked. I'd had drink problems, I'd been in trouble with the police – who'd have believed me?'

'You'll have to give a statement now.'

'I know.'

When they got back to the fish market, the auction was over. Arias headed to the office at the side of the hall to collect his receipts before the auctioneer left.

'Do you know when the trial will be?' he asked as they made their way out of the market building.

'It's out of our hands now,' said Caldas. 'I expect you'll be receiving a letter with a summons.'

Arias grimaced.

'You weren't thinking of staying?'

'I will for now,' said the fisherman. 'After that, we'll see.'

*

The policemen walked to the end of the jetty. There were no anglers. Caldas lit a cigarette and leaned on the wall, looking at the sea. Rebeca Neira's body lay out there somewhere. He recalled the ending of *Captains Courageous*, the boy with his father, throwing flowers into the sea in memory of Manuel the Portuguese fisherman. Caldas pictured Diego Neira in some other harbour, alone, and clicked his tongue at the thought.

They headed back to the car and, as they passed the yacht club, they looked over the fence. The sliding door to the workshop was shut. Neira had left the village, not wanting to be the subject of gossip.

'He came to get his cat and say goodbye,' said a voice behind them. 'I'm sorry he left. He was a real craftsman.'

'I know,' said Caldas, smiling at Manuel Trabazo. 'Going out fishing this early?'

'I think it might rain later on,' replied the doctor.

'Yes, it might well,' said Caldas, glancing up.

Estevez looked up, too, but all he could see were a couple of seagulls wheeling about in a clear blue sky.

'How can you tell it's going to rain?' he asked.

Trabazo looked at him out of the corner of his eye.

'You're not from around here, are you?'

'No, I'm from Aragon. From Zaragoza.'

Free

After lunch on Friday, his father came to collect him outside the police station.

'How's Uncle Alberto?' asked Caldas as he got into the car.

'Not too bad. Free of the mask. He's only got a nasal tube now, so he can speak and eat without that horrible noise.'

'That's good.'

'Yes. In a few days, he might not even need the oxygen.'

'Will he go back to his place?' asked the inspector, opening the window a couple of centimetres.

'Not unless he wants to.'

They arrived at the estate and parked beside the camellia bush.

When his father opened the door, the brown dog, which had run up to the car, began jumping around him, licking his hands, whining and lashing its tail.

'How long have you been away?' asked Caldas.

'Only since this morning,' replied his father, trying to push the dog away.

'Well, that's quite a welcome,' muttered the inspector. 'Does it know it doesn't belong to you?'

'How the hell should I know what a dog's thinking, Leo?'

'I don't think it does know,' Caldas said and smiled, heading towards the terrace that overlooked the vineyard.

Leaning on the wall, he contemplated the ranks of leafless vines, each tied to a post. It was a cold day, and so clear that you could count the trees on the hill across the river. It smelled like the days of his childhood.

His father came to stand beside him.

'The estate's looking lovely, isn't it?' he said, patting the brown dog's side in an attempt to stop it rubbing against his legs.

'Yes.'

'Have you seen the new area I've planted, down by the river?'

'No,' Caldas lied once again.

'Well, let's go in and say hello to Alberto, and then we can walk down and take a look. You're going to love it.'

As they got to the house, his father said, 'By the way, we spoke to Alba yesterday.'

'Did she call you?'

'Yes,' said his father. 'To see how Alberto was.'

'Right.'

'You haven't called her, have you?'

'No, not yet.'

'Don't you think you should?'

THE OXFORD MURDERS

Winner of the Planeta Prize

Guillermo Martínez

'An enthralling conflict between the heart and the mind'
Observer

Using rules and axioms, there will always be some propositions that can't be proved either true or false. But can this apply to murder? Gödel's Theorem of Incompleteness is familiar territory to the young mathematician who arrives in Oxford. Murder, however, is not.

Yet barely has he greeted his elderly landlady when he is bidding her a posthumous farewell. Mrs Eagleton is murdered in her wheelchair. The only clue to the crime is a cryptic symbol and the words 'the first in the series'. It's not much to go on, but it's enough to appeal to Arthur Seldom, one of the leading minds in logic. His most famous work of philosophy contains a chapter on serial killers. This killer, clearly, has read it . . .

Abacus
978-0-349-11723-2

DEATH IN THE LATIN QUARTER

Raphaël Cardetti

'An original and fascinating treasure-hunt tale'
Literary Review

Early one morning in Paris, the tranquillity of the Sorbonne University is shattered by a death. But why would Albert Cadas, a quiet, crumpled professor of medieval literature, have any reason to kill himself? Meanwhile, Valentine Savi, a talented young restorer, receives a visit from an enigmatic elderly gentleman with a unique commission: to restore a priceless manuscript that promises to reveal the truth of a mystery that has fascinated scholars and writers for centuries.

Valentine soon learns that the shadowy figures who seek to possess the book's secrets are darker and more ruthless than she ever imagined, and finds herself on a terrifying and thrilling adventure through the narrow streets and gloomily palatial mansions of the Latin Quarter.

'A crime novel worthy of Arturo Pérez-Reverte'
L'Express

Abacus
978-0-349-12256-4

A DEATH IN CALABRIA

Michele Giuttari

'The leading Italian crime writer'
The Times

One of the wildest and most beautiful regions in Italy, known for its rugged coastline and mountains, Calabria is also home to the deadly 'Ndrangheta. An organised Mafia crime operation more feared in Italy than the Cosa Nostra or the Camorra, it is shrouded in mystery.

Chief Superintendent Michele Ferrara of Italy's elite Anti-Mafia Investigation Department is tasked with investigating the deaths of several Calabria citizens – some in New York, some in the isolated villages that dot the Calabrian countryside. To get to the bottom of the case, Ferrara must infiltrate the village of San Piero d'Aspromonte, deep in the Calabrian mountains. And there, he must put his life on the line to learn more about a family at the centre of an ancient, bloody feud . . .

Abacus
978-0-349-12309-7

THE DEATH OF A MAFIA DON

Michele Giuttari

A bomb explodes in the centre of Florence, hitting the car of Chief Superintendent Michele Ferrara. The attack rocks the ancient city to its foundations. Ferrara was clearly the target – and he did, after all, controversially imprison notorious Mafia boss Salvatore Laprua. A week later, another bomb explodes, bringing tragedy for Ferrara and a renewed determination to find the culprit. But that same morning, Salvatore Laprua is found dead in his prison cell. So who is the mysterious influence behind the bombings – someone even the Mafia fear?

An ingenious, gripping mystery, *The Death of a Mafia Don* has been a bestseller in Italy and across Europe. Written by former Florence police chief Michele Giuttari, it offers a fascinating insight into the secret world of the Mafia, and life in Florence.

Abacus
978-0-349-12197-0